12

AMERICAN
DETECTIVE
STORIES

EDWARD D. HOCH has published nearly 800 short stories himself, and is a past president of Mystery Writers of America. He has edited twenty-five short story anthologies, including *The Year's Best Mystery and Suspense Stories* series, and his own stories have been collected in a dozen volumes, most recently *The Night My Friend* (1991), *Diagnosis: Impossible* (1996), and *The Ripper of Storyville* (1997).

12

AMERICAN DETECTIVE STORIES

Selected and introduced by

EDWARD D. HOCH

Oxford   New York

OXFORD UNIVERSITY PRESS

1997

Oxford University Press, Great Clarendon Street, Oxford OX2 6DP

Oxford New York

Athens Auckland Bangkok Bogota Bombay Buenos Aires
Calcutta Cape Town Dar es Salaam Delhi Florence Hong Kong Istanbul
Karachi Kuala Lumpur Madras Madrid Melbourne Mexico City
Nairobi Paris Singapore Taipei Tokyo Toronto Warsaw

and associated companies in
Berlin Ibadan

Oxford is a trade mark of Oxford University Press

© Introduction and selection
Edward D. Hoch 1997

First published as an Oxford University Press paperback 1997

British Library Cataloguing in Publication Data
Data available

Library of Congress Cataloging in Publication Data
Data available

ISBN 0-19-288064-0

1 3 5 7 9 10 8 6 4 2

Typeset by Jayvee, Trivandrum, India
Printed in Great Britain by
Caledonian International Book Manufacturing Ltd.
Glasgow

CONTENTS

Contents

INTRODUCTION

These days, more than a century and a half after Edgar Allan Poe penned the first detective story, there is a tendency to classify much American work in the genre under the broad umbrella of 'crime fiction'. The formal detective story is often thought of mainly as a British product, encompassing as it does Arthur Conan Doyle, G. K. Chesterton, Agatha Christie, Dorothy L. Sayers, P. D. James, and a host of others. It detracts nothing from the skills of its British practitioners when we point to the long and noble history of detective fiction in America.

By definition a detective story, be it a novel or a shorter work, is one which features a detective—official or unofficial—who performs acts of detection in solving a crime. The crime is usually murder, though in four of the stories that follow it is a lesser offence. Ideally, the author treats the reader fairly and presents the clues by which the crime can be solved. This, however, is not always the case. Sherlock Holmes and others often withheld clues and observations from the reader.

In this gathering of American detective fiction we have attempted to entertain the reader while at the same time illustrating a wide range of styles and subjects. The twelve examples of American detective fiction included here were all published more than thirty-five years ago. Though the form is still popular today, it is a sad truth that many recent novels and tales published as detective stories contain little or no detection.

As American as these stories are, two of them—by C. Daly King and Raymond Chandler—were first published in England. Another of our American authors, Carter Dickson, lived a large portion of his adult life in England and often used British settings.

It is fitting that such a collection opens with a lesser-known story by Edgar Allan Poe, one in which he plays fair and presents an essential clue to be detected by astute readers. Poe's sleuth remains nameless, as does the detective in the final story by Cornell Woolrich. Perhaps they can be viewed as some form of detection's Everyman.

In stories from the early years of this century, two American originals, Jacques Futrelle's 'The Thinking Machine' and Melville Davisson Post's Uncle Abner, demonstrate the intellectual versus the intuitive approach to the science of detection. Anna Katharine Green presents one of the earliest female sleuths, Violet Strange, in a case that is strange indeed. The next two, series sleuths who existed only in the short-story form, are all but forgotten today. Yet both T. S. Stribling's Professor Poggioli and C. Daly King's Trevis Tarrant are worth rediscovering—Poggioli for his surprise endings and Tarrant for his bizarre plots.

Craig Rice is another author who is seldom read today, though fifty years ago her picture graced the cover of *Time* magazine and she was hailed as a leading American mystery writer. If her career lasted a relatively short eighteen years, Ellery Queen and John Dickson Carr ('Carter Dickson') each had careers of active professional writing covering forty-two years. Both must rank high in any survey of American detective fiction, and the exploits of popular sleuths Ellery Queen and Sir Henry Merrivale are well deserving of their place here.

It was Mary Roberts Rinehart more than anyone else who regularly brought the American detective story to women's magazines and the best-seller lists. A trick of chronology places Rinehart just ahead of Raymond Chandler in our line-up, and no two authors could have been more different, in intent and execution. Both Rinehart and Chandler are represented here by the final stories they wrote before their death.

Lastly, there is Cornell Woolrich, whose stories of suspense and despair did more than anything else to inspire the *film noir* in Hollywood and France. Woolrich never used series characters and rarely wrote formal detective tales, but in 'One Drop of Blood' he created a masterpiece of an inverted detective story in which the question is not 'whodunit?', but rather 'how will he be discovered?'

This, then, is the American detective story, from Poe to Woolrich, full of murder and kidnapping and theft, where the victims are innocent babies or double-crossing mobsters, where the setting can be a department store at Christmastime or a death cell at the state prison, where locked rooms and surprise endings abound, and the important clue can be as tiny as a single bullet or a splinter of wood.

EDWARD D. HOCH

1

EDGAR ALLAN POE

'Thou Art the Man'

I will now play the Œdipus to the Rattleborough enigma. I will expound to you—as I alone can—the secret of the enginery that effected the Rattleborough miracle—the one, the true, the admitted, the undisputed, the indisputable miracle, which put a definite end to infidelity among the Rattleburghers and converted to the orthodoxy of the grandames all the carnal-minded who had ventured to be skeptical before.

This event—which I should be sorry to discuss in a tone of unsuitable levity—occurred in the summer of 18—. Mr Barnabas Shuttleworthy—one of the wealthiest and most respectable citizens of the borough—had been missing for several days under circumstances which gave rise to suspicion of foul play. Mr Shuttleworthy had set out from Rattleborough very early one Saturday morning, on horseback, with the avowed intention of proceeding to the city of ——, about fifteen miles distant, and of returning the night of the same day. Two hours after his departure, however, his horse returned without him, and without the saddle-bags which had been strapped on his back at starting. The animal was wounded, too, and covered with mud. These circumstances naturally gave rise to much alarm among the friends of the missing man; and when it was found, on Sunday morning, that he had not yet made his appearance, the whole borough arose *en masse* to go and look for his body.

The foremost and most energetic in instituting this search was the bosom friend of Mr Shuttleworthy—a Mr Charles Goodfellow, or, as he was universally called, 'Charley Goodfellow', or 'Old Charley Goodfellow'. Now, whether it is a marvellous coincidence, or

1

whether it is that the name itself has an imperceptible effect upon the character, I have never yet been able to ascertain; but the fact is unquestionable, that there never yet was any person named Charles who was not an open, manly, honest, good-natured, and frank-hearted fellow, with a rich, clear voice, that did you good to hear it, and an eye that looked you always straight in the face, as much as to say: 'I have a clear conscience myself, am afraid of no man, and am altogether above doing a mean action.' And thus all the hearty, careless, 'walking gentlemen' of the stage are very certain to be called Charles.

Now, 'Old Charley Goodfellow', although he had been in Rattleborough not longer than six months or thereabouts, and although nobody knew anything about him before he came to settle in the neighborhood, had experienced no difficulty in the world in making the acquaintance of all the respectable people in the borough. Not a man of them but would have taken his bare word for a thousand at any moment; and as for the women, there is no saying what they would not have done to oblige him. And all this came of his having been christened Charles, and of his possessing, in consequence, that ingenuous face which is proverbially the very 'best letter of recommendation'.

I have already said that Mr Shuttleworthy was one of the most respectable and, undoubtedly, he was the most wealthy man in Rattleborough, while 'Old Charley Goodfellow' was upon as intimate terms with him as if he had been his own brother. The two old gentlemen were next-door neighbors, and, although Mr Shuttleworthy seldom, if ever, visited 'Old Charley', and never was known to take a meal in his house, still this did not prevent the two friends from being exceedingly intimate, as I have just observed; for 'Old Charley' never let a day pass without stepping in three or four times to see how his neighbor came on, and very often he would stay to breakfast or tea, and almost always to dinner; and then the amount of wine that was made way with by the two cronies at a sitting, it would really be a difficult thing to ascertain. 'Old Charley's' favorite beverage was *Château Margaux*, and it appeared to do Mr Shuttleworthy's heart good to see the old fellow swallow it, as he did, quart after quart; so that, one day, when the wine was *in* and the wit, as a natural consequence, somewhat *out*, he said to his crony, as he slapped him upon the back: 'I tell you what it is, "Old Charley", you are, by all odds, the heartiest old fellow I ever came across in all my born days; and, since you love to guzzle the wine at that fashion, I'll be darned if I don't have to make thee a present of a big box of the Château Margaux. Od rot me'—(Mr Shuttleworthy had a sad habit of swearing, although he seldom went beyond 'Od rot me', or 'By gosh', or 'By the jolly golly')—'Od rot me,' says he, 'if I don't send an order to town this very afternoon for a double box of the best that can be got, and I'll make ye a present of it, I will!—ye needn't say a word now—I *will*, I tell ye, and there's an end of it; so look out for it—it will come to hand some of these fine days, precisely when ye are looking for it the least!' I mention this little bit of liberality on the part of Mr Shuttleworthy, just by way of showing you how *very* intimate an understanding existed between the two friends.

Well, on the Sunday morning in question, when it came to be fairly understood that Mr Shuttleworthy had met with foul play, I never saw any one so profoundly affected as 'Old Charley Goodfellow'. When he first heard that the horse had come home without his master, and without his master's saddle-bags, and all bloody from a pistol-shot, that had gone clean through and through the poor animal's chest without quite killing him—when he heard all this, he turned as pale as if the missing man had been his own dear brother or father, and shivered and shook all over as if he had had a fit of the ague.

At first he was too much overpowered with grief to be able to do anything at all, or to decide upon any plan of action; so that for a long time he endeavored to dissuade Mr Shuttleworthy's other friends from making a stir about the matter, thinking it best to wait awhile— say for a week or two, or a month, or two—to see if something wouldn't turn up, or if Mr Shuttleworthy wouldn't come in the natural way, and explain his reasons for sending his horse on before. I dare say you have often observed this disposition to temporize, or to procrastinate, in people who are laboring under any very poignant sorrow. Their powers of mind seem to be rendered torpid, so that they have a horror of anything like action, and like nothing in the world so well as to lie quietly in bed and 'nurse their grief', as the old ladies express it—that is to say, ruminate over the trouble.

The people of Rattleborough had, indeed, so high an opinion of the wisdom and discretion of 'Old Charley', that the greater part of them felt disposed to agree with him, and not make a stir in the business 'until something should turn up', as the honest old gentleman worded it; and I believe that, after all, this would have been the general determination, but for the very suspicious interference of Mr Shuttleworthy's nephew, a young man of very dissipated habits, and otherwise of rather bad character. This nephew, whose name was Pennifeather, would listen to nothing like reason in the matter of 'lying quiet', but insisted upon making immediate search for the 'corpse of the murdered man'. This was the expression he employed; and Mr Goodfellow acutely remarked at the time, that it was 'a *singular* expression, to say no more'. This remark of 'Old Charley's', too, had great effect upon the crowd; and one of the party was heard to ask, very impressively, 'how it happened that young Mr Pennifeather was so intimately cognizant of all the circumstances connected with his wealthy uncle's disappearance, as to feel authorized to assert, distinctly and unequivocally, that his uncle *was* "a murdered man" '. Hereupon some little squibbling and bickering occurred among various members of the crowd, and especially between 'Old Charley' and Mr Pennifeather—although this latter occurrence was, indeed, by no means a novelty, for little good-will had subsisted between the parties for the last three or four months; and matters had even gone so far that Mr Pennifeather had actually knocked down his uncle's friend for some alleged excess of liberty that the latter had taken in the uncle's house, of which the nephew was an inmate. Upon this occasion 'Old Charley' is said to have behaved with exemplary moderation and Christian charity. He arose from the blow, adjusted his clothes, and made no attempt at retaliation at all—merely muttering a few words about 'taking summary vengeance at the first convenient opportunity'—a natural and very justifiable ebullition of anger, which meant nothing, however, and, beyond doubt, was no sooner given vent to than forgotten.

However these matters may be (which have no reference to the point now at issue), it is quite certain that the people of Rattleborough, principally through the persuasion of Mr Pennifeather, came at length to the determination of dispersion over the adjacent country in

search of the missing Mr Shuttleworthy. I say they came to this determination in the first instance. After it had been fully resolved that a
search should be made, it was considered almost a matter of course
that the seekers should disperse—that is to say, distribute themselves
in parties—for the more thorough examination of the region round
about. I forget, however, by what ingenious train of reasoning it was
that 'Old Charley' finally convinced the assembly that this was the
most injudicious plan that could be pursued. Convince them, however, he did—all except Mr Pennifeather; and, in the end, it was
arranged that a search should be instituted, carefully and very thoroughly, by the burghers *en masse*, 'Old Charley' himself leading the
way.

As for the matter of that, there could have been no better pioneer
than 'Old Charley', whom everybody knew to have the eye of a lynx;
but, although he led them into all manner of out-of-the-way holes and
corners, by routes that nobody had ever suspected of existing in the
neighborhood, and although the search was incessantly kept up day
and night for nearly a week, still no trace of Mr Shuttleworthy could
be discovered. When I say no trace, however, I must not be understood
to speak literally; for trace, to some extent, there certainly was. The
poor gentleman had been tracked, by his horse's shoes (which were
peculiar), to a spot about three miles to the east of the borough, on the
main road leading to the city. Here the track made off into a by-path
through a piece of woodland—the path coming out again into the
main road, and cutting off about half a mile of the regular distance.
Following the shoe-marks down this lane, the party came at length to
a pool of stagnant water, half hidden by the brambles, to the right of
the lane, and opposite this pool all vestige of the track was lost sight of.
It appeared, however, that a struggle of some nature had here taken
place, and it seemed as if some large and heavy body, much larger and
heavier than a man, had been drawn from the by-path to the pool.
This latter was carefully dragged twice, but nothing was found; and
the party were upon the point of going away, in despair of coming to
any result, when Providence suggested to Mr Goodfellow the expedi-
ency of draining the water off altogether. This project was received
with cheers, and many high compliments to 'Old Charley' upon his
sagacity and consideration. As many of the burghers had brought

spades with them, supposing that they might possibly be called upon to disinter a corpse, the drain was easily and speedily effected; and no sooner was the bottom visible, than right in the middle of the mud that remained was discovered a black silk velvet waistcoat, which nearly every one present immediately recognized as the property of Mr Pennifeather. This waistcoat was much torn and stained with blood, and there were several persons among the party who had a distinct remembrance of its having been worn by its owner on the very morning of Mr Shuttleworthy's departure for the city; while there were others, again, ready to testify upon oath, if required, that Mr P. did *not* wear the garment in question at any period during the *remainder* of that memorable day; nor could any one be found to say that he had seen it upon Mr P.'s person at any period at all subsequent to Mr Shuttleworthy's disappearance.

Matters now wore a very serious aspect for Mr Pennifeather, and it was observed, as an indubitable confirmation of the suspicions which were excited against him, that he grew exceedingly pale, and when asked what he had to say for himself, was utterly incapable of saying a word. Hereupon, the few friends his riotous mode of living had left him deserted him at once to a man, and were even more clamorous than his ancient and avowed enemies for his instantaneous arrest. But, on the other hand, the magnanimity of Mr Goodfellow shone forth with only the more brilliant lustre through contrast. He made a warm and intensely eloquent defence of Mr Pennifeather, in which he alluded more than once to his own sincere forgiveness of that wild young gentleman—'the heir of the worthy Mr Shuttleworthy'—for the insult which he (the young gentleman) had, no doubt in the heat of passion, thought proper to put upon him (Mr Goodfellow). 'He forgave him for it,' he said, 'from the very bottom of his heart; and for himself (Mr Goodfellow), so far from pushing the suspicious circumstances to extremity, which he was sorry to say, really *had* arisen against Mr Pennifeather, he (Mr Goodfellow) would make every exertion in his power, would employ all the little eloquence in his possession to—to—to—soften down, as much as he could conscientiously do so, the worst features of this really exceedingly perplexing piece of business.'

Mr Goodfellow went on for some half hour longer in this strain, very much to the credit both of his head and of his heart; but your warm-hearted people are seldom apposite in their observations—they run into all sorts of blunders, *contre-temps* and *mal àpropos-isms*, in the hot headedness of their zeal to serve a friend—thus, often with the kindest intentions in the world, doing infinitely more to prejudice his cause than to advance it.

So, in the present instance, it turned out with all the eloquence of 'Old Charley'; for, although he labored earnestly in behalf of the suspected, yet it so happened, somehow or other, that every syllable he uttered of which the direct but unwitting tendency was not to exalt the speaker in the good opinion of his audience, had the effect of deepening the suspicion already attached to the individual whose cause he plead, and of arousing against him the fury of the mob.

One of the most unaccountable errors committed by the orator was his allusion to the suspected as 'the heir of the worthy old gentleman Mr Shuttleworthy'. The people had really never thought of this before. They had only remembered certain threats of disinheritance uttered a year or two previously by the uncle (who had no living relative except the nephew), and they had, therefore, always looked upon this disinheritance as a matter that was settled—so single-minded a race of beings were the Rattleburghers; but the remark of 'Old Charley' brought them at once to a consideration of this point, and thus gave them to see the possibility of the threats having been nothing *more* than a threat. And straightway, hereupon, arose the natural question of *cui bono?*—a question that tended even more than the waistcoat to fasten the terrible crime upon the young man. And here, lest I may be misunderstood, permit me to digress for one moment merely to observe that the exceedingly brief and simple Latin phrase which I have employed, is invariably mistranslated and misconceived. '*Cui bono?*' in all the crack novels and elsewhere—in those of Mrs Gore, for example, (the author of 'Cecil') a lady who quotes all tongues from the Chaldæan to Chickasaw, and is helped to her learning, 'as needed', upon a systematic plan, by Mr Beckford—in *all* the crack novels, I say, from those of Bulwer and Dickens to those of Turnapenny and Ainsworth, the two little Latin words *cui bono* are rendered 'to what purpose?' or, (as if *quo bono*) 'to what good?' Their true meaning, nevertheless, is 'for whose advantage'. *Cui*, to whom; *bono*,

7

is it for a benefit? It is a purely legal phrase, and applicable precisely in cases such as we have now under consideration, where the probability of the doer of a deed hinges upon the probability of the benefit accruing to this individual or to that from the deed's accomplishment. Now in the present instance, the question *cui bono?* very pointedly implicated Mr Pennifeather. His uncle had threatened him, after making a will in his favor, with disinheritance. But the threat had not been actually kept; the original will, it appeared, had not been altered. *Had* it been altered, the only supposable motive for murder on the part of the suspected would have been the ordinary one of revenge; and even this would have been counteracted by the hope of reinstation into the good graces of the uncle. But the will being unaltered, while the threat to alter remained suspended over the nephew's head, there appears at once the very strongest possible inducement for the atrocity; and so concluded, very sagaciously, the worthy citizens of the borough of Rattle.

Mr Pennifeather was, accordingly, arrested upon the spot, and the crowd, after some further search, proceeded homeward, having him in custody. On the route, however, another circumstance occurred tending to confirm the suspicion entertained. Mr Goodfellow, whose zeal led him to be always a little in advance of the party, was seen suddenly to run forward a few paces, stoop, and then apparently pick up some small object from the grass. Having quickly examined it, he was observed, too, to make a sort of half attempt at concealing it in his coat pocket; but this action was noticed, as I say, and consequently prevented, when the object picked up was found to be a Spanish knife which a dozen persons at once recognized as belonging to Mr Pennifeather. Moreover, his initials were engraved upon the handle. The blade of this knife was open and bloody.

No doubt now remained of the guilt of the nephew, and immediately upon reaching Rattleborough he was taken before a magistrate for examination.

Here matters again took a most unfavorable turn. The prisoner, being questioned as to his whereabouts on the morning of Mr Shuttleworthy's disappearance, had absolutely the audacity to acknowledge that on that very morning he had been out with his rifle deer stalking, in the immediate neighborhood of the pool where the bloodstained waistcoat had been discovered through the sagacity of Mr Goodfellow.

This latter now came forward, and, with tears in his eyes, asked permission to be examined. He said that a stern sense of the duty he owed his Maker, not less than his fellow-men, would permit him no longer to remain silent. Hitherto, the sincerest affection for the young man (notwithstanding the latter's ill-treatment of himself, Mr Goodfellow) had induced him to make every hypothesis which imagination could suggest, by way of endeavoring to account for what appeared suspicious in the circumstances that told so seriously against Mr Pennifeather; but these circumstances were now altogether *too* convincing—*too* damning; he would hesitate no longer—he would tell all he knew, although his heart (Mr Goodfellow's) should absolutely burst asunder in the effort. He then went on to state that, on the afternoon of the day previous to Mr Shuttleworthy's departure for the city, that worthy old gentleman had mentioned to his nephew, in *his* hearing (Mr Goodfellow's), that his object in going to town on the morrow was to make a deposit of an unusually large sum of money in the 'Farmers' and Merchants' Bank', and that, then and there, the said Mr Shuttleworthy had distinctly avowed to the said nephew his irrevocable determination of rescinding the will originally made, and of cutting him off with a shilling. He (the witness) now solemnly called upon the accused to state whether what he (the witness) had just stated was or was not the truth in every substantial particular. Much to the astonishment of every one present, Mr Pennifeather frankly admitted that *it was*.

The magistrate now considered it his duty to send a couple of constables to search the chamber of the accused in the house of his uncle. From this search they almost immediately returned with the well-known steel-bound russet leather pocket-book which the old gentleman had been in the habit of carrying for years. Its valuable contents, however, had been abstracted, and the magistrate in vain endeavored to extort from the prisoner the use which had been made of them, or the place of their concealment. Indeed, he obstinately denied all knowledge of the matter. The constables, also, discovered, between the bed and the sacking of the unhappy man, a shirt and neck-handkerchief both marked with the initials of his name, and both hideously besmeared with the blood of the victim.

At this juncture, it was announced that the horse of the murdered man had just expired in the stable from the effects of the wound he had received, and it was proposed by Mr Goodfellow that a post-mortem examination of the beast should be immediately made, with the view, if possible, of discovering the ball. This was accordingly done; and, as if to demonstrate beyond a question the guilt of the accused, Mr Goodfellow, after considerable searching in the cavity of the chest, was enabled to detect and to pull forth a bullet of very extra-ordinary size, which, upon trial, was found to be exactly adapted to the bore of Mr Pennifeather's rifle, while it was far too large for that of any other person in the borough or its vicinity. To render the matter even surer yet, however, this bullet was discovered to have a flaw or seam at right angles to the usual suture, and upon examination, this seam corresponded precisely with an accidental ridge or elevation in a pair of moulds acknowledged by the accused himself to be his own property. Upon the finding of this bullet, the examining magistrate refused to listen to any further testimony, and immediately commit-ted the prisoner for trial—declining resolutely to take any bail in the case, although against this severity Mr Goodfellow very warmly remonstrated, and offered to become surety in whatever amount might be required. This generosity on the part of 'Old Charley' was only in accordance with the whole tenor of his amiable and chivalrous conduct during the entire period of his sojourn in the borough of Rattle. In the present instance the worthy man was so entirely carried away by the excessive warmth of his sympathy, that he seemed to have quite forgotten, when he offered to go bail for his young friend, that he himself (Mr Goodfellow) did not possess a single dollar's worth of property upon the face of the earth.

The result of the committal may be readily foreseen. Mr Pennifeather, amid the loud execrations of all Rattleborough, was brought to trial at the next criminal sessions, when the chain of cir-cumstantial evidence (strengthened as it was by some additional damning facts, which Mr Goodfellow's sensitive conscientiousness forbade him to withhold from the court) was considered so unbroken and so thoroughly conclusive, that the jury, without leaving their seats, returned an immediate verdict of *'Guilty of murder in the first degree'*. Soon afterward the unhappy wretch received sentence of death, and was remanded to the county jail to await the inexorable vengeance of the law.

In the meantime, the noble behaviour of 'Old Charley Goodfellow' had doubly endeared him to the honest citizens of the borough. He became ten times a greater favorite than ever; and, as a natural result of the hospitality with which he was treated, he relaxed, as it were, perforce, the extremely parsimonious habits which his poverty had hitherto impelled him to observe, and very frequently had little *réunions* at his own house, when wit and jollity reigned supreme—dampened a little, *of course*, by the occasional remembrance of the untoward and melancholy fate which impended over the nephew of the late lamented bosom friend of the generous host.

One fine day, this magnanimous old gentleman was agreeably surprised at the receipt of the following letter:

Charles Goodfellow, Esq., Rattleborough.
From H, F., B., & Co.
Chât. Mar. A—No. 1—6 doz. bottles (½ Gross).

> *'Charles Goodfellow, Esquire:*
>
> *'Dear Sir—In conformity with an order transmitted to our firm about two months since, by our esteemed correspondent, Mr Barnabas Shuttleworthy, we have the honor of forwarding this morning, to your address, a double box of Château-Margaux, of the antelope brand, violet seal. Box numbered and marked as per margin.*
>
> > *'We remain, sir,*
> > *'Your most ob'nt ser'ts,*
> > *'*HOGGS, FROGS, BOGS, & CO.
>
> *'City of——, June 21, 18—.*
>
> *'P.S.—The box will reach you, by wagon, on the day after your receipt of this letter. Our respects to Mr Shuttleworthy.*
>
> > *'*H., F., B., & CO.*'*

The fact is, that Mr Goodfellow had, since the death of Mr Shuttleworthy, given over all expectation of ever receiving the promised Château-Margaux; and, he, therefore, looked upon it *now* as a sort of especial dispensation of Providence in his behalf. He was highly delighted, of course, and in the exuberance of his joy invited a large party of friends to a *petit souper* on the morrow, for the purpose of broaching the good old Mr Shuttleworthy's present. Not that he *said* anything about 'the good old Mr Shuttleworthy' when he issued the invitations. The fact is, he thought much and concluded to say nothing at all. He did *not* mention to any one—if I remember aright—that he had received a *present* of Château-Margaux. He merely asked his friends to come and help him drink some of a remarkably fine quality and rich flavor that he had ordered up from the city a couple of months ago, and of which he would be in the receipt upon the morrow. I have often puzzled myself to imagine *why* it was that 'Old Charley' came to the conclusion to say nothing about having received the wine from his old friend, but I could never precisely understand his reason for the silence, although he had *some* excellent and very magnanimous reason, no doubt.

The morrow at length arrived, and with it a very large and highly respectable company at Mr Goodfellow's house. Indeed, half the borough was there—I myself among the number—but, much to the vexation of the host, the Château-Margaux did not arrive until a late hour, and when the sumptuous supper supplied by 'Old Charley' had been done very ample justice by the guests. It came at length, however—a monstrously big box of it there was, too—and as the whole party were in excessively good humor, it was decided, *nem. con.*, that it should be lifted upon the table and its contents disembowelled forthwith.

No sooner said than done. I lent a helping hand; and, in a trice, we had the box upon the table, in the midst of all the bottles and glasses, not a few of which were demolished in the scuffle. 'Old Charley', who was pretty much intoxicated, and excessively red in the face, now took a seat, with an air of mock dignity, at the head of the board, and thumped furiously upon it with a decanter, calling upon the company to keep order 'during the ceremony of disinterring the treasure'.

After some vociferation, quiet was at length fully restored, and, as very often happens in similar cases, a profound and remarkable silence ensued. Being then requested to force open the lid, I complied, of course, 'with an infinite deal of pleasure'. I inserted a chisel, and giving it a few slight taps with a hammer, the top of the box flew suddenly off, and, at the same instant, there sprang up into a sitting position, directly facing the host, the bruised, bloody, and nearly putrid corpse of the murdered Mr Shuttleworthy himself. It gazed for a few seconds, fixedly and sorrowfully, with its decaying and lack-lustre eyes, full into the countenance of Mr Goodfellow; uttered slowly, but clearly and impressively, the words—'Thou art the man!' and then, falling over the side of the chest as if thoroughly satisfied, stretched out its limbs quiveringly upon the table.

The scene that ensued is altogether beyond description. The rush for the doors and windows was terrific, and many of the most robust men in the room fainted outright through sheer horror. But after the first wild, shrieking burst of affright, all eyes were directed to Mr Goodfellow. If I live a thousand years, I can never forget the more than mortal agony which was depicted in that ghastly face of his, so lately rubicund with triumph and wine. For several minutes he sat rigidly as a statue of marble; his eyes seeming, in the intense vacancy of their gaze, to be turned inward and absorbed in the contemplation of his own miserable, murderous soul. At length their expression appeared to flash suddenly out into the external world, when, with a quick leap, he sprang from his chair, and falling heavily with his head and shoulders upon the table, and in contact with the corpse, poured out rapidly and vehemently a detailed confession of the hideous crime for which Mr Pennifeather was then imprisoned and doomed to die.

What he recounted was in substance this:—He followed his victim to the vicinity of the pool; there shot his horse with a pistol; despatched its rider with the butt end; possessed himself of the pocket-book; and, supposing the horse dead, dragged it with great labor to the brambles by the pond. Upon his own beast he slung the corpse of Mr Shuttleworthy, and thus bore it to a secure place of concealment a long distance off through the woods.

The waistcoat, the knife, the pocket-book, and bullet, had been placed by himself where found, with the view of avenging himself upon Mr Pennifeather. He had also contrived the discovery of the stained handkerchief and shirt.

Toward the end of the blood-chilling recital, the words of the guilty wretch faltered and grew hollow. When the record was finally exhausted, he arose, staggered backward from the table, and fell—
dead.

The means by which this happily timed confession was extorted, although efficient, were simple indeed. Mr Goodfellow's excess of frankness had disgusted me, and excited my suspicions from the first. I was present when Mr Pennifeather had struck him, and the fiendish expression which then arose upon his countenance, although momentary, assured me that his threat of vengeance would, if possible, be rigidly fulfilled. I was thus prepared to view the *manœuvring* of 'Old Charley' in a very different light from that in which it was regarded by the good citizens of Rattleborough. I saw at once that all the criminating discoveries arose, either directly or indirectly, from himself. But the fact which clearly opened my eyes to the true state of the case, was the affair of the bullet, *found* by Mr G. in the carcass of the horse. I had not forgotten, although the Rattleburghers *had*, that there was a hole where the ball had entered the horse, and another where it *went out*. If it were found in the animal then, after having made its exit, I saw clearly that it must have been deposited by the person who found it. The bloody shirt and handkerchief confirmed the idea suggested by the bullet; for the blood on examination proved to be capital claret, and no more. When I came to think of these things, and also of the late increase of liberality and expenditure on the part of Mr Goodfellow, I entertained a suspicion which was none the less strong because I kept it altogether to myself.

In the meantime, I instituted a rigorous private search for the corpse of Mr Shuttleworthy, and, for good reasons, searched in quarters as divergent as possible from those to which Mr Goodfellow conducted his party. The result was that, after some days, I came across an old dry well, the mouth of which was nearly hidden by brambles; and here, at the bottom, I discovered what I sought.

Now it so happened that I had overheard the colloquy between the two cronies, when Mr Goodfellow had contrived to cajole his host into the promise of a box of Château-Margaux. Upon this hint I acted. I procured a stiff piece of whalebone, thrust it down the throat of the corpse, and deposited the latter in an old wine box—taking care so to double the body up as to double the whalebone with it. In this manner I had to press forcibly upon the lid to keep it down while I secured it with nails; and I anticipated, of course, that as soon as these latter were removed, the top would fly *off* and the body *up*.

Having thus arranged the box, I marked, numbered, and addressed it as already told; and then writing a letter in the name of the wine-merchants with whom Mr Shuttleworthy dealt, I gave instructions to my servant to wheel the box to Mr Goodfellow's door, in a barrow, at a given signal from myself. For the words which I intended the corpse to speak, I confidently depended upon my ventriloquial abilities; for their effect, I counted upon the conscience of the murderous wretch.

I believe there is nothing more to be explained. Mr Pennifeather was released upon the spot, inherited the fortune of his uncle, profited by the lessons of experience, turned over a new leaf, and led happily ever afterwards a new life.

2

JACQUES FUTRELLE

The Stolen Rubens

Matthew Kale made fifty million dollars out of axle grease, after which he began to patronize the high arts. It was simple enough: he had the money, and Europe had the old masters. His method of buying was simplicity itself. There were five thousand square yards, more or less, in the huge gallery of his marble mansion which were to be covered, so he bought five thousand yards, more or less, of art. Some of it was good, some of it fair, and much of it bad. The chief picture of the collection was a Rubens, which he had picked up in Rome for fifty thousand dollars.

Soon after acquiring his collection, Kale decided to make certain alterations in the vast room where the pictures hung. They were all taken down and stored in the ballroom, equally vast, with their faces toward the wall. Meanwhile Kale and his family took refuge in a nearby hotel.

It was at this hotel that Kale met Jules de Lesseps. De Lesseps was distinctly the sort of Frenchman whose conversation resembles calisthenics. He was nervous, quick, and agile, and he told Kale in confidence that he was not only a painter himself, but a connoisseur in the high arts. Pompous in the pride of possession, Kale went to a good deal of trouble to exhibit his private collection for de Lesseps' delectation. It happened in the ballroom, and the true artist's delight shone in the Frenchman's eyes as he handled the pieces which were good. Some of the others made him smile, but it was an inoffensive sort of smile.

With his own hands Kale lifted the precious Rubens and held it before the Frenchman's eyes. It was a 'Madonna and Child', one of those wonderful creations which have endured through the years with all the sparkle and color beauty of their pristine days. Kale seemed disappointed because de Lesseps was not particularly enthusiastic about this picture.

'Why, it's a Rubens!' he exclaimed.

'Yes, I see,' replied de Lesseps.

'It cost me fifty thousand dollars.'

'It is perhaps worth more than that,' and the Frenchman shrugged his shoulders as he turned away.

Kale looked at him in chagrin. Could it be that de Lesseps did not understand that it was a Rubens, and that Rubens was a painter? Or was it that he had failed to hear him say that it cost him fifty thousand dollars. Kale was accustomed to seeing people bob their heads and open their eyes when he said fifty thousand dollars; therefore, 'Don't you like it?' he asked.

'Very much indeed,' replied de Lesseps; 'but I have seen it before. I saw it in Rome just a week or so before you purchased it.'

They rummaged on through the pictures, and at last a Whistler was turned up for their inspection. It was one of the famous Thames series, a water color. De Lesseps' face radiated excitement, and several times he glanced from the water color to the Rubens as if mentally comparing the exquisitely penciled and colored newer work with the bold, masterly technic of the older painting.

Kale misunderstood his silence. 'I don't think much of this one myself,' he explained apologetically. 'It's a Whistler, and all that, and it cost me five thousand dollars, and I sort of had to have it, but still it isn't just the kind of thing that I like. What do you think of it?'

'I think it is perfectly wonderful!' replied the Frenchman enthusiastically. 'It is the essence, the superlative, of Whistler's work. I wonder if it would be possible', and he turned to face Kale, 'for me to make a copy of that? I have some slight skill in painting myself, and dare say I could make a fairly creditable copy of it.'

Kale was flattered. He was more and more impressed each moment with the picture. 'Why certainly,' he replied. 'I will have it sent up to the hotel, and you can—'

'No, no, no!' interrupted de Lesseps quickly. 'I wouldn't care to accept the responsibility of having the picture in my charge. There is always a danger of fire. But if you would give me permission to come here—this room is large and airy and light—and besides it is quiet—'

'Just as you like,' said Kale magnanimously. 'I merely thought the other way would be most convenient for you.'

De Lesseps laid one hand on the millionaire's arm. 'My dear friend,' he said earnestly, 'if these pictures were my pictures, I shouldn't try to accommodate anybody where they were concerned. I dare say the collection as it stands cost you—'

'Six hundred and eighty-seven thousand dollars,' volunteered Kale proudly.

'And surely they must be well protected here in your house during your absence.'

'There are about twenty servants in the house, while the workmen are making the alterations,' said Kale, 'and three of them don't do anything but watch this room. No one can go in or out except by the door we entered—the others are locked and barred—and then only with my permission, or a written order from me. No sir, nobody can get away with anything in this room.'

'Excellent—excellent!' said de Lesseps admiringly. He smiled a little. 'I am afraid I did not give you credit for being the far-sighted businessman that you are.' He turned and glanced over the collection of pictures abstractedly. 'A clever thief, though,' he ventured, 'might cut a valuable painting, for instance the Rubens, out of the frame, roll it up, conceal it under his coat, and escape.'

Kale laughed and shook his head.

It was a couple of days later at the hotel that de Lesseps brought up the subject of copying the Whistler. He was profuse in his thanks when Kale volunteered to accompany him into the mansion and witness the preliminary stages of the work. They paused at the ballroom door.

'Jennings,' said Kale to the liveried servant there, 'this is Mr de Lesseps. He is to come and go as he likes. He is going to do some work in the ballroom here. See that he isn't disturbed.'

De Lesseps noticed the Rubens leaning carelessly against some other pictures, with the holy face of the Madonna turned toward them. 'Really, Mr Kale,' he protested, 'that picture is too valuable to be left about like that. If you will let your servants bring me some canvas, I shall wrap it and place it up on this table off the floor. Suppose there were mice here!'

Kale thanked him. The necessary orders were given, and finally the picture was carefully wrapped and placed beyond harm's reach, whereupon de Lesseps adjusted himself, paper, easel, stool, and all, and began his work of copying. There Kale left him.

Three days later Kale found the artist still at his labor.

'I just dropped by,' he explained, 'to see how the work in the gallery was getting along. It will be finished in another week. I hope I am not disturbing you?'

'Not at all,' said de Lesseps; 'I have nearly finished. See how I am getting along?' He turned the easel toward Kale.

The millionaire gazed from that toward the original which stood on a chair near by, and frank admiration for the artist's efforts was in his eyes. 'Why, it's fine!' he exclaimed. 'It's just as good as the other one, and I bet you don't want any five thousand dollars for it—eh?'

That was all that was said about it at the time. Kale wandered about the house for an hour or so, then dropped into the ballroom where de Lesseps was getting his paraphernalia together, and they walked back to the hotel. The artist carried under one arm his copy of the Whistler, loosely rolled up.

Another week passed, and the workmen who had been engaged in refinishing and decorating the gallery had gone. De Lesseps volunteered to assist in the work of rehanging the pictures, and Kale gladly turned the matter over to him. It was in the afternoon of the day this work began that de Lesseps, chatting pleasantly with Kale, ripped loose the canvas which enshrouded the precious Rubens. Then he paused with an exclamation of dismay. The picture was gone; the frame which had held it was empty. A thin strip of canvas around the inside edge showed that a sharp penknife had been used to cut out the painting.

All of these facts came to the attention of Professor Augustus S. F. X. Van Dusen—The Thinking Machine. This was a day or so after Kale had rushed into Detective Mallory's office at police headquarters with the statement that his Rubens had been stolen. He banged his fist down on the detective's desk, and roared at him.

'It cost me fifty thousand dollars! Why don't you do something? What are you sitting there staring at me for?'

'Don't excite yourself, Mr Kale,' the detective advised. 'I will put my men at work right now to recover the—the—What is a Rubens, anyway?'

'It's a picture!' bellowed Kale. 'A piece of canvas with some paint on it, and it cost me fifty thousand dollars—don't you forget that!'

So the police machinery was set in motion to recover the picture. And in time the matter fell under the watchful eye of Hutchinson Hatch, reporter. He learned the facts preceding the disappearance of the picture and then called on de Lesseps. He found the artist in a state of excitement bordering on hysteria; an intimation from the reporter of the object of his visit caused de Lesseps to burst into words.

'*Mon Dieu!* It is outrageous! What can I do? I was the only one in the room for several days. I was the one who took such pains to protect the picture. And now it is gone! The loss is irreparable. What can I do?'

Hatch didn't have any very definite idea as to just what he could do, so he let him go on. 'As I understand it, Mr de Lesseps,' he interrupted at last, 'no one else was in the room, except you and Mr Kale, all the time you were there?'

'No one else.'

'And I think Mr Kale said that you were making a copy of some famous water color; weren't you?'

'Yes, a Thames scene by Whistler,' was the reply. 'That is it, hanging over the fireplace.'

Hatch glanced at the picture admiringly. It was an exquisite copy, and showed the deft touch of a man who was himself an artist of great ability.

De Lesseps read the admiration in his face. 'It is not bad,' he said modestly. 'I studied with Carolus Duran.'

With all else that was known, and this little additional information, which seemed of no particular value to the reporter, the entire matter was laid before The Thinking Machine. That distinguished man listened from beginning to end without comment.

'Who had access to the room?' he asked finally.

'That is what the police are working on now,' said Hutchinson Hatch. 'There are a couple of dozen servants in the house, and I suppose, in spite of Kale's rigid orders, there was a certain laxity in their enforcement.'

'Of course that makes it more difficult,' said The Thinking Machine in the perpetually irritated voice which was so characteristic a part of himself. 'Perhaps it would be best for us to go to Mr Kale's home and personally investigate.'

Kale received them with the reserve which rich men usually show in the presence of representatives of the press. He stared frankly and somewhat curiously at the diminutive figure of the scientist, who explained the object of their visit.

'I guess you fellows can't do anything with this,' the millionaire assured them. 'I've got some regular detectives on it.'

'Is Mr Mallory here now?' asked The Thinking Machine curtly.

'Yes, he is upstairs in the servants' quarters.'

'May we see the room from which the picture was taken?' enquired the scientist, with a suave intonation which Hatch knew well.

Kale granted the permission with a wave of the hand, and ushered them into the ballroom, where the pictures had been stored. From the center of this room The Thinking Machine surveyed it all. The windows were high. Half a dozen doors leading out into the hallways, the conservatory, quiet nooks of the mansion offered innumerable possibilities of access. After this one long comprehensive squint, The Thinking Machine went over and picked up the frame from which the Rubens had been cut. For a long time he examined it. Kale's impatience was evident. Finally the scientist turned to him.

'How well do you know M. de Lesseps?'

'I've known him for only a month or so. Why?'

'Did he bring you letters of introduction, or did you meet him merely casually?'

Kale regarded him with displeasure. 'My own personal affairs have nothing whatever to do with this matter! Mr de Lesseps is a gentleman of integrity, and certainly he is the last whom I would suspect of any connection with the disappearance of the picture.'

'That is usually the case,' remarked The Thinking Machine tartly. He turned to Hatch. 'Just how good a copy was that he made of the Whistler picture?'

'I have never seen the original,' Hatch replied; 'but the workman-ship was superb. Perhaps Mr Kale wouldn't object to us seeing—'

'Oh, of course not,' said Kale resignedly. 'Come in; it's in the gallery.'

Hatch submitted the picture to a careful scrutiny. 'I should say the copy is well-nigh perfect,' was his verdict. 'Of course, in its absence, I can't say exactly; but it is certainly a superb work.'

The curtains of a wide door almost in front of them were thrown aside suddenly, and Detective Mallory entered. He carried something in his hand, but at sight of them concealed it behind him. Unrepressed triumph was in his face.

'Ah, professor, we meet often; don't we?' he said.

'This reporter here and his friend seem to be trying to drag de Lesseps into this affair somehow,' Kale complained to the detective. 'I don't want anything like that to happen. He is liable to go out and print anything. They always do.'

The Thinking Machine glared at him unwaveringly for an instant, then extended his hand toward Mallory. 'Where did you find it?' he asked.

'Sorry to disappoint you, professor,' said the detective sarcas-tically, 'but this is the time when you were a little late,' and he produced the object which he held behind him. 'Here is your picture, Mr Kale.'

Kale gasped in relief and astonishment, and held up the canvas with both hands to examine it. 'Fine!' he told the detective. 'I'll see that you don't lose anything by this. Why, that thing cost me fifty thousand dollars!'

The Thinking Machine leaned forward to squint at the upper right-hand corner of the canvas. 'Where did you find it?' he asked again.

'Rolled up tight, and concealed in the bottom of a trunk in the room of one of the servants,' explained Mallory. 'The servant's name is Jennings. He is now under arrest.'

'Jennings!' exclaimed Kale. 'Why, he has been with me for years.'

'Did he confess?' asked the scientist imperturbably.

'Of course not,' said Mallory. 'He says some of the other servants must have hidden it there.'

The Thinking Machine nodded at Hatch. 'I think perhaps that is all,' he remarked. 'I congratulate you, Mr Mallory, upon bringing the matter to such a quick and satisfactory conclusion.'

Ten minutes later they left the house and took a taxi for the scientist's home. Hatch was a little chagrined at the unexpected termination of the affair.

'Mallory does show an occasional gleam of human intelligence, doesn't he?'

'Not that I ever noticed,' remarked The Thinking Machine crustily.

'But he found the picture,' Hatch insisted.

'Of course he found it. It was put there for him to find.'

'Put there for him to find!' repeated the reporter. 'Didn't Jennings steal it?'

'If he did, he's a fool.'

'Well, if he didn't steal it, who put it there?'

'De Lesseps.'

'De Lesseps!' echoed Hatch. 'Why the deuce did he steal a fifty thousand dollar picture and put it in a servant's trunk to be found?'

The Thinking Machine twisted around in his seat and squinted at him coldly for a moment. 'At times, Mr Hatch, I am absolutely amazed at your stupidity. I can understand it in a man like Mallory, but I have always given you credit for being an astute, quick-witted man.'

Hatch smiled at the reproach. It was not the first time he had heard it. But nothing bearing on the problem in hand was said until they reached The Thinking Machine's house.

'The only real question in my mind, Mr Hatch,' said the scientist then, 'is whether or not I should take the trouble to restore Mr Kale's picture at all. He is perfectly satisfied, and will probably never know the difference. So—'

Suddenly Hatch saw something. 'Great Scott!' he exclaimed. 'Do you mean that the picture Mallory found was—'

'A copy of the original,' snapped the scientist. 'Personally I know nothing whatever about art; therefore, I could not say from observation that it is a copy, but I know it from the logic of the thing. When the original was cut from the frame, the knife swerved a little at the upper right-hand corner. The canvas remaining in the frame told me that. The picture that Mr Mallory found did not correspond in this detail with the canvas in the frame. The conclusion is obvious.'

'And de Lesseps has the original?'

'De Lesseps has the original. How did he get it? In any one of a dozen ways. He might have rolled it up and stuck it under his coat. He might have had a confederate. But I don't think that any ordinary method of theft would have appealed to him. I am giving him credit for being clever, as I must when we review the whole case.

'For instance, he asked for permission to copy the Whistler, which you saw was the same size as the Rubens. It was granted. He copied it practically under guard, always with the chance that Mr Kale himself would drop in. It took him three days to copy it, so he says. He was alone in the room all that time. He knew that Mr Kale had not the faintest idea of art. Taking advantage of that, what would have been simpler than to have copied the Rubens in oil? He could have removed it from the frame immediately after he canvased it over, and kept it in a position near him where it could be quickly concealed if he was interrupted. Remember, the picture is worth fifty thousand dollars; therefore, was worth the trouble.

'De Lesseps is an artist—we know that—and dealing with a man who knew nothing whatever of art, he had no fears. We may suppose his idea all along was to use the copy of the Rubens as a sort of decoy after he got away with the original. You saw that Mallory didn't know the difference, and it was safe for him to suppose that Mr Kale wouldn't. His only danger until he could get away gracefully was of some critic or connoisseur, perhaps, seeing the copy. His boldness we see readily in the fact that he permitted himself to discover the theft; that he discovered it after he had volunteered to assist Mr Kale in the general work of rehanging the pictures in the gallery. Just how he put the picture in Jenning's trunk I don't happen to know. We can imagine many ways.' He lay back in his chair for a minute without speaking, eyes steadily turned upward, fingers placed precisely tip to tip.

'But how did he take the picture from the Kale home?' asked Hatch.

'He took it with him probably under his arm the day he left the house with Mr Kale,' was the astonishing reply.

Hatch was staring at him in amazement. After a moment the

scientist rose and passed into the adjoining room, and the telephone bell there jingled. When he joined Hatch again he picked up his hat and they went out together.

De Lesseps was in when their cards were sent up, and received them. They conversed about the case generally for ten minutes, while the scientist's eyes were turned enquiringly here and there about the room. At last there came a knock on the door.

'It is Detective Mallory, Mr Hatch,' remarked The Thinking Machine. 'Open the door for him.'

De Lesseps seemed startled for just one instant, then quickly recovered. Mallory's eyes were full of questions when he entered.

'I should like, Mr Mallory,' began The Thinking Machine quietly, 'to call your attention to this copy of Mr Kale's picture by Whistler—over the mantel here. Isn't it excellent? You have seen the original?'

Mallory grunted. De Lesseps face, instead of expressing appreciation of the compliment, blanched, and his hands closed tightly. Again he recovered himself and smiled.

'The beauty of this picture lies not only in its faithfulness to the original,' the scientist went on, 'but also in the fact that it was painted under extraordinary circumstances. For instance, I don't know if you know, Mr Mallory, that it is possible so to combine glue and putty and a few other commonplace things into a paste which will effectually blot out an oil painting, and offer at the same time an excellent surface for water color work!'

There was a moment's pause, during which the three men stared at him silently—with conflicting emotions.

'This water color—this copy of Whistler,' continued the scientist evenly—'is painted on such a paste as I have described. That paste in turn covers the original Rubens picture. It can be removed with water without damage to the picture, which is in oil, so that instead of a copy of the Whistler painting, we have an original by Rubens, worth fifty thousand dollars. That is true; isn't it, M. de Lesseps?'

There was no reply to the question—none was needed.

It was an hour later, after de Lesseps was safely in his cell, that Hatch called up The Thinking Machine and asked one question.

'How did you know that the water color was painted over the Rubens?'

'Because it was the only absolutely safe way in which the Rubens could be hopelessly lost to those who were looking for it, and at the same time perfectly preserved,' was the answer. 'I told you de Lesseps was a clever man, and a little logic did the rest. Two and two always make four, Mr Hatch, not sometimes, but all the time.'

3

ANNA KATHARINE GREEN

The Second Bullet

'You must see her.'

'No. No.'

'She's a most unhappy woman. Husband and child both taken from her in a moment; and now, all means of living as well, unless some happy thought of yours—some inspiration of your genius—shows us a way of re-establishing her claims to the policy voided by this cry of suicide.'

But the small wise head of Violet Strange continued its slow shake of decided refusal.

'I'm sorry,' she protested, 'but it's quite out of my province. I'm too young to meddle with so serious a matter.'

'Not when you can save a bereaved woman the only possible compensation left her by untoward fate?'

'Let the police try their hand at that.'

'They have had no success with the case.'

'Or you?'

'Nor I either.'

'And you expect——'

'Yes, Miss Strange. I expect *you* to find the missing bullet which will settle the fact that murder and not suicide ended George Hammond's life. If you cannot, then a long litigation awaits this poor widow, ending, as such litigation usually does, in favour of the stronger party. There's the alternative. If you once saw her——'

'But that's what I'm not willing to do. If I once saw her I should yield to her importunities and attempt the seemingly impossible. My instincts bid me say no. Give me something easier.'

'Easier things are not so remunerative. There's money in this affair, if the insurance company is forced to pay up. I can offer you——'

'What?'

There was eagerness in the tone despite her effort at nonchalance. The other smiled imperceptibly, and briefly named the sum.

It was larger than she had expected. This her visitor saw by the way her eyelids fell and the peculiar stillness which, for an instant, held her vivacity in check.

'And you think I can earn that?'

Her eyes were fixed on his in an eagerness as honest as it was unrestrained.

He could hardly conceal his amazement, her desire was so evident and the cause of it so difficult to understand. He knew she wanted money—that was her avowed reason for entering into this uncongenial work. But to want it *so much!* He glanced at her person; it was simply clad but very expensively—how expensively it was his business to know. Then he took in the room in which they sat. Simplicity again, but the simplicity of high art—the drawing-room of one rich enough to indulge in the final luxury of a highly cultivated taste, viz.: unostentatious elegance and the subjection of each carefully chosen ornament to the general effect.

What did this favoured child of fortune lack that she could be reached by such a plea, when her whole being revolted from the nature of the task he offered her? It was a question not new to him; but one he had never heard answered and was not likely to hear answered now. But the fact remained that the consent he had thought dependent upon sympathetic interest could be reached much more readily by the promise of large emolument—and he owned to a feeling of secret disappointment even while he recognized the value of the discovery.

But his satisfaction in the latter, if satisfaction it were, was of very short duration. Almost immediately he observed a change in her. The sparkle which had shone in the eye whose depths he had never been able to penetrate, had dissipated itself in something like a tear and she spoke up in that vigorous tone no one but himself had ever heard, as she said:

'No. The sum is a good one and I could use it; but I will not waste my energy on a case I do not believe in. The man shot himself. He was a speculator, and probably had good reason for his act. Even his wife acknowledges that he has lately had more losses than gains.'

'See her. She has something to tell you which never got into the papers.'

'You say that? You know that?'

'On my honour, Miss Strange.'

Violet pondered; then suddenly succumbed.

'Let her come, then. Prompt to the hour. I will receive her at three. Later I have a tea and two party calls to make.'

Her visitor rose to leave. He had been able to subdue all evidence of his extreme gratification, and now took on a formal air. In dismissing a guest, Miss Strange was invariably the society belle and that only. This he had come to recognize.

The case (well known at the time) was, in the fewest possible words, as follows:

On a sultry night in September, a young couple living in one of the large apartment houses in the extreme upper portion of Manhattan were so annoyed by the incessant crying of a child in the adjoining suite, that they got up, he to smoke, and she to sit in the window for a possible breath of cool air. They were congratulating themselves upon the wisdom they had shown in thus giving up all thought of sleep—for the child's crying had not ceased—when (it may have been two o'clock and it may have been a little later) there came from somewhere near, the sharp and somewhat peculiar detonation of a pistol-shot.

He thought it came from above; she, from the rear, and they were staring at each other in the helpless wonder of the moment, when they were struck by the silence. The baby had ceased to cry. All was as still in the adjoining apartment as in their own—too still—much too still. Their mutual stare turned to one of horror. 'It came from there!' whispered the wife. 'Some accident has occurred to Mr or Mrs Hammond—we ought to go——'

Her words—very tremulous ones—were broken by a shout from below. They were standing in their window and had evidently been seen by a passing policeman. 'Anything wrong up there?' they heard him cry. Mr Saunders immediately looked out. 'Nothing wrong here,' he called down. (They were but two stories from the pavement.) 'But I'm not so sure about the rear apartment. We thought we heard a shot. Hadn't you better come up, officer? My wife is nervous about it. I'll meet you at the stair-head and show you the way.'

The officer nodded and stepped in. The young couple hastily donned some wraps, and, by the time he appeared on their floor, they were ready to accompany him.

Meanwhile, no disturbance was apparent anywhere else in the house, until the policeman rang the bell of the Hammond apartment. Then, voices began to be heard, and doors to open above and below, but not the one before which the policeman stood.

Another ring, and this time an insistent one; and still no response. The officer's hand was rising for the third time when there came a sound of fluttering from behind the panels against which he had laid his ear, and finally a choked voice uttering unintelligible words. Then a hand began to struggle with the lock, and the door, slowly opening, disclosed a woman clad in a hastily donned wrapper and giving every evidence of extreme fright.

'Oh!' she exclaimed, seeing only the compassionate faces of her neighbours. 'You heard it, too! a pistol-shot from there—*there* my husband's room. I have not dared to go—I—I—O, have mercy and see if anything is wrong! It is so still—so still, and only a moment ago the baby was crying. Mrs Saunders, Mrs Saunders, why is it so still?'

She had fallen into her neighbour's arms. The hand with which she had pointed out a certain door had sunk to her side and she appeared to be on the verge of collapse.

The officer eyed her sternly, while noting her appearance, which was that of a woman hastily risen from bed.

'Where were you?' he asked. 'Not with your husband and child, or you would know what had happened there.'

'I was sleeping down the hall,' she managed to gasp out. 'I'm not well—I—Oh, why do you all stand still and do nothing? My baby's in there. Go! go!' and, with a sudden energy, she sprang upright, her eyes wide open and burning, her small well-featured face white as the linen she sought to hide.

The officer demurred no longer. In another instant he was trying the door at which she was again pointing.

It was locked.

Glancing back at the woman, now cowering almost to the floor, he pounded at the door and asked the man inside to open.

No answer came back.

With a sharp turn he glanced again at the wife.

'You say that your husband is in this room?'

She nodded, gasping faintly, 'And the child!'

He turned back, listened, then beckoned to Mr Saunders. 'We shall have to break our way in,' said he. 'Put your shoulder well to the door. *Now!*'

The hinges of the door creaked; the lock gave way (this special officer weighed two hundred and seventy-five, as he found out, next day), and a prolonged and sweeping crash told the rest.

Mrs Hammond gave a low cry; and, straining forward from where she crouched in terror on the floor, searched the faces of the two men for some hint of what they saw in the dimly-lighted space beyond.

Something dreadful, something which made Mr Saunders come rushing back with a shout:

'Take her away! Take her to our apartment, Jennie. She must not see——'

Not see! He realized the futility of his words as his gaze fell on the young woman who had risen up at his approach and now stood gazing at him without speech, without movement, but with a glare of terror in her eyes, which gave him his first realization of human misery.

His own glance fell before it. If he had followed his instinct he would have fled the house rather than answer the question of her look and the attitude of her whole frozen body.

Perhaps in mercy to his speechless terror, perhaps in mercy to herself, she was the one who at last found the word which voiced their mutual anguish.

'Dead?'

No answer. None was needed.

'And my baby?'

O, that cry! It curdled the hearts of all who heard it. It shook the souls of men and women both inside and outside the apartment; then all was forgotten in the wild rush she made. The wife and mother had flung herself upon the scene, and, side by side with the not unmoved policeman, stood looking down upon the desolation made in one fatal instant in her home and heart.

They lay there together, both past help, both quite dead. The child had simply been strangled by the weight of his father's arm which lay directly across the upturned little throat. But the father was a victim of the shot they had heard. There was blood on his breast, and a pistol in his hand.

Suicide! The horrible truth was patent. No wonder they wanted to hold the young widow back. Her neighbour, Mrs Saunders, crept in on tiptoe and put her arms about the swaying, fainting woman; but there was nothing to say—absolutely nothing.

At least, they thought not. But when they saw her throw herself down, not by her husband, but by the child, and drag it out from under that strangling arm and hug and kiss it and call out wildly for a doctor, the officer endeavoured to interfere and yet could not find the heart to do so, though he knew the child was dead and should not, according to all the rules of the coroner's office, be moved before that official arrived. Yet because no mother could be convinced of a fact like this, he let her sit with it on the floor and try all her little arts to revive it, while he gave orders to the janitor and waited himself for the arrival of doctor and coroner.

She was still sitting there in wide-eyed misery, alternately fondling the little body and drawing back to consult its small set features for some sign of life, when the doctor came, and, after one look at the child, drew it softly from her arms and laid it quietly in the crib from which its father had evidently lifted it but a short time before. Then he turned back to her, and found her on her feet, upheld by her two friends. She had understood his action, and without a groan had accepted her fate. Indeed, she seemed incapable of any further speech or action. She was staring down at her husband's body, which she, for the first time, seemed fully to see. Was her look one of grief or of resentment for the part he had played so unintentionally in her child's death? It was hard to tell; and when, with slowly rising finger, she pointed to the pistol so tightly clutched in the other outstretched hand, no one there—and by this time the room was full—could foretell what her words would be when her tongue regained its usage and she could speak.

What she did say was this:

'Is there a bullet gone? Did he fire off that pistol?' A question so manifestly one of delirium that no one answered it, which seemed to surprise her, though she said nothing till her glance had passed all around the walls of the room to where a window stood open to the night—its lower sash being entirely raised. 'There! look there!' she cried, with a commanding accent, and, throwing up her hands, sank a dead weight into the arms of those supporting her.

No one understood; but naturally more than one rushed to the window. An open space was before them. Here lay the fields not yet parcelled out into lots and built upon; but it was not upon these they looked, but upon the strong trellis which they found there, which, if it supported no vine, formed a veritable ladder between this window and the ground.

Could she have meant to call attention to this fact; and were her words expressive of another idea than the obvious one of suicide?

If so, to what lengths a woman's imagination can go! Or so their combined looks seemed to proclaim, when to their utter astonishment they saw the officer, who had presented a calm appearance up till now, shift his position and with a surprised grunt direct their eyes to a portion of the wall just visible beyond the half-drawn curtains of the bed. The mirror hanging there showed a star-shaped breakage, such as follows the sharp impact of a bullet or a fiercely projected stone.

'He fired two shots. One went wild; the other straight home.'

It was the officer delivering his opinion.

Mr Saunders, returning from the distant room where he had assisted in carrying Mrs Hammond, cast a look at the shattered glass, and remarked forcibly:

'I heard but one; and I was sitting up, disturbed by that poor infant. Jennie, did you hear more than one shot?' he asked, turning toward his wife.

'No,' she answered, but not with the readiness he had evidently expected. 'I heard only one, but that was not quite usual in its tone. I'm used to guns,' she explained, turning to the officer. 'My father was an army man, and he taught me very early to load and fire a pistol. There was a prolonged sound to this shot; something like an echo of itself, following close upon the first ping. Didn't you notice that, Warren?'

'I remember something of the kind,' her husband allowed.

'He shot twice and quickly,' interposed the policeman sententiously. 'We shall find a spent bullet back of that mirror.'

But when, upon the arrival of the coroner, an investigation was made of the mirror and the wall behind, no bullet was found either there or anywhere else in the room, save in the dead man's breast. Nor had more than one been shot from his pistol, as five full chambers testified. The case which seemed so simple had its mysteries, but the assertion made by Mrs Saunders no longer carried weight, nor was the evidence offered by the broken mirror considered as indubitably establishing the fact that a second shot had been fired in the room.

Yet it was equally evident that the charge which had entered the dead speculator's breast had not been delivered at the close range of the pistol found clutched in his hand. There were no powder-marks to be discerned on his pajama-jacket, or on the flesh beneath. Thus anomaly confronted anomaly, leaving open but one other theory: that the bullet found in Mr Hammond's breast came from the window and the one he shot went out of it. But this would necessitate his having shot his pistol from a point far removed from where he was found; and his wound was such as made it difficult to believe that he would stagger far, if at all, after its infliction.

Yet, because the coroner was both conscientious and alert, he caused a most rigorous search to be made of the ground overlooked by the above-mentioned window; a search in which the police joined, but which was without any result save that of rousing the attention of people in the neighbourhood and leading to a story being circulated of a man seen sometime the night before crossing the fields in a great hurry. But as no further particulars were forthcoming, and not even a description of the man to be had, no emphasis would have been laid upon this story had it not transpired that the moment a report of it had come to Mrs Hammond's ears (why is there always some one to carry these reports?) she roused from the torpor into which she had fallen, and in wild fashion exclaimed:

'I knew it! I expected it! He was shot through the window and by that wretch. He never shot himself.' Violent declarations which trailed off into the one continuous wail, 'O, my baby! my poor baby!'

Such words, even though the fruit of delirium, merited some sort of attention, or so this good coroner thought, and as soon as opportunity offered and she was sufficiently sane and quiet to respond to his questions, he asked her whom she had meant by *that wretch*, and what reason she had, or thought she had, of attributing her husband's death to any other agency than his own disgust with life.

And then it was that his sympathies, although greatly roused in her favour began to wane. She met the question with a cold stare followed by a few ambiguous words out of which he could make nothing. Had she said *wretch*? She did not remember. They must not be influenced by anything she might have uttered in her first grief. She was well-nigh insane at the time. But of one thing they might be sure: her husband had not shot himself; he was too much afraid of death for such an act. Besides, he was too happy. Whatever folks might say he was too fond of his family to wish to leave it.

Nor did the coroner or any other official succeed in eliciting anything further from her. Even when she was asked, with cruel insistence, how she explained the fact that the baby was found lying on the floor instead of in its crib, her only answer was: 'His father was trying to soothe it. The child was crying dreadfully, as you have heard from those who were kept awake by him that night, and my husband was carrying him about when the shot came which caused George to fall and overlay the baby in his struggles.'

'Carrying a baby about with a loaded pistol in his hand?' came back in stern retort.

She had no answer for this. She admitted when informed that the bullet extracted from her husband's body had been found to correspond exactly with those remaining in the five chambers of the pistol taken from his hand, that he was not only the owner of this pistol but was in the habit of sleeping with it under his pillow; but, beyond that, nothing; and this reticence, as well as her manner which was cold and repellent, told against her.

A verdict of suicide was rendered by the coroner's jury, and the life-insurance company, in which Mr Hammond had but lately insured himself for a large sum, taking advantage of the suicide clause embodied in the policy, announced its determination of not paying the same.

Such was the situation, as known to Violet Strange and the general public, on the day she was asked to see Mrs Hammond and learn what might alter her opinion as to the justice of this verdict and the stand taken by the Shuler Life Insurance Company.

The clock on the mantel in Miss Strange's rose-coloured boudoir had struck three, and Violet was gazing in some impatience at the door, when there came a gentle knock upon it, and the maid (one of the elderly, not youthful, kind) ushered in her expected visitor.

'You are Mrs Hammond?' she asked, in natural awe of the too black figure outlined so sharply against the deep pink of the sea-shell room.

The answer was a slow lifting of the veil which shadowed the features she knew only from the cuts she had seen in newspapers.

'You are—Miss Strange?' stammered her visitor; 'the young lady who——'

'I am,' chimed in a voice as ringing as it was sweet. 'I am the person you have come here to see. And this is my home. But that does not make me less interested in the unhappy, or less desirous of serving them. Certainly you have met with the two greatest losses which can come to a woman—I know your story well enough to say that—; but what have you to tell me in proof that you should not lose your anticipated income as well? Something vital, I hope, else I cannot help you; something which you should have told the coroner's jury—and did not.'

The flush which was the sole answer these words called forth did not take from the refinement of the young widow's expression, but rather added to it; Violet watched it in its ebb and flow and, seriously affected by it (why, she did not know, for Mrs Hammond had made no other appeal either by look or gesture), pushed forward a chair and begged her visitor to be seated.

'We can converse in perfect safety here,' she said. 'When you feel quite equal to it, let me hear what you have to communicate. It will never go any further. I could not do the work I do if I felt it necessary to have a confidant.'

'But you are so young and so—so——'

'So inexperienced you would say and so evidently a member of

36

what New Yorkers call "society". Do not let that trouble you. My inexperience is not likely to last long and my social pleasures are more apt to add to my efficiency than to detract from it.'

With this Violet's face broke into a smile. It was not the brilliant one so often seen upon her lips, but there was something in its quality which carried encouragement to the widow and led her to say with obvious eagerness:

'You know the facts?'

'I have read all the papers.'

'I was not believed on the stand.'

'It was your manner——'

'I could not help my manner. I was keeping something back, and, being unused to deceit, I could not act quite naturally.'

'Why did you keep something back? When you saw the unfavourable impression made by your reticence, why did you not speak up and frankly tell your story?'

'Because I was ashamed. Because I thought it would hurt me more to speak than to keep silent. I do not think so now; but I did then—and so made my great mistake. You must remember not only the awful shock of my double loss, but the sense of guilt accompanying it; for my husband and I had quarreled that night, quarreled bitterly—that was why I had run away into another room and not because I was feeling ill and impatient of the baby's fretful cries.'

'So people have thought.' In saying this, Miss Strange was perhaps cruelly emphatic. 'You wish to explain that quarrel? You think it will be doing any good to your cause to go into that matter with me now?'

'I cannot say; but I must first clear my conscience and then try to convince you that quarrel or no quarrel, *he* never took his own life. He was not that kind. He had an abnormal fear of death. I do not like to say it but he was a physical coward. I have seen him turn pale at the least hint of danger. He could no more have turned that muzzle upon his own breast than he could have turned it upon his baby. Some other hand shot him, Miss Strange. Remember the open window, the shattered mirror; and *I think I know that hand.*'

Her head had fallen forward on her breast. The emotion she showed was not so eloquent of grief as of deep personal shame.

'You think you know the *man*?' In saying this, Violet's voice sunk to a whisper. It was an accusation of murder she had just heard.

'To my great distress, yes. When Mr Hammond and I were married,' the widow now proceeded in a more determined tone, 'there was another man—a very violent one—who vowed even at the church door that George and I should never live out two full years together. We have not. Our second anniversary would have been in November.'

'But——'

'Let me say this: the quarrel of which I speak was not serious enough to occasion any such act of despair on his part. A man would be mad to end his life on account of so slight a disagreement. It was not even on account of the person of whom I've just spoken, though that person had been mentioned between us earlier in the evening, Mr Hammond having come across him face to face that very afternoon in the subway. Up to this time neither of us had seen or heard of him since our wedding-day.'

'And you think this person whom you barely mentioned, so mindful of his old grudge that he sought out your domicile, and, with the intention of murder, climbed the trellis leading to your room and turned his pistol upon the shadowy figure which was all he could see in the semi-obscurity of a much lowered gas-jet?'

'A man in the dark does not need a bright light to see his enemy when he is intent upon revenge.'

Miss Strange altered her tone.

'And your husband? You must acknowledge that he shot off his pistol whether the other did or not.'

'It was in self-defence. He would shoot to save his own life—or the baby's.'

'Then he must have heard or seen——'

'A man at the window.'

'And would have shot there?'

'Or tried to.'

'Tried to?'

'Yes; the other shot first—oh, I've thought it all out—causing my husband's bullet to go wild. It was his which broke the mirror.'

Violet's eyes, bright as stars, suddenly narrowed.

'And what happened then?' she asked. 'Why cannot they find the bullet?'

'Because it went out of the window;—glanced off and went out of the window.' Mrs Hammond's tone was triumphant; her look spirited and intense.

Violet eyed her compassionately.

'Would a bullet glancing off from a mirror, however hung, be apt to reach a window so far on the opposite side?'

'I don't know; I only know that it did,' was the contradictory, almost absurd, reply.

'What *was* the cause of the quarrel you speak of between your husband and yourself? You see, I must know the exact truth and all the truth to be of any assistance to you.'

'It was—it was about the care I gave, or didn't give, the baby. I feel awfully to have to say it, but George did not think I did my full duty by the child. He said there was no need of its crying so; that if I gave it the proper attention it would not keep the neighbours and himself awake half the night. And I—I got angry and insisted that I did the best I could; that the child was naturally fretful and that if he wasn't satisfied with my way of looking after it, he might try his. All of which was very wrong and unreasonable on my part, as witness the awful punishment which followed.'

'And what made you get up and leave him?'

'The growl he gave me in reply. When I heard that, I bounded out of bed and said I was going to the spare room to sleep; and if the baby cried he might just try what he could do himself to stop it.'

'And he answered?'

'This, just this—I shall never forget his words as long as I live—"If you go, you need not expect me to let you in again no matter what happens." '

'He said that?'

'And locked the door after me. You see I could not tell all that.'

'It might have been better if you had. It was such a natural quarrel and so unprovocative of actual tragedy.'

Mrs Hammond was silent. It was not difficult to see that she had no very keen regrets for her husband personally. But then he was not a very estimable man nor in any respect her equal.

'You were not happy with him,' Violet ventured to remark.

'I was not a fully contented woman. But for all that he had no cause to complain of me except for the reason I have mentioned. I was not a very intelligent mother. But if the baby were living now—O, if he were living now—with what devotion I should care for him.'

She was on her feet, her arms were raised, her face impassioned with feeling. Violet, gazing at her, heaved a little sigh. It was perhaps in keeping with the situation, perhaps extraneous to it, but whatever its source, it marked a change in her manner. With no further check upon her sympathy, she said very softly: 'It is well with the child.'

The mother stiffened, swayed, and then burst into wild weeping.

'But not with me,' she cried, 'not with me. I am desolate and bereft. I have not even a home in which to hide my grief and no prospect of one.'

'But,' interposed Violet, 'surely your husband left you something? You cannot be quite penniless?'

'My husband left nothing,' was the answer, uttered without bitterness, but with all the hardness of fact. 'He had debts. I shall pay those debts. When these and other necessary expenses are liquidated, there will be but little left. He made no secret of the fact that he lived close up to his means. That is why he was induced to take on a life insurance. Not a friend of his but knows his improvidence. I—I have not even jewels. I have only my determination and an absolute conviction as to the real nature of my husband's death.'

'What is the name of the man you secretly believe to have shot your husband from the trellis?'

Mrs Hammond told her.

It was a new one to Violet. She said so and then asked:

'What else can you tell me about him?'

'Nothing, but that he is a very dark man and has a club-foot.'

'Oh, what a mistake you've made.'

'Mistake? Yes, I acknowledge that.'

'I mean in not giving this last bit of information at once to the police. A man can be identified by such a defect. Even his footsteps can be traced. He might have been found that very day. Now, what have we to go upon?'

'You are right, but not expecting to have any difficulty about the insurance money I thought it would be generous in me to keep still. Besides, this is only surmise on my part. I feel certain that my husband was shot by another hand than his own, but I know of no way of proving it. Do you?'

Then Violet talked seriously with her, explaining how their only hope lay in the discovery of a second bullet in the room which had already been ransacked for this very purpose and without the shadow of a result.

A tea, a musicale, and an evening dance kept Violet Strange in a whirl for the remainder of the day. No brighter eye nor more contagious wit lent brilliance to these occasions, but with the passing of the midnight hour no one who had seen her in the blaze of electric lights would have recognized this favoured child of fortune in the earnest figure sitting in the obscurity of an uptown apartment, studying the walls, the ceilings, and the floors by the dim light of a lowered gas-jet. Violet Strange in society was a very different person from Violet Strange under the tension of her secret and peculiar work.

She had told them at home that she was going to spend the night with a friend; but only her old coachman knew who that friend was. Therefore a very natural sense of guilt mingled with her emotions at finding herself alone on a scene whose gruesome mystery she could solve only by identifying herself with the place and the man who had perished there.

Dismissing from her mind all thought of self, she strove to think as he thought, and act as he acted on the night when he found himself (a man of but little courage) left in this room with an ailing child.

At odds with himself, his wife, and possibly with the child screaming away in its crib, what would he be apt to do in his present emergency? Nothing at first, but as the screaming continued he would remember the old tales of fathers walking the floor at night with crying babies, and hasten to follow suit. Violet, in her anxiety to reach his inmost thought, crossed to where the crib had stood, and, taking that as a start, began pacing the room in search of the spot from which a bullet, if shot, would glance aside from the mirror in the direction of the window. (Not that she was ready to accept this theory of Mrs Hammond, but that she did not wish to entirely dismiss it without putting it to the test.)

She found it in an unexpected quarter of the room and much nearer the bed-head than where his body was found. This, which might seem to confuse matters, served, on the contrary to remove from the case one of its most serious difficulties. Standing here, he was within reach of the pillow under which his pistol lay hidden, and if startled, as his wife believed him to have been by a noise at the other end of the room, had but to crouch and reach behind him in order to find himself armed and ready for a possible intruder.

Imitating his action in this as in other things, she had herself crouched low at the bedside and was on the point of withdrawing her hand from under the pillow, when a new surprise checked her movement and held her fixed in her position, with eyes staring straight at the adjoining wall. She had seen there what he must have seen in making this same turn—the dark bars of the opposite window-frame outlined in the mirror—and understood at once what had happened. In the nervousness and terror of the moment, George Hammond had mistaken this reflection of the window for the window itself, and shot impulsively at the man he undoubtedly saw covering him from the trellis without. But while this explained the shattering of the mirror, how about the other and still more vital question, of where the bullet went afterward? Was the angle at which it had been fired acute enough to send it out of a window diagonally opposed? No; even if the pistol had been held closer to the man firing it than she had reason to believe, the angle still would be oblique enough to carry it on to the further wall.

But no sign of any such impact had been discovered on this wall. Consequently, the force of the bullet had been expended before reaching it, and when it fell——

Here, her glance, slowly travelling along the floor, impetuously paused. It had reached the spot where the two bodies had been found, and unconsciously her eyes rested there, conjuring up the picture of the bleeding father and the strangled child. How piteous and how dreadful it all was. If she could only understand—— Suddenly she rose straight up, staring and immovable in the dim light. Had the idea—the explanation—the only possible explanation covering the whole phenomena come to her at last?

It would seem so, for as she so stood, a look of conviction settled over her features, and with this look, evidences of a horror which for all her fast accumulating knowledge of life and its possibilities made her appear very small and very helpless.

A half-hour later, when Mrs Hammond, in her anxiety at hearing nothing more from Miss Strange, opened the door of her room, it was to find, lying on the edge of the sill, the little detective's card with these words hastily written across it:

I do not feel as well as I could wish, and so have telephoned to my own coachman to come and take me home. I will either see or write you within a few days. But do not allow yourself to hope. I pray you do not allow yourself the least hope; the outcome is still very problematical.

When Violet's employer entered his office the next morning it was to find a veiled figure awaiting him which he at once recognized as that of his little deputy. She was slow in lifting her veil and when it finally came free he felt a momentary doubt as to his wisdom in giving her just such a matter as this to investigate. He was quite sure of his mistake when he saw her face, it was so drawn and pitiful.

'You have failed,' said he.

'Of that you must judge,' she answered; and drawing near she whispered in his ear.

'No!' he cried in his amazement.

'Think,' she murmured, 'think. Only so can all the facts be accounted for.'

'I will look into it; I will certainly look into it,' was his earnest reply. 'If you are right—— But never mind that. Go home and take a horseback ride in the Park. When I have news in regard to this I will let you know. Till then forget it all. Hear me, I charge you to forget everything but your balls and your parties.'

And Violet obeyed him.

Some few days after this, the following statement appeared in all the papers:

Owing to some remarkable work done by the firm of —— & ——, the well-known private detective agency, the claim made by Mrs George Hammond against the Shuler Life Insurance Company is likely to be allowed without further litigation. As our readers will remember, the contestant has insisted from the first that the bullet causing her husband's death came from another pistol than the one found clutched in his own hand. But while reasons were not lacking to substantiate this assertion, the failure to discover more than the disputed track of a second bullet led to a verdict of suicide, and a refusal of the company to pay.

But now that bullet has been found. And where? In the most startling place in the world, viz.: in the larynx of the child found lying dead upon the floor beside his father, strangled as was supposed by the weight of that father's arm. The theory is, and there seems to be none other, that the father, hearing a suspicious noise at the window, set down the child he was endeavoring to soothe and made for the bed and his own pistol, and, mistaking a reflection of the assassin for the assassin himself, sent his shot sidewise at a mirror just as the other let go the trigger which drove a similar bullet into his breast. The course of the one was straight and fatal and that of the other deflected. Striking the mirror at an oblique angle, the bullet fell to the floor where it was picked up by the crawling child, and, as was most natural, thrust at once into his mouth. Perhaps it felt hot to the little tongue; perhaps the child was simply frightened by some convulsive movement of the father who evidently spent his last moment in an endeavour to reach the child, but, whatever the cause, in the quick gasp it gave, the bullet was drawn into the larynx, strangling him.

That the father's arm, in his last struggle, should have fallen directly across the little throat is one of those anomalies which confounds reason and misleads justice by stopping investigation at the very point where truth lies and mystery disappears.

Mrs Hammond is to be congratulated that there are detectives who do not give too much credence to outward appearances.

We expect soon to hear of the capture of the man who sped home the death-dealing bullet.

4

MELVILLE DAVISSON POST

The Age of Miracles

The girl was standing apart from the crowd in the great avenue of the poplars that led up to the house. She seemed embarrassed and uncertain what to do, a thing of April emerging into Summer.

Abner and Randolph marked her as they entered along the gravel road.

They had left their horses at the gate, but she had brought hers inside, as though from some habit unconsciously upon her.

But halfway to the house she had remembered and got down. And she stood now against the horse's shoulder. It was a black hunter, big and old, but age marred no beauty of his lines. He was like a horse of ebony, enchanted out of the earth by some Arabian magic, but not yet by that magic awakened into life.

The girl wore a long, dark riding skirt, after the fashion of the time, and a coat of hunter's pink. Her dark hair was in a great wrist-thick plait. Her eyes, too, were big and dark, and her body firm and lithe from the out-of-doors.

'Ah!' cried Randolph, making his characteristic gesture, 'Prospero has been piping in this grove. Here is a daughter of the immortal morning! We grow old, Abner, and it is youth that the gods love.'

My uncle, his hands behind him, his eyes on the gravel road, looked up at the bewitching picture.

'Poor child,' he said. 'The gods that love her must be gods of the valleys and not gods of the hills.'

'Ruth amid the alien corn! Is it a better figure, Abner? Well, she has a finer inheritance than these lands—she has youth!'

'She ought to have both,' replied my uncle. 'It was sheer robbery to take her inheritance.'

'It was a proceeding at law,' replied the Justice. 'It was the law that did the thing, and we cannot hold the law in disrespect.'

'But the man who uses the law to accomplish a wrong, we can so hold,' said my Uncle Abner. 'He is an outlaw, as the highwayman and the pirate are.'

He extended his arm toward the great house sitting at the end of the avenue.

'In spite of the sanction of the law I hold this dead man for a robber. And I would have wrested these lands from him, if I could. But your law, Randolph, stood before him.'

'Well,' replied the Justice, 'he takes no gain from it. He lies yonder waiting for the grave.'

'But his brother takes,' said Abner, 'and this child loses.'

The Justice, elegant in the costume of the time, turned his ebony stick in his fingers.

'One should forgive the dead,' he commented in a facetious tone. 'It is a mandate of the Scripture.'

'I am not concerned about the dead,' replied Abner. 'The dead are in God's hands. It is the living who concern me.'

'Then,' cried the Justice, 'you should forgive the brother who takes.'

'And I shall forgive him,' replied Abner, 'when he returns what he has taken.'

'Returns what he has taken!' Randolph laughed. 'Why, Abner, the devil could not filch a coin out of the clutches of old Benton Wolf.'

'The devil,' said my uncle, 'is not an authority that I depend on.'

'A miracle of Heaven, then,' said the Justice. 'But, alas, it is not the age of miracles.'

'Perhaps,' replied Abner, 'but I am not so certain.'

They had come now to where the girl stood, her back against the black shoulder of the horse. The morning air moved the yellow leaves about her feet. She darted out to meet them, her face aglow.

'Damme!' cried Randolph. 'William of Avon knew only witches of the second order! How do you do, Julia? I have hardly seen you since you were no taller than my stick, and told me that your name was

"Pete-George", and that you were a circus horse, and offered to do tricks for me.'

A shadow crossed the girl's face.

'I remember,' she said, 'it was up there on the porch!'

'Egad!' cried Randolph, embarassed. 'And so it was.'

He kissed the girl's fingers and the shadow in her face fled for a moment.

For the man's heart was good, and he had the manner of a gentleman. But it was Uncle Abner whom she turned to in her dilemma.

'I forgot,' she said, 'and almost rode into the house. Do you think I could leave the horse here? He will stand if I drop the rein.'

Then she went on to make her explanation. She wanted to see the old house that had been so long her home. This was the only opportunity, today, when all the countryside came to the dead man's burial. She thought she might come, too, although her motive was no tribute of respect.

She put her hand through Abner's arm and he looked down upon her, grave, and troubled.

'My child,' he said, 'leave the horse where he stands and come with me—for my motive, also, is no tribute of respect; and you go with a better right than I do.'

'I suppose,' the girl hesitated, 'that one ought to respect the dead, but this man—these men—I cannot.'

'Nor can I,' replied my uncle. 'If I do not respect a man when he is living, I shall not pretend to when he is dead. One does not make a claim upon my honor by going out of life.'

They went up the avenue among the yellow poplar leaves and the ragweed and fennel springing up along the unkept gravel.

It was a crisp and glorious morning. The frost lay on the rail fence. The spider webs stretched here and there across the high grasses of the meadows in intricate and bewildering lacework. The sun was clear and bright, but it carried no oppressive heat as it drew on in its course toward noon.

The countryside had gathered to see Adam Wolf buried. It was a company of tenants, the idle and worthless mostly, drawn by curiosity. For in life the two old men who had seized upon this property by virtue of a defective acknowledgement to a deed permitted no invasion of their boundary.

Everywhere the lands were posted; no urchin fished and no schoolboy hunted. The green perch, fattened in the deep creek that threaded the rich bottom lands, no man disturbed. But the quail, the pheasant, the robin, and the meadow lark, old Adam pursued with his fowling piece.

He had tramped about with it in all seasons. One would have believed that all the birds of heaven had done the man some unending harm and in revenge he had declared a war. And so the accident by which he met his death was a jeopardy of the old man's habits, and to be looked for when one lived with a fowling piece in one's hands and grew careless in its use.

The two men lived alone and thus all sorts of mystery sprang up around them, elaborated by fancy and gaining in grim detail at every storyteller's hand. It had the charm and thrilling interest of an adventure, then, for the countryside to get this entry.

The brothers lived in striking contrast. Adam was violent, and his cries and curses, his hard and brutal manner were the terror of those who passed at night that way, or the urchin overtaken by darkness on his road home. But Benton got about his affairs in silence, with a certain humility of manner, and a mild concern for the opinion of his fellows.

Still, somehow, the traveler and the urchin held him in a great terror. Perhaps because he had got his coffin made and kept in his house, together with his clothes for burial. It seemed uncanny thus to prepare against his dissolution and to bargain for the outfit, with anxiety to have his shilling's worth.

And yet, with this gruesome furniture at hand, the old man, it would seem, was in no contemplation of his death. He spoke sometimes with a marked savor and an unctuous kneading of the hands of that time when he should own the land, for he was the younger and by rule should have the expectancy of life.

There was a crowd about the door and filling the hall inside, a crowd that elbowed and jostled, taken with a quivering interest, and there to feed its maw of curiosity with every item.

The girl wished to remain on the portico, where she could see the ancient garden and the orchard and all the paths and byways that had been her wonderland of youth, but Abner asked her to go in.

Randolph turned away, but my uncle and the girl remained some time by the coffin. The rim of the dead man's forehead and his jaw were riddled with bird shot, but his eyes and an area of his face below them, where the thin nose came down and with its lines and furrows made up the main identity of features, were not disfigured. And these preserved the hard stamp of his violent nature, untouched by the accident that had dispossessed him of his life.

He lay in the burial clothes and the coffin that Benton Wolf had provided for himself, all except the gloves upon his hands. These Benton had forgotten to provide in advance. And now when he came to prepare his brother for a public burial, for no other had touched the man, he must needs take what he could find out about the house—a pair of old knit gloves with every rent and moth hole carefully darned, as though the man had sat down there with pains to give his brother the best appearance that he could.

This little touch affected the girl to tears, so strange is a woman's heart. 'Poor thing!' she said. And for this triviality she would forget the injury that the dead man and his brother had done to her, forget the loss they had inflicted, and her long distress.

She took a closer hold upon Abner's arm, and dabbed her eyes with a tiny handkerchief.

'I am sorry for him,' she said, 'for the living brother. It is so pathetic.'

And she indicated the old, coarse gloves so crudely darned and patched together.

But my uncle looked down at her, strangely, and with a cold, inexorable face.

'My child,' he said, 'there is a curious virtue in this thing that moves you. Perhaps it will also move the man whose handiwork it is. Let us go up and see him.'

Then he called the Justice.

'Randolph, come with us.'

The Justice turned about. 'Where do you go?' he asked.

'Why, sir,' Abner answered, 'this child is weeping at the sight of the dead man's gloves, and I thought, perhaps, that old Benton might weep at them too, and in the softened mood return what he has stolen.'

The Justice looked upon Abner as upon one gone mad.

'And be sorry for his sins! And pluck out his eye and give it to you for a bauble! Why, Abner, where is your common sense. This thing would take a miracle of God.'

My uncle was undisturbed.

'Well,' he said, 'come with me, Randolph, and help me to perform that miracle.'

He went out into the hall, and up the wide old stairway, with the girl, in tears, upon his arm. And the Justice followed, like one who goes upon a patent and ridiculous fool's errand.

They came into an upper chamber, where a great bulk of a man sat in a padded chair looking down upon his avenue of trees. He looked with satisfaction. He turned his head about when the three came in and then his eyes widened among the folds of fat.

'Abner and Mr Randolph and Miss Julia Clayborne!' he gurgled. 'You come to do honor to the dead!'

'No, Wolf,' replied my uncle, 'we come to do justice to the living.'

The room was big and empty but for chairs and an open secretary of some English make. The pictures on the wall had been turned about as though from lack of interest in the tenant. But there hung in a frame above the secretary—with its sheets of foolscap, its iron ink-pot and quill pens—a map in detail, and the written deed for the estate that these men had taken in their lawsuit. It was not the skill of any painter that gave pleasure to this mountain of a man; not fields or groves imagined or copied for their charm, but the fields and groves that he now possessed and mastered.

The old man's eyelids fluttered an instant as with some indecision, then he replied, 'It was kind to have this thought of me. I have been long neglected. A little justice of recognition, even now, does much to soften the sorrow at my brother's death.'

Randolph caught at his jaw to keep in the laughter. And the huge old man, his head crouched into his billowy shoulders, his little reptilian eye shining like glass, went on with his speech.

'I am the greater moved,' he said, 'because you have been aloof and distant with me. You, Abner, have not visited my house, nor you,

Randolph, although you live at no great distance. It is not thus that one gentleman should treat another. And especially when I and my dead brother, Adam, were from distant parts and came among you without a friend to take us by the hand and bring us to your door.'

He sighed and put the fingers of his hands together.

'Ah, Abner,' he went on, 'it was a cruel negligence, and one from which I and my brother Adam suffered. You, who have a hand and a word at every turning, can feel no longing for this human comfort. But to the stranger alone, and without the land of his nativity, it is a bitter lack.'

He indicated the chairs about him.

'I beg you to be seated, gentlemen and Miss Clayborne. And overlook that I do not rise. I am shaken at Adam's death.'

Randolph remained planted on his feet, his face now under control. But Abner put the child into a chair and stood behind it, as though he were some close and masterful familiar.

'Wolf,' he said, 'I am glad that your heart is softened.'

'My heart—softened!' cried the man. 'Why, Abner, I have the tenderest heart of any of God's creatures. I cannot endure to kill a sparrow. My brother Adam was not like that. He would be for hunting the wild creatures to their death with firearms. But I took no pleasure in it.'

'Well,' said Randolph, 'the creatures of the air got their revenge of him. It was a foolish accident to die by.'

'Randolph,' replied the man, 'it was the very end and the extreme of carelessness. To look into a fowling piece, a finger on the hammer, a left hand holding the barrel halfway up to see if it was empty. It was a foolish and simple habit of my brother, and one that I abhorred and begged him to forgo, again and again, when I have seen him do it.

'But he had no fear of any firearms, as though by use and habit he had got their spirit tamed—as trainers, I am told, grow careless of wild beasts, and jugglers of the fangs and poison of their reptiles. He was growing old and would forget if they were loaded.'

He spoke to Randolph, but he looked at Julia Clayborne and Abner behind her chair.

The girl sat straight and composed, in silence. The body of my uncle was to her a great protecting presence. He stood with his broad shoulders above her, his hands on the back of the chair, his face lifted. And he was big and dominant, as painters are accustomed to draw Michael in Satan's wars.

The pose held the old man's eye, and he moved in his chair; then he went on, speaking to the girl.

'It was kind of you, Abner, and you, Randolph, to come in to see me in my distress, but it was fine and noble in Miss Julia Clayborne. Men will understand the justice of the law and by what right it gives and takes. But a child will hardly understand that. It would be in nature for Miss Clayborne, in her youth, to hold the issue of this lawsuit against me and my brother Adam, to feel that we had wronged her; had by some unfairness taken what her father bequeathed to her at his death, and always regarded as his own. A child would not see how the title had never vested, as our judges do. How possession is one thing, and the title in fee simple another and distinct. And so I am touched by this consideration.'

Abner spoke then.

'Wolf,' he said, 'I am glad to find you in this mood, for now Randolph can write his deed, with consideration of love and affection instead of the real one I came with.'

The old man's beady eye glimmered and slipped about.

'I do not understand, Abner. What deed?'

'The one Randolph came to write,' replied my uncle.

'But, Abner,' interrupted the Justice, 'I did not come to write a deed.' And he looked at my uncle in amazement.

'Oh, yes,' returned Abner, 'that is precisely what you came to do.'

He indicated the open secretary with his hand.

'And the grantor, as it happens, has got everything ready for you. Here are foolscap and quill pens and ink. And here, exhibited for your convenience, is a map of the lands with all the metes and bounds. And here,' he pointed to the wall, 'in a frame, as though it were a work of art with charm, is the court's deed. Sit down, Randolph, and write.'

And such virtue is there in a dominant command that the Justice sat down before the secretary and began to select a goose quill. Then he realized the absurdity of the direction and turned about.

'What do you mean, Abner?' he cried.

'I mean precisely what I say,' replied my uncle. 'I want you to write a deed.'

'But what sort of deed,' cried the astonished Justice, 'and by what grantor, and to whom, and for what lands?'

'You will draw a conveyance,' replied Abner, 'in form, with covenants of general warranty for the manor and lands set out in the deed before you and given in the plat. The grantor will be Benton Wolf, Esquire, and the grantee, Julia Clayborne, and mark you, Randolph, the consideration will be love and affection, with a dollar added for the form.'

Old man Benton was amazed. His head, bedded into his huge shoulders, swung about; his pudgy features worked; his expression and his manner changed; his reptilian eyes hardened; he puffed with his breath in gusts.

'Not so fast, my fine gentlemen!' he gurgled. 'There will be no such deed.'

'Go on, Randolph,' said my uncle, as though there had been no interruption, 'get this business over.'

'But, Abner,' returned the Justice, 'it is fool's work—the grantor will not sign.'

'He will sign,' said my uncle, 'when you have finished, and seal and acknowledge—go on!'

And such authority was in the man to impose his will that the bewildered Justice spread out his sheet of foolscap, dipped his quill into the ink, and began to draw the instrument. And while he wrote, Abner turned back to the gross old man.

'Wolf,' he said, 'must I persuade you to sign the deed?'

'Abner,' cried the man, 'do you take me for a fool?'

'I do not,' replied my uncle, 'and therefore I think that you will sign.'

The obese old man spat violently on the floor, his face a horror of great folds.

'Sign!' he sputtered. 'Idiot, madman! Why should I sign away my lands?'

'There are many reasons,' replied Abner calmly. 'The property is not yours. You got it by a legal trick—the judge who heard you was bound by the technicalities of language. But you are old, Wolf, and the next Judge will go beyond the record. He will be hard to face. He has expressed himself on these affairs. "If the widow and the orphan cry to me, I will surely hear their cry." Sinister words, Wolf, for one who comes with a case like yours into the Court of Final Equity.'

'Abner,' cried the old man, 'begone with your sermons!'

My uncle's big fingers tightened on the back of the chair.

'Then, Wolf,' he said, 'if that does not move you, let me urge the esteem of men and this child's sorrow, and our high regard.'

The old man's jaw chattered and he snapped his fingers.

'I would not give that for the things you name,' he cried, and he set off a tiny measure of his index finger with the thumb. 'Why, sir, my whim, idle and ridiculous, is a greater power to move me than this drivel.'

Abner did not move, but his voice took on depth and volume.

'Wolf,' he said, 'a whim is sometimes a great lever to move a man. Now, I am taken with a whim myself. I have a fancy, Wolf, that your brother Adam ought to go out of the world barehanded as he came into it.'

The old man twisted his great head, as though he would get Abner wholly within the sweep of his reptilian eye.

'What?' he gurgled. 'What is that?'

'Why, this,' replied my uncle. 'I have a whim—"idle and ridiculous", did you say, Wolf? Well, then, idle and ridiculous, if you like, that your brother ought not to be buried in his gloves.'

Abner looked hard at the man and, although he did not move, the threat and menace of his presence seemed somehow to advance him. And the effect on the huge old man was like some work of sorcery. The whole mountain of him began to quiver and the folds of his face seemed spread over him with thin oil. He sat piled up in the chair and the oily sweat gathered and thickened on him. His jaw jerked and fell into a baggy gaping and the great expanse of him worked as with an ague.

Finally, out of the pudgy, undulating mass, a voice issued, thin and shaken.

'Abner,' it said, 'has any other man this fancy?'

'No,' replied my uncle, 'but I hold it, Wolf, at your decision.'

'And, Abner,' his thin voice trebled, 'you will let my brother be buried as he is?'

'If you sign!' said my uncle.

The man reeked with the terror on him, and one thought that his billowy body would never again be at peace. 'Randolph,' he quavered, 'bring me the deed.'

Outside, the girl sobbed in Abner's arms. She asked for no explanation. She wished to believe her fortune a miracle of God, forever—to the end of all things. But Randolph turned on my uncle when she was gone.

'Abner! Abner!' he cried. 'Why in the name of the Eternal was the old creature so shaken at the gloves?'

'Because he saw the hangman behind them,' replied my uncle. 'Did you notice how the rim of the dead man's face was riddled by the bird shot and the center of it clean? How could that happen, Randolph?'

'It was a curious accident of gunfire,' replied the Justice.

'It was no accident at all,' said Abner. 'That area of the man's face is clean because it was *protected*. Because the dead man put up his hands to cover his face when he saw that his brother was about to shoot him. The backs of old Adam's hands, hidden by the gloves, will be riddled with bird shot like the rim of his face.'

5

T. S. STRIBLING

The Shadow

With wind and rain whipping at his umbrella, the bank clerk Samuels opened the door of his apartment house and handed Mr Poggioli inside. He followed after him, opened the inner door, permitting its gush of light to fill the dark street, then closed it again, leaving himself and the psychiatrist still standing in the dark entry.

'Now we ought to see him in a moment,' he whispered.

The two men shook the water from their clothes, moved their feet with the slight motions of men settling for a watch.

'You opened this inside door to make a show of going in?' queried Poggioli in a low tone.

'Well, I waited the other night—several minutes . . . Finally I did that and he came.'

'I see.'

'He may have just happened to get here then.'

'Mm-hm,' murmured the psychiatrist.

The two men stood listening to the rain thrum the windows and curse the pavement. Finally the clerk began in an undertone of nervous complaint:

'Look here, isn't there some law against this sort of thing? Can anybody shadow anybody else for no reason at all?'

The psychologist reflected.

'I'm no lawyer. Might bring an action of nuisance, possibly . . . Never heard of such a thing . . . You don't know why he is doing this—can't think of anything you've done?'

'Oh, no.'

The psychologist gave a whispered laugh.

'The reason I asked—almost any man can think up something he's done that deserves—oh, almost anything.'

The younger man seemed not amused. He remained quiet a moment, then said: 'You—you would be in a better position to give me advice if—if you knew what possibly might have caused it?'

'I—imagine so. Of course, I can't tell until I hear what it is. The thing you have in mind may have no connection with this beagle that's trailing—'

The bank clerk interrupted him nervously:

'It—it's a sanitarium.'

Mr Poggioli shifted his gaze from the street to his host.

'A what?'

'Sanitarium.'

The psychologist stood for upward of a minute fitting this unexpected bit of information into the shadowy hypotheses he had in mind.

'Is it a—a New York sanitarium?'

'Yes.'

'Park Avenue?'

'Fifth.'

'Same thing.' Poggioli frowned. Finally he broke out, puzzled: 'Look here—you're not keeping somebody in a private sanitarium?'

Mr Samuels was shocked.

'Oh, my Lord, no. There was a—a friend of mine in the sanitarium. . . . We—went out for a taxi-ride to break the monotony.'

'This friend—was a woman, of course, Mr Samuels?'

'If it'd been a man, I'd have sat in his room and talked.'

'Certainly. . . . And you've known this lady for a long time.'

'How did you come by that?'

'A man doesn't go into a hospital to make new acquaintances, but to see very old ones.'

'That's true . . . I've known her ever since we were children.'

'I see—children. . . . Then—then she comes from Pennsylvania, the same as you?'

The bank clerk was astonished.

'You guessed that by my accent?'

'Certainly.'

'I didn't know I had one.'

'Well, nobody does. . . . They think other people have them.'

The bank clerk gave a little laugh.

'You must have made a study of it?'

'I have. It's very convenient sometimes to know where a man comes from without asking him. Now and then it is still more convenient to know where he comes from after you've asked him.'

The younger man began laughing again, then broke off in the middle of his mirth. After a moment he continued soberly:

'Yes, both of us came from Everbrook, Pennsylvania. I came a year or two before she did.'

'H'm—then let me see—what sort of family did this young lady come from—wealthy, middle-class, laborers—'

'Middle-class. . . . Her father was a doctor.'

Mr Poggioli nodded thoughtfully.

'Then in that instance she must be married and wealthy. I should surmise that she married a wealthy man and came to New York to live.'

Came a moment's pause; then the bank clerk asked in an odd voice:

'Why do you jump to that conclusion?'

'Money had to come in somehow, Mr Samuels,' argued the psychologist. 'A Fifth Avenue sanitarium is a very expensive thing. It wasn't likely the girl made the money herself, or she wouldn't have been in a sanitarium in the first place. The fact that she went there at all suggests she was married—unhappily married; and a Fifth Avenue sanitarium certifies to a husband of wealth.'

The clerk was astonished.

'Well, I declare—that is simple, isn't it? One thing follows the other just as natural as two old shoes—if you happen to think of it.'

The psychologist smiled at the naïve compliment.

'Now, let me see: the last thing *you* were saying was, you took this lady, this Mrs—'

'Hessland—Margaret Hessland.'

'—out for a taxi-ride. Then you told me before that the man who is shadowing you—if he had any reason for doing such a thing at all—was doing it because of the sanitarium. That, I'll confess, I don't understand. Why a sanitarium should shadow you—'

Samuels drew a breath.

'Well, it's simple enough when I explain it. We drove out together—but we didn't drive back together.'

'Did you send her back by herself?'

'No. . . . I—I drove back without her.'

'Why didn't you bring her back with you?'

'I couldn't.' Samuels moistened his lips. 'She had—disappeared.'

'What! She didn't step out of the cab and leave you?'

'No; that wouldn't be disappearing. She disappeared—vanished! It was this way: I found I needed some matches, and stopped the chauffeur and went into a cigar store. I don't suppose I was away three minutes. When I came back outside, cab, girl, and chauffeur were gone.'

'And what did you do?'

'I telephoned the sanitarium.'

'And what did the authorities there say?'

'Told me to come back at once for an interview.'

'You went back?'

'Certainly, and explained what had happened.'

'But since you think this—this man who is trailing you is working for the sanitarium, evidently the superintendent didn't believe you?'

'I—suppose not,' agreed Samuels gloomily.

'What do you suppose the superintendent does believe?'

'I have no idea at all.'

'He couldn't be—well, looking for his patient, could he?'

Samuels lifted a nervous hand.

'I—I don't know. . . . I suppose maybe he is.'

'But you have no idea what became of Mrs Hessland?'

'Not the slightest.'

The two men stood quiet, peering out into the dark street.

'Did Mrs Hessland ask you to come to take her for a drive, or did you suggest it?'

Samuels considered.

'Now that you mention it, I believe she did. . . . Yes, I think she did.'

'And who wanted the matches—she or you?'

'Why-y—she did.'

'Were you two riding in a new type of cab?'

'Yes.'

'Well, look here: when she asked you to get out and get her some matches, didn't you *know* she was going to drive off and leave you?'

The bank clerk turned.

'No. Why should I?'

'Because women enjoy little gadgets like cigarette lighters; she would never have dreamed of sending you after matches unless—'

The bank clerk lifted a hand.

'But, Mr Poggioli, we are not all of us analytical psychologists; and besides that, it's a lot clearer what she was up to, on looking back at it, than looking forward at it.'

Poggioli tapped the floor with his foot impatiently.

'But look here, man, that's the point: you wouldn't have needed to think. You would have handed her the lighter automatically; then if she had asked for matches—if she had asked after that for you to stop the car and get out and buy matches, you couldn't have helped knowing—'

'But I didn't.'

'Yes, I see you didn't,' agreed the psychologist in a flattened tone. 'Look here, there is no earthly use in your trying to confuse me as to the motives behind your actions. In the first place, you couldn't if you wanted to. In the second place, you came to me as your psychiatrist. You are paying me money to get rid of your nervousness and depression. So tell me why you deliberately stepped out of that taxicab, walked into the cigar store and allowed Mrs Hessland to drive away?'

Samuels began a stammering, then drew a sharp breath:

'Look, look yonder!' he whispered. 'There he is!'

Both men fell silent and watched a dim figure on the opposite side of the street. At times the curtain of the rain almost obscured him.

'Now what will he do?' whispered Poggioli, whose heat at the bank clerk was purely professional and vanished the moment another notion entered his head.

'Nothing, just stand at the corner and watch this house.'

'Trying to find out where you have—er—concealed Mrs—er—do you suppose?'

'Damn it, I suppose that's his idea,' jerked out the bank clerk.

'But look here, if he is looking for Mrs Hessland, why doesn't he follow you off somewhere—why does he watch this apartment?'

'Oh, hell! I don't know! I suppose he thinks I've got her in my rooms!'

'You haven't, have you?'

'No! No! Of course not! How long would a bank clerk hold his job with a— Aw, the man's a fool!'

'He must be. . . . Hello, this fellow doesn't seem to be stopping on the other side of the street!'

'He isn't?' The younger man peered out, then drew back a step, stood staring, but finally drew a breath of relief. 'Oh, that's all right. He's not the man who's been following me. It was a much bigger man than he is—as big as you are.'

Poggioli watched the figure crossing the street toward them, then went back to the point they were discussing:

'You were telling me, I believe, that you stepped out of the taxi to allow Mrs Hessland to drive away—'

'My God, no, I wasn't telling you anything like that!' ejaculated the bank clerk.

'Not in so many words, perhaps. . . . But why should I probe into that? It has nothing to do with your nervousness, has it?'

'Absolutely nothing,' assured the younger man.

The third man had now crossed the street and was climbing the stoop of the apartment house. He stepped into the entrance, blinked, stood a moment letting the water run from his overcoat, and said:

'Will you tell me—is this Number 215? I can't make it out in the dark.'

'Yes, it is.'

'Does Mr Oliver Samuels live here?'

The bank clerk looked at the newcomer.

'I'm Oliver Samuels.'

'Mr Samuels, I have a paper here to serve on you. It makes you co-respondent in the case. . . . Lemme see—' The fellow held his paper up toward the dim top light of the entry. ' "*Hessland versus Hessland.*" . . . I'll read it to you.' And he began unfolding his summons.

The bank clerk stood with a hand on the inner door as if holding himself upright.

'Hessland,' he repeated.

'I think it's Hessland. . . . Yes, it's Hessland.'

'Why, I don't know where Mrs Hessland is . . . I haven't the faintest notion.'

'Well, you know, sir, I haven't got nothing to do with that. I'm the process-server.'

'But listen,' pleaded the bank clerk, 'I don't know—I really don't. And if I get made co-respondent—what is it, a divorce suit?'

'Why, I suppose so, sir, by you being made a co-respondent.'

'I'll lose my job. . . . I'm sure to lose my job in the bank. Listen—couldn't you fail to find me—would that help?'

'But I have found you, sir.'

'Suppose you've found fifty, or a—a hundred dollars instead. . . . You understand how this is, Mr Poggioli—I simply don't know *anything* about the woman, and why should I lose my position for something that will do nobody any good?'

The smallish man smacked his lips.

'Why-y-y . . . no, sir, I fancy not. . . . I know some of the boys who—who have gone out and found—er—money instead o' men; but in the long run, sir, it really don't pay—especially in comp'ny like we are, sir.'

The fellow made a notation, gave Samuels a copy of the paper, and turned about once more into the rain.

The bank clerk stood holding the paper, staring into the darkness where the process-server had disappeared. The psychologist studied his companion intently.

'You really didn't expect that fellow, did you?' he asked in a puzzled tone.

Samuels got a breath.

'Why—why, Mr Poggioli, if—if the roof had fallen in on me—'

The psychiatrist nodded.

'Yes—I see. You really are amazed and shocked.'

'I certainly am.'

Poggioli pulled slowly at his chin.

'That creates rather a riddle, Samuels: Your actions in the cab with Mrs Hessland assert one thing, but your shock at being mentioned in divorce proceedings testifies with equal truth to its opposite.' The scientist made a little gesture. 'Now somehow both those things are true, but I am frank to admit at first glance I don't see it.'

Samuels looked at his companion, evidently without seeing or hearing him. He stirred himself out of his consternation, batted his eyes and looked around.

'Well,' he said uncertainly, 'I—I don't suppose there is any use watching any longer.' He peered into the darkness again. 'Suppose we go up to my rooms?'

The psychiatrist gave a nod of acquiescence, and they went through an inner hallway to an automatic elevator. In the little cage Samuels asked suddenly: 'What was it you said to me just then?'

'When?'

'A few moments ago—you were asking—something?'

'Oh, yes, I was puzzled. . . . I'm not so much now.'

'Why, what have you found out?'

'I've found out why you invented that story about Mrs Hessland wanting matches and how she drove off while you were gone to get them.'

Samuels looked intently at his companion.

'The story is perfectly true! Why do you *think* I invented it?'

'You and Mrs Hessland invented it together—to tell at the hospital when you returned to explain her disappearance.'

'But she did drive away!'

'I know it; but you both had planned for her to do it. You knew she would go on the moment you went into the cigar stand—that is if you actually went into a cigar stand. I imagine you just stepped out of the cab and let her ride on.'

Samuels broke out in an annoyed voice:

'Why do you say that? You know I wouldn't deliberately desert an invalid from a sanitarium on the street!'

Poggioli shrugged patiently.

'You did it because you didn't want to be seen entering the new apartment with her for the first time.'

'What apartment?'

'The one you had furnished for her, of course.'

Samuels frowned, and moistened his lips.

'Why shouldn't I enter it with her the first time—if there was any such apartment?'

'Oh, that was bank-clerkly caution,' hazarded the psychologist dryly. 'Anybody is allowed to have an establishment in New York except a bank clerk. You thought after Mrs Hessland had settled, and a few other friends had called, you might drop in—casually—and avoid the appearance of evil.'

The elevator clicked to a halt, and Samuels stood looking at the scientist with a dropped face.

'Well, ye-es, we had planned something like that.'

The scientist nodded.

'Those were your plans; but—something went wrong. . . . She never appeared at the apartment you furnished.'

'What makes you say that?' asked the bank clerk, almost in terror.

'Why, your shock at being mentioned with her in the divorce papers. That tells me with equal certitude that you don't know where she is now, and you've never been with her at all.'

The bank clerk caught the psychologist's arm.

'Mr Poggioli, if you know that, for God's sake tell me where she went—and what made her go! You don't know the uncertainty, the suspense—waiting day after day, running blind ads in the papers—'

The psychologist opened the elevator-door, and the two men moved automatically into the upper hallway.

'Where she went I can't tell you, Mr Samuels. When she found herself free, she may have decided to make a new start, alone.'

'But she loved me! She had been ill-treated, and I loved her!'

'If she really loved you, that would be a reason for a certain type of woman not to live with you illicitly, Mr Samuels.'

'But where is she now? Has she got herself a job somewhere? How can I find her again?'

The psychologist held up his hand and shook it to signify that he could not answer.

'But you've told everything else—why can't you tell that?'

Samuels led the way to his apartment, and unlocked the door.

'Look here,' said Poggioli, 'I believe there is a little gap in the logic of this disappearance. If she suggested it, why—why should she be the one to disappear?'

Samuels looked at him blankly.

'She suggested it?'

'Yes—didn't she?'

'Why, no. I did, of course.'

Poggioli smiled slightly, and shook his head.

'You think that, Samuels, because men always believe they originate such ideas. But you were concerned about her health, about her physical well-being; you were wrought up because she was miserable. . . . You still are. . . . That feeling would never have suggested an elopement. . . . I think it must have come about through her.'

The bank clerk was bewildered.

'Why, I know I'm the one who sug—'

'How did you communicate with her?'

'Through notes.'

'Well, you probably saved those notes. Working in a bank would cause you to—'

'I did; certainly I would save Margaret's letters.'

'Could you find out just who did originate the idea of an elopement?'

'Sit down,' invited the host. He went to a closet and returned with a filing-case of letters, drew a chair to a reading-lamp and began going through them with the carefulness of a teller investigating an account. Presently he turned rather blankly to Poggioli.

'This seems to be the first letter mentioning—such a thing.'

'So she did write it, after all?'

'Apparently.'

'May I see it?'

Samuels hesitated, but finally folded the paper so Poggioli could see only one sentence. It read:

. . . continue like this when we could be together. I don't know what New York may have done to your ideas about things, Oliver, but I feel as if Everbrook were a thousand miles away—

Here the lower fold cut off the sentence.

Poggioli sat frowning blankly at the writing.

'That's extraordinary,' he said slowly.

'Why?' enquired the bank clerk.

'A woman—a girl suggesting an elopement, and breaking off to say she doesn't know what New York has done to your ideas about things. . . . You didn't give me a copy of your letter to her, did you, Samuels, by mistake?'

'Oh, no, certainly not. . . . Why do you say that?'

'Because to consider how the idea came into one's head, to break off a suggestion to consider that—a man might think of that, Samuels, but a woman would not.'

'Yes, but she did.'

'H'm! So it appears. . . . And she disappeared afterward—in the midst of carrying out her plans?'

The bank clerk assented dully.

Poggioli pulled at his chin and nodded slowly as he stared at and through the paper. Finally he turned to his host.

'Let me see two or three more of her letters, noncommittal ones, near the beginning of the correspondence.'

Samuels selected a half-dozen and handed them across. Poggioli made a place on the table beside him and spread out the letters. He let his glance brush over them, then shook his head.

'You know, Samuels, it's a difficult task to counterfeit another person's signature; it's still harder to reproduce her general handwriting, and that is the mere mechanical side of it. The mental and spiritual side, for a man to duplicate the thoughts a woman would think and write—that, I am sure, is an impossibility.'

The bank clerk strode over to the table and looked at the exhibits.

'Do you mean to say her letter was—' He checked himself to ejaculate: 'Why, it was forged, wasn't it?'

'Exactly! I knew some man had dictated this note, when I read it.'

'But who forged it?'

'There is only one person in the world who could have any interest in the matter.'

'Who's that?'

'Hessland, of course.'

Samuels looked at his companion with horror in his eyes.

'You mean her own husband—you think he would deliberately inject the idea of an elopement into—'

'Certainly. That would give him easy grounds for divorce—and avoid the possibility of alimony.'

'But how did he get into the correspondence?'

'Why, through the nurses at the hospital. They doubtless read all the notes that passed between you and Mrs Hessland. . . . He paid them, you know.'

'Then—then what has happened to her? Did he follow her to the apartment—and take some sort of revenge?'

'That I can't say. . . . Let me see. . . . What do you know about Hessland? You say he posed as a man of wealth?'

'Yes, Margaret married him under the impression that he was very wealthy.'

Poggioli nodded and quirked his lips.

'That doesn't get us very far. There are so many men who pose as wealthy, you couldn't possibly deduce Hessland's type from that. . . . What about the woman herself? Would she incite revenge if she betrayed a husband?'

'I don't know.'

'Was she young?'

'Twenty-three—her birthday was the fourteenth of May.'

'Pretty?'

The bank clerk drew a breath.

'The most beautiful girl I have ever known.'

'Happen to have a photograph of her?'

'Yes, I'll show it to you.'

The clerk went back to his closet and brought out a 'cabinet' portrait. Poggioli took it, looked at the fluffy lace dress and flowers in the figure's hands. He glanced at the back of the picture.

'This was made by a photographer in Everbrook; it must have been done some time ago?'

'Yes, when she finished high school. . . . It was taken for our Annual.'

'She probably doesn't look like this now. Have you anything later?'

'No, I haven't.' Samuels took the high school portrait. As he replaced it in its folder, he remembered something. 'Yes, I have a recent picture of her, too; but it isn't much good.' He handed Poggioli a postcard picture of a very pretty woman.

The psychologist took the cheap photograph, glanced at it; then something seemed to catch his attention, for he gave it a closer look and asked:

'Where did you get this one?'

'Why, she handed it to me when she came out of the sanitarium and got into the taxicab with me. She said she had got a picture made for me, too—' The bank clerk came to a full stop, and ejaculated: 'Why, of course—she was fixing to leave me right then—it was her way of telling me goodbye.'

As the psychologist continued to study the picture, he shook his head slowly.

'No—no—that's not probable. When she handed you this picture, Mr Samuels, she must have been in a light mood; she did it casually. Really at the time she must have meant to live with you, as you had planned.'

'Why do you say that?'

'Because this picture is plainly no prettier than Mrs Hessland is herself; it has not even been retouched.'

'Well, what's that got to do with it? Why couldn't she have said goodbye with—'

'Because no woman would have given you a farewell picture that was not as pretty as she could have it made. She would want to be remembered at her best, naturally. No; when Mrs Hessland got into the taxicab with you, she had not the slightest idea of deserting you, Mr Samuels; this picture is proof positive of that.'

The smallish man was puzzled, and annoyed at this hopeful logic which was obviously false.

'But look here, she did leave me, Mr Poggioli; there's no use your sitting there saying she didn't mean to leave me, when she did!'

Poggioli waved a patient forefinger at his client.

'I didn't say she didn't leave you; I merely said she didn't mean to leave you when she handed you this postcard. . . . What happened in the taxi?'

'Why, nothing!'

'You didn't—make her angry?'

'Why, of course not. I—I drew shut the— No, I didn't make her angry at all, not in the least.'

The psychologist frowned.

'H'm. If she left you and did not intend to leave you, then some-body—some third person must have—'

Samuels leaned across the table.

'You are not suggesting that somebody did something to Margaret? How could they, driving through the street in a public taxi, to the apartment I had furnished?'

The psychiatrist waved down this lead to ask carefully:

'She couldn't have got this picture made just for you; did she say what she did with the others?'

'Why, as a matter of fact, she didn't have the pictures made at all, Mr Poggioli; the sanitarium did that. When they were turned in, she simply kept one out for me.'

'The sanitarium? You mean the authorities there in the sanitar-ium?'

'Yes, of course that was what she meant.'

'And did she happen to tell you what the authorities wanted with a picture like this?'

The bank clerk considered.

'Yes,' he recalled, 'she said she was giving me this to show me how she looked in the sanitarium records.'

'Their records?'

'Yes; she said the sanitarium kept a photograph of each patient in their records.'

'But she wasn't just entering the sanitarium, was she?'

'Oh, no; she had been there about a year.'

'And after a year's residence the authorities suddenly decided they must have a postcard photograph of Mrs Hessland for their records?'

Samuels looked at his guest.

'That is a queer thing, isn't it?'

'No, it isn't queer at all; it is simply a bald misstatement to throw Mrs Hessland off the track. . . . They had some reason—'

The bank clerk suddenly sat up. 'Look here, you don't suppose they *knew* she was going to run away . . . and with me . . . and they wanted her photograph so the police could trace her!' He broke off, wetting his lips.

'The idea of taking a photograph to trace her when they had her in their hands!' Poggioli pointed out.

'Yes, that is so,' agreed the smaller man, breathing a little more easily but still apprehensive.

The scientist sat tapping his lips and studying the photograph. Then he suddenly opened his eyes and ejaculated abruptly:

'Why, my God, making all this mystery out of this, when here the thing is before us!'

'What?'

'Why, this: if the sanitarium didn't want the photograph for their records, and Mrs Hessland didn't order it, then there is only one thing left for it to be used for!'

'What's that?' asked Samuels blankly.

'Why, a passport, of course! It's passport size, passport finish—'

'Passport!' echoed Mr Samuels, becoming alarmed on a new tack.

'Certainly. Then the husband must have really had it made. He got a passport for her—Mrs Hessland has gone abroad.'

Samuels' hands fell limply on the table.

'Then she did run away from me after all!'

'No, no, she didn't run away from you—not after giving you that picture for a keepsake.'

'But her husband has taken her back—he's gone abroad with her!'

'Good Lord, man, not after he had arranged for you two to elope . . . No man in his position would be so wishy-washy.'

'How do you know?'

'Because it takes persistence and nerve and a lack of sentiment to keep up an appearance of wealth on nothing a year. No, Hessland is unprincipled. He had arranged for you to elope with his wife and save himself alimony; then—then something or other popped into his head that seemed even better than that—something or other—' Poggioli beat a nervous tattoo on the desk with his fingers. 'Whatever it was, probably—yes, by God, it would be that—it would bring him in money!'

'It was what? What would bring him in money?'

'Why, when he read your letter and found she would go to the apartment alone, he hurried her passport through, and—sold her!'

'What!'

'Certainly, kidnapped her, shanghaied her, sold her! When did you say she disappeared?'

'Day before yesterday!'

'Have you got the papers for that day?'

'Certainly—but Mr Poggioli, where in the world could he sell—'

'Bring me the sailing-lists. . . . What boats sailed at midnight day before yesterday?'

Samuels produced the papers—opened them shakily at the shipping news.

Poggioli skimmed down the list.

'*Megantic* . . . . *Cape Verde* . . . . *Queen of India* . . . . *Uruguay* . . . . *Montevideo* . . . . I imagine, I am almost sure, she will be on a South American steamer.'

'What makes you say that?'

'Because Europe has plenty of women of its own. . . . By the way, we might save radioing to all of these steamers . . . Where does Hessland live in New York?'

'Park Avenue near Eightieth.'

'What's the nearest telegraph to Park and Eightieth?' He picked up the Manhattan telephone-lists, answered his own question, and dialed a number. He sat listening to the buzz for ten or fifteen seconds, then began:

'Western Union, this is William Hessland speaking. . . . I am expecting a wireless. . . . Oh, you've sent it up to me already. . . . Was it from the *Montevideo*? . . . The *Uruguay*? . . . Very well—take this message, will you:

Captain *Uruguay*, a young woman is aboard your ship in charge of man or woman who purports to be her medical attendant. She was brought aboard under color of being very ill or insane. Her passport is forged. She is a victim of abduction. Arrest attendant, liberate prisoner. Will have police wire you confirmation of this order.

Sign the name, "*Henry Poggioli*". Yes, that's correct, operator: the Captain of the *Uruguay*, whoever he is, will know Henry Poggioli.'

Samuels leaned across the table with eyes starting from his head.

'My God—sold her—shipped her like an animal! Haven't you made some horrible mistake?'

Poggioli turned and snapped out:

'How could I have made a mistake? If she gave you that photograph, she didn't know she was going away; since it was for a passport, someone else got it for her; if they forged her passport, they kidnapped her; if her husband had her kidnapped, he had her sold. There is no other solution.'

Samuels sat staring wordlessly.

Poggioli leaned back, regarding the clerk with a thoughtful half-frown.

'And look here,' he proceeded presently, 'this couldn't have been Hessland's first offense. The whole thing worked too smoothly. I'll venture he's got a record of divorces from missing wives.' He leaned forward on some impulse and picked up the receiver again.

Samuels watched him a moment apathetically; then he roused himself to ask:

'Who are you telephoning now?'

'The police. I'm going to have his record sent over.'

He began dialing again; then Samuels stood up with a white face.

'You—you're not asking a policeman to—to come here?'

Poggioli lifted his hand and continued his dialing.

'Sit down, sit down. This may be the final solution of your nervousness, Mr Samuels.'

The bank clerk drew a quick breath.

'My nervousness! What do you mean?'

'You asked me to come here and examine you because you were nervous, didn't you?'

'Why—y-yes—certainly.'

'And I have discovered why you are nervous. You spent rather too much money on Mrs Hessland's apartment—money that didn't really belong to you. . . . That's true, isn't it?'

Samuels wet his lips, swallowed, stared at Poggioli.

'Do—do you suppose the—the bank knows about that? Do you suppose *they* sent out that man to—to follow me around—to shadow me?'

Poggioli sat with receiver to ear.

'The bank employs me to look after the irregularities in its clerical force, Mr Samuels. . . . I am the man who has been following you around.'

6

C. DALY KING

The Episode of the Nail
and the Requiem

Characters of the Episode

JERRY PHELAN, the narrator
GLEEB, manager of Tarrant's apartment house
WICKS, apartment house electrician
BARBARA BREBANT, wealthy débutante of bohemian tastes
MICHAEL SALTI, an artist in oils
MULLINS, a lieutenant of police; large and loud
PEAKE, deputy inspector; tall, thin, soft voiced
WEBER, patrolman; a regular cop
TREVIS TARRANT, interested in sealed rooms
KATOH, his butler-valet

THE EPISODE OF THE NAIL AND THE REQUIEM

The episode of the nail and the requiem was one of the most characteristic of all those in which, over a relatively brief period, I was privileged to watch Trevis Tarrant at work. Characteristic, in that it
brought out so well the unusual aptitude of the man to see clearly, to
welcome *all* the facts, no matter how apparently contradictory, and to
think his way through to the only possible solution by sheer logic,
while everyone else boggled at impossibilities and sought to forget
them. From the gruesome beginning that November morning, when
he was confronted by the puzzle of the sealed studio, to the equally
gruesome denouement that occurred despite his own grave warning
twenty-four hours later, his brain clicked successively and infallibly
along the rails of reason to the inevitable, true goal.

Tarrant had been good enough to meet us at the boat when Valerie and I had returned from our wedding trip; and a week later I had been delighted with the opportunity of spending the night at his apartment, telling him of the trip and our plans and hearing of his own activities during the interval. After all, he was largely responsible for my having won Valerie when I did; our friendship had grown to intimacy during those few days when the three of us, and Katoh too, had struggled with the thickening horror in Valerie's modernistic house.

It was that most splendid time of year when the suburban air is tinged with the smoke of leaves, when the country beyond flaunts beauty along the roads, when the high windows of the city look out every evening through violet dusk past myriad twinkling lights at the gorgeous painting of sunset. We had been to a private address at the Metropolitan Museum by a returning Egyptologist; we had come back to the apartment and talked late into the night. Now, at eight-thirty the next morning, we sat at breakfast in Tarrant's lounge while the steam hissed comfortably in the wall radiators and the brisk, bright sky poured light through the big window beside us.

I remember that we had nearly finished eating and that Tarrant was saying: 'Cause and effect rule this world; they may be a mirage but they are a consistent mirage; everywhere, except possibly in sub-atomic physics, there is a cause for each effect, and that cause can be found,' when the manager came in. He wore a fashionable morning coat and looked quite handsome; he was introduced to me as Mr Gleeb. Apparently he had merely dropped in, as was his custom, to assure himself that all was satisfactory with a valued tenant, but the greetings were scarcely over when the phone rang and Katoh indicated that he was being called. His monosyllabic answers gave no indication of the conversation from the other end; he finished with 'All right; I'll be up in a minute.'

He turned back to us. 'I'm sorry,' he said, 'but there is some trouble at the penthouse. Or else my electrician has lost his mind. He says there is a horrible kind of music being played there and that he can get no response to his ringing at the door. I shall have to go up and see what it is all about.'

The statement was a peculiar one and Tarrant's eyes, I thought,

74

held an immediate gleam of curiosity. He got out of his seat in a leisurely fashion, however, and declared: 'You know, Gleeb, I'd like a breath of fresh air after breakfast. Mind if we come up with you? There's a terrace, I believe, where we can take a step or so while you're untangling the matter.'

'Not at all, Mr Tarrant. Come right along. I hardly imagine it's of any importance, but I can guarantee plenty of air.'

There was, in fact a considerable wind blowing across the open terrace that, guarded by a three foot parapet, surrounded the penthouse on all sides except the north, where its wall was flush with that of the building. The penthouse itself was rather small, containing as I later found, besides the studio which comprised its whole northern end, only a sleeping room with a kitchenette and a lavatory off its east and west sides respectively. The entrance was on the west side of the studio and here stood the electrician who had come to the roof to repair the radio antennæ of the apartment house and had been arrested by the strange sounds from within. As we strolled about the terrace, we observed the penthouse itself as well as the wide view below. Its southern portion possessed the usual windows but the studio part had only blank brick walls; a skylight was just visible above it and there was, indeed, a very large window, covering most of the northern wall, but this, of course, was invisible and inaccessible from the terrace.

Presently the manager beckoned us over to the entrance door and, motioning us to be silent, asked: 'What do you make of that, Mr Tarrant?'

In the silence the sound of doleful music was more than audible. It appeared to emanate from within the studio; slow, sad and mournful, it was obviously a dirge and its full-throated quality suggested that it was being rendered by a large orchestra. After a few moments' listening Tarrant said: 'That is the rendition of a requiem mass and very competently done, too. Unless I'm mistaken, it is the requiem of Palestrina.... There; there's the end of it.... Now it's beginning again.'

'Sure, it goes on like that all the time,' contributed Wicks, the electrician. 'There must be someone in there, but I can't get no answer.' He banged on the door with his fist, but obviously without hope of response.

'Have you looked in at the windows?'

'Sure.'

We, too, stepped to the available windows and peered in, but beyond a bedroom that had not been used, nothing was visible. The door from the bedroom to the studio was closed. The windows were all locked.

'I suggest,' said Tarrant, 'that we break in.'

The manager hesitated. 'I don't know. After all, he has a right to play any music he likes, and if he doesn't want to answer the door——'

'Who has the penthouse, anyhow?'

'A man named Michael Salti. An eccentric fellow, like many of these artists. I don't know much about him, to tell the truth; we can't insist on as many references as we used to, nowadays. He paid a year's rent in advance and he hasn't bothered anyone in the building, that's about all I can tell you.'

'Well,' Tarrant considered, 'this performance *is* a little peculiar. How does he know we may not be trying to deliver an important message? How about his phone?'

'Tried it,' Wicks answered. 'The operator says there isn't any answer.'

'I'm in favour of taking a peek. Look here, Gleeb, if you don't want to take the responsibility of breaking in, let us procure a ladder and have a look through the skylight. Ten to one that will pass unobserved; and if everything seems all right we can simply sneak away.'

To this proposal the manager consented, although it seemed to me that he did so most reluctantly. Possibly the eerie sounds that continued to issue through the closed door finally swayed him, for their quality, though difficult to convey, was certainly upsetting. In any event the ladder was brought and Tarrant himself mounted it, once it had been set in place. I saw him looking through the skylight, then leaning closer, peering intently through hands cupped about his eyes. Presently he straightened and came down the ladder in some haste.

His face, when he stood beside us, was strained. 'I think you should call the police,' he grated. 'At once. And wait till they get here before you go in.'

'The police? But—what is it?'

'It's not pleasant,' Tarrant said slowly. 'I think it's murder.'

Nor would he say anything further until the police, in the person of a traffic patrolman from Park Avenue, arrived. Then we all went in together, Gleeb's pass-key having failed and the door being broken open.

The studio was a large, square room, and high, and the light, sweeping in through the north wall and the skylight, illuminated it almost garishly. It was sparsely furnished; a couch, a chair, a stool, an easel and a cabinet for paints and supplies stood on a hardwood floor which two rugs scarcely covered. The question of the music was soon settled; in one corner was an electric victrola with an automatic arrangement for turning the record and starting it off again when it had reached its end. The record was of Palestrina's Requiem Mass, played by a well-known orchestra. Someone, I think it was Tarrant, crossed the room and turned it off, while we stood huddled near the door, gazing stupidly at the twisted, bloody figure on the couch.

It was that of a girl, altogether naked; although she was young— not older than twenty-two certainly—her body was precociously voluptuous. One of her legs was contorted into a bent position, her mouth was awry, her right hand held a portion of the couch covering in an agonized clutch. Just beneath her left breast the hilt of a knife protruded shockingly. The bleeding had been copious.

It was Tarrant again who extinguished the four tall candles, set on the floor and burning at the corners of the couch. As he did so he murmured: 'You will remember that the candles were burning at eight-forty-seven, officer. I dislike mockery.'

Then I was out on the terrace again, leaning heavily against the western parapet. In the far distance the Orange mountains stood against the bright horizon; somewhat nearer, across the river, huddled the building masses that marked Newark; overhead a plane droned south-westward. I gagged and forced my thoughts determinedly toward that plane. It was a transport plane, it was going to Newark Airport; probably it was an early plane from Boston. On it were people, prosaic people, thank God. One of them was perhaps a button salesman; presently he would enter the offices of Messrs Simon and Morgetz and display his buttons on a card for the benefit of Mr Simon. . . . Now my insides were behaving less drastically. I could gasp; and I did gasp, deep intakes of clear, cold air.

When I came back into the studio, a merciful blanket covered the girl's body. And for the first time I noticed the easel. It stood in the south-east corner of the room, diagonally opposite the couch and across the studio from the entrance doorway. It should have faced north-west, to receive the light from the big north window, and in fact the stool to its right indicated that position. But the easel had been partly turned, so that it faced south-west, toward the bedroom door; and one must walk almost to that door to observe its canvas.

This, stretched tightly on its frame, bore a painting in oil of the murdered girl. She was portrayed in a nude, half-crouching pose, her arms extended, and her features held a revoltingly lascivious leer. The portrait was entitled 'La Séduction'. In the identical place where the knife had pierced her actual body, a large nail had been driven through the web of the canvas. It was half-way through, the head protruding two inches on the obverse side of the picture; and a red gush of blood had been painted down the torso from the point where the nail entered.

Tarrant stood with his hands in his pockets, surveying this work of art. His gaze seemed focused upon the nail, incongruous in its strange position and destined to play so large a part in the tragedy. He was murmuring to himself and his voice was so low that I scarcely caught his words.

'Madman's work. . . . But why is the easel turned away from the room. . . . Why is that? . . .'

It was late afternoon in Tarrant's apartment and much activity had gone forward. The Homicide Squad in charge of Lieutenant Mullins had arrived and unceremoniously ejected everyone else from the penthouse, Tarrant included. Thereupon he had called a friend at Headquarters and been assured of a visit from Deputy Inspector Peake, who would be in command of the case, a visit which had not yet eventuated.

I had gone about my business in the city somewhat dazedly. But I had met Valerie for luncheon downtown and her presence was like a fragrant, reviving draft of pure ozone. She had left again for Norrisville, after insisting that I stay with Tarrant another night when she saw how excited I had become over the occurrences of the morning. Back in the apartment Katoh, who, for all that he was a man of our own class in Japan, was certainly an excellent butler in New York, had immediately provided me with a fine bottle of Irish whisky (Bushmills, bottled in 1919). I was sipping my second highball and Tarrant was quietly reading across the room, when Inspector Peake rang the bell.

He advanced into the room with hand outstretched. 'Mr Tarrant, I believe? . . . Ah. Glad to know you, Mr Phelan.' He was a tall, thin man in mufti, with a voice unexpectedly soft. I don't know why, but I was also surprised that a policeman should wear so well-cut a suit of tweeds. As he sank into a chair, he continued, 'I understand you were among the first to enter the penthouse, Mr Tarrant. But I'm afraid there isn't much to add now. The case is cut and dried.'

'You have the murderer?'

'Not yet. But the drag-net is out. We shall have him, if not today, then tomorrow or the next day.'

'The artist, I suppose?'

'Michael Salti, yes. An eccentric man, quite mad. . . . By the way, I must thank you for that point about the candles. In conjunction with the medical examiner's evidence it checked the murder definitely at between one and two a.m.'

'There is no doubt, then, I take it, about the identity of the criminal.'

'No,' Peake asserted, 'none at all. He was seen alone with his model at 10.50 p.m. by one of the apartment house staff and the elevator operators are certain no one was taken to the penthouse during the evening or night. His fingerprints were all over the knife, the candle-sticks, the victrola record. There was a lot more corroboration, too.'

'And was he seen to leave the building after the crime?'

'No, he wasn't. That's the one missing link. But since he isn't here, he must have left. Perhaps by the fire-stairs; we've checked it and it's possible. . . . The girl is Barbara Brebant—a wealthy family.' The inspector shook his head. 'A wild one, though; typical Prohibition product. She has played around with dubious artistics from the

Village and elsewhere for some years; gave most of 'em more than they could take, by all accounts. Young, too; made her debut only about a year ago. Apparently she has made something of a name for herself in the matter of viciousness; three of our men brought in the very same description—a vicious beauty.'

'The old Roman type,' Tarrant surmised. 'Not so anachronistic in this town, at that. . . . Living with Salti?'

'No. She lived at home. When she bothered to go home. No one doubts, though, that she was Salti's mistress. And from what I've learned, when she was any man's mistress he was pretty certain to be dragged through the mire. Salti, being mad, finally killed her.'

'Yes, that clicks,' Tarrant agreed. 'The lascivious picture and the nail driven through it. Madmen, of course, act perfectly logically. He was probably a loose liver himself, but she showed him depths he had not suspected. Then remorse. His insanity taking the form of an absence of the usual values, he made her into a symbol of his own vice, through the painting, and then killed her, just as he mutilated the painting with the nail. . . . Yes, Salti is your man all right.'

Peake ground out a cigarette. 'A nasty affair. But not especially mysterious. I wish all our cases were as simple.' He was preparing to take his leave.

Tarrant also got up. He said: 'Just a moment. There were one or two things——'

'Yes?'

'I wonder if I could impose upon you a little more, Inspector. Just to check some things I noticed this morning. Can I be admitted to the penthouse now?'

Peake shrugged, as if the request were a useless one, but took it with a certain good grace. 'Yes, I'll take you up. All our men have left now, except a patrolman who will guard the premises until we make the arrest. I still have an hour to spare.'

It was two hours, however, before they returned. The inspector didn't come in, but I caught Tarrant's parting words at the entrance. 'You will surely assign another man to the duty tonight, won't you?' The policeman's reply sounded like a grunt of acquiescence.

I looked at my friend in amazement when he came into the lounge. His clothes, even his face, were covered with dirt; his nose was a long, black smudge. By the time he had bathed and changed and we sat down to one of Katoh's dinners, it was nearly half-past nine.

During dinner Tarrant was unaccustomedly silent. Even after we had finished and Katoh had brought our coffee and liqueurs, he sat at a modernistic tabouret stirring the black liquid reflectively, and in the light of the standing lamp behind him I thought his face wore a slight frown.

Presently he gave that peculiar whistle that summoned his man and the butler-valet appeared almost immediately from the passage to the kitchen.

'Sit down, doctor,' he spoke without looking up.

Doubtless a small shift in my posture expressed my surprise, for he continued, for my benefit, 'I've told you that Katoh is a doctor in his own country, a well-educated man who is over here really on account of this absurd spy custom. Because of that nonsense I am privileged to hire him as a servant, but when I wish his advice as a friend, I call him doctor—a title to which he is fully entitled—and institute a social truce. Usually I do it when I'm worried . . . I'm worried now.'

Katoh, meantime, had hoisted himself on to the divan, where he sat smiling and helping himself to one of Tarrant's Dimitrinoes. 'Sozhial custom matter of convenience,' he acknowledged. 'Conference about what?'

'About this penthouse murder,' said Tarrant without further ado. 'You know the facts related by Inspector Peake. You heard them?'

'I listen. Part my job.'

'Yes, well that portion is all right. Salti's the man. There's no mystery about that, not even interesting, in fact. But there's something else, something that isn't right. It stares you in the face, but the police don't care. Their business is to arrest the murderer; they know who he is and they're out looking for him. That's enough for them. But there *is* a mystery up above, a real one. I'm not concerned with chasing crooks, but their own case won't hold unless this curious fact fits in. It is as strange as anything I've ever met.'

Katoh's grin had faded; his face was entirely serious. 'What this mystery?'

'It's the most perfect sealed room, or rather sealed house, problem ever reported. There was no way out and yet the man isn't there. No possibility of suicide; the fingerprints on the knife are only one element that rules that out. No, he was present all right. But where did he go, and how? . . . Listen carefully. I've checked this from my own observation, from the police investigations, and from my later search with Peake.

'When we entered the penthouse this morning, Gleeb's pass-key didn't suffice; we had to break the entrance door in because it was bolted on the inside by a strong bar. The walls of the studio are of brick and they have no windows except on the northern side where there is a sheer drop to the ground. The window there was fastened on the inside and the skylight was similarly fastened. The only other exit from the studio is the door to the bedroom. This was closed and the key turned in the lock; the key was on the studio side of the door.

'Yes, I know,' Tarrant went on, apparently forestalling an interruption; 'it is sometimes possible to turn a key in a lock from the wrong side, by means of pincers or some similar contrivance. That makes the bedroom, the lavatory and the kitchenette adjoining it, possibilities. There is no exit from any of them except by the windows. They were all secured from the inside and I am satisfied that they cannot be so secured by anyone already out of the penthouse.'

He paused and looked over at Katoh, whose head nodded up and down as he made the successive points. 'Two persons in penthouse when murder committed. One is victim, other is Salti man. After murder only victim is visible. One door, windows and skylight are only exits and they are all secured on inside. Cannot be secured from outside. Therefore, Salti man still in penthouse when you enter.'

'But he wasn't there when we entered. The place was thoroughly searched. I was there then myself.'

'Maybe trapdoor. Maybe space under floor or entrance to floor below.'

'Yes,' said Tarrant, 'well, now get this. There are no trapdoors in the flooring of the penthouse, there are none in the walls and there are not even any in the roof. I have satisfied myself of that with Peake. Gleeb, the manager, who was on the spot when the penthouse was built, further assures me of it.'

'Only place is floor,' Katoh insisted. 'Salti man could make this himself.'

'He couldn't make a trapdoor without leaving at least a minute crack,' was Tarrant's counter. 'At least I don't see how he could. The flooring of the studio is hardwood, the planks closely fitted together, and I have been over every inch of it. Naturally there are cracks between the planks, lengthwise; but there are no transverse cracks anywhere. Gleeb has shown me the specifications of that floor. The planks are grooved together and it is impossible to raise any plank without splintering the grooving. From my own examination I am sure none of the planks has been, or can be, lifted.

'All this was necessary because there *is* a space of something like two and a half feet between the floor of the penthouse and the roof of the apartment building proper. One has to mount a couple of steps at the entrance of the penthouse. Furthermore, I have been in part of this space. Let me make it perfectly clear how I got there.

'The bedroom adjoins the studio on the south, and the lavatory occupies the north-west corner of the bedroom. It is walled off, of course. Along the northern wall of the lavatory (which is part of the southern wall of the studio) is the bath-tub; and the part of the flooring under the bath-tub has been cut away, leaving an aperture to the space beneath.'

I made my first contribution. 'But how can that be? Wouldn't the bath-tub fall through?'

'No. The bath-tub is an old-fashioned one, installed by Salti himself only a few weeks ago. It is not flush with the floor, as they make them now, but stands on four legs. The flooring has only been cut away in the middle of the tub, say two or three planks, and the opening extended only to the outer edge of the tub. Not quite that far, in fact.'

'There is Salti man's trapdoor,' grinned Katoh. 'Not even door; just trap.'

'So I thought,' Tarrant agreed grimly. 'But it isn't. Or if it is he didn't use it. As no one could get through the opening without moving the tub—which hadn't been done, by the way—Peake and I pulled up some more of the cut plank by main force and I squeezed myself into the space beneath the lavatory and bedroom. There was nothing there but dirt; I got plenty of that.'

'How about space below studio?'

'Nothing doing. The penthouse is built on a foundation, as I said, about two and a half feet high, of concrete building blocks. A line of these blocks runs underneath the penthouse, directly below the wall between the studio and bedroom. As the aperture in the floor is on the southern side of that wall, it is likewise to the south of the transverse line of building blocks in the foundation. The space beneath the studio is to the north of these blocks, and they form a solid wall that is impassable. I spent a good twenty minutes scrummaging along the entire length of it.'

'Most likely place,' Katoh confided, 'just where hole in lavatory floor.'

'Yes, I should think so too. I examined it carefully. I could see the ends of the planks that form the studio floor partway over the beam above the building blocks. But there isn't a trace of a loose block at that point, any more than there is anywhere else. . . . To make everything certain, we also examined the other three sides of the foundation of the bedroom portion of the penthouse. They are solid and haven't been touched since it was constructed. So the whole thing is just a cul-de-sac; there is no possibility of exit from the penthouse even through the aperture beneath the bath-tub.'

'You examine also foundations under studio part?'

'Yes, we did that, too. No result. It didn't mean much, though, for there is no entrance to the space beneath the studio from the studio itself, nor is there such an entrance from the other space beneath the bedroom portion. That opening under the bath-tub must mean something, especially in view of the recent installation of the tub. But what does it mean?'

He looked at Katoh long and searchingly and the other, after a pause, replied slowly: 'Can only see this. Salti man construct this trap, probably for present use. Then he do not use. Must go some other way.'

'But there *is* no other way.'

'Then Salti man still there.'

'He isn't there.'

'Harumph,' said Katoh reflectively. It was evident that he felt the same respect for a syllogism that animated Tarrant, and was stopped, for the time being at any rate. He went off on a new tack. 'What else specially strange about setting?'

'There are two other things that strike me as peculiar,' Tarrant answered, and his eyes narrowed. 'On the floor, about one foot from the northern window, there is a fairly deep indentation in the floor of the studio. It is a small impression and is almost certainly made by a nail partly driven through the planking and then pulled up again.'

I thought of the nail through the picture. 'Could he have put the picture down on that part of the floor in order to drive the nail through it? But what if he did?'

'I can see no necessity for it, in any case. The nail would go through the canvas easily enough just as it stood on the easel.'

Katoh said: 'With nail in plank, perhaps plank could be pulled up. You say no?'

'I tried it. Even driving the nail in sideways, instead of vertically, as the original indentation was made, the plank can't be lifted at all.'

'O.K. You say some other thing strange, also.'

'Yes. The position of the easel that holds the painting of the dead girl. When we broke in this morning, it was turned away from the room, toward the bedroom door, so that the picture was scarcely visible even from the studio entrance, let alone the rest of the room. I don't believe that was the murderer's intention. He had set the rest of the stage too carefully. The requiem; the candles. It doesn't fit; I'm sure he meant the first person who entered to be confronted by the whole scene, and especially by that symbolic portrait. It doesn't accord even with the position of the stool, which agrees with the intended position of the easel. It doesn't fit at all with the mentality of the murderer. It seems a small thing but I'm sure it's important. I'm certain the position of the easel is an important clue.'

'To mystery of disappearance?'

'Yes. To the mystery of the murderer's escape from that sealed room.'

'Not see how,' Katoh declared after some thought. As for me, I couldn't even appreciate the suggestion of any connection.

'Neither do I,' grated Tarrant. He had risen and began to pace the floor. 'Well, there you have it all. A little hole in the floor near the north window, an easel turned out of position and a sealed room without an occupant who certainly ought to be there. . . . There's an answer to this; damn it, there must be an answer.'

Suddenly he glanced at an electric clock on the table he was passing and stopped abruptly. 'My word,' he exclaimed, 'it's nearly three o'clock. Didn't mean to keep you up like this, Jerry. You either, doctor. Well, the conference is over. We've got nowhere.'

Katoh was on his feet, in an instant once more the butler. 'Sorry could not help. You wish night-cap, Misster Tarrant?'

'No. Bring the Scotch, Katoh. And a siphon. And ice. I'm not turning in.'

I had been puzzling my wits without intermission ever since dinner over the problem above, and the break found me more tired than I realized. I yawned prodigiously. I made a half-hearted attempt to persuade Tarrant to come to bed, but it was plain that he would have none of it.

I said, 'Good-night, Katoh. I'm no good for anything until I get a little sleep. . . . Night, Tarrant.'

I left him once more pacing the floor; his face, in the last glimpse I had of it, was set in the stern lines of thought.

It seemed no more than ten seconds after I got into bed that I felt my shoulder being shaken and, through the fog of sleep, heard Katoh's hissing accents. '——Misster Tarrant just come from penthouse. He excited. Maybe you wish wake up.' As I rolled out and shook myself free from slumber, I noticed that my wrist watch pointed to six-thirty.

When I had thrown on some clothes and come into the living-room, I found Tarrant standing with the telephone instrument to his head, his whole posture one of grimness. Although I did not realize it at once, he had been endeavouring for some time to reach Deputy Inspector Peake. He accomplished this finally a moment or so after I reached the room.

'Hallo, Peake? Inspector Peake? . . . This is Tarrant. How many men did you leave to guard that penthouse last night?' . . . 'What, only one? But I said two, man. Damn it all, I don't make suggestions like that for amusement!' . . . 'All right, there's nothing to be accomplished arguing about it. You'd better get here, and get here pronto.' . . . 'That's *all* I'll say.' He slammed down the receiver viciously.

I had never before seen Tarrant upset; my surprise was a measure of his own disturbance, which resembled consternation. He paced the floor, muttering below his breath, his long legs carrying him swiftly up and down the apartment. . . . 'Damned fools . . . everything must fit. . . . Or else . . .' For once I had sense enough to keep my questions to myself for the time being.

Fortunately I had not long to wait. Hardly had Katoh had opportunity to brew some coffee, with which he appeared somewhat in the manner of a dog wagging its tail deprecatingly, than Peake's ring sounded at the entrance. He came in hurriedly, but his smile, as well as his words, indicated his opinion that he had been roused by a false alarm.

'Well, well, Mr Tarrant, what *is* this trouble over?'

Tarrant snapped, 'Your man's gone. Disappeared. How do you like that?'

'The patrolman on guard?' The policeman's expression was incredulous.

'The *single* patrolman you left on guard.'

Peake stepped over to the telephone, called Headquarters. After a few brief words he turned back to us, his incredulity at Tarrant's statement apparently confirmed.

'You must be mistaken, sir,' he asserted. 'There have been no reports from Officer Weber. He would never leave the premises without reporting such an occasion.'

Tarrant's answer was purely practical. 'Come and see.'

And when we reached the terrace on the building's roof, there was, in fact, no sign of the patrolman who should have been at his station. We entered the penthouse and, the lights having been turned on, Peake himself made a complete search of the premises. While Tarrant watched the proceedings in a grim silence, I walked over to the north window of the studio, grey in the early morning light, and sought for the nail hole he had mentioned as being in the floor. There it was, a small, clean indentation, about an inch or an inch and a half deep, in one of the hardwood planks. This, and everything else about the place, appeared just as Tarrant had described it to us some hours before, previous to my turning in. I was just in time to see Peake emerge from the enlarged opening in the lavatory floor, dusty and sorely puzzled.

'Our man is certainly not here,' the inspector acknowledged. 'I cannot understand it. This is a serious breach of discipline.'

'Hell,' said Tarrant sharply, speaking for the first time since we had come to the roof. 'This is a serious breach of intelligence, not discipline.'

'I shall broadcast an immediate order for the detention of Patrolman Weber.' Peake stepped into the bedroom and approached the phone to carry out his intention.

'You needn't broadcast it. I have already spoken to the night operator in the lobby on the ground floor. He told me a policeman left the building in great haste about 3.30 this morning. If you will have the local precinct check up on the all-night lunch-rooms along Lexington Avenue in this vicinity, you will soon pick up the first step of the trail that man left. . . . You will probably take my advice, now that it is too late.'

Peake did so, putting the call through at once; but his bewilderment was no whit lessened. Nor was mine. As he put down the instrument, he said: 'All right. But it doesn't make sense. Why should he leave his post without notifying us? And why should he go to a lunch-room?'

'Because he was hungry.'

'But there has been a crazy murderer here already. And now Weber, an ordinary cop, if I ever saw one. Does this place make everybody mad?'

'Not as mad as you're going to be in a minute. But perhaps you weren't using the word in that sense?'

Peake let it pass. 'Everything,' he commented slowly, 'is just as we left it yesterday evening. Except for Weber's disappearance.'

'Is that so?' Tarrant led us to the entrance from the roof to the studio and pointed downwards. The light was now bright enough to disclose an unmistakable spattering of blood on one of the steps before the door. 'That blood wasn't there when we left last night. I came up here about five-thirty, the moment I got on to this thing,' he continued bitterly. 'Of course I was too late. . . . Damnation, let us make an end to this farce. I'll show you some more things that have altered during the night.'

We followed him into the studio again as he strode over to the easel with its lewd picture, opposite the entrance. He pointed to the nail still protruding through the canvas. 'I don't know how closely you observed the hole made in this painting by the nail yesterday. But it's a little larger now and the edges are more frayed. In other words the nail has been removed and once more inserted.'

I turned about to find that Gleeb, somehow apprised of the excitement, had entered the penthouse and now stood a little behind us. Tarrant acknowledged his presence with a curt nod; and in the air of tension that his tenant was building up the manager ventured no questions.

'Now,' Tarrant continued, pointing out the locations as he spoke, 'possibly they have dried, but when I first got here this morning there was a trail of moist spots still leading from the entrance doorway to the vicinity of the north window. You will find that they were places where a trail of blood had been wiped away with a wet cloth.'

He turned to the picture beside him and withdrew the nail, pulling himself up as if for a repugnant job. He walked over to the north window and motioned us to take our places on either side of him. Then he bent down and inserted the nail, point first, into the indentation in the plank, as firmly as he could. He braced himself and apparently strove to pull the nail toward the south, away from the window.

I was struggling with an obvious doubt. I said, 'But you told us the planks could not be lifted.'

'Can't,' Tarrant grunted. 'But they can be *slid*.'

Under his efforts the plank was, in fact, sliding. Its end appeared from under the footboard at the base of the north wall below the window and continued to move over a space of several feet. When this had been accomplished, he grasped the edges of the planks on both sides of the one already moved and slid them back also. An opening quite large enough to squeeze through was revealed.

But that was not all. The huddled body of a man lay just beneath; the man was clad only in underwear and was obviously dead from the beating in of his head.

As we bent over, gasping at the unexpectedly gory sight, Gleeb suddenly cried, 'But that is not Michael Salti! What is this, a murder farm? I don't know this man.'

Inspector Peake's voice was ominous with anger. 'I do. That is the body of Officer Weber. But how could he——'

Tarrant had straightened up and was regarding us with a look that said plainly he was anxious to get an unpleasant piece of work finished. 'It was simple enough,' he ground out. 'Salti cut out the planks beneath the bath-tub in the lavatory so that *these* planks in the studio could be slid back over the beam along the foundation under the south wall; their farther ends in this position will now be covering the hole in the lavatory floor. The floor here is well fitted and the planks are grooved, thus making the sliding possible. They can be moved back into their original position by someone in the space below here; doubtless we shall find a small block nailed to the under portion of all three planks for that purpose.

'He murdered his model, set the scene and started his phonograph, which will run interminably on the electric current. Then he crawled into his hiding-place. The discovery of the crime could not be put off any later than the chambermaid's visit in the morning, and I have no doubt he took a sadistic pleasure in anticipating her hysterics when she entered. By chance your radio man, Gleeb, caused us to enter first.

'When the place was searched and the murderer not discovered, his pursuit passed elsewhere, while he himself lay concealed here all day. It was even better than doubling back upon his tracks, for he had never left the starting post. Eventually, of course, he had to get out, but by that time the vicinity of this building would be the last place in which he was being searched for.

'Early this morning he pushed back the planks from underneath and came forth. I don't know whether he had expected anyone to be left on guard, but that helped rather than hindered him. Creeping up upon the unsuspecting guard, he knocked him out—doubtless with that mallet I can just see beside the body—and beat him to death. Then he put his second victim in the hiding-place, returning the instrument that closes it from above, the nail, to its position in the painting. He had already stripped off his own clothes, which you will find down in that hole, and in the officer's uniform and coat he found no difficulty in leaving the building. His first action was to hurry to a lunch-room, naturally, since after a day and a night without food under the floor here, he must have been famished. I have no doubt that your men will get a report of him along Lexington Avenue, Peake; but, even so, he now has some hours' start on you.'

'We'll get him,' Peake assured us. 'But if you knew all this, why in heaven's name didn't you have this place opened up last night, before he had any chance to commit a second murder? We should have taken him red-handed.'

'Yes, but I didn't know it last night,' Tarrant reminded him. 'It was not until late yesterday afternoon that I had any proper opportunity to examine the penthouse. What I found was a sealed room and a sealed house. There was no exit that had not been blocked nor, after our search, could I understand how the man could still be in the penthouse. On the other hand, I could not understand how it was possible that he had left. As a precaution, in case he were still here in some manner I had not fathomed, I urged you to leave at least two men on guard, and it was my understanding that you agreed. I think it is obvious, although I was unable then to justify myself, that the precaution was called for.'

Peake said, 'It was.'

'I have been up all night working this out. What puzzled me completely was the absence of any trapdoors. Certainly we looked for them thoroughly. But it was there right in front of us all the time; we even investigated a portion of it, the aperture in the lavatory floor, which we supposed to be a trapdoor itself, although actually it was only a part of the real arrangement. As usual the trick was based upon taking advantage of habits of thought, of our habitized notion of a trapdoor as something that is lifted or swung back. I have never heard before of a trapdoor that slides back. Nevertheless, that was the simple answer, and it took me until five-thirty to reach it.'

Katoh, whom for the moment I had forgotten completely, stirred uneasily and spoke up. 'I not see, Misster Tarrant, how you reach answer then.'

'Four things,' was the reply. 'First of all, the logical assumption that, since there was no way out, the man was still here. As to the mechanism by which he managed to remain undiscovered, three things.

We mentioned them last night. First, the nail hole in the plank; second, the position of the easel; third, the hole in the lavatory floor. I tried many ways to make them fit together, for I felt sure they must *all* fit.

'It was the position of the easel that finally gave me the truth. You remember we agreed that it was wrong, that the murderer had never intended to leave it facing away from the room. But if the murderer had left it as he intended, if no one had entered until we did, and still its position was wrong, what could have moved it in the meantime? Except for the phonograph, which could scarcely be responsible, the room held nothing but motionless objects. *But if the floor under one of its legs had moved, the easel would have been slid around.* That fitted with the other two items, the nail hole in the plank, the opening under the bath-tub.

'The moment it clicked, I got an automatic and ran up here. I was too late. As I said, I've been up all night. I'm tired; and I'm going to bed.'

He walked off without another word, scarcely with a parting nod. Tarrant, as I know now, did not often fail. He was a man who offered few excuses for himself, and he was humiliated.

It was a week or so later when I had an opportunity to ask him if Salti had been captured. I had seen nothing of it in the newspapers, and the case had now passed to the back pages with the usual celerity of sensations.

Tarrant said, 'I don't know.'

'But haven't you followed it up with that man, Peake?'

'I'm not interested. It's nothing but a straight police chase now. This part of it might make a good film for a Hollywood audience, but there isn't the slightest intellectual interest left.'

He stopped and added after an appreciable pause, 'Damn it, Jerry, I don't like to think of it even now. I've blamed the stupidity of the police all I can; their throwing me out when I might have made a real investigation in the morning, that delay; then the negligence in overlooking my suggestion for a pair of guards, which I made as emphatic as I could. But it's no use. I should have solved it in time, even so. There could only be that one answer and I took too long to find it.

'The human brain works too slowly, Jerry, even when it works straight. . . . It works too slowly.'

CRAIG RICE

His Heart Could Break

> *'As I passed by the ol' state's prison,*
> *Ridin' on a stream-line' train——'*

John J. Malone shuddered. He wished he could get the insidious melody out of his mind—or, remember the rest of the words. It had been annoying him since three o'clock that morning, when he'd heard it sung by the janitor of Joe the Angel's City Hall Bar.

It seemed like a bad omen, and it made him uncomfortable. Or maybe it was the cheap gin he'd switched to between two and four a.m. that was making him uncomfortable. Whichever it was, he felt terrible.

'I bet your client's happy today,' the guard said cordially, leading the way towards the death house.

'He ought to be,' Malone growled. He reminded himself that he too ought to be happy. He wasn't. Maybe it was being in a prison that depressed him. John J. Malone, criminal lawyer, didn't like prisons. He devoted his life to keeping his clients out of them.

> *Then the warden told me gently——*

That song again! How did the next line go?

'Well,' the guard said, 'they say you've never lost a client yet.' It wouldn't do any harm, he thought, to get on the good side of a smart guy like John J. Malone.

'Not yet,' Malone said. He'd had a close call with this one, though.

'You sure did a wonderful job, turning up the evidence to get a new trial,' the guard rattled on. Maybe Malone could get him a better appointment, with his political drag. 'Your client sure felt swell when he heard about it last night, he sure did.'

'That's good,' Malone said noncommittally. It hadn't been evidence that had turned the trick, though. Just a little matter of knowing some interesting facts about the judge's private life. The evidence would have to be manufactured before the trial, but that was the least of his worries. By that time, he might even find out the truth of what had happened. He hummed softly under his breath. Ah, there were the next lines!

> *Then the warden told me gently,*
> *He seemed too young, too young to die,*
> *We cut the rope and let him down——*

John J. Malone tried to remember the rhyme for 'die'. By, cry, lie, my and sigh. Then he let loose a few loud and indignant remarks about whoever had written that song, realized that he was entering the death house, and stopped, embarrassed. That particular cell block always inspired him with the same behavior he would have shown at a high-class funeral. He took off his hat and walked softly.

And at that moment hell broke loose. Two prisoners in the block began yelling like banshees. The alarms began to sound loudly, causing the outside siren to chime in with its hideous wail. Guards were running through the corridor, and John J. Malone instinctively ran with them toward the center of disturbance, the fourth cell on the left.

Before the little lawyer got there, one of the guards had the door open. Another guard cut quickly through the bright new rope from which the prisoner was dangling, and eased the limp body down to the floor.

The racket outside was almost deafening now, but John J. Malone scarcely heard it. The guard turned the body over, and Malone recognized the very young and rather stupid face of Paul Palmer.

'He's hung himself,' one of the guards said.

'With me for a lawyer?' Malone said angrily. 'Hung himself,——'
He started to say 'hell', then remembered he was in the presence of death.

'Hey,' the other guard said excitedly. 'He's alive. His neck's broke, but he's breathing a little.'

Malone shoved the guard aside and knelt down beside the dying man. Paul Palmer's blue eyes opened slowly, with an expression of terrible bewilderment. His lips parted.

'It wouldn't break,' Paul Palmer whispered. He seemed to recognize Malone, and stared at him, with a look of frightful urgency. '*It wouldn't break,*' he whispered to Malone. Then he died.

'You're damned right I'm going to sit in on the investigation,' Malone said angrily. He gave Warden Garrity's wastebasket a vicious kick. 'The inefficient way you run your prison has done me out of a client.' Out of a fat fee, too, he reminded himself miserably. He hadn't been paid yet, and now there would be a long tussle with the lawyer handling Paul Palmer's estate, who hadn't wanted him engaged for the defense in the first place. Malone felt in his pocket, found three crumpled bills and a small handful of change. He wished now that he hadn't got into that poker game last week.

The warden's dreary office was crowded. Malone looked around, recognized an assistant warden, the prison doctor—a handsome grey-haired man named Dickson—the guards from the death house, and the guard who had been ushering him in—Bowers was his name, Malone remembered, a tall, flat-faced, gangling man.

'Imagine him hanging himself,' Bowers was saying incredulously. 'Just after he found out he was gonna get a new trial.'

Malone had been wondering the same thing. 'Maybe he didn't get my wire,' he suggested coldly.

'I gave it to him myself,' Bowers stated positively. 'Just last night. Never saw a man so happy in my life.'

Dr Dickson cleared his throat. Everyone turned to look at him.

'Poor Palmer was mentally unstable,' the doctor said sadly. 'You may recall I recommended, several days ago, that he be moved to the prison hospital. When I visited him last night he appeared hilariously—hysterically—happy. This morning, however, he was distinctly depressed.'

'You mean the guy was nuts?' Warden Garrity asked hopefully.

'He was nothing of the sort,' Malone said indignantly. Just let a hint get around that Paul Palmer had been of unsound mind, and he'd never collect that five thousand dollar fee from the estate. 'He was saner than anyone in this room, with the possible exception of myself.'

Dr Dickson shrugged his shoulders. 'I didn't suggest that he was insane. I only meant he was subject to moods.'

Malone wheeled to face the doctor. 'Say. Were you in the habit of visiting Palmer in his cell a couple of times a day?'

'I was,' the doctor said, nodding. 'He was suffering from a serious nervous condition. It was necessary to administer sedatives from time to time.'

Malone snorted. 'You mean he was suffering from the effect of being sober for the first time since he was sixteen.'

'Put it any way you like,' Dr Dickson said pleasantly. 'You remember, too, that I had a certain personal interest.'

'That's right,' Malone said slowly. 'He was going to marry your niece.'

'No one was happier than I to hear about the new trial,' the doctor said. He caught Malone's eye and added, 'No, I wasn't fond enough of him to smuggle in a rope. Especially when he'd just been granted a chance to clear himself.'

'Look here,' Warden Garrity said irritably. 'I can't sit around listening to all this stuff. I've got to report the result of an investigation. Where the hell did he get that rope?'

There was a little silence, and then one of the guards said, 'Maybe from the guy who was let in to see him last night.'

'What guy?' the warden snapped.

'Why——' The guard paused, confused. 'He had an order from you, admitting him. His name was La Cerra.'

Malone felt a sudden tingling along his spine. Georgie La Cerra was one of Max Hook's boys. What possible connection could there be between Paul Palmer, socialite, and the big gambling boss?

Warden Garrity had recognized the name too. 'Oh, yes,' he said quickly. 'That must have been it. But I doubt if we could prove it.' He paused just an instant, and looked fixedly at Malone, as though daring him to speak. 'The report will read that Paul Palmer obtained a rope, by means which have not yet been ascertained, and committed suicide while of unsound mind.'

Malone opened his mouth and shut it again. He knew when he was licked. Temporarily licked, anyway. 'For the love of Mike,' he said, 'leave out the unsound mind.'

'I'm afraid that's impossible,' the warden said coldly.

Malone had kept his temper as long as he could. 'All right,' he said, 'but I'll start an investigation that'll be a pip.' He snorted. 'Letting a gangster smuggle a rope in to a guy in the death house!' He glared at Dr Dickson. 'And you, foxy, with two escapes from the prison hospital in six months.' He kicked the wastebasket again, this time sending it halfway across the room. 'I'll show you from investigations! And I'm just the guy who can do it, too.'

Dr Dickson said quickly, 'We'll substitute "temporarily depressed" for the "unsound mind".'

But Malone was mad, now. He made one last, loud comment regarding the warden's personal life and probably immoral origin, and slammed the door so hard when he went out that the steel engraving of Chester A. Arthur over the warden's desk shattered to the floor.

'Mr Malone,' Bowers said in a low voice as they went down the hall, 'I searched that cell, after they took the body out. Whoever smuggled in that rope smuggled in a letter, too. I found it hid in his mattress, and it wasn't there yesterday because the mattress was changed.' He paused, and added 'And the rope couldn't of been there last night either, because there was no place he could of hid it.'

Malone glanced at the envelope the guard held out to him—pale grey expensive stationery, with 'Paul Palmer' written across the front of it in delicate, curving handwriting.

'I haven't any money with me,' the lawyer said.

Bowers shook his head. 'I don't want no dough. But there's gonna be an assistant warden's job open in about three weeks.'

'You'll get it,' Malone said. He took the envelope and stuffed it in an inside pocket. Then he paused, frowned, and finally added, 'And keep your eyes open and your mouth shut. Because there's going to be an awful stink when I prove Paul Palmer was murdered.'

The pretty, black-haired girl in Malone's anteroom looked up as he opened the door. 'Oh, Mr Malone,' she said quickly. 'I read about it in the paper. I'm so sorry.'

'Never mind, Maggie,' the lawyer said. 'No use crying over spilled clients.' He went into his private office and shut the door.

Fate was treating him very shabbily, evidently from some obscure motive of personal spite. He'd been counting heavily on that five thousand buck fee.

He took a bottle of rye out of the filing cabinet marked 'Personal', poured himself a drink, noted that there was only one more left in the bottle, and stretched out on the worn red leather davenport to think things over.

Paul Palmer had been an amiable, stupid young drunk of good family, whose inherited wealth had been held in trust for him by an uncle considered to be the stingiest man in Chicago. The money was to be turned over to him on his thirtieth birthday—some five years off—or on the death of the uncle, Carter Brown. Silly arrangement, Malone reflected, but rich men's lawyers were always doing silly things.

Uncle Carter had cramped the young man's style considerably, but he'd managed pretty well. Then he'd met Madelaine Starr.

Malone lit a cigar and stared dreamily through the smoke. The Starrs were definitely social, but without money. A good keen eye for graft, too. Madelaine's uncle was probably making a very good thing out of that political appointment as prison doctor.

Malone sighed, wished he weren't a lawyer, and thought about Madelaine Starr. An orphan, with a tiny income which she augmented by modelling in an exclusive dress shop—a fashionable and acceptable way of making a living. She had expensive tastes. (The little lawyer could spot expensive tastes in girls a mile away.)

She'd had to be damned poor to want to marry Palmer, Malone reflected, and damned beautiful to get him. Well, she was both.

But there had been another girl, one who had to be paid off. Lillian Claire by name, and a very lovely hunk of girl, too. Lovely, and smart enough to demand a sizable piece of money for letting the Starr-Palmer nuptials go through without a scandalous fuss.

Malone shook his head sadly. It had looked bad at the trial. Paul Palmer had taken his bride-to-be night-clubbing, delivering her back to her kitchenette apartment just before twelve. He'd been a shade high, then, and by the time he'd stopped off at three or four bars, he was several shades higher. Then he'd paid a visit to Lillian Claire, who claimed later at the trial that he'd attempted—unsuccessfully—to talk her out of the large piece of cash money, and had drunk up all the whiskey in the house. She'd put him in a cab and sent him home.

No one knew just when Paul Palmer had arrived at the big, gloomy apartment he shared with Carter Brown. The manservant had the night off. It was the manservant who discovered, next morning, that Uncle Carter had been shot neatly through the forehead with Paul Palmer's gun, and that Paul Palmer had climbed into his own bed, fully dressed, and was snoring drunk.

Everything had been against him, Malone reflected sadly. Not only had the jury been composed of hard-working, poverty-stricken men who liked nothing better than to convict a rich young wastrel of murder, but worse still, they'd all been too honest to be bribed. The trial had been his most notable failure. And now, this.

But Paul Palmer would never have hanged himself. Malone was sure of it. He'd never lost hope. And now, especially, when a new trial had been granted, he'd have wanted to live.

It had been murder. But how had it been done?

Malone sat up, stretched, reached in his pocket for the pale grey envelope Bowers had given him, and read the note through again.

My dearest Paul:
   I'm getting this note to you this way because I'm in terrible trouble and danger. I need you—no one else can help me. I know there's to be a new trial, but even another week may be too late. Isn't there *any* way?

                                                              Your own

                                                                              M.

'M', Malone decided, would be Madelaine Starr. She'd use that kind of pale grey paper, too.

He looked at the note and frowned. If Madelaine Starr had smuggled that note to her lover, would she have smuggled in a rope by the same messenger? Or had someone else brought in the rope?

There were three people he wanted to see. Madelaine Starr was one. Lillian Claire was the second. And Max Hook was the third.

He went out into the anteroom, stopped halfway across it and said aloud, 'But it's a physical impossibility. If someone smuggled that rope into Paul Palmer's cell and then Palmer hanged himself, it isn't murder. But it must have been murder.' He stared at Maggie without seeing her. 'Damn it, though, no one could have got into Paul Palmer's cell and hanged him.'

Maggie looked at him sympathetically, familiar from long experience with her employer's processes of thought. 'Keep on thinking and it'll come to you.'

'Maggie, have you got any money?'

'I have ten dollars, but you can't borrow it. Besides, you haven't paid my last week's salary yet.'

The little lawyer muttered something about ungrateful and heartless wenches, and flung himself out of the office.

Something had to be done about ready cash. He ran his mind over a list of prospective lenders. The only possibility was Max Hook. No, the last time he'd borrowed money from the Hook, he'd got into no end of trouble. Besides, he was going to ask another kind of favor from the gambling boss.

Malone went down Washington Street, turned the corner, went into Joe the Angel's City Hall Bar, and cornered its proprietor at the far end of the room.

'Cash a hundred dollar check for me, and hold it until a week from'—Malone made a rapid mental calculation—'Thursday?'

'Sure,' Joe the Angel said. 'Happy to do you a favor.' He got out ten ten-dollar bills while Malone wrote the check. 'Want I should take your bar bill out of this?'

Malone shook his head. 'I'll pay next week. And add a double rye to it.'

As he set down the empty glass, he heard the colored janitor's voice coming faintly from the back room.

> *They hanged him for the thing you done,*
> *You knew it was a sin,*
> *You didn't know his heart could break——*

The voice stopped suddenly. For a moment Malone considered calling for the singer and asking to hear the whole thing, all the way through. No, there wasn't time for it now. Later, perhaps. He went out on the street, humming the tune.

What was it Paul Palmer had whispered in that last moment?

'*It wouldn't break!*' Malone scowled. He had a curious feeling that there was some connection between those words and the words of that damned song. Or was it his Irish imagination, tripping him up again? '*You didn't know his heart could break.*' But it was Paul Palmer's neck that had been broken.

Malone hailed a taxi and told the driver to take him to the swank Lake Shore Drive apartment-hotel where Max Hook lived.

The gambling boss was big in two ways. He took in a cut from every crooked gambling device in Cook County, and most of the honest ones. And he was a mountain of flesh, over six feet tall and three times too fat for his height. His pink head was completely bald and he had the expression of a pleased cherub.

His living room was a masterpiece of the gilt-and-brocade school of interior decoration, marred only by a huge, battle-scarred roll-top desk in one corner. Max Hook swung around from the desk to smile cordially at the lawyer.

'How delightful to see you! What will you have to drink?'

'Rye,' Malone said, 'and it's nice to see you too. Only this isn't exactly a social call.'

He knew better, though, than to get down to business before the drinks had arrived. (Max Hook stuck to pink champagne.) That wasn't the way Max Hook liked to do things. But when the rye was down, and the gambling boss had lighted a slender, tinted (and, Malone suspected, perfumed) cigarette in a rose quartz holder, he plunged right in.

'I suppose you read in the papers about what happened to my client, Palmer,' he said.

'I never read the papers,' Max Hook told him, 'but one of my boys informed me. Tragic, wasn't it.'

'Tragic is no name for it,' Malone said bitterly. 'He hadn't paid me a dime.'

Max Hook's eyebrows lifted. 'So?' Automatically he reached for the green metal box in the left-hand drawer. 'How much do you need?'

'No, no,' Malone said hastily, 'that isn't it. I just want to know if one of your boys—Little Georgie La Cerra—smuggled the rope in to him. That's all.'

Max Hook looked surprised, and a little hurt. 'My dear Malone,' he said at last, 'why do you imagine he'd do such a thing?'

'For money,' Malone said promptly, 'if he did do it. I don't care, I just want to know.'

'You can take my word for it,' Max Hook said, 'he did nothing of the kind. He did deliver a note from a certain young lady to Mr Palmer, at my request—a bit of nuisance, too, getting hold of that admittance order signed by the warden. I assure you, though, there was no rope. I give you my word, and you know I'm an honest man.'

'Well, I was just asking,' Malone said. One thing about the big gangster, he always told the truth. If he said Little Georgie La Cerra hadn't smuggled in that rope, then Little Georgie hadn't. Nor was there any chance that Little Georgie had engaged in private enterprises on the side. As Max Hook often remarked, he liked to keep a careful watch on his boys. 'One thing more, though,' the lawyer said, 'if you don't mind. Why did the young lady come to you to get her note delivered?'

Max Hook shrugged his enormous shoulders. 'We have a certain—business connection. To be exact, she owes me a large sum of money. Like most extremely mercenary people she loves gambling, but she is not particularly lucky. When she told me that the only chance for that money to be paid was for the note to be delivered, naturally I obliged.'

'Naturally,' Malone agreed. 'You didn't happen to know what was in the note, did you?'

Max Hook was shocked. 'My dear Malone! You don't think I read other people's personal mail!'

No, Malone reflected, Max Hook probably didn't. And not having read the note, the big gambler probably wouldn't know what kind of 'terrible trouble and danger' Madelaine Starr was in. He decided to ask, though, just to be on the safe side.

'Trouble?' Max Hook repeated after him. 'No, outside of having her fiancé condemned to death, I don't know of any trouble she's in.'

Malone shrugged his shoulders at the reproof, rose and walked to the door. Then he paused, suddenly. 'Listen, Max. Do you know the words to a tune that goes like this?' He hummed a bit of it.

Max Hook frowned, then nodded. 'Mmm—I know the tune. An entertainer at one of my places used to sing it.' He thought hard, and finally came up with a few lines.

He was leaning against the prison bars,
Dressed up in his new prison clothes——

'Sorry,' Max Hook said at last, 'that's all I remember. I guess those two lines stuck in my head because they reminded me of the first time I was in jail.'

Outside in the taxi, Malone sang the two lines over a couple of times. If he kept on, eventually he'd have the whole song. But Paul Palmer hadn't been leaning against the prison bars. He'd been hanging from the water pipe.

Damn, and double damn that song!

It was well past eight o'clock, and he'd had no dinner, but he didn't feel hungry. He had a grim suspicion that he wouldn't feel hungry until he'd settled this business. When the cab paused for the next red light, he flipped a coin to decide whether he'd call first on Madelaine Starr or Lillian Claire, and Madelaine won.

He stepped out of the cab in front of the small apartment building on Walton Place, paid the driver, and started across the sidewalk just as a tall, white-haired man emerged from the door. Malone recognized Orlo Featherstone, the lawyer handling Paul Palmer's estate, considered ducking out of sight, realized there wasn't time, and finally managed to look as pleased as he was surprised.

'I was just going to offer Miss Starr my condolences,' he said.

'I'd leave her undisturbed, if I were you,' Orlo Featherstone said coldly. He had only one conception of what a lawyer should be, and Malone wasn't anything like it. 'I only called myself because I am, so to speak and in a sense, a second father to her.'

If anyone else had said that, Malone thought, it would have called for an answer. From Orlo Featherstone, it sounded natural. He nodded sympathetically and said, 'Then I won't bother her.' He tossed away a ragged cigar and said 'Tragic affair, wasn't it.'

Orlo Featherstone unbent at least half a degree. 'Distinctly so. Personally, I cannot imagine Paul Palmer doing such a thing. When I visited him yesterday, he seemed quite cheerful and full of hope.'

'You—visited him yesterday?' Malone asked casually. He drew a cigar from his pocket and began unwrapping it with exquisite care.

'Yes,' Featherstone said, 'about the will. He had to sign it, you know. Fortunate for her,' he indicated Madelaine Starr with a gesture toward the building, 'that he did so. He left her everything, of course.'

'Of course,' Malone said. He lighted his cigar on the second try. 'You don't think Paul Palmer could have been murdered, do you?'

'Murdered!' Orlo Featherstone repeated, as though it was an obscene word, 'Absurd! No Palmer has ever been murdered.'

Malone watched him climb into a shiny 1928 Rolls Royce, then started walking briskly toward State Street. The big limousine passed him just as he reached the corner, it turned north on State Street and stopped. Malone paused by the newsstand long enough to see Mr Orlo Featherstone get out and cross the sidewalk to the corner drug store. After a moment's thought he followed and paused at the cigar counter, from where he could see clearly into the adjacent telephone booth.

Orlo Featherstone, in the booth, consulted a little notebook. Then he took down the receiver, dropped a nickel in the slot, and began dialling. Malone watched carefully. D-E-L—9-6-0——It was Lillian Claire's number.

The little lawyer cursed all sound-proof phone booths, and headed for a bar on the opposite corner. He felt definitely unnerved.

After a double rye, and halfway through a second one, he came to the heartening conclusion that when he visited Lillian Claire, later in the evening, he'd be able to coax from her the reason why Orlo Featherstone, of all people, had telephoned her, just after leaving the late Paul Palmer's fiancée. A third rye braced him for his call on the fiancée herself.

Riding up in the self-service elevator to her apartment, another heartening thought came to him. If Madelaine Starr was going to inherit all the Palmer dough—then it might not be such a trick to collect his five thousand bucks. He might even be able to collect it by a week from Thursday.

And he reminded himself, as she opened the door, this was going to be one time when he wouldn't be a sucker for a pretty face.

Madelaine Starr's apartment was tiny, but tasteful. Almost too tasteful, Malone thought. Everything in it was cheap, but perfectly correct and in exactly the right place, even to the Van Gogh print over the midget fireplace. Madelaine Starr was in exactly the right taste, too.

She was a tall girl, with a figure that still made Malone blink, in spite of the times he'd admired it in the courtroom. Her bronze-brown hair was smooth and well-brushed, her pale face was calm and composed. Serene, polished, suave. Malone had a private idea that if he made a pass at her, she wouldn't scream. She was wearing black rayon house-pajamas. He wondered if they were her idea of mourning.

Malone got the necessary condolences and trite remarks out of the way fast, and then said, 'What kind of terrible trouble and danger are you in, Miss Starr?'

That startled her. She wasn't able to come up with anything more original than 'What do you mean?'

'I mean what you wrote in your note to Paul Palmer,' the lawyer said.

She looked at the floor and said, 'I hoped it had been destroyed.'

'It will be,' Malone said gallantly, 'if you say so.'

'Oh,' she said. 'Do you have it with you?'

'No,' Malone lied. 'It's in my office safe. But I'll go back there and burn it.' He didn't add when.

'It really didn't have anything to do with his death, you know,' she said.

Malone said, 'Of course not. You didn't send him the rope too, did you?'

She stared at him. 'How awful of you.'

'I'm sorry,' Malone said contritely.

She relaxed. 'I'm sorry too. I didn't mean to snap at you. I'm a little unnerved, naturally.' She paused. 'May I offer you a drink?'

'You may,' Malone said, 'and I'll take it.'

He watched her while she mixed a lot of scotch and a little soda in two glasses, wondering how soon after her fiancé's death he could safely ask her for a date. Maybe she wouldn't say Yes to a broken-down criminal lawyer, though. He took the drink, downed half of it, and said to himself indignantly, 'Who's broken-down?'

'Oh, Mr Malone,' she breathed, 'you don't believe my note had anything to do with it?'

'Of course not,' Malone said. 'That note would have made him want to live, and get out of jail.' He considered bringing up the matter of his five thousand dollar fee, and then decided this was not the time. 'Nice that you'll be able to pay back what you owe Max Hook. He's a bad man to owe money to.'

She looked at him sharply and said nothing. Malone finished his drink, and walked to the door.

'One thing, though,' he said, hand on the knob. 'This—terrible trouble and danger you're in. You'd better tell me. Because I might be able to help, you know.'

'Oh, no,' she said. She was standing very close to him, and her perfume began to mingle dangerously with the rye and scotch in his brain. 'I'm afraid not.' He had a definite impression that she was thinking fast. 'No one can help, now.' She looked away, delicately. 'You know—a girl—alone in the world——'

Malone felt his cheeks reddening. He opened the door and said, 'Oh.' Just plain Oh.

'Just a minute,' she said quickly. 'Why did you ask all these questions?'

'Because,' Malone said, just as quickly, 'I thought the answers might be useful—in case Paul Palmer was murdered.'

That, he told himself, riding down the self-service elevator, would give her something to think about.

He hailed a cab and gave the address of the apartment building where Lillian Claire lived, on Goethe Street. In the lobby of the building he paused long enough to call a certain well-known politician at his home and make sure that he was there. It would be just as well not to run into that particular politician at Lillian Claire's apartment, since he was paying for it.

It was a nice apartment, too, Malone decided, as the slim mulatto maid ushered him in. Big, soft modernistic divans and chairs, panelled mirrors, and a built-in bar. Not half as nice, though, as Lillian Claire herself.

She was a cuddly little thing, small, and a bit on the plump side, with curly blonde hair and a deceptively simple stare. She said, 'Oh, Mr Malone, I've always wanted a chance to get acquainted with you.' Malone had a pleasant feeling that if he tickled her, just a little, she'd giggle.

She mixed him a drink, lighted his cigar, sat close to him on the biggest and most luxurious divan, and said, 'Tell me, how on earth did Paul Palmer get that rope?'

'I don't know,' Malone said. 'Did you send it to him, baked in a cake?'

She looked at him reprovingly. 'You don't think I wanted him to kill himself and let that awful woman inherit all that money?'

Malone said, 'She isn't so awful. But this is tough on you, though. Now you'll never be able to sue him.'

'I never intended to,' she said. 'I didn't want to be paid off. I just thought it might scare her away from him.'

Malone put down his glass, she hopped up and refilled it. 'Were you in love with him?' he said.

'Don't be silly.' She curled up beside him again. 'I liked him. He was much too nice to have someone like that marry him for his money.'

Malone nodded slowly. The room was beginning to swim—not unpleasantly—before his eyes. Maybe he should have eaten dinner after all.

'Just the same,' he said, 'you didn't think that idea up all by yourself. Somebody put you up to asking for money.'

She pulled away from him a little—not too much. 'That's perfect nonsense,' she said unconvincingly.

'All right,' Malone said agreeably. 'Tell me just one thing——'

'I'll tell you this one thing,' she said. 'Paul never murdered his uncle. I don't know who did, but it wasn't Paul. Because I took him home that night. He came to see me, yes. But I didn't put him in a cab and send him home. I took him home, and got him to his own room. Nobody saw me. It was late—almost daylight.' She paused and lit a cigarette. 'I peeked into his uncle's room to make sure I hadn't been seen, and his uncle was dead. I never told anybody because I didn't want to get mixed up in it worse than I was already.'

Malone sat bolt upright. 'Fine thing,' he said, indignantly and a bit thickly. 'You could have alibied him and you let him be convicted.'

'Why bother?' she said serenely. 'I knew he had you for a lawyer. Why would he need an alibi?'

Malone shoved her back against the cushions of the davenport and glared at her. 'A'right,' he said. 'But that wasn't the thing I was gonna ask. Why did old man Featherstone call you up tonight?'

Her shoulders stiffened under his hands. 'He just asked me for a dinner date,' she said.

'You're a liar,' Malone said, not unpleasantly. He ran an experimental finger along her ribs. She did giggle. Then he kissed her.

All this time spent, Malone told himself reprovingly, and you haven't learned one thing worth the effort. Paul Palmer hadn't killed his uncle. But he'd been sure of that all along, and anyway it wouldn't do any good now. Madelaine Starr needed money, and now she was going to inherit a lot of it. Orlo Featherstone was on friendly terms with Lillian Claire.

The little lawyer leaned his elbows on the table and rested his head on his hands. At three o'clock in the morning, Joe the Angel's was a desolate and almost deserted place. He knew now, definitely, that he should have eaten dinner. Nothing, he decided, would cure the way he felt except a quick drink, a long sleep, or sudden death.

He would probably never learn who had killed Paul Palmer's uncle, or why. He would probably never learn what had happened to Paul Palmer. After all, the man had hanged himself. No one else could have got into that cell. It wasn't murder to give a man enough rope to hang himself with.

No, he would probably never learn what had happened to Paul Palmer, and he probably would never collect that five thousand dollar fee. But there was one thing that he could do. He'd learn the words of that song.

He called for a drink, the janitor, and the janitor's guitar. Then he sat back and listened.

> *As I passed by the ol' State's prison,*
> *Ridin' on a stream-lin' train——*

It was a long, rambling ballad, requiring two drinks for the janitor and two more for Malone. The lawyer listened, remembering a line here and there.

> *When they hanged him in the mornin',*
>   *His last words were for you,*
> *Then the sheriff took his shiny knife*
>   *An' cut that ol' rope through.*

A sad story, Malone reflected, finishing the second drink. Personally, he'd have preferred 'My Wild Irish Rose' right now. But he yelled to Joe for another drink, and went on listening.

> *They hanged him for the thing you done,*
>   *You knew it was a sin,*
> *How well you knew his heart could break,*
>   *Lady, why did you turn him in——*

The little lawyer jumped to his feet. That was the line he'd been trying to remember! And what had Paul Palmer whispered? *'It wouldn't break.'*

Malone knew, now.

He dived behind the bar, opened the cash drawer, and scooped out a handful of telephone slugs.

'You're drunk,' Joe the Angel said indignantly.

'That may be,' Malone said happily, 'and it's a good idea too. But I know what I'm doing.'

He got one of the slugs into the phone on the third try, dialled Orlo Featherstone's number, and waited till the elderly lawyer got out of bed and answered the phone.

It took ten minutes, and several more phone slugs to convince Featherstone that it was necessary to get Madelaine Starr out of bed and make the three-hour drive to the state's prison, right now. It took another ten minutes to wake up Lillian Claire and induce her to join the party. Then he placed a long-distance call to the sheriff of Statesville County and invited him to drop in at the prison and pick up a murderer.

Malone strode to the door. As he reached it, Joe the Angel hailed him.

'I forgot,' he said, 'I got sumpin' for you.' Joe the Angel rummaged back of the cash register and brought out a long envelope. 'That cute secretary of yours was looking for you all over town to give you this. Finally she left it with me. She knew you'd get here sooner or later.'

Craig Rice

Malone said 'Thanks,' took the envelope, glanced at it, and winced. 'First National Bank.' Registered mail. He knew he was overdrawn, but——

Oh, well, maybe there was still a chance to get that five thousand bucks.

The drive to Statesville wasn't so bad, in spite of the fact that Orlo Featherstone snored most of the way. Lillian snuggled up against Malone's left shoulder like a kitten, and with his right hand he held Madelaine Starr's hand under the auto robe. But the arrival, a bit before seven a.m., was depressing. The prison looked its worst in the early morning, under a light fog.

Besides, the little lawyer wasn't happy over what he had to do.

Warden Garrity's office was even more depressing. There was the warden, eyeing Malone coldly and belligerently, and Madelaine Starr and her uncle, Dr Dickson, looking a bit annoyed. Orlo Featherstone was frankly skeptical. The sheriff of Statesville County was sleepy and bored, Lillian Claire was sleepy and suspicious. Even the guard, Bowers, looked bewildered.

And all these people, Malone realized, were waiting for him to pull a rabbit out of his whiskers.

He pulled it out fast. 'Paul Palmer was murdered,' he said flatly.

Warden Garrity looked faintly amused. 'A bunch of pixies crawled in his cell and tied the rope around his neck?'

'No,' Malone said, lighting a cigar. 'This murderer made one try— murder by frame-up. He killed Paul Palmer's uncle for two reasons, one of them being to send Paul Palmer to the chair. It nearly worked. Then I got him a new trial. So another method had to be tried, fast, and that one did work.'

'You're insane,' Orlo Featherstone said. 'Palmer hanged himself.'

'I'm not insane,' Malone said indignantly, 'I'm drunk. There's a distinction. And Paul Palmer hanged himself because he thought he wouldn't die, and could escape from prison.' He looked at Bowers and said, 'Watch all these people, someone may make a move.'

Lillian Claire said, 'I don't get it.'

'You will,' Malone promised. He kept a watchful eye on Bowers and began talking fast. 'The whole thing was arranged by someone who was mercenary and owed money. Someone who knew Paul

110

Palmer would be too drunk to know what had happened the night his uncle was killed, and who was close enough to him to have a key to the apartment. That person went in and killed the uncle with Paul Palmer's gun. And, as that person had planned, Paul Palmer was tried and convicted and would have been electrocuted, if he hadn't had a damn smart lawyer.'

He flung his cigar into the cuspidor and went on, 'Then Paul Palmer was granted a new trial. So the mercenary person who wanted Paul Palmer's death convinced him that he had to break out of prison, and another person showed him how the escape could be arranged—by pretending to hang himself, and being moved to the prison hospital—*watch her, Bowers!*'

Madelaine Starr had flung herself at Dr Dickson. 'Damn you,' she screamed, her face white. 'I knew you'd break down and talk. But you'll never talk again——'

There were three shots. One from the little gun Madelaine had carried in her pocket, and two from Bowers' service revolver.

Then the room was quite still.

Malone walked slowly across the room, looked down at the two bodies, and shook his head sadly. 'Maybe it's just as well,' he said. 'They'd probably have hired another defense lawyer anyway.'

'This is all very fine,' the Statesville County sheriff said. 'But I still don't see how you figured it. Have another beer?'

'Thanks,' Malone said. 'It was easy. A song tipped me off. Know this?' He hummed a few measures.

'Oh, sure,' the sheriff said. 'The name of it is, "The Statesville Prison".' He sang the first four verses.

'Well, I'll be double-damned,' Malone said. The bartender put the two glasses of beer on the table. 'Bring me a double gin for a chaser,' the lawyer told him.

'Me too,' the sheriff said. 'What does the song have to do with it, Malone?'

Malone said, 'It was the crank on the adding machine, pal. Know what I mean? You put down a lot of stuff to add up and nothing happens, and then somebody turns the crank and it all adds up to what you want to know. See how simple it is?'

'I don't,' the sheriff said, 'but go on.'

'I had all the facts,' Malone said, 'I knew everything I needed to know, but I couldn't add it up. I needed one thing, that one thing.' He spoke almost reverently, downing his gin. 'Paul Palmer said "*It wouldn't break*"—just before he died. And he looked terribly surprised. For a long time, I didn't know what he meant. Then I heard that song again, and I did know.' He sang a few lines. '*The sheriff took his shiny knife, and cut that ol' rope through.*' Then he finished his beer, and sang on '*They hanged him for the thing you done, you knew it was a sin. You didn't know his heart could break, Lady why did you turn him in.*' He ended on a blue note.

'Very pretty,' the sheriff said. 'Only I heard it, "*You knew that his poor heart could break*".'

'Same thing,' Malone said, waving a hand. 'Only, that song was what turned the crank on the adding machine. When I heard it again, I knew what Palmer meant by "*it wouldn't break*".'

'His heart?' the sheriff said helpfully.

'No,' Malone said, 'the rope.'

He waved at the bartender and said 'Two more of the same.' Then to the sheriff, 'He expected the rope to break. He thought it would be artfully frayed so that he would drop to the floor unharmed. Then he could have been moved to the prison hospital—from which there had been two escapes in the past six months. He had to escape, you see, because his sweetheart had written him that she was in terrible trouble and danger—the same sweetheart whose evidence had helped convict him at the trial.

'Madelaine Starr wanted his money,' Malone went on, 'but she didn't want Paul. So her murder of his uncle served two purposes. It released Paul's money, and it framed him. Using poor old innocent Orlo Featherstone, she planted in Lillian Claire's head the idea of holding up Paul for money, so Paul would be faced with a need for ready cash. Everything worked fine, until I gummixed up the whole works by getting my client a new trial.'

'Your client shouldn't of had such a smart lawyer,' the sheriff said, over his beer glass.

Malone tossed aside the compliment with a shrug of his cigar. 'Maybe he should of had a better one. Anyway, she and her uncle,

Dr Dickson, fixed it all up. She sent that note to Paul, so he'd think he had to break out of the clink. Then her uncle, Dickson, told Paul he'd arrange the escape, with the rope trick. To the world, it would have looked as though Paul Palmer had committed suicide in a fit of depression. Only he did have a good lawyer, and he lived long enough to say *"It wouldn't break".'*

Malone looked into his empty glass and lapsed into a melancholy silence.

The phone rang—someone hijacked a truck over on the Springfield Road—and the sheriff was called away. Left by himself, Malone cried a little into his beer. Lillian Claire had gone back to Chicago with Orlo Featherstone, who really had called her up for a date, and no other reason.

Malone reminded himself he hadn't had any sleep, his head was splitting, and what was left of Joe the Angel's hundred dollars would just take him back to Chicago. And there was that letter from the bank, probably threatening a summons. He took it out of his pocket and sighed as he tore it open.

'Might as well face realities,' Malone said to the bartender. 'And bring me another double gin.'

He drank the gin, tore open the envelope, and took out a certified check for five thousand dollars, with a note from the bank to the effect that Paul Palmer had directed its payment. It was dated the day before his death.

Malone waltzed to the door, waltzed back to pay the bartender and kiss him good-bye.

'Do you feel all right?' the bartender asked anxiously.

'All right!' Malone said. 'I'm a new man!'

What was more, he'd just remembered the rest of that song. He sang it, happily, as he went up the street toward the railroad station.

> *As I passed by the ol' State's prison,*
> *Ridin' on a stream-lin' train*
> *I waved my hand, and said out loud,*
> *I'm never comin' back again,*
> *I'm never comin' back a—gain!*

8

CARTER DICKSON

The House in Goblin Wood

In Pall Mall, that hot July afternoon three years before the war, an open saloon car was drawn up to the curb just opposite the Senior Conservatives' Club.

And in the car sat two conspirators.

It was the drowsy post-lunch hour among the clubs, where only the sun remained brilliant. The Rag lay somnolent; the Athanaeum slept outright. But these two conspirators, a dark-haired young man in his early thirties and a fair-haired girl perhaps half a dozen years younger, never moved. They stared intently at the Gothic-like front of the Senior Conservatives'.

'Look here, Eve,' muttered the young man, and punched at the steering wheel. 'Do you think this is going to work?'

'I don't know,' the fair-haired girl confessed. 'He absolutely *loathes* picnics.'

'Anyway, we've probably missed him.'

'Why so?'

'He can't have taken as long over lunch as that!' her companion protested, looking at a wrist-watch. The young man was rather shocked. 'It's a quarter to four! Even if . . .'

'Bill! There! Look there!'

Their patience was rewarded by an inspiring sight.

Out of the portals of the Senior Conservatives' Club, in awful majesty, marched a large, stout, barrel-shaped gentleman in a white linen suit.

His corporation preceded him like the figurehead of a man-of-war. His shell-rimmed spectacles were pulled down on a broad nose, all being shaded by a Panama hat. At the top of the stone steps he surveyed the street with a lordly sneer.

'Sir Henry!' called the girl.

'Hey?' said Sir Henry Merrivale.

'I'm Eve Drayton. Don't you remember me? You knew my father!'

'Oh, ah,' said the great man.

'We've been waiting here a terribly long time,' Eve pleaded. 'Couldn't you see us for just five minutes?—The thing to do,' she whispered to her companion, 'is to keep him in a good humor. Just keep him in a good humor!'

As a matter of fact, H.M. was in a good humor, having just triumphed over the Home Secretary in an argument. But not even his own mother could have guessed it. Majestically, with the same lordly sneer, he began in grandeur to descend the steps of the Senior Conservatives'. He did this, in fact, until his foot encountered an unnoticed object lying some three feet from the bottom.

It was a banana skin.

'Oh, dear!' said the girl.

Now it must be stated with regret that in the old days certain urchins, of what were then called the 'lower orders', had a habit of placing such objects on the steps in the hope that some eminent statesman would take a toss on his way to Whitehall. This was a venial but deplorable practice, probably accounting for what Mr Gladstone said in 1882.

In any case, it accounted for what Sir Henry Merrivale said now.

From the pavement, where H.M. landed in a seated position, arose in H.M.'s bellowing voice such a torrent of profanity, such a flood of invective and vile obscenities, as has seldom before blasted the holy calm of Pall Mall. It brought the hall-porter hurrying down the steps, and Eve Drayton flying out of the car.

Heads were now appearing at the windows of the Athenaeum across the street.

'Is it all right?' cried the girl, with concern in her blue eyes. 'Are you hurt?'

H.M. merely looked at her. His hat had fallen off, disclosing a large bald head; and he merely sat on the pavement and looked at her.

'Anyway, H.M., get up! Please get up!'

'Yes, sir,' begged the hall-porter, 'for heaven's sake get up!'

'Get up?' bellowed H.M., in a voice audible as far as St James' Street. 'Burn it all, how *can* I get up?'

'But why not?'

'My behind's out of joint,' said H.M. simply. 'I'm hurt awful bad. I'm probably goin' to have spinal dislocation for the rest of my life.'

'But, sir, people are looking!'

H.M. explained what these people could do. He eyed Eve Drayton with a glare of indescribable malignancy over his spectacles.

'I suppose, my wench, *you're* responsible for this?'

Eve regarded him in consternation.

'You don't mean the banana skin?' she cried.

'Oh, yes, I do,' said H.M., folding his arms like a prosecuting counsel.

'But we—we only wanted to invite you to a picnic!'

H.M. closed his eyes.

'That's fine,' he said in a hollow voice. 'All the same, don't you think it'd have been a subtler kind of hint just to pour mayonnaise over my head or shove ants down the back of my neck? Oh, lord love a duck!'

'I didn't mean that! I meant . . .'

'Let me help you up, sir,' interposed the calm, reassuring voice of the dark-haired and blue-chinned young man who had been with Eve in the car.

'So you want to help too, hey? And who are *you*?'

'I'm awfully sorry!' said Eve. 'I should have introduced you! This is my fiancé. Dr William Sage.'

H.M.'s face turned purple.

'I'm glad to see,' he observed, 'you had the uncommon decency to bring along a doctor. I appreciate that, I do. And the car's there, I suppose, to assist with the examination when I take off my pants?'

The hall-porter uttered a cry of horror.

Bill Sage, either from jumpiness and nerves or from sheer inability to keep straight face, laughed loudly.

'I keep telling Eve a dozen times a day,' he said, 'that I'm not to be called "doctor". I happen to be a surgeon—'

(Here H.M. really did look alarmed.)

'—but I don't think we need operate. Nor, in my opinion,' Bill gravely addressed the hall-porter, 'will it be necessary to remove Sir Henry's trousers in front of the Senior Conservatives' Club.'

'Thank you very much, sir.'

'We had an infernal nerve to come here,' the young man confessed to H.M. 'But I honestly think, Sir Henry, you'd be more comfortable in the car. What about it? Let me give you a hand up?'

Yet even ten minutes later, when H.M. sat glowering in the back of the car and two heads were craned round towards him, peace was not restored.

'All right!' said Eve. Her pretty, rather stolid face was flushed; her mouth looked miserable. 'If you won't come to the picnic, you won't. But I did believe you might do it to oblige me.'

'Well . . . now!' muttered the great man uncomfortably.

'And I did think, too, you'd be interested in the other person who was coming with us. But Vicky's—difficult. She won't come either, if you don't.'

'Oh? And who's this other guest?'

'Vicky Adams.'

H.M.'s hand, which had been lifted for an oratorical gesture, dropped to his side.

'Vicky Adams? That's not the gal who . . .?'

'Yes!' Eve nodded. 'They say it was one of the great mysteries, twenty years ago, that the police failed to solve.'

'It was, my wench,' H.M. agreed sombrely. 'It was.'

'And now Vicky's grown up. And we thought if you of all people went along, and spoke to her nicely, she'd tell us what really happened on that night.'

H.M.'s small, sharp eyes fixed disconcertingly on Eve.

'I say, my wench. What's your interest in all this?'

'Oh, reasons.' Eve glanced quickly at Bill Sage, who was again punching moodily at the steering wheel, and checked herself. 'Anyway, what difference does it make now? If you won't go with us . . .'

H.M. assumed a martyred air.

'I never said I *wasn't* goin' with you, did I?' he demanded. (This was inaccurate, but no matter.) 'Even after you practically made a cripple of me, I never said I *wasn't* goin'?' His manner grew flurried and hasty. 'But I got to leave now,' he added apologetically. 'I got to get back to my office.'

'We'll drive you there, H.M.'

'No, no, no,' said the practical cripple, getting out of the car with surprising celerity. 'Walkin' is good for my stomach if it's not so good for my behind. I'm a forgivin' man. You pick me up at my house tomorrow morning. G'bye.'

And he lumbered off in the direction of the Haymarket.

It needed no close observer to see that H.M. was deeply abstracted. He remained so abstracted, indeed, as to be nearly murdered by a taxi at the Admiralty Arch; and he was half-way down Whitehall before a familiar voice stopped him.

'Afternoon, Sir Henry!'

Burly, urbane, buttoned up in blue serge, with his bowler hat and his boiled blue eye, stood Chief Inspector Masters.

'Bit odd,' the Chief Inspector remarked affably, 'to see you taking a constitutional on a day like this. And how are you, sir?'

'Awful,' said H.M. instantly. 'But that's not the point. Masters, you crawlin' snake! You're the very man I wanted to see.'

Few things startled the Chief Inspector. This one did.

'You,' he repeated, 'wanted to see *me*?'

'Uh-huh.'

'And what about?'

'Masters, do you remember the Victoria Adams case about twenty years ago?'

The Chief Inspector's manner suddenly changed and grew wary.

'Victoria Adams case?' he ruminated. 'No, sir, I can't say I do.'

'Son, you're lyin'! You were sergeant to old Chief Inspector Rutherford in those days, and well I remember it!'

Masters stood on his dignity.

'That's as may be, sir. But twenty years ago . . .'

'A little girl of twelve or thirteen, the child of very wealthy parents, disappeared one night out of a country cottage with all the doors and windows locked on the inside. A week later, while everybody was havin' screaming hysterics, the child reappeared again: through the locks and bolts, tucked up in her bed as usual. And to this day nobody's ever known what really happened.'

There was a silence, while Masters shut his jaws hard.

'This family, the Adamses,' persisted H.M., 'owned the cottage down Aylesbury way, on the edge of Goblin Wood, opposite the lake. Or was it?'

'Oh, ah,' growled Masters. 'It was.'

H.M. looked at him curiously.

'They used the cottage as a base for bathin' in summer, and ice-skatin' in winter. It was black winter when the child vanished, and the place was all locked up inside against drafts. They say her old man nearly went loopy when he found her there a week later, lying asleep under the lamp. But all she'd say, when they asked her where she'd been, was, "*I don't know*".'

Again there was a silence, while red buses thundered through the traffic press of Whitehall.

'You've got to admit, Masters, there was a flaming public rumpus. I say: did you ever read Barrie's *Mary Rose*?'

'No.'

'Well, it was a situation straight out of Barrie. Some people, y'see, said that Vicky Adams was a child of faërie who'd been spirited away by the pixies . . .'

Whereupon Masters exploded.

He removed his bowler hat and made remarks about pixies, in detail, which could not have been bettered by H.M. himself.

'I know, son, I know.' H.M. was soothing. Then his big voice sharpened. 'Now tell me. Was all this talk strictly true?'

'What talk?'

'Locked windows? Bolted doors? No attic-trap? No cellar? Solid walls and floor?'

'Yes, sir,' answered Masters, regaining his dignity with a powerful effort, 'I'm bound to admit it *was* true.'

'Then there wasn't any jiggery-pokery about the cottage?'

'In your eye there wasn't,' said Masters.

'How d'ye mean?'

'Listen, sir.' Masters lowered his voice. 'Before the Adamses took over that place, it was a hideout for Chuck Randall. At that time he was the swellest of the swell mob; we lagged him a couple of years later. Do you think Chuck wouldn't have rigged up some gadget for a getaway? Just so! Only . . .'

'Well? Hey?'

'We couldn't find it,' grunted Masters.

'And I'll bet that pleased old Chief Inspector Rutherford?'

'I tell you straight: he was fair up the pole. Especially as the kid herself was a pretty kid, all big eyes and dark hair. You couldn't help trusting her story.'

'Yes,' said H.M. 'That's what worries me.'

'Worries you?'

'Oh, my son!' said H.M. dismally. 'Here's Vicky Adams, the spoiled daughter of dotin' parents. She's supposed to be "odd" and "fey". She's even encouraged to be. During her adolescence, the most impressionable time of her life, she gets wrapped round with the gauze of a mystery that people talk about even yet. What's that woman like now, Masters? What's that woman like now?'

'Dear Sir Henry!' murmured Miss Vicky Adams in her softest voice.

She said this just as William Sage's car, with Bill and Eve Drayton in the front seat, and Vicky and H.M. in the back seat, turned off the main road. Behind them lay the smoky-red roofs of Aylesbury, against a brightness of late afternoon. The car turned down a side road, a damp tunnel of greenery, and into another road which was little more than a lane between hedgerows.

H.M.—though cheered by three good-sized picnic hampers from Fortnum & Mason, their wickerwork lids bulging with a feast—did not seem happy. Nobody in that car was happy, with the possible exception of Miss Adams herself.

Vicky, unlike Eve, was small and dark and vivacious. Her large light-brown eyes, with very black lashes, could be arch and coy; or they could be dreamily intense. The late Sir James Barrie might have called her a sprite. Those of more sober views would have recognized a different quality: she had an inordinate sex-appeal, which was as palpable as a physical touch to any male within yards. And despite her smallness, Vicky had a full voice like Eve's. All these qualities she used even in so simple a matter as giving traffic directions.

'First right,' she would say, leaning forward to put her hands on Bill Sage's shoulders. 'Then straight on until the next traffic light. Ah, clever boy!'

'Not at all, not at all!' Bill would disclaim, with red ears and rather an erratic style of driving.

'Oh, yes, you are!' And Vicky would twist the lobe of his ear, playfully, before sitting back again.

(Eve Drayton did not say anything. She did not even turn round. Yet the atmosphere, even of that quiet English picnic-party, had already become a trifle hysterical.)

'Dear Sir Henry!' murmured Vicky, as they turned down into the deep lane between the hedgerows. 'I do wish you wouldn't be so materialistic! I do, really. Haven't you the tiniest bit of spirituality in your nature?'

'Me?' said H.M. in astonishment. 'I got a very lofty spiritual nature. But what I want just now, my wench, is grub.—Oi!'

Bill Sage glanced round.

'By that speedometer,' H.M. pointed, 'we've now come forty-six miles and a bit. We didn't even leave town until people of decency and sanity were having their tea. Where are we *going*?'

'But didn't you know?' asked Vicky, with wide-open eyes. 'We're going to the cottage where I had such a dreadful experience when I was a child.'

'Was it such a dreadful experience, Vicky dear?' enquired Eve.

Vicky's eyes seemed far away.

'I don't remember, really. I was only a child, you see. I didn't understand. I hadn't developed the power for myself then.'

'What power?' H.M. asked sharply.

'To dematerialize,' said Vicky. 'Of course.'

In that warm sun-dusted lane, between the hawthorn hedges, the car jolted over a rut. Crockery rattled.

'Uh-huh. I see,' observed H.M. without inflection. 'And where do you go, my wench, when you dematerialize?'

'Into a strange country. Through a little door. You wouldn't understand. Oh, you *are* such Philistines!' moaned Vicky. Then, with a sudden change of mood, she leaned forward and her whole physical allurement flowed again towards Bill Sage. '*You* wouldn't like me to disappear, would you, Bill?'

(Easy! Easy!)

'Only,' said Bill, with a sort of wild gallantry, 'if you promised to reappear again straightaway.'

'Oh, I should have to do that.' Vicky sat back. She was trembling. 'The power wouldn't be strong enough. But even a poor little thing like me might be able to teach you a lesson. Look there!'

And she pointed ahead.

On their left, as the lane widened, stretched the ten-acre gloom of what is fancifully known as Goblin Wood. On their right lay a small lake, on private property and therefore deserted.

The cottage—set well back into a clearing of the wood so as to face the road, screened from it by a line of beeches—was in fact a bungalow of rough-hewn stone, with a slate roof. Across the front of it ran a wooden porch. It had a seedy air, like the long yellow-green grass of its front lawn. Bill parked the car at the side of the road, since there was no driveway.

'It's a bit lonely, ain't it?' demanded H.M. His voice boomed out against that utter stillness, under the hot sun.

'Oh, yes!' breathed Vicky. She jumped out of the car in a whirl of skirts. 'That's why *they* were able to come and take me. When I was a child.'

'They?'

'Dear Sir Henry! Do I need to explain?'

Then Vicky looked at Bill.

'I must apologize,' she said, 'for the state the house is in. I haven't been out here for months and months. There's a modern bathroom, I'm glad to say. Only paraffin lamps, of course. But then,' a dreamy smile flashed across her face, 'you won't need lamps, will you? Unless. . . .'

'You mean,' said Bill, who was taking a black case out of the car, 'unless you disappear again?'

'Yes, Bill. And promise me you won't be frightened when I do.'

The young man uttered a ringing oath which was shushed by Sir Henry Merrivale, who austerely said he disapproved of profanity. Eve Drayton was very quiet.

'But in the meantime,' Vicky said wistfully, 'let's forget it all, shall we? Let's laugh and dance and sing and pretend we're children! And surely our guest must be even more hungry by this time?'

It was in this emotional state that they sat down to their picnic.

H.M., if the truth must be told, did not fare too badly. Instead of sitting on some hummock of ground, they dragged a table and chairs to the shaded porch. All spoke in strained voices. But no word of controversy was said. It was only afterwards, when the cloth was cleared, the furniture and hampers pushed indoors, the empty bottles flung away, that danger tapped a warning.

From under the porch Vicky fished out two half-rotted deckchairs, which she set up in the long grass of the lawn. These were to be occupied by Eve and H.M., while Vicky took Bill Sage to inspect a plum tree of some remarkable quality she did not specify.

Eve sat down without comment. H.M., who was smoking a black cigar opposite her, waited some time before he spoke.

'Y' know,' he said, taking the cigar out of his mouth, 'you're behaving remarkably well.'

'Yes.' Eve laughed. 'Aren't I?'

'Are you pretty well acquainted with this Adams gal?'

'I'm her first cousin,' Eve answered simply. 'Now that her parents are dead, I'm the only relative she's got. I know *all* about her.'

From far across the lawn floated two voices saying something about wild strawberries. Eve, her fair hair and fair complexion vivid against the dark line of Goblin Wood, clenched her hands on her knees.

'You see, H.M.,' she hesitated, 'there was another reason why I invited you here. I—I don't quite know how to approach it.'

'I'm the old man,' said H.M., tapping himself impressively on the chest. 'You tell me.'

'Eve, darling!' interposed Vicky's voice, crying across the ragged lawn. 'Coo-ee! Eve!'

'Yes, dear?'

'I've just remembered,' cried Vicky, 'that I haven't shown Bill over the cottage! You don't mind if I steal him away from you for a little while?'

'No, dear! Of course not!'

It was H.M., sitting so as to face the bungalow, who saw Vicky and Bill go in. He saw Vicky's wistful smile as she closed the door after them. Eve did not even look round. The sun was declining, making fiery chinks through the thickness of Goblin Wood behind the cottage.

'I won't let her have him,' Eve suddenly cried. 'I won't! I won't! I won't!'

'Does she want him, my wench? Or, which is more to the point, does he want her?'

'He never has,' Eve said with emphasis. 'Not really. And he never will.'

H.M., motionless, puffed out cigar smoke.

'Vicky's a faker,' said Eve. 'Does that sound catty?'

'Not necessarily. I was just thinkin' the same thing myself.'

'I'm patient,' said Eve. Her blue eyes were fixed. 'I'm terribly, terribly patient. I can wait years for what I want. Bill's not making much money now, and I haven't got a bean. But Bill's got great talent under that easy-going manner of his. He *must* have the right girl to help him. If only . . .'

'If only the elfin sprite would let him alone. Hey?'

'Vicky acts like that,' said Eve, 'toward practically every man she ever meets. That's why she never married. She says it leaves her soul free to commune with other souls. This occultism—'

Then it all poured out, the family story of the Adamses. This repressed girl spoke at length, spoke as perhaps she had never spoken before. Vicky Adams, the child who wanted to attract attention, her father Uncle Fred and her mother Aunt Margaret seemed to walk in vividness as the shadows gathered.

'I was too young to know her at the time of the "disappearance", of course. But, oh, I knew her afterwards! And I thought . . .'

'Well?'

'If I could get *you* here,' said Eve, 'I thought she'd try to show off with some game. And then you'd expose her. And Bill would see what an awful faker she is. But it's hopeless! It's hopeless!'

'Looky here,' observed H.M., who was smoking his third cigar. He sat up. 'Doesn't it strike you those two are being a rummy-awful long time just in lookin' through a little bungalow?'

Eve, roused out of a dream, stared back at him. She sprang to her feet. She was not now, you could guess, thinking of any disappearance.

124

'Excuse me a moment,' she said curtly.

Eve hurried across to the cottage, went up on the porch, and opened the front door. H.M. heard her heels rap down the length of the small passage inside. She marched straight back again, closed the front door, and rejoined H.M.

'All the doors of the rooms are shut,' she announced in a high voice. 'I really don't think I ought to disturb them.'

'Easy, my wench!'

'I have absolutely no interest,' declared Eve, with the tears coming into her eyes, 'in what happens to either of them now. Shall we take the car and go back to town without them?'

H.M. threw away his cigar, got up, and seized her by the shoulders.

'I'm the old man,' he said, leering like an ogre. 'Will you listen to me?'

'No!'

'If I'm any reader of the human dial,' persisted H.M., 'that young feller's no more gone on Vicky Adams than I am. He was scared, my wench. Scared.' Doubt, indecision crossed H.M.'s face. 'I dunno what he's scared of. Burn me, I don't! But . . .'

'Hoy!' called the voice of Bill Sage.

It did not come from the direction of the cottage.

They were surrounded on three sides by Goblin Wood, now blurred with twilight. From the north side the voice bawled at them, followed by crackling in dry undergrowth. Bill, his hair and sports coat and flannels more than a little dirty, regarded them with a face of bitterness.

'Here are her blasted wild strawberries,' he announced, extending his hand. 'Three of 'em. The fruitful (excuse me) result of three quarters of an hour's hard labor. I absolutely refuse to chase 'em in the dark.'

For a moment Eve Drayton's mouth moved without speech.

'Then you weren't . . . in the cottage all this time?'

'In the cottage?' Bill glanced at it. 'I was in that cottage,' he said, 'about five minutes. Vicky had a woman's whim. She wanted some wild strawberries out of what she called the "forest".'

'Wait a minute, son!' said H.M. very sharply. 'You didn't come out that front door. Nobody did.'

'No! I went out the back door! It opens straight on the wood.'

'Yes. And what happened then?'

'Well, I went to look for these damned . . .'

'No, no! What did *she* do?'

'Vicky? She locked and bolted the back door on the inside. I remember her grinning at me through the glass panel. She—'

Bill stopped short. His eyes widened, and then narrowed, as though at the impact of an idea. All three of them turned to look at the rough-stone cottage.

'By the way,' said Bill. He cleared his throat vigorously. 'By the way, have you seen Vicky since then?'

'No.'

'This couldn't be . . .?'

'It could be, son,' said H.M. 'We'd all better go in there and have a look.'

They hesitated for a moment on the porch. A warm, moist fragrance breathed up from the ground after sunset. In half an hour it would be completely dark.

Bill Sage threw open the front door and shouted Vicky's name. That sound seemed to penetrate, reverberating, through every room. The intense heat and stuffiness of the cottage, where no window had been raised in months, blew out at them. But nobody answered.

'Get inside,' snapped H.M. 'And stop yowlin'.' The Old Maestro was nervous. 'I'm dead sure she didn't get out by the front door; but we'll just make certain there's no slippin' out now.'

Stumbling over the table and chairs they had used on the porch, he fastened the front door. They were in a narrow passage, once handsome with parquet floor and pine-paneled walls, leading to a door with a glass panel at the rear. H.M. lumbered forward to inspect this door and found it locked and bolted, as Bill had said.

Goblin Wood grew darker.

Keeping well together, they searched the cottage. It was not large, having two good-sized rooms on one side of the passage, and two small rooms on the other side, so as to make space for bathroom and kitchenette. H.M., raising fogs of dust, ransacked every inch where a person could possibly hide.

126

And all the windows were locked on the inside. And the chimney-flues were too narrow to admit anybody.

And Vicky Adams wasn't there.

'Oh, my eye!' breathed Sir Henry Merrivale.

They had gathered, by what idiotic impulse not even H.M. could have said, just outside the open door of the bathroom. A bath-tap dripped monotonously. The last light through a frosted-glass window showed three faces hung there as though disembodied.

'Bill,' said Eve in an unsteady voice, 'this is a trick. Oh, I've longed for her to be exposed! This is a trick!'

'Then where is she?'

'H.M. can tell us! Can't you, H.M.?'

'Well . . . now,' muttered the great man.

Across H.M.'s Panama hat was a large black handprint, made there when he had pressed down the hat after investigating a chimney. He glowered under it.

'Son,' he said to Bill, 'there's just one question I want you to answer in all this hokey-pokey. When you went out pickin' wild strawberries, will you swear Vicky Adams didn't go with you?'

'As God is my judge, she didn't,' returned Bill, with fervency and obvious truth. 'Besides, how the devil could she? Look at the lock and bolt on the back door!'

H.M. made two more violent black handprints on his hat.

He lumbered forward, his head down, two or three paces in the narrow passage. His foot half-skidded on something that had been lying there unnoticed, and he picked it up. It was a large, square section of thin, waterproof oilskin, jagged at one corner.

'Have you found anything?' demanded Bill in a strained voice.

'No. Not to make any sense, that is. But just a minute!'

At the rear of the passage, on the left-hand side, was the bedroom from which Vicky Adams had vanished as a child. Though H.M. had searched this room once before, he opened the door again.

It was now almost dark in Goblin Wood.

He saw dimly a room of twenty years before: a room of flounces, of lace curtains, of once-polished mahogany, its mirrors glimmering against white-papered walls. H.M. seemed especially interested in the windows.

He ran his hands carefully round the frame of each, even climbing laboriously up on a chair to examine the tops. He borrowed a box of matches from Bill; and the little spurts of light, following the rasp of the match, rasped against nerves as well. The hope died out of his face, and his companions saw it.

'H.M.,' Bill said for the dozenth time, 'where is she?'

'Son,' replied H.M. despondently, 'I don't know.'

'Let's get out of here,' Eve said abruptly. Her voice was a small scream. 'I kn-know it's all a trick! I know Vicky's a faker! But let's get out of here. For God's sake let's get out of here!'

'As a matter of fact,' Bill cleared his throat, 'I agree. Anyway, we won't hear from Vicky until tomorrow morning.'

'*Oh, yes, you will,*' whispered Vicky's voice out of the darkness.

Eve screamed.

They lighted a lamp.

But there was nobody there.

Their retreat from the cottage, it must be admitted, was not very dignified.

How they stumbled down that ragged lawn in the dark, how they piled rugs and picnic-hampers into the car, how they eventually found the main road again, is best left undescribed.

Sir Henry Merrivale has since sneered at this—'a bit of a goosy feeling; nothin' much'—and it is true that he has no nerves to speak of. But he can be worried, badly worried; and that he was worried on this occasion may be deduced from what happened later.

H.M., after dropping in at Claridge's for a modest late supper of lobster and *Pêche Melba*, returned to his house in Brook Street and slept a hideous sleep. It was three o'clock in the morning, even before the summer dawn, when the ringing of the bedside telephone roused him.

What he heard sent his blood pressure soaring.

'Dear Sir Henry!' crooned a familiar and sprite-like voice.

H.M. was himself again, full of gall and bile. He switched on the bedside lamp and put on his spectacles with care, so as adequately to address the 'phone.

'Have I got the honor,' he said with dangerous politeness, 'of addressin' Miss Vicky Adams?'

'Oh, yes!'

'I sincerely trust,' said H.M., 'you've been havin' a good time? Are you materialized yet?'

'Oh, yes!'

'Where are you now?'

'I'm afraid,' there was coy laughter in the voice, 'that must be a little secret for a day or two. I want to teach you a really *good* lesson. Blessings, dear.'

And she hung up the receiver.

H.M. did not say anything. He climbed out of bed. He stalked up and down the room, his corporation majestic under an old-fashioned nightshirt stretching to his heels. Then, since he himself had been waked up at three o'clock in the morning, the obvious course was to wake up somebody else; so he dialed the home number of Chief Inspector Masters.

'No, sir,' retorted Masters grimly, after coughing the frog out of his throat, 'I do *not* mind you ringing up. Not a bit of it!' He spoke with a certain pleasure. 'Because I've got a bit of news for you.'

H.M. eyed the 'phone suspiciously.

'Masters, are you trying to do me in the eye again?'

'It's what you always try to do to me, isn't it?'

'All right, all right!' growled H.M. 'What's the news?'

'Do you remember mentioning the Vicky Adams case yesterday?'

'Sort of. Yes.'

'Oh, ah! Well, I had a word or two round among our people. I was tipped the wink to go and see a certain solicitor. He was old Mr Fred Adams's solicitor before Mr Adams died about six or seven years ago.'

Here Masters's voice grew triumphant.

'I always said, Sir Henry, that Chuck Randall had planted some gadget in that cottage for a quick getaway. And I was right. The gadget was . . .'

'You were quite right, Masters. The gadget was a trick window.'

The telephone, so to speak, gave a start.

'What's that?'

'A trick window.' H.M. spoke patiently. 'You press a spring. And the whole frame of the window, two leaves locked together, slides down between the walls far enough so you can climb over. Then you push it back up again.'

'How in lum's name do you know that?'

'Oh, my son! They used to build windows like it in country houses during the persecution of Catholic priests. It was a good enough *second* guess. Only . . . it won't work.'

Masters seemed annoyed. 'It won't work now,' Masters agreed. 'And do you know why?'

'I can guess. Tell me.'

'Because, just before Mr Adams died, he discovered how his darling daughter had flummoxed him. He never told anybody except his lawyer. He took a handful of four-inch nails, and sealed up the top of that frame so tight an orangoutang couldn't move it, and painted 'em over so they wouldn't be noticed.'

'Uh-huh. You can notice 'em now.'

'I doubt if the young lady herself ever knew. But, by George!' Masters said savagely, 'I'd like to see anybody try the same game now!'

'You would, hey? Then will it interest you to know that the same gal has just disappeared out of the same house again?'

H.M. began a long narrative of the facts, but he had to break off because the telephone was raving.

'Honest, Masters,' H.M. said seriously, 'I'm not joking. She didn't get out through that window. But she did get out. You'd better meet me,' he gave directions, 'tomorrow morning. In the meantime, son, sleep well.'

It was, therefore, a worn-faced Masters who went into the Visitors' Room at the Senior Conservatives' Club just before lunch on the following day.

The Visitors' Room is a dark sepulchral place, opening on an air-well, where the visitor is surrounded by pictures of dyspeptic-looking gentlemen with beards. It has a pervading mustiness of wood and leather. Though whiskey and soda stood on the table, H.M. sat in a leather chair far away from it, ruffling his hands across his bald head.

'Now, Masters, keep your shirt on!' he warned. 'This business may be rummy. But it's not a police matter—yet.'

'I know it's not a police matter,' Masters said grimly. 'All the same, I've had a word with the Superintendent at Aylesbury.'

'Fowler?'

'You know him?'

'Sure. I know everybody. Is he goin' to keep an eye out?'

'He's going to have a look at that ruddy cottage. I've asked for any telephone calls to be put through here. In the meantime, sir—'

It was at this point, as though diabolically inspired, that the telephone rang. H.M. reached it before Masters.

'It's the old man,' he said, unconsciously assuming a stance of grandeur. 'Yes, yes! Masters is here, but he's drunk. You tell me first. What's that?'

The telephone talked thinly.

'Sure I looked in the kitchen cupboard,' bellowed H.M. 'Though I didn't honestly expect to find Vicky Adams hidin' there. What's that? Say it again! Plates? Cups that had been . . .'

An almost frightening change had come over H.M.'s expression. He stood motionless. All the posturing went out of him. He was not even listening to the voice that still talked thinly, while his eyes and his brain moved to put together facts. At length (though the voice still talked) he hung up the receiver.

H.M. blundered back to the centre table, where he drew out a chair and sat down.

'Masters,' he said very quietly, 'I've come close to makin' the silliest mistake of my life.'

Here he cleared his throat.

'I shouldn't have made it, son. I really shouldn't. But don't yell at me for cuttin' off Fowler. I can tell you know how Vicky Adams disappeared. And she said one true thing when she said she was going into a strange country.'

'How do you mean?'

'She's dead,' answered H.M.

The word fell with heavy weight into that dingy room, where the bearded faces looked down.

'Y'see,' H.M. went on blankly, 'a lot of us were right when we thought Vicky Adams was a faker. She was. To attract attention to herself, she played that trick on her family with the hocused window. She's lived and traded on it ever since. That's what sent me straight in the wrong direction. I was on the alert for some *trick* Vicky Adams might play. So it never occurred to me that this elegant pair of beauties, Miss Eve Drayton and Mr William Sage, were deliberately conspirin' to murder *her*.'

131

Masters got slowly to his feet.

'Did you say . . . murder?'

'Oh, yes.'

Again H.M. cleared his throat.

'It was all arranged beforehand for me to be a witness. They knew Vicky Adams couldn't resist a challenge to disappear, especially as Vicky always believed she could get out by the trick window. They wanted Vicky to *say* she was goin' to disappear. They never knew anything about the trick window, Masters. But they knew their own plan very well.

'Eve Drayton even told me the motive. She hated Vicky, of course. But that wasn't the main point. She was Vicky Adams's only relative; she'd inherit an awful big scoopful of money. Eve said she could be patient. (And, burn me, how her eyes meant it when she said that!) Rather than risk any slightest suspicion of murder, she was willing to wait seven years until a disappeared person can be presumed dead.

'Our Eve, I think, was the fiery drivin' force of that conspiracy. She was only scared part of the time. Sage was scared all of the time. But it was Sage who did the real dirty work. He lured Vicky Adams into that cottage, while Eve kept me in close conversation on the lawn . . .'

H.M. paused.

Intolerably vivid in the mind of Chief Inspector Masters, who had seen it years before, rose the picture of the rough-stone bungalow against the darkling wood.

'Masters,' said H.M., 'why should a bath-tap be dripping in a house that hadn't been occupied for months?'

'Well?'

'Sage, y'see, is a surgeon. I saw him take his black case of instruments out of the car. He took Vicky Adams into that house. In the bathroom he stabbed her, he stripped her, and *he dismembered her body in the bath tub.—* Easy, son!'

'Go on,' said Masters without moving.

'The head, the torso, the folded arms and legs, were wrapped up in three large square pieces of thin transparent oilskin. Each was sewed up with coarse thread so the blood wouldn't drip. Last night I found one of the oilskin pieces he'd ruined when his needle slipped at the corner. Then he walked out of the house, with the back door still standin' unlocked, to get his wild-strawberry alibi.'

'Sage went out of there,' shouted Masters, 'leaving the body in the house?'

'Oh, yes,' agreed H.M.

'But where did he leave it?'

H.M. ignored this.

'In the meantime, son, what about Eve Drayton? At the end of the arranged three-quarters of an hour, she indicated there was hanky-panky between her fiancé and Vicky Adams. She flew into the house. But what did she do?

'She walked to the back of the passage. I heard her. *There she simply locked and bolted the back door.* And then she marched out to join me with tears in her eyes. And these two beauties were ready for investigation.'

'Investigation?' said Masters. '*With that body still in the house?*'

'Oh, yes.'

Masters lifted both fists.

'It must have given young Sage a shock,' said H.M., 'when I found that piece of waterproof oilskin he'd washed but dropped. Anyway, these two had only two more bits of hokey-pokey. The "vanished" gal had to speak—to show she was still alive. If you'd been there, son, you'd have noticed that Eve Drayton's got a voice just like Vicky Adams's. If somebody speaks in a dark room, carefully imitatin' a coy tone she never uses herself, the illusion's goin' to be pretty good. The same goes for a telephone.

'It was finished, Masters. All that had to be done was remove the body from the house, and get it far away from there . . .'

'But that's just what I'm asking you, sir! Where was the body all this time? And who in blazes *did* remove the body from the house?'

'All of us did,' answered H.M.

'What's that?'

'Masters,' said H.M., 'aren't you forgettin' the picnic hampers?'

And now, the Chief Inspector saw, H.M. was as white as a ghost. His next words took Masters like a blow between the eyes.

'Three good-sized wickerwork hampers, with lids. After our big meal on the porch, those hampers were shoved inside the house where Sage could get at 'em. He had to leave most of the used crockery behind, in the kitchen cupboard. But three wickerwork hampers from a picnic, and three butcher's parcels to go inside 'em. I carried one down to the car myself. It felt a bit funny . . .'

H.M. stretched out his hand, not steadily, towards the whiskey.

'Y'know,' he said, 'I'll always wonder if I was carryin' the—head.'

134

9

ELLERY QUEEN

The Dauphin's Doll

There is a law among story-tellers, originally passed by Editors at the cries (they say) of their constituents, which states that stories about Christmas shall have children in them. This Christmas story is no exception; indeed, misopedists will complain that we have overdone it. And we confess in advance that this is also a story about Dolls, and that Santa Claus comes into it, and even a Thief; though as to this last, whoever he was—and that was one of the questions—he was certainly not Barabbas, even parabolically.

Another section of the statute governing Christmas stories provides that they shall incline toward Sweetness and Light. The first arises, of course, from the orphans and the never-souring savor of the annual Miracle; as for Light, it will be provided at the end, as usual, by that luminous prodigy, Ellery Queen. The reader of gloomier temper will also find a large measure of Darkness, in the person and works of one who, at least in Inspector Queen's harassed view, was surely the winged Prince of that region. His name, by the way, was not Satan, it was Comus; and this is paradox enow, since the original Comus, as everyone knows, was the god of festive joy and mirth, emotions not commonly associated with the Underworld. As Ellery struggled to embrace his phantom foe, he puzzled over this *non sequitur* in vain; in vain, that is, until Nikki Porter, no scorner of the obvious, suggested that he *might* seek the answer where any ordinary mortal would go at once. And there, to the great man's mortification, it was indeed to be found: On page 262b of Volume 6, *Coleb to Damasci*, of the 175th Anniversary edition of the *Encyclopaedia Britannica*. A French conjuror of that name, performing in London in the year 1789, caused his wife to vanish from the top of a table—the very first time, it appeared, that this feat, uxorial or otherwise, had been accomplished without the aid of mirrors. To track his dark adversary's *nom de nuit* to its historic lair gave Ellery his only glint of satisfaction until that blessed moment when light burst all around him and exorcised the darkness, Prince and all.

But this is chaos.

Our story properly begins not with our invisible character but with our dead one.

Miss Ypson had not always been dead; *au contraire*. She had lived for seventy-eight years, for most of them breathing hard. As her father used to remark, 'She was a very active little verb.' Miss Ypson's father was a professor of Greek at a small Mid-western university. He had conjugated his daughter with the rather bewildered assistance of one of his brawnier students, an Iowa poultry heiress.

Professor Ypson was a man of distinction. Unlike most professors of Greek, he was a Greek professor of Greek, having been born Gerasymos Aghamos Ypsilonomon in Polykhnitos, on the island of Mytilini, 'where', he was fond of recalling on certain occasions, 'burning Sappho loved and sung'—a quotation he found unfailingly useful in his extracurricular activities; and, the Hellenic ideal notwithstanding, Professor Ypson believed wholeheartedly in immoderation in all things. This hereditary and cultural background explains the professor's interest in fatherhood—to his wife's chagrin, for Mrs Ypson's own breeding prowess was confined almost exclusively to the barnyards on which her income was based; he held their daughter to be nothing less than a biological miracle.

The professor's mental processes also tended to confuse Mrs Ypson. She never ceased to wonder why, instead of shortening his name to Ypson, her husband had not sensibly changed it to Jones. 'My dear,' the professor once replied, 'you are an Iowa snob.' 'But nobody,' Mrs Ypson cried, 'can spell it or pronounce it!' 'This is a cross,' murmured Professor Ypson, 'which we must bear with Ypsilanti.' 'Oh,' said Mrs Ypson.

There was invariably something Sibylline about his conversation. His favorite adjective for his wife was 'ypsiliform', a term, he explained, which referred to the germinal spot at one of the fecundation stages in a ripening egg and which was, therefore, exquisitely à propos. Mrs Ypson continued to look bewildered; she died at an early age.

And the professor ran off with a Kansas City variety girl of considerable talent, leaving his baptized chick to be reared by an eggish relative of her mother's named Jukes.

The only time Miss Ypson heard from her father—except when he wrote charming and erudite little notes requesting, as he termed it, *lucrum*—was in the fourth decade of his Odyssey, when he sent her a handsome addition to her collection, a terracotta play doll of Greek origin over three thousand years old which, unhappily, Miss Ypson felt duty-bound to return to the Brooklyn museum from which it had unaccountably vanished. The note accompanying her father's gift had said, whimsically: *'Timeo Danaos et dona ferentes.'*

There was poetry behind Miss Ypson's dolls. At her birth the professor, ever harmonious, signalized his devotion to fecundity by naming her Cytherea. This proved the Olympian irony. For, it turned out, her father's philoprogenitiveness throbbed frustrate in her mother's stony womb: even though Miss Ypson interred five husbands of quite adequate vigor, she remained infertile to the end of her days. Hence it is classically tragic to find her, when all passion was spent, a sweet little old lady with a vague if eager smile who, under the name of her father, pattered about a vast and echoing New York apartment playing enthusiastically with dolls.

In the beginning they were dolls of common clay: a Billiken, a kewpie, a Kathe Kruse, a Patsy, a Foxy Grandpa, and so forth. But then, as her need increased, Miss Ypson began her fierce sack of the past.

Down into the land of Pharaoh she went for two pieces of thin desiccated board, carved and painted and with hair of strung beads, and legless—so that they might not run away—which any connoisseur will tell you are the most superb specimens of ancient Egyptian paddle doll extant, far superior to those in the British Museum, although this fact will be denied in certain quarters.

Miss Ypson unearthed a foremother of 'Letitia Penn', until her discovery held to be the oldest doll in America, having been brought to Philadelphia from England in 1699 by William Penn as a gift for a playmate of his small daughter's. Miss Ypson's find was a wooden-hearted 'little lady' in brocade and velvet which had been sent by Sir Walter Raleigh to the first English child born in the New World. Since Virginia Dare had been born in 1587, not even the Smithsonian dared impugn Miss Ypson's triumph.

On the old lady's racks, in her plate-glass cases, might be seen the wealth of a thousand childhoods, and some riches—for such is the genetics of dolls—possessed by children grown. Here could be found 'fashion babies' from fourteenth-century France, sacred dolls of the Orange Free State Fingo tribe, Satsuma paper dolls and court dolls from old Japan, beady-eyed 'Kalifa' dolls of the Egyptian Sudan, Swedish birchbark dolls, 'Katcina' dolls of the Hopis, mammoth-tooth dolls of the Eskimos, feather dolls of the Chippewa, tumble dolls of the ancient Chinese, Coptic bone dolls, Roman dolls dedicated to Diana, *pantin* dolls which had been the street toys of Parisian exquisites before Madame Guillotine swept the boulevards, early Christian dolls in their crèches representing the Holy Family—to specify the merest handful of Miss Ypson's Briarean collection. She possessed dolls of pasteboard, dolls of animal skin, spool dolls, crab-claw dolls, eggshell dolls, cornhusk dolls, rag dolls, pine-cone dolls with moss hair, stocking dolls, dolls of bisque, dolls of palm leaf, dolls of papier mâché, even dolls made of seed pods. There were dolls forty inches tall, and there were dolls so little Miss Ypson could hide them in her gold thimble.

Cytherea Ypson's collection bestrode the centuries and took tribute of history. There was no greater—not the fabled playthings of Montezuma, or Victoria's, or Eugene Field's; not the collection at the Metropolitan, or the South Kensington, or the royal palace in old Bucharest, or anywhere outside the enchantment of little girls' dreams.

It was made of Iowan eggs and the Attic shore, corn-fed and myrtle-clothed; and it brings us at last to Attorney John Somerset Bondling and his visit to the Queen residence one December twenty-third not so very long ago.

December the twenty-third is ordinarily not a good time to seek the Queens. Inspector Richard Queen likes his Christmas old-fashioned;

his turkey stuffing, for instance, calls for twenty-two hours of over-all preparation and some of its ingredients are not readily found at the corner grocer's. And Ellery is a frustrated gift-wrapper. For a month before Christmas he turns his sleuthing genius to tracking down unusual wrapping papers, fine ribbons, and artistic stickers; and he spends the last two days creating beauty.

So it was that when Attorney John S. Bondling called, Inspector Queen was in his kitchen, swathed in a barbecue apron, up to his elbows in *fines herbes*, while Ellery, behind the locked door of his study, composed a secret symphony in glittering fuchsia metallic paper, forest-green moiré ribbon, and pine cones.

'It's almost useless,' shrugged Nikki, studying Attorney Bondling's card, which was as crackly-looking as Attorney Bondling. 'You say you know the Inspector personally, Mr Bondling?'

'Just tell him Bondling the estate lawyer,' said Bondling neurotically. 'Park Row. He'll know.'

'Don't blame me,' said Nikki, 'if you wind up in his stuffing. Goodness knows he's used everything else.' And she went for Inspector Queen.

While she was gone, the study door opened noiselessly for one inch. A suspicious eye reconnoitered from the crack.

'Don't be alarmed,' said the owner of the eye, slipping through the crack and locking the door hastily behind him. 'Can't trust them, you know. Children, just children.'

'Children!' Attorney Bondling snarled. 'You're Ellery Queen, aren't you?'

'Yes.'

'Interested in youth? Christmas? Orphans, dolls, that sort of thing?' Mr Bondling went on in a remarkably nasty way.

'I suppose so.'

'The more fool you. Ah, here's your father. Inspector Queen——!'

'Oh, that Bondling,' said the old gentleman absently, shaking his visitor's hand. 'My office called to say someone was coming up. Here, use my handkerchief; that's a bit of turkey liver. Know my son? His secretary, Miss Porter? What's on your mind, Mr Bondling?'

'Inspector, I'm in charge of handling the Cytherea Ypson estate, and——'

'Cytherea Ypson,' frowned the Inspector. 'Oh, yes. She died only recently.'

'Leaving me with the headache,' said Mr Bondling bitterly, 'of disposing of her Dollection.'

'Her what?' asked Ellery.

'Dolls—collection. Dollection. She coined the word.'

Ellery strolled over to his armchair.

'Do I take this down?' sighed Nikki.

'Dollection,' said Ellery.

'Spent about thirty years at it. Dolls!'

'Yes, Nikki, take it down.'

'Well, well, Mr Bondling,' said Inspector Queen. 'What's the problem? Christmas comes but once a year, you know.'

'Will provides the Dollection be sold at auction,' grated the attorney, 'and the proceeds used to set up a fund for orphan children. I'm holding the public sale right after New Year's.'

'Dolls and orphans, eh?' said the Inspector, thinking of Javanese black pepper and Country Gentleman Seasoning Salt.

'That's *nice*,' beamed Nikki.

'Oh, is it?' said Mr Bondling softly. 'Apparently, young woman, you've never tried to satisfy a Surrogate. I've administered estates for nineteen years without a whisper against me, but let an estate involve the interests of just one little fatherless child, and you'd think from the Surrogate's attitude I was Bill Sikes himself!'

'My stuffing,' began the Inspector.

'I've had those dolls catalogued. The result is ominous! Did you know there's no set market for the damnable things? And aside from a few personal possessions, the Dollection constitutes the old lady's entire estate. Sank every nickel she had in it.'

'But it should be worth a fortune,' remarked Ellery.

'To whom, Mr Queen? Museums always want such things as free and unencumbered gifts. I tell you, except for one item, those hypothetical orphans won't realize enough from that sale to keep them in—in bubble gum for two days!'

'Which item would that be, Mr Bondling?'

'Number Six-seventy-four,' the lawyer snapped. 'This one.'

'Number Six-seventy-four,' read Inspector Queen from the fat catalogue Bondling had fished out of a large greatcoat pocket. 'The Dauphin's Doll. Unique. Ivory figure of a boy Prince eight inches tall, clad in court dress, genuine ermine, brocade, velvet. Court sword in gold strapped to waist. Gold circlet crown surmounted by single blue brilliant diamond of finest water, weight approximately forty-nine carats—'

'How many carats?' exclaimed Nikki.

'Larger than the Hope and the Star of South Africa,' said Ellery, with a certain excitement.

'—appraised,' continued his father, 'at one hundred and ten thousand dollars.'

'Expensive dollie.'

'Indecent!' said Nikki.

'This indecent—I mean exquisite royal doll,' the Inspector read on, 'was a birthday gift from King Louis XVI of France to Louis Charles, his second son, who became dauphin at the death of his elder brother in 1789. The little dauphin was proclaimed Louis XVII by the royalists during the French Revolution while in custody of the *sans-culottes*. His fate is shrouded in mystery. Romantic, historic item.'

'*Le prince perdu.* I'll say,' muttered Ellery. 'Mr Bondling, is this on the level?'

'I'm an attorney, not an antiquarian,' snapped their visitor. 'There are documents attached, one of them a sworn statement—holograph—by Lady Charlotte Atkyns, the English actress-friend of the Capet family—she was in France during the Revolution—or purporting to be in Lady Atkyns's hand. It doesn't matter, Mr Queen. Even if the history is bad, the diamond's good!'

'I take it this hundred-and-ten-thousand-dollar dollie constitutes the bone, as it were, or that therein lies the rub?'

'You said it!' cried Mr Bondling, cracking his knuckles in a sort of agony. 'For my money the Dauphin's Doll is the only negotiable asset of that collection. And what's the old lady do? She provides by will that on the day preceding Christmas the Cytherea Ypson Dollection is to be publicly displayed . . . on the main floor of Nash's Department Store! *The day before Christmas, gentlemen!* Think of it!'

'But why?' asked Nikki, puzzled.

'Why? Who knows why? For the entertainment of New York's

army of little beggars, I suppose! Have you any notion how many peasants pass through Nash's on the day before Christmas? My cook tells me—she's a very religious woman—it's like Armageddon.'

'Day before Christmas,' frowned Ellery. 'That's tomorrow.'

'It does sound chancy,' said Nikki anxiously. Then she brightened. 'Oh, well, maybe Nash's won't cooperate, Mr Bondling.'

'Oh, won't they!' howled Mr Bondling. 'Why, old lady Ypson had this stunt cooked up with that gang of peasant-purveyors for years! They've been snapping at my heels ever since the day she was put away!'

'It'll draw every crook in New York,' said the Inspector, his gaze on the kitchen door.

'Orphans,' said Nikki. 'The orphans' interests *must* be protected.' She looked at her employer accusingly.

'Special measures, dad,' he said.

'Sure, sure,' said the Inspector, rising. 'Don't you worry about this, Mr Bondling. Now if you'll be kind enough to excu—'

'Inspector Queen,' hissed Mr Bondling, leaning forward tensely, 'that is not all.'

'Ah,' said Ellery briskly, lighting a cigarette. 'There's a specific villain in this piece, Mr Bondling, and you know who he is.'

'I do,' said the lawyer hollowly, 'and then again I don't. I mean, it's Comus.'

'*Comus!*' the Inspector screamed.

'Comus?' said Ellery slowly.

'Comus?' said Nikki. 'Who dat?'

'Comus,' nodded Mr Bondling. 'First thing this morning. Marched right into my office, bold as day—must have followed me, I hadn't got my coat off, my secretary wasn't even in. Marched in and tossed this card on my desk.'

Ellery seized it. 'The usual, dad.'

'His trademark,' growled the Inspector, his lips working.

'But the card just says "Comus",' complained Nikki. 'Who—?'

'Go on, Mr Bondling!' thundered the Inspector.

'And he calmly announced to me,' said Bondling, blotting his cheeks with an exhausted handkerchief, 'that he's going to steal the Dauphin's Doll tomorrow, in Nash's.'

142

'Oh, a maniac,' said Nikki.

'Mr Bondling,' said the old gentleman in a terrible voice, 'just what did this fellow look like?'

'Foreigner—black beard—spoke with a European accent of some sort. To tell you the truth, I was so thunderstruck I didn't notice details. Didn't even chase him till it was too late.'

The Queens shrugged at each other, Gallically.

'The old story,' said the Inspector; the corners of his nostrils were greenish. 'The brass of the colonel's monkey and when he does show himself nobody remembers anything but beards and foreign accents. Well, Mr Bondling, with Comus in the game it's serious business. Where's the collection right now?'

'In the vaults of the Life Bank and Trust, Forty-third Street branch.'

'What time are you to move it over to Nash's?'

'They wanted it this evening. I said nothing doing. I've made special arrangements with the bank, and the collection's to be moved at seven thirty tomorrow morning.'

'Won't be much time to set up,' said Ellery thoughtfully, 'before the store opens its doors.' He glanced at his father.

'You leave Operation Dollie to us, Mr Bondling,' said the Inspector grimly. 'Better give me a buzz this afternoon.'

'I can't tell you, Inspector, how relieved I am—'

'Are you?' said the old gentleman sourly. 'What makes you think he won't get it?'

When Attorney Bondling had left, the Queens put their heads together, Ellery doing most of the talking, as usual. Finally, the Inspector went into the bedroom for a session with his direct line to headquarters.

'Anybody would think,' sniffed Nikki, 'you two were planning the defense of the Bastille. Who on earth is this Comus, anyway?'

'We don't know, Nikki,' said Ellery slowly. 'Might be anybody. Began his criminal career about five years ago. He's in the grand tradition of Lupin—a saucy, highly intelligent rascal who's made stealing an art. He seems to take a special delight in stealing valuable things under virtually impossible conditions. Master of make-up— he's appeared in a dozen different disguises. And he's an uncanny mimic. Never been caught, photographed, or fingerprinted. Imaginative, daring—I'd say he's the most dangerous thief operating right now in the United States.'

'If he's never been caught,' said Nikki skeptically, 'how do you know he commits these crimes?'

'You mean and not someone else?' Ellery smiled pallidly. 'The techniques mark the thefts as his work. And then, like Arsène, he leaves a card—with the name "Comus" on it—on the scene of each visit.'

'Does he usually announce in advance that he's going to swipe the crown jewels?'

'No.' Ellery frowned. 'To my knowledge, this is the first such instance. Since he's never done anything without a reason, that visit to Bondling's office this morning must be part of his greater plan. I wonder if—'

The telephone in the living room rang clear and loud.

Nikki looked at Ellery. Ellery looked at the telephone.

'Do you suppose—?' began Nikki. But then she said, 'Oh, it's too absurd.'

'Where Comus is involved,' said Ellery wildly, 'nothing is too absurd!' and he leaped for the phone. 'Hello!'

'A call from an old friend,' announced a deep and hollowish male voice. 'Comus.'

'Well,' said Ellery. 'Hello again.'

'Did Mr Bondling,' asked the voice jovially, 'persuade you to "prevent" me from stealing the Dauphin's Doll in Nash's tomorrow?'

'So you know Bondling's been here.'

'No miracle involved, Queen. I followed him. Are you taking the case?'

'See here, Comus,' said Ellery. 'Under ordinary circumstances I'd welcome the sporting chance to put you where you belong. But these circumstances are not ordinary. That doll represents the major asset of a future fund for orphaned children. I'd rather we didn't play catch with it. Comus, what do you say we call this one off?'

'Shall we say,' asked the voice gently, 'Nash's Department Store—tomorrow?'

Thus the early morning of December twenty-fourth finds Messrs Queen and Bondling, and Nikki Porter, huddled on the iron sidewalk of Forty-third Street before the holly-decked windows of the Life Bank & Trust Company, just outside a double line of armed guards. The guards form a channel between the bank entrance and an armored truck, down which Cytherea Ypson's Dollection flows swiftly. And all about gapes New York, stamping callously on the aged, icy face of the street against the uncharitable Christmas wind.

Now is the winter of his discontent, and Mr Queen curses.

'I don't know what you're beefing about,' moans Miss Porter. 'You and Mr Bondling are bundled up like Yukon prospectors. Look at *me*.'

'It's that rat-hearted public relations tripe from Nash's,' says Mr Queen murderously. 'They all swore themselves to secrecy, Brother Rat included. Honor! Spirit of Christmas!'

'It was all over the radio last night,' whimpers Mr Bondling. 'And in this morning's papers.'

'I'll cut his creep's heart out. Here! Velie, keep those people away!'

Sergeant Velie says good-naturedly from the doorway of the bank, 'You jerks stand back.' Little does the Sergeant know the fate in store for him.

'Armored trucks,' says Miss Porter bluishly. 'Shotguns.'

'Nikki, Comus made a point of informing us in advance that he meant to steal the Dauphin's Doll in Nash's Department Store. It would be just like him to have said that in order to make it easier to steal the doll en route.'

'Why don't they hurry?' shivers Mr Bondling. 'Ah!' Inspector Queen appears suddenly in the doorway. His hands clasp treasure.

'Oh!' cries Nikki.

New York whistles.

It is magnificent, an affront to democracy. But street mobs, like children, are royalists at heart.

New York whistles, and Sergeant Thomas Velie steps menacingly before Inspector Queen, Police Positive drawn, and Inspector Queen dashes across the sidewalk between the bristling lines of guards.

Queen the Younger vanishes, to materialize an instant later at the door of the armored truck.

'It's just immorally, hideously beautiful, Mr Bondling,' breathes Miss Porter, sparkly-eyed.

Mr Bondling cranes, thinly.

ENTER *Santa Claus, with bell.*

Santa. Oyez, oyez. Peace, good will. Is that the dollie the radio's been yappin' about, folks?

Mr B. Scram.

Miss P. Why, Mr Bondling.

Mr B. Well, he's got no business here. Stand back, er, Santa. Back!

Santa. What eateth you, my lean and angry friend? Have you no compassion at this season of the year?

Mr B. Oh . . . Here! (*Clink.*) Now will you kindly . . .?

Santa. Mighty pretty dollie. Where they takin' it, girlie?

Miss P. Over to Nash's, Santa.

Mr B. You asked for it. Officer!!!

Santa. (*Hurriedly*) Little present for you, girlie. Compliments of old Santy. Merry, merry.

Miss P. For *me*? (EXIT *Santa, rapidly, with bell.*) Really, Mr Bondling, was it necessary to . . .?

Mr B. Opium for the masses! What did that flatulent faker hand you, Miss Porter? What's in that unmentionable envelope?

Miss P. I'm sure I don't know, but isn't it the most touching idea? Why, it's addressed to *Ellery.* Oh! Elleryyyyyy!

Mr B. (EXIT *excitedly*) Where is he? You—! Officer! Where did that baby-deceiver disappear to? A Santa Claus . . .

Mr Q. (*Entering on the run*) Yes? Nikki, what is it? What's happened?

Miss P. A man dressed as Santa Claus just handed me this envelope. It's addressed to you.

Mr Q. Note? (*He snatches it, withdraws a miserable slice of paper from it on which is block-lettered in pencil a message which he reads aloud with considerable expression.*) 'Dear Ellery, Don't you trust me? I said I'd steal the Dauphin in Nash's emporium today and that's exactly where I'm going to do it. Yours—' Signed . . .

Miss P. (*Craning*) 'Comus.' That Santa?

Mr Q. (*Sets his manly lips. An icy wind blows*)

Even the master had to acknowledge that their defenses against Comus were ingenious.

From the Display Department of Nash's they had requisitioned four miter-jointed counters of uniform length. These they had fitted together, and in the center of the hollow square thus formed they had erected a platform six feet high. On the counters, in plastic tiers, stretched the long lines of Miss Ypson's babies. Atop the platform, dominant, stood a great chair of hand-carved oak, filched from the Swedish Modern section of the Fine Furniture Department; and on this Valhalla-like throne, a huge and rosy rotundity, sat Sergeant Thomas Velie of police headquarters, morosely grateful for the anonymity endowed by the scarlet suit and the jolly mask and whiskers of his appointed role.

Nor was this all. At a distance of six feet outside the counters shimmered a surrounding rampart of plate glass, borrowed in its various elements from *The Glass Home of the Future* display on the sixth floor rear, and assembled to shape an eight-foot wall quoined with chrome, its glistening surfaces flawless except at one point, where a thick glass door had been installed. But the edges fitted intimately and there was a formidable lock in the door, the key to which lay buried in Mr Queen's right trouser pocket.

It was 8:54 a.m. The Queens, Nikki Porter, and Attorney Bondling stood among store officials and an army of plain-clothesmen on Nash's main floor surveying the product of their labors.

'I think that about does it,' muttered Inspector Queen at last. 'Men! Positions around the glass partition.'

Twenty-four assorted gendarmes in mufti jostled one another. They took marked places about the wall, facing it and grinning up at Sergeant Velie. Sergeant Velie, from his throne, glared back.

'Hagstrom and Piggott—the door.'

Two detectives detached themselves from a group of reserves. As they marched to the glass door, Mr Bondling plucked at the Inspector's overcoat sleeve. 'Can all these men be trusted, Inspector Queen?' he whispered. 'I mean, this fellow Comus—'

'Mr Bondling,' replied the old gentleman coldly, 'you do your job and let me do mine.'

'But—'

'Picked men, Mr Bondling! I picked 'em myself.'

'Yes, yes, Inspector. I merely thought I'd—'

'Lieutenant Farber.'

147

A little man with watery eyes stepped forward.

'Mr Bondling, this is Lieutenant Geronimo Farber, headquarters jewelry expert. Ellery?'

Ellery took the Dauphin's Doll from his greatcoat pocket, but he said, 'If you don't mind, dad, I'll keep holding on to it.'

Somebody said, 'Wow,' and then there was silence.

'Lieutenant, this doll in my son's hand is the famous Dauphin's Doll with the diamond crown that—'

'Don't touch it, Lieutenant, please,' said Ellery. 'I'd rather nobody touched it.'

'The doll,' continued the Inspector, 'has just been brought here from a bank vault which it ought never to have left, and Mr Bondling, who's handling the Ypson estate, claims it's the genuine article. Lieutenant, examine the diamond and give us your opinion.'

Lieutenant Farber produced a loupe. Ellery held the dauphin securely, and Farber did not touch it.

Finally, the expert said: 'I can't pass an opinion about the doll itself, of course, but the diamond's a beauty. Easily worth a hundred thousand dollars at the present state of the market—maybe more. Looks like a very strong setting, by the way.'

'Thanks, Lieutenant. Okay, son,' said the Inspector. 'Go into your waltz.'

Clutching the dauphin, Ellery strode over to the glass gate and unlocked it.

'This fellow Farber,' whispered Attorney Bondling in the Inspector's hairy ear. 'Inspector, are you absolutely sure he's—?'

'He's really Lieutenant Farber?' The Inspector controlled himself. 'Mr Bondling, I've known Gerry Farber for eighteen years. Calm yourself.'

Ellery was crawling perilously over the nearest counter. Then, bearing the dauphin aloft, he hurried across the floor of the enclosure to the platform.

Sergeant Velie whined, 'Maestro, how in hell am I going to sit here all day without washin' my hands?'

But Mr Queen merely stooped and lifted from the floor a heavy little structure faced with black velvet consisting of a floor and a backdrop, with a two-armed chromium support. This object he placed on the platform directly between Sergeant Velie's massive legs.

Carefully, he stood the Dauphin's Doll in the velvet niche. Then he clambered back across the counter, went through the glass door, locked it with the key, and turned to examine his handiwork.

Proudly the prince's plaything stood, the jewel in his little golden crown darting 'on pale electric streams' under the concentrated tide of a dozen of the most powerful floodlights in the possession of the great store.

'Velie,' said Inspector Queen, 'you're not to touch that doll. Don't lay a finger on it.'

The sergeant said, 'Gaaaaa'.

'You men on duty. Don't worry about the crowds. Your job is to keep watching that doll. You're not to take your eyes off it all day. Mr Bondling, are you satisfied?' Mr Bondling seemed about to say something, but then he hastily nodded. 'Ellery?'

The great man smiled. 'The only way he can get that bawbie,' he said, 'is by spells and incantations. Raise the portcullis!'

Then began the interminable day, *dies irae*, the last shopping day before Christmas. This is traditionally the day of the inert, the procrastinating, the undecided, and the forgetful, sucked at last into the mercantile machine by the perpetual pump of Time. If there is peace upon earth, it descends only afterward; and at no time, on the part of anyone embroiled, is there good will toward men. As Miss Porter expresses it, a cat fight in a bird cage would be more Christian.

But on this December twenty-fourth, in Nash's the normal bedlam was augmented by the vast shrilling of thousands of Children. It may be, as the Psalmist insists, that happy is the man that hath his quiver full of them; but no bowmen surrounded Miss Ypson's darlings this day, only detectives carrying revolvers, not a few of whom forbore to use same only by the most heroic self-discipline. In the black floods of humanity overflowing the main floor little folks darted about like electrically charged minnows, pursued by exasperated maternal shrieks and the imprecations of those whose shins and rumps and toes were at the mercy of hot, happy little limbs; indeed, nothing was sacred, and Attorney Bondling was seen to quail and wrap his greatcoat defensively about him against the savage innocence of childhood. But the guardians of the law, having been ordered to simulate store employees, possessed no such armor; and many a man earned his citation that day for unique cause. They stood in the very millrace of the tide; it churned about them, shouting, 'Dollies! *Dollies!*' until the very word lost its familiar meaning and became the insensate scream of a thousand Loreleis beckoning strong men to destruction below the eye-level of their diamond Light.

But they stood fast.

And Comus was thwarted. Oh, he tried. At 11:18 a.m. a tottering old man holding fast to the hand of a small boy tried to wheedle Detective Hagstrom into unlocking the glass door 'so my grandson here—he's terrible nearsighted—can get a closer look at the pretty dollies'. Detective Hagstrom roared, 'Rube!' and the old gentleman dropped the little boy's hand violently and with remarkable agility lost himself in the crowd. A spot investigation revealed that, coming upon the boy, who had been crying for his mommy, the old gentleman had promised to find her. The little boy, whose name—he said—was Lance Morganstern, was removed to the Lost and Found Department; and everyone was satisfied that the great thief had finally launched his attack. Everyone, that is, but Ellery Queen. He seemed puzzled. When Nikki asked him why, he merely said: 'Stupidity, Nikki. It's not in character.'

At 1:46 p.m., Sergeant Velie sent up a distress signal. Inspector Queen read the message aright and signaled back: 'O.K. Fifteen minutes.' Sergeant Santa C. Velie scrambled off his perch, clawed his way over the counter, and pounded urgently on the inner side of the glass door. Ellery let him out, relocking the door immediately, and the Sergeant's red-clad figure disappeared on the double in the general direction of the main-floor gentlemen's relief station, leaving the dauphin in solitary possession of the dais.

During the Sergeant's recess Inspector Queen circulated among his men repeating the order of the day.

The episode of Velie's response to the summons of Nature caused a temporary crisis. For at the end of the specified fifteen minutes he had not returned. Nor was there a sign of him at the end of a half-hour. An aide dispatched to the relief station reported back that the Sergeant was not there. Fears of foul play were voiced at an emergency staff conference held then and there and countermeasures were being planned even as, at 2:35 p.m. the familiar Santa-clad bulk of the Sergeant was observed battling through the lines, pawing at his mask.

'Velie,' snarled Inspector Queen, 'where have you been?'

'Eating my lunch,' growled the Sergeant's voice, defensively. 'I been taking my punishment like a good soldier all day, Inspector, but I draw the line at starvin' to death even in line of duty.'

'Velie—!' choked the Inspector; but then he waved his hand feebly and said, 'Ellery, let him back in there.'

And that was very nearly all. The only other incident of note occurred at 4:22 p.m. A well-upholstered woman with a red face yelled, 'Stop! Thief! He grabbed my pocketbook! Police!' about fifty feet from the Ypson exhibit. Ellery instantly shouted, '*It's a trick! Men, don't take your eyes off that doll!*'

'It's Comus disguised as a woman,' exclaimed Attorney Bondling, as Inspector Queen and Detective Hesse wrestled the female figure through the mob. She was now a wonderful shade of magenta. 'What are you *doing?*' she screamed. 'Don't arrest *me!*—catch that crook who stole my pocketbook!' 'No dice, Comus,' said the Inspector. 'Wipe off that makeup.' 'McComas?' said the woman loudly. 'My name is Rafferty, and all these folks saw it. He was a fat man with a mustache.' 'Inspector,' said Nikki Porter, making a surreptitious scientific test. 'This is a female. Believe me.' And so, indeed, it proved. All agreed that the mustachioed fat man had been Comus, creating a diversion in the desperate hope that the resulting confusion would give him an opportunity to steal the little dauphin.

'Stupid, stupid,' muttered Ellery, gnawing his fingernails.

'Sure,' grinned the Inspector. 'We've got him nibbling his tail, Ellery. This was his do-or-die pitch. He's through.'

'Frankly,' sniffed Nikki, 'I'm a little disappointed.'

'Worried,' said Ellery, 'would be the word for me.'

Inspector Queen was too case-hardened a sinner's nemesis to lower his guard at his most vulnerable moment. When the 5:30 bells bonged and the crowds began struggling toward the exits, he barked: 'Men, stay at your posts. Keep watching that doll!' So all hands were on the *qui vive* even as the store emptied. The reserves kept hustling people out. Ellery, standing on an Information booth, spotted bottlenecks and waved his arms.

At 5:50 p.m. the main floor was declared out of the battle zone. All stragglers had been herded out. The only persons visible were the refugees trapped by the closing bell on the upper floors, and these were pouring out of elevators and funneled by a solid line of detectives and accredited store personnel to the doors. By 6:05 they were a trickle; by 6:10 even the trickle had dried up. And the personnel itself began to disperse.

'No, men!' called Ellery sharply from his observation post. 'Stay where you are till all the store employees are out!' The counter clerks had long since disappeared.

Sergeant Velie's plaintive voice called from the other side of the glass door. 'I got to get home and decorate my tree. Maestro, make with the key.'

Ellery jumped down and hurried over to release him. Detective Piggott jeered, 'Going to play Santa to your kids tomorrow morning, Velie?' at which the Sergeant managed even through his mask to project a four-letter word distinctly, forgetful of Miss Porter's presence, and stamped off toward the gentlemen's relief station.

'Where you going, Velie?' asked the Inspector, smiling.

'I got to get out of these x-and-dash Santy clothes somewheres, don't I?' came back the Sergeant's mask-muffled tones, and he vanished in a thunderclap of his fellow-officers' laughter.

'Still worried, Mr Queen?' chuckled the Inspector.

'I don't understand it.' Ellery shook his head. 'Well, Mr Bondling, there's your dauphin, untouched by human hands.'

'Yes. Well!' Attorney Bondling wiped his forehead happily. 'I don't profess to understand it, either, Mr Queen. Unless it's simply another case of an inflated reputation . . .' He clutched the Inspector suddenly. 'Those men!' he whispered. '*Who are they?*'

'Relax, Mr Bondling,' said the Inspector good-naturedly. 'It's just the men to move the dolls back to the bank. Wait a minute, you men! Perhaps, Mr Bondling, we'd better see the dauphin back to the vaults ourselves.'

'Keep those fellows back,' said Ellery to the headquarters men, quietly, and he followed the Inspector and Mr Bondling into the enclosure. They pulled two of the counters apart at one corner and strolled over to the platform. The dauphin was winking at them in a friendly way. They stood looking at him.

'Cute little devil,' said the Inspector.

'Seems silly now,' beamed Attorney Bondling. 'Being so worried all day.'

'Comus must have had *some* plan,' mumbled Ellery.

'Sure,' said the Inspector. 'That old man disguise. And that purse-snatching act.'

'No, no, dad. Something clever. He's always pulled something clever.'

'Well, there's the diamond,' said the lawyer comfortably. 'He didn't.'

'Disguise . . .' muttered Ellery. 'It's always been a disguise. Santa Claus costume—he used that once—this morning in front of the bank. . . . Did we see a Santa Claus around here today?'

'Just Velie,' said the Inspector, grinning. 'And I hardly think—'

'Wait a moment, please,' said Attorney Bondling in a very odd voice.

He was staring at the Dauphin's Doll.

'Wait for what, Mr Bondling?'

'What's the matter?' said Ellery, also in a very odd voice.

'But . . . not possible . . .' stammered Bondling. He snatched the doll from its black velvet repository. '*No!*' he howled. '*This isn't the dauphin! It's a fake—a copy!*'

Something happened in Mr Queen's head—a little *click!* like the sound of a switch. And there was light.

'Some of you men!' he roared. '*After Santa Claus!*'

'After who, Ellery?' gasped Inspector Queen.

'Don't stand here! *Get him!*' screamed Ellery, dancing up and down. 'The man I just let out of here! The Santa who made for the men's room!'

Detectives started running, wildly.

'But Ellery,' said a small voice, and Nikki found that it was her own, 'that was Sergeant Velie.'

'It was *not* Velie, Nikki! When Velie ducked out just before two o'clock, *Comus waylaid him!* It was Comus who came back in Velie's

Santa Claus rig, wearing Velie's whiskers and mask! *Comus has been on this platform all afternoon!*' He tore the dauphin from Attorney Bondling's grasp. 'Copy . . . He did it, he did it!'

'But Mr Queen,' whispered Attorney Bondling, 'his voice. He spoke to us . . . in Sergeant Velie's voice.'

'Yes, Ellery,' Nikki heard herself saying.

'I told you yesterday Comus is a great mimic, Nikki. Lieutenant Farber! Is Farber still here?'

The jewelry expert, who had been gaping from a distance, shook his head and shuffled into the enclosure.

'Lieutenant,' said Ellery in a strangled voice. 'Examine this diamond. . . . I mean, *is* it a diamond?'

Inspector Queen removed his hands from his face and said froggily, 'Well, Gerry?'

Lieutenant Farber squinted once through his loupe. 'The hell you say. It's strass—'

'It's what?' said the Inspector piteously.

'Strass, Dick—lead glass—paste. Beautiful job of imitation—as nice as I've ever seen.'

'Lead me to that Santa Claus,' whispered Inspector Queen.

But Santa Claus was being led to him. Struggling in the grip of a dozen detectives, his red coat ripped off, his red pants around his ankles, but his whiskery mask still on his face, came a large shouting man.

'But I tell you,' he was roaring, 'I'm Sergeant Tom Velie! Just take the mask off—that's all!'

'It's a pleasure,' growled Detective Hagstrom, trying to break their prisoner's arm, 'we're reservin' for the Inspector.'

'Hold him, boys,' whispered the Inspector. He struck like a cobra. His hand came away with Santa's face.

And there, indeed, was Sergeant Velie.

'Why, it's Velie,' said the Inspector wonderingly.

'I only told you that a thousand times,' said the Sergeant, folding his great hairy arms across his great hairy chest. 'Now who's the so-and-so who tried to bust my arm?' Then he said, 'My pants!' and as Miss Porter turned delicately away, Detective Hagstrom humbly stooped and raised Sergeant Velie's pants.

'Never mind that,' said a cold, remote voice.

It was the master, himself.

'Yeah?' said Sergeant Velie.

'Velie, weren't you attacked when you went to the men's room just before two?'

'Do I look like the attackable type?'

'You did go to lunch?—in person?'

'And a lousy lunch it was.'

'It was *you* up here among the dolls all afternoon?'

'Nobody else, Maestro. Now, my friends, I want action. Fast patter. What's this all about? Before,' said Sergeant Velie softly, 'I lose my temper.'

While divers headquarters orators delivered impromptu periods before the silent Sergeant, Inspector Richard Queen spoke.

'Ellery. Son. How in the name of the second sin did he do it?'

'Pa,' replied the master, 'you got me.'

Deck the hall with boughs of holly, but not if your name is Queen on the evening of a certain December twenty-fourth. If your name is Queen on that lamentable evening you are seated in the living room of a New York apartment uttering no falalas but staring miserably into a somber fire. And you have company. The guest list is short, but select. It numbers two, a Miss Porter and a Sergeant Velie, and they are no comfort.

No, no ancient Yuletide carol is being trolled; only the silence sings.

Wail in your crypt, Cytherea Ypson; all was for nought; your little dauphin's treasure lies not in the empty coffers of the orphans but in the hot clutch of one who took his evil inspiration from a long-crumbled specialist in vanishments.

Fact: Lieutenant Geronimo Farber of police headquarters had examined the diamond in the genuine dauphin's crown a matter of seconds before it was conveyed to its sanctuary in the enclosure. Lieutenant Farber had pronounced the diamond a diamond, and not merely a diamond, but a diamond worth in his opinion over one hundred thousand dollars.

Fact: It was this genuine diamond and this genuine Dauphin's Doll which Ellery with his own hands had carried into the glass-enclosed fortress and deposited between the authenticated Sergeant Velie's verified feet.

Fact: All day—specifically, between the moment the dauphin had been deposited in his niche until the moment he was discovered to be a fraud; that is, during the total period in which a theft-and-substitution was even theoretically possible—no person whatsoever, male or female, adult or child, had set foot within the enclosure except Sergeant Thomas Velie, alias Santa Claus; and some dozens of persons with police training and specific instructions, not to mention the Queens themselves, Miss Porter, and Attorney Bondling, testified unqualifiedly that Sergeant Velie had not touched the doll, at any time, all day.

Fact: All those deputized to watch the doll swore that they had done so without lapse or hindrance the everlasting day; moreover, that at no time had anything touched the doll—human or mechanical—either from inside or outside the enclosure.

Fact: Despite all the foregoing, at the end of the day they had found the real dauphin gone and a worthless copy in its place.

'It's brilliantly, unthinkably clever,' said Ellery at last. 'A master illusion. For, of course, it *was* an illusion. . . .'

'Witchcraft,' groaned the Inspector.

'Mass mesmerism,' suggested Nikki Porter.

'Mass bird gravel,' growled the Sergeant.

Two hours later Ellery spoke again.

'So Comus had a worthless copy of the dauphin all ready for the switch,' he muttered. 'It's a world-famous dollie, been illustrated countless times, minutely described, photographed. . . . All ready for the switch, but how did he make it? How? How?'

'You said that,' said the Sergeant, 'once or forty-two times.'

'The bells are tolling,' sighed Nikki, 'but for whom? Not for us.' And indeed, while they slumped there, Time, which Seneca named father of truth, had crossed the threshold of Christmas; and Nikki looked alarmed, for as that glorious song of old came upon the midnight clear, a great light spread from Ellery's eyes and beatified the whole contorted countenance, so that peace sat there, the peace that approximateth understanding; and he threw back that noble head and laughed with the merriment of an innocent child.

'Hey,' said Sergeant Velie, staring.

'Son,' began Inspector Queen, half-rising from his armchair; when the telephone rang.

'Beautiful!' roared Ellery. 'Oh, exquisite! How did Comus make the switch, eh? Nikki—'

'From somewhere,' said Nikki, handing him the telephone receiver, 'a voice is calling, and if you ask me it's saying "Comus". Why not ask him?'

'Comus,' whispered the Inspector, shrinking.

'Comus,' echoed the Sergeant, baffled.

'Comus?' said Ellery heartily. 'How nice. Hello there! Congratulations.'

'Why, thank you,' said the familiar deep and hollow voice. 'I called to express my appreciation for a wonderful day's sport and to wish you the merriest kind of Yuletide.'

'You anticipate a rather merry Christmas yourself, I take it.'

'*Laeti triumphantes*,' said Comus jovially.

'And the orphans?'

'They have my best wishes. But I won't detain you, Ellery. If you'll look at the doormat outside your apartment door, you'll find on it— in the spirit of the season—a little gift, with the compliments of Comus. Will you remember me to Inspector Queen and to Attorney Bondling?'

Ellery hung up, smiling.

On the doormat he found the true Dauphin's Doll, intact except for a contemptible detail. The jewel in the little golden crown was missing.

'It was,' said Ellery later, over pastrami sandwiches, 'a fundamentally simple problem. All great illusions are. A valuable object is placed in full view in the heart of an impenetrable enclosure, it is watched hawkishly by dozens of thoroughly screened and reliable trained persons, it is never out of their view, it is not once touched by human hand or any other agency, and yet, at the expiration of the danger period, it is gone—exchanged for a worthless copy. Wonderful. Amazing. It defies the imagination. Actually, it's susceptible—like all magical hocus-pocus—to immediate solution if only one is able—as I was not—to ignore the wonder and stick to the fact. But then, the wonder is there for precisely that purpose: to stand in the way of the fact.

'What is the fact?' continued Ellery, helping himself to a dill pickle. 'The fact is that between the time the doll was placed on the exhibit platform and the time the theft was discovered no one and no thing touched it. Therefore between the time the doll was placed on the platform and the time the theft was discovered *the dauphin could not have been stolen*. It follows, simply and inevitably, that the dauphin must have been stolen *outside that period*.

'Before the period began? No. I placed the authentic dauphin inside the enclosure with my own hands; at or about the beginning of the period, then, no hand but mine had touched the doll—not even, you'll recall, Lieutenant Farber's.

'Then the dauphin must have been stolen after the period closed.'

Ellery brandished half the pickle. 'And who,' he demanded solemnly, 'is the only one besides myself who handled that doll after the period closed and before Lieutenant Farber pronounced the diamond to be paste? *The only one?*'

The Inspector and the Sergeant exchanged puzzled glances, and Nikki looked blank.

'Why, Mr Bondling,' said Nikki, 'and he doesn't count.'

'He counts very much, Nikki,' said Ellery, reaching for the mustard, 'because the facts say Bondling stole the dauphin at that time.'

'Bondling!' The Inspector paled.

'I don't get it,' complained Sergeant Velie.

'Ellery, you must be wrong,' said Nikki. 'At the time Mr Bondling grabbed the doll off the platform, the theft had already taken place. It was the worthless copy he picked up.'

'That,' said Ellery, reaching for another sandwich, 'was the focal point of his illusion. How do we know it was the worthless copy he picked up? Why, he said so. Simple, eh? He said so and like the dumb bunnies we were, we took his unsupported word as gospel.'

'That's right!' mumbled his father. 'We didn't actually examine the doll till quite a few seconds later.'

'Exactly,' said Ellery in a munchy voice. 'There was a short period of beautiful confusion, as Bondling knew there would be. I yelled to the boys to follow and grab Santa Claus—I mean, the Sergeant here.

The detectives were momentarily demoralized. You, dad, were stunned. Nikki looked as if the roof had fallen in. I essayed an excited explanation. Some detectives ran; others milled around. And while all this was happening—during those few moments when nobody was watching the genuine doll in Bondling's hand because everyone thought it was a fake—Bondling calmly slipped it into one of his greatcoat pockets and from the other produced the worthless copy which he'd been carrying there all day. When I did turn back to him, it was the copy I grabbed from his hand. And his illusion was complete.

'I know,' said Ellery dryly, 'it's rather on the let-down side. That's why illusionists guard their professional secrets so closely; knowledge is disenchantment. No doubt the incredulous amazement aroused in his periwigged London audience by Comus the French conjuror's dematerialization of his wife from the top of a table would have suffered the same fate if he'd revealed the trapdoor through which she had dropped. A good trick, like a good woman, is best in the dark. Sergeant, have another pastrami.'

'Seems like funny chow to be eating early Christmas morning,' said the Sergeant, reaching. Then he stopped. Then he said, 'Bondling', and shook his head.

'Now that we know it was Bondling,' said the Inspector, who had recovered a little, 'it's a cinch to get that diamond back. He hasn't had time to dispose of it yet. I'll just give downtown a buzz—'

'Wait, dad,' said Ellery.

'Wait for what?'

'Whom are you going to sic the hounds on?'

'What?'

'You're going to call headquarters, get a warrant, and so on. Who's your man?'

The Inspector felt his head. 'Why . . . Bondling, didn't you say?'

'It might be wise,' said Ellery, thoughtfully searching with his tongue for a pickle seed, 'to specify his alias.'

'Alias?' said Nikki. 'Does he have one?'

'What alias, son?'

'Comus.'

'*Comus!*'

'*Comus?*'

159

'Oh, come off it,' said Nikki, pouring herself a shot of coffee, straight, for she was in training for the Inspector's Christmas dinner. 'How could Bondling be Comus when Bondling was with us all day?—and Comus kept making disguised appearances all over the place . . . that Santa who gave me the note in front of the bank—the old man who kidnapped Lance Morganstern—the fat man with the mustache who snatched Mrs Rafferty's purse.'

'Yeah,' said the Sergeant. 'How?'

'These illusions die hard,' said Ellery. 'Wasn't it Comus who phoned a few minutes ago to rag me about the theft? Wasn't it Comus who said he'd left the stolen dauphin—minus the diamond—on our doormat? Therefore Comus is Bondling.

'I told you Comus never does anything without a good reason,' said Ellery. 'Why did "Comus" announce to "Bondling" that he was *going* to steal the Dauphin's Doll? Bondling told us that—putting the finger on his *alter ego*—because he wanted us to believe he and Comus were separate individuals. He wanted us to watch for *Comus* and take *Bondling* for granted. In tactical execution of this strategy Bondling provided us with three "Comus" appearances during the day—obviously, confederates.

'Yes,' said Ellery, 'I think, dad, you'll find on backtracking that the great thief you've been trying to catch for five years has been a respectable estate attorney on Park Row all the time, shedding his quiddities and his quillets at night in favor of the soft shoe and the dark lantern. And now he'll have to exchange them all for a number and a grilled door. Well, well, it couldn't have happened at a more appropriate season; there's an old English proverb that says the Devil makes his Christmas pie of lawyers' tongues. Nikki, pass the pastrami.'

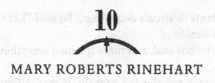

10

MARY ROBERTS RINEHART

The Splinter

The doorbell roused young Doctor Mitchell from an exhausted nap on the old sofa in his office. It also set off a series of yaps and squeals from the dogs in the hospital behind him, and he waited for the third peal of the bell before he grunted and got up. There was something urgent about the last one, as though someone was practically leaning against the bell. It annoyed him. For the past three days and nights, along with other men, he had ranged the wooded hills behind the town, looking for a lost child. Now he was stiff and tired.

'What the hell!' he muttered, as the bell rang again.

He limped to the street door and flung it open with unreasonable fury.

'Look,' he began, 'get your finger off that thing and . . .'

He stopped abruptly. A small and rather frightened boy was standing there. In the early morning light he looked pale, and the freckles on his face stood out distinctly.

'Can I come in, mister?' he said. 'I don't want anybody to see me.'

Mitchell stepped aside and the boy darted into the office. Only then did Mitchell realize that the boy was carrying a small dog, and that he looked a little frightened.

'Sit down, son,' he said. 'Got your dog there, I see. Well, that's my business. What's wrong? Eat something he shouldn't?'

The boy sat down. He looked rather better now. A little of his color had come back.

'He's not mine,' he said. 'I guess you could say I stole him.'

But Mitchell had recognized the dog by that time. He stared at the boy.

'That's Johnny Watson's dog, Wags,' he said. 'Let's hear about it. Why did you steal him?'

'I had to,' the boy said, as if that explained everything, and then he sat very still.

Mitchell inspected the lad gravely. It was Johnny Watson for whom he and the posse of citizens had been searching. At first, the search had been more or less desultory, for Johnny was known to have a roving foot. At the age of seven he had already set a local record for the number of times he had been missing, but previously he had always come home of his own accord or been discovered and brought back.

Usually, Johnny's excursions were brief. He was picked up and returned home within a few hours. But this time was different. The entire town knew that he always took his dog with him, and on the evening of the day he disappeared a deer hunter found the dog up on Bald Hill, a mile or so back of the town, and carried him down. Carried him, because the dog was too lame and exhausted to walk.

The hunter took him to the police station in the county courthouse, and the chief of police sent for the boy's aunt, a Mrs Hunt, with whom he lived.

'This Johnny's dog?' he asked.

She eyed the tired little creature without pleasure.

'I suppose it is,' she said. 'You can keep him. I don't want him. If you ask me Johnny's been kidnaped.'

'Kidnaped? What for?' the chief snapped. 'He hasn't any money, nor have you, Hattie. Don't be a fool. And you're taking the dog back, whether you want him or not.'

That was the evening of the first day, but by the end of the second the town began to rouse. People were talking, for everybody knew Johnny, with his wide blue eyes and his endearing grin. Everybody knew Wags too, and when another day had gone by, a posse was formed to search the hills. No Johnny was found, however. Now he had been missing for five days, and hope had practically been abandoned.

Knowing all this, Doc Mitchell eyed the boy who was holding Johnny's dog in his arms. The youngster was nine, possibly ten, a well-built sturdy lad with a tousled head and a pudgy nose.

'All right,' Mitchell said. 'So you stole him. I suppose you had a reason. Better be a good one, son.'

'I think Mrs Hunt wants him to die,' he said simply. 'She keeps him tied in the yard day and night, in the cold. And he's lame, too. His foot's awful sore.'

Carefully he put the dog on the floor, and Mitchell saw that he was standing on three legs.

'Why on earth do you think she wants him to die?' he asked sharply.

'All the kids think so, mister,' the boy said quietly. 'They think she knows where Johnny is, and she doesn't care if he's found or not.'

'That's a pretty bad thing to say,' Mitchell snapped. He got up and lifted the dog. He was thin, and one paw was badly swollen; but he seemed to realize he was in friendly hands, and wagged his stubby tail.

'Hello, Wags,' the young veterinary said. 'In a bit of trouble, eh? Want me to look at it?' He glanced at the boy, who looked more cheerful.

'I thought if you would fix his foot, and maybe hide him here for a while, I'd pay for him. I've got two dollars.'

Mitchell smiled.

'Let's not bother about that just yet,' he said. 'I like dogs, and I've always got one or two free boarders around the place. Anyhow, Wags and I are old friends. Johnny used to bring him in now and then. Want to stick around while I look at the foot?'

'I'd like to, if it's all right with you.'

Mitchell took the boy to the small operating room, and as he prepared the table he learned who he was. His name was Harold Johnson, but he was usually called Pete. He lived in the house next to the Hunt place, and he knew Johnny well and liked him. Mitchell eyed Pete.

'Have the kids got any idea where Johnny went?' he said casually. But to his surprise the boy's face went suddenly blank.

'No, sir,' he said flatly. 'Only Wags kept trying to get up into the hills, before she tied him.'

Mitchell did not press the subject. He picked up the dog and put him on his side on the table. Wags did not move. It was as though he knew something good was going to be done to him, and except for a low whine he was quiet while Mitchell examined the paw.

'Looks like he's got something in it,' he said. 'I'll have to open it, son. Want to hold him while I get after it?'

'Yes, sir. I'd like to.'

Looking down at him, Mitchell had an absurd desire to pat the boy's hair, which needed cutting and had a cowlick to boot. He restrained himself and picked up a scalpel.

'Better not look,' he said. 'It'll take only a couple of seconds.' And a few moments later, 'All over, son. Now let's see what we found.'

What he drew out with the forceps was a long wooden splinter, and Pete gave him a sickly grin.

'So that's what it was,' the boy said, and letting go of the dog found a chair and sat down.

Mitchell held the splinter up and examined it, and he rather thought the dog looked at it too. At least he raised his head. Then he dropped it back again and closed his eyes.

'Looks as though this came off a board somewhere,' he said. 'No houses up in the hills, are there? Nobody lives there that I know of.'

Pete didn't know. Except for visits to a picnic ground not far away, the town children were not allowed in the hills. There were stories of bears, and one had been shot there not too long ago. Pete was looking better now, but he waited until Wags had been put into a cage before he came out with what was in his mind.

'Look, mister,' he said. 'Maybe Johnny comes back, or maybe he doesn't. But could you keep this a sort of secret? Mrs Hunt could have me arrested.'

'Why wouldn't Johnny come back? Any place we could have missed looking for him?'

Pete looked unhappy.

'I guess not, if he was where you could see him,' he said.

'What does that mean?' Mitchell asked sharply. But Pete slid off his chair and picked up his cap.

'That's just talk,' he said. 'And thanks a lot. It's time I went home for my breakfast.'

Mitchell watched the boy leave. He was a likable kid, he thought. But before he went upstairs to his apartment for a shower he called Joe, his assistant, into his office.

'We've got a new boarder,' he said. 'He needs sleep right now, but when he wakes up give him a good feed. And if anyone enquires for him we haven't got him.'

'What's the idea?' said Joe. 'We got him and we ain't got him. We got plenty, Doc, without stealing them.'

'He's Wags, Johnny Watson's dog,' Mitchell said. 'And I wish to God he could talk. He knows something, Joe.'

Joe looked startled.

'You think he knows where the boy went, Doc?'

'I think he knows where the boy is. That may be something different. And stop calling me "Doc".'

The next morning, after coffee in his apartment upstairs, Mitchell made his rounds of his small hospital, doing dressings, putting a new cast on the broken leg of a Great Dane, inspecting a blue Persian cat who had had difficulty with her first litter of kittens, and feeding a banana to a small chimp left there by a traveling carnival. Johnny Watson had loved the chimp. The last time he had been in they had been sitting together, and the boy had had his arms around the small ape.

It made Mitchell feel a little heartsick to remember.

By noon he took off his professional coat and dressed for the street, and soon after he was in the office of the chief of police.

The chief looked tired.

'Look, Doc,' he said, 'I hope this is important. I ain't as young as I used to be, and this last three days have about finished me. All I want is to get home and soak in a hot bath.'

Mitchell nodded.

'Maybe it's important, maybe not, Chief,' he said. 'You know these hills pretty well. Any cabins in them?'

'Cabins? No, not that I know of. Hunters who go in there use tents. Was a bunk-house on Bald Hill for workers in the old quarry about twenty years ago, but they moved out after the highway was finished. Only a ruin now. Roof's fallen in.' He eyed Mitchell curiously. 'Why? We searched the quarry and the bunk-house too, what's left of it. Combed the whole place. The boy's not there.'

'That's not far from where the dog was found, is it?'

'Still got a bee in your bonnet, Doc, haven't you?' the chief said quizzically. 'Yep. Used to be a road up there to the quarry, but it's gone now. Only a sort of track. Dog was near it, all tuckered out.'

Mitchell lit a cigarette and smoked it absently.

'That's a mile or so away,' he said. 'What was the dog doing there?'

The chief grunted.

'Chasing a squirrel or a rabbit, and got lost. That's easy.'

Mitchell got up.

'It's too easy, Chief,' he said. 'Why did the boy keep running away? Got any ideas about it? I suppose a psychiatrist would say there was a reason for it.'

'I'm no psychiatrist,' the chief said, yawning. 'I'm only a cop. How the hell should I know?'

Mitchell persisted. 'What about the Hunt woman? Think she had anything to do with it? Was she good to the boy?'

The chief looked indignant.

'Now look,' he said, 'I've known Hattie Hunt all my life. She's pretty well on in years to raise a kid. But she fed him and took care of him. She did her duty to him, and that's a fact.'

Mitchell was thoughtful.

'Orphan, wasn't he?'

'Yep. Plane crash. Both parents killed. Damned lucky for the boy he wasn't with them. The father had the promise of a job on the Coast, and during a stopover in Nebraska the kid fell and broke his leg. They had to leave him in a hospital in Omaha, so when the authorities found the mother's purse in the wreck, with a letter in it from Hattie, they notified me and sent me the letter. I told Hattie, and she went out and got him. Got the dog too. Seems a nurse in the hospital gave it to him. Pretty hard on the old girl, if you ask me.'

'Where did all this happen?'

'Somewhere out near Omaha, I forget the place.'

'You still have the letter?'

The chief stared at him.

'Look, Doc,' he said. 'That's three years ago, and what the hell has it got to do with the boy's disappearance?'

'Only what I said—that it's queer for a child to keep running away time after time.'

'You get them now and then,' the chief said indifferently. 'Kids with a wandering foot.' He grinned. 'Lots of dogs do that too, don't they? Only they usually have a damn good reason!'

This small jest seemed to please the chief; he got up and straightened himself with a grunt.

'I'm going home and get a hot bath and a decent meal for a change,' he said. 'But maybe I do have the letter. I'll see.'

He went stiffly to an ancient wooden file in a corner and fumbled with one of the drawers lettered *H*, from which he took out a pair of bedroom slippers and a soiled shirt, which last he greeted with pleasure.

'So that's where the damned thing was,' he said, gratified. 'If you'd heard my wife going on about it you'd have thought I was involved with another woman. Well, let's see.'

In due time he located a folder and brought it back to the desk. The letter *H* seemed to cover a number of things, from a stolen horse to a prescription for falling hair; but at last he produced a letter and passed it triumphantly to Mitchell. It had come from the Police Department of Omaha, Nebraska, and was a brief description of the parents' death and the boy's situation. Enclosed was the letter from Mrs Hunt to the dead woman. It was not a particularly affectionate one.

Dear Emily, it said. *In answer to your request I can only say I am totally unable to help you. As you know I objected and still object to your marriage. Aside from that I have barely adequate means to live on, and your suggestion that I help you because you have a child is outrageous. That is your fault and your husband's responsibility. Certainly not mine.*

There was no closing—it was merely signed Hattie Hunt, and the writing was small and crabbed. Mitchell handed back the letter, but made a note of the date of the one from the Omaha police. The chief watched him with amusement.

'So what?' he said. 'There was a receipt from the hospital in the purse too, so they located the boy and Hattie went West and got the kid. Only thing she objected to was the dog, but Johnny wouldn't let go of him. Raised hell when she tried to leave him behind. Maybe you can understand that, Mitch. You must like dogs, to be in your business.'

'I like them better than some people,' Mitchell said drily.

He left soon after that, feeling a little foolish. All he had was a dog with a sore paw, a rather large splinter from a board of some sort, and a boy named Pete who almost certainly believed Johnny was dead.

Still, that in itself was curious. Children did not usually think in such terms. However, what with radio and television these days . . .

That afternoon Mitchell put the splinter from Wags' paw under his microscope and examined it carefully. It was pine, he thought, from an old piece of pine board, and of course there were a dozen explanations for it. Only one thing was sure. It had been in the dog's foot for several days, to have caused the fester it had.

What had Pete meant about the Hunt woman? Mitchell knew her merely by sight, a dour-looking woman of sixty or thereabouts, always shabbily dressed in rusty black, and with a hard unsmiling face. Not the loving sort, to judge by her letter, and that was an understatement if he ever heard one. But it was a long way from murder. And why murder anyhow? What possible motive would she have for getting rid of the boy?

He sat back, considering. Up to the finding of Wags on Bald Hill, Johnny's disappearance had been regarded as one of his normal wayward excursions. It was only afterwards that things looked ominous, since boy and dog were inseparable, and then search parties had started out. Maybe the kids had something, he thought, and after some hesitation he wrote out and telephoned a night letter to the police in Omaha, wording it carefully because of the local operator.

'Seven-year-old boy named John Watson missing here. Was injured in accident your neighborhood three years ago and taken to hospital your city. Possibly trying to make his way back. Be glad of any details of said accident and name of hospital. Please wire collect.'

He gave his name and address, and was rewarded by the warmth in the night operator's voice after she read it back to him.

'You know,' she said. 'I never thought of that. I'll bet that's just what Johnny's doing.'

'It's a possibility, anyhow,' he said. 'Just keep it to yourself, will you? I don't want to hurt the chief's feelings.'

'That old blabbermouth!'

Mitchell made his final rounds at ten o'clock that night, and Wags seemed comfortable. He decided to walk off his uneasiness, and it was a half hour later when he found himself near the Hunt property. It stood back from the street, as did the other houses in the vicinity, and in the moonless night it looked dark and gloomy, a two-story frame building once white and now a dirty gray against its background of low hills. It was unlighted save for a dim glow from a rear window—the kitchen, he thought—and rather amused at himself, he turned in and went quietly to the back of the house.

Seen through a window, the kitchen proved to be empty and he was about to leave when he became aware of a small figure beside him.

'She's out looking for Wags,' Pete whispered. 'She's gone up the hill with a flashlight. Why would she think he goes up there? It's kinda funny, isn't it?'

'I wouldn't know, son,' Mitchell said frankly. 'It's pretty rough going. I'll wait here a while, so you'd better go home. You don't want your mother coming out after you, do you?'

Left alone, the young doctor watched the hill behind the house, but no light appeared, and after a few minutes he stepped onto the porch and tried the kitchen door. It was unlocked, and with a prayer that Pete was not watching he stepped inside. It was a dreary room, floored with old linoleum, and with a tin coffee pot on a rusty stove. It looked as though little cooking was done there, and with a final look at the hillside he moved into the house itself.

He had no flashlight, but by using a match here and there he got a fair idea of the rooms. They showed neatness but a sort of genteel poverty, and even in the basement there was no sign of a board from which Wags could have got the splinter. Only on the second floor did he find anything odd. If Johnny Watson had ever lived there there was no sign of it. Just one room, obviously Mrs Hunt's, showed any signs of occupancy. The others were bleak and empty, even to the closets.

It seemed incredible that the boy's room should be empty. Had she sent him away, *clothes and all?* It was the only explanation he could think of, and he began to think his previous apprehension might have been absurd. Nevertheless, he was infuriated—remembering the long hard search and the anxious town, while in all probability she had known all along where the boy was.

He got out of the house just in time. There was a light coming down the hill. It came steadily to the edge of the woods. Then whoever carried it stopped and extinguished it. Mitchell slid around the corner of the house and waited until, by the light from the kitchen window, he recognized Mrs Hunt. She was in a heavy coat, with a handkerchief tied over her head, and at the foot of the steps he confronted her. He could hear her gasp as he greeted her.

'Good evening,' he said. 'Sorry if I frightened you. I was taking a walk, and I saw your light in the woods. Nothing wrong, is there?'

For a moment she could not speak. She had obviously been badly scared, and she dropped the flashlight, as though she could no longer hold it. When he picked it up she made no move to take it.

'Who are you?' she said. 'Whoever you are you've no business here. What are you doing—spying on me?'

'Not at all.' His voice was casual. 'I thought someone might be in trouble. My name's Mitchell—Doctor Mitchell. If you're all right I'll be going on.'

But she had recovered by that time and eyed him suspiciously.

'So that's who you are!' she said angrily. 'Maybe you know where my dog is. Maybe that boy next door stole him and took him to you. If you've got him I want him back, or I'll make plenty of trouble.'

He laughed.

'That's rather fantastic, isn't it?' he said. 'Why should the boy do anything like that? Was the dog sick?'

She ignored that, sitting down abruptly on the kitchen steps, and Mitchell held out the flashlight to her. In doing so he snapped the light on, and he had a momentary glimpse of her. Wherever she had been she had had no easy time. The heavy coat had accumulated considerable brush and pine needles, and below it her stockings were torn to rags. She looked exhausted too, her elderly face an ugly gray. He cut off her protests as he gave her the flashlight.

'If it's Johnny's dog you're talking about,' he said, 'I'd be a little slow about accusing this boy, whoever he is. Any kid who knew Wags—and a lot of them did—might have taken him.'

She seemed to be thinking that over. Then she got up and climbed the steps.

'Well, let whoever has him keep him,' she said. 'I don't like dogs. I never did.'

It was no use going on, he realized, and she ended the conversation by going into the house and slamming the kitchen door. In a sense he felt relieved. If she had sent the boy away he was probably all right, and with this hope, and because he was tired from the days of searching, Mitchell slept rather late the next morning.

The answer from Omaha arrived at noon that day. It was fully detailed, having been sent collect, and it verified the airplane crash and the deaths of the Watsons; also the boy's broken leg and his having been claimed by a relative named Mrs Hunt. It added something however which puzzled him. It said: *Left for East by car.*

He wandered in again to see the chief that afternoon. Evidently his wife had taken him in hand, for the chief wore a clean shirt and even a necktie. He was in a bad humor, however.

'Now see here, Doc,' he said, 'the Johnny Watson case is closed, and I'm damned glad of it. Unless,' he added suspiciously, 'you've got the dog. In that case you're under arrest, and no fooling.'

Mitchell managed to look surprised.

'Dog?' he said. 'What dog?'

'All right, so you haven't got him,' the chief growled. 'Probably chewed the rope and got away. What brings you here anyhow?'

'I just had an idea,' Mitchell said. 'What would you do with a kid you didn't want? How would you get rid of him? By car?'

The chief eyed him.

'Well, God knows there are times when I could spare some of mine,' he said. 'What are you talking about? The Hunt woman didn't get rid of Johnny. You can bet on that. She had nothing to gain by it. Besides, she has no car, if that's what you mean, and couldn't drive it if she had one.'

Mitchell was puzzled as he left. How could Mrs Hunt have spirited Johnny away?—if she had done so. Not by bus, or train, that was sure. Both trainmen and bus drivers knew the little blond boy and his dog by sight. Yet the empty room in the Hunt house certainly meant she did not expect him back. There was only one other explanation—and that was one he did not have to accept.

As a result he motored into the city that afternoon, carrying the splinter from Wags' foot in a cellophane envelope, and went to the crime laboratory at police headquarters. After a long delay he got to a technician and had it put under a microscope, where a young man in a white coat worked over it.

'Nothing very interesting about it,' he said after a time. 'Looks like blood and pus on it, if that's what you want.'

'No, I want to know about the splinter itself. What is it?'

'Pine,' said the laboratory man. 'Probably came off a board. Apparently been varnished at one time. Mean anything to you?'

'Not unless I can find where it came from,' Mitchell said grimly, and took his departure.

Down on the street he stood by his car and wondered what else he could do. After all, the youngster had been gone before, although never as long as this. And there was no real reason to believe this was not simply another runaway. All Mitchell had was a small boy's belief something had happened to Johnny, a dog with a splinter which might have come from anywhere, and a woman who apparently did not expect the child to come back.

So strongly was all this in his mind that he was not really surprised to see her in person. She did not notice him, but she had come out of a garage across the street, and it seemed so strange a place for her to be that he waited until he saw her take the bus back home before he went in himself.

There were a couple of chauffeurs loafing there, and somewhere in the back an employee was working on the tube of a tire. In a corner was a small glass-enclosed office with a clerk at a desk, and after looking about Mitchell went in there. The man looked up annoyed, after making an entry in a ledger, and Mitchell's voice was apologetic.

'Sorry to bother you,' he said, 'but I was to take my aunt home in my car. I'm afraid I missed her. Elderly woman in black.'

The clerk nodded.

'You missed her all right, brother,' he said. 'At least it sounds like her.'

Mitchell nodded.

'I try to keep an eye on her,' he said. 'She's peculiar at times. She wasn't trying to buy a car, was she?'

'Buy a car!' The clerk grinned. 'She's had an old second-hand one here in dead storage for three years. Never took it out, but comes in now and then to pay her storage bill. Name's Barnes. That right?'

'Not my aunt, then,' Mitchell said, and was about to leave when the man spoke again.

'Funny thing about this old dame,' he said. 'Keeps it here all that time, and now she wants it. Came in ten days ago or so and ordered it put in condition in a hurry. Then never showed up again until today!'

'Did she say when she wanted it?' Mitchell hoped his voice was steady. 'Might be my aunt after all. She gets ideas like that.'

'No. Just wanted it ready. Said she might need it soon. That's all.'

Mitchell went rather dazedly into the street. Some things were clear, of course. What had happened to the car in which she had brought the boy East, for instance. And she had meant to use it again a few days ago, only Wags had been found and as a result the search had been started. She had not dared make a move then, but that either the boy or his body was hidden away somewhere Mitchell no longer doubted, and his blood froze as he considered the possibilities.

Why had she wanted to get rid of the child? And why had the body not been found? She gained nothing by his death, if that was what had happened. Or did she? Some inkling of the truth stirred in him, and it frightened him with its implications. As soon as he got home he called the hospital in Omaha and listened with interest to the reply.

'Caused some excitement, I suppose?' he said.

'What do you think?' said the remote voice.

That afternoon for the first time he really believed Johnny Watson was dead. It was without any enthusiasm that he received Joe's report on Wags.

'Foot's fine,' Joe said. 'Only he ain't too happy, Doc. He ain't eatin' right, for one thing. I gave him a mess of good hamburger today, and he just looked at it.'

'I'm going to need him tonight, Joe,' Mitchell said. 'I'll carry him if I have to, but you don't know where he is. Get that?'

Joe looked bewildered.

'That woman, she's raisin' hell about him,' he said dolefully. 'You want to get into trouble?'

'Very likely,' Mitchell said drily. 'I don't know just when I'll be taking him, but I have an idea where he wants to go.'

At 6 o'clock—supper time in the town—he called Pete on the phone and asked him if Pete was busy that night. When the boy said he was not, only some homework, Mitchell said he had a job for him.

'I want to know if Mrs Hunt leaves her house tonight,' he said. 'Can you do it? And if she does will you telephone me at once?'

'Sure. That's easy,' Pete said excitedly.

'All right. Only don't try to follow her. Just call me up here. I'll be waiting.'

Nothing happened that night, however, and the next day was endless. Mitchell did his usual work without enthusiasm, and late in the afternoon dropped in on a harassed police chief, who scowled when he saw him.

'If it's about the Watson kid,' he said sourly, 'why don't you mind your own business, which is dogs?'

Mitchell grinned and lit a cigarette.

'All right,' he said. 'Now I'll ask you one. Where up in the hills would the dog Wags get a splinter of varnished wood in his foot?'

'Well, for God's sake!' the chief exploded. 'Where does any dog pick up a splinter?'

'It lamed him so badly he couldn't walk. Remember where he was found. The fellow who found him had to carry him back to town. Remember that?'

'It just occurs to me,' the chief said suspiciously, 'that you know too damned much about this dog. How'd you learn about a splinter?'

'I took it out of his foot,' Mitchell said, and slammed out of the office.

He expected trouble after that, but evidently the chief was not interested. At 6 o'clock Pete called up to say he would be on the job again that night, if it was okay. Mitchell said it was certainly okay with him, and rang off grinning. But after that the evening seemed endless. He stayed near the telephone, trying to read a copy of *Veterinary Medicine*, but when by 9 o'clock there was no message from Pete he finally called the boy's home. Pete, however, was not there, and his mother was worried.

'He left quite a while ago,' she said. 'I don't know what got into him. I was using the phone about the young people's meeting at the church, and he acted very excited. Then when I finished he was gone.'

'He didn't say where he was going?'

'No. But he said if you called I was to tell you somebody had started up the hill. I wasn't really listening. Only he knows he isn't allowed up there, and it's too late for him to go to the movies.'

Mitchell was sure where Pete had gone, and he felt a cold chill down his spine. How long had he been gone? And what would happen if he overtook the Hunt woman? She must be desperate by this time, if what Mitchell believed was true. Wherever Johnny was hidden, alive or dead, she would be on her way there now, and Pete was not safe in the hands of a half-crazed woman.

He never remembered much that followed. He must have picked up Wags and got into his car, and some time later he was climbing through woods and dense underbrush, using his flashlight cautiously. But it seemed an interminable time and an endless struggle when, with the dog in his arms, he saw a light moving slowly, ahead and above him.

The dog saw it too and whined, and Mitchell put a hand over his muzzle. After that he was even more cautious, climbing carefully and without his flash. Once he fell headlong and almost lost the dog.

It seemed an hour or more before he reached the edge of the clearing on Bald Hill and stopped. Mrs Hunt was there, near the ruined bunk-house, sitting as though exhausted on a fallen timber, and his heart contracted sharply as he saw that she held a long-handled spade in her hands.

There was no sign of Pete, but Wags had recognized the place. He gave a short sharp bark and leaped out of Mitchell's arms. In a second he had shot past the woman and was scratching furiously at the door of a small shack adjoining the bunk-house. The woman leaped to her feet and caught up the spade.

'You little devil!' she said hoarsely. 'Just stay there till I get you.'

Then Mitchell heard Pete's shrill young voice from somewhere among the trees.

'Don't you touch him,' he screamed at her. 'Let him alone. And I'm getting the police. You're a bad wicked woman.'

From the stirring in the underbrush Mitchell realized that Pete was running down the hill, and drew a long breath. The woman seemed stunned. She barely noticed him as he approached her.

'All right,' he said. 'Where is he, Mrs Hunt?'

She did not speak, but after a moment she raised a heavy hand and pointed to the shack near the bunk-house, where the dog was scratching wildly at an improvised door of old pine boards. And where a little boy inside was calling weakly:

'Hello, Wags,' he said. 'I knew you'd come back.'

Early the next morning Mitchell sat in the chief's office, looking smug.

'So you combed the whole place!' he said. 'Why on earth didn't you look in that shack?'

'Why the hell should I?' the chief said irritably. 'It was boarded up and bolted on the outside. The boy couldn't lock himself in from the outside, could he? Why didn't he yell?'

'Probably afraid it was her,' Mitchell said. 'He was always afraid of her. That's why he kept running off. Or he may have been given a dose of sleeping pills. I don't suppose we'll ever know. But I imagine she didn't mean to do anything drastic in the beginning. Maybe take him by car to the Coast and get rid of him in a home, or something of the sort. But when she learned from the insurance company a day or so ago that she had to produce a body or wait seven years for the money . . .'

'Money! What money?'

'Oh, didn't I tell you?' Mitchell said, as if surprised. 'His parents took out airplane accident insurance before they left Omaha, naming the boy as beneficiary. Twenty-five thousand each. It didn't cost much. And the company paid it to Johnny in the hospital, with your friend Hattie as guardian, or something like that. I imagine,' he added smoothly, 'that fifty thousand dollars has been eating her heart out. She's his only relative.'

'Are you saying she meant to *murder* him?' the chief said incredulously.

'I am. Only you'll never jail her. She'll go to an institution somewhere.'

He ignored the chief's shocked face and dropped something on the desk.

'You might like to have this,' he said. 'It's the splinter that saved Johnny Watson's life.'

He left the chief staring at it in complete bewilderment and drove

The Splinter

back to his hospital, where Joe eyed him skeptically, his torn clothes, his dirty face, and unshaven jaw.

'Must have had a big night, Doc,' he said. 'How's the other fellow?'

'Doing fine in the hospital,' Mitchell said cheerfully. 'How's Wags?'

'Looks like he's had a big night too,' he said. 'But he's sleepin' fine.'

'Good for him,' Mitchell said, and went upstairs.

Downstairs it was feeding time, with the usual pandemonium of whines and barks, and he was reminded of the talk he had had with the chief of police a day or so ago. He had said then that he liked some dogs better than some people, and all at once he knew why.

11

RAYMOND CHANDLER

The Pencil

He was a slightly fat man with a dishonest smile that pulled the corners of his mouth out half an inch leaving the thick lips tight and his eyes bleak. For a fattish man he had a slow walk. Most fat men are brisk and light on their feet. He wore a gray herringbone suit and a handpainted tie with part of a diving girl visible on it. His shirt was clean, which comforted me, and his brown loafers, as wrong as the tie for his suit, shone from a recent polishing.

He sidled past me as I held the door between the waiting room and my thinking parlor. Once inside, he took a quick look around. I'd have placed him as a mobster, second grade, if I had been asked. For once I was right. If he carried a gun, it was inside his pants. His coat was too tight to hide the bulge of an underarm holster.

He sat down carefully and I sat opposite and we looked at each other. His face had a sort of foxy eagerness. He was sweating a little. The expression on my face was meant to be interested but not clubby. I reached for a pipe and the leather humidor in which I kept my Pearce's tobacco. I pushed the cigarettes at him.

'I don't smoke.' He had a rusty voice. I didn't like it any more than I liked his clothes, or his face. While I filled the pipe he reached inside his coat, prowled in a pocket, came out with a bill, glanced at it, and dropped it across the desk in front of me. It was a nice bill and clean and new. One thousand dollars.

'Ever save a guy's life?'
'Once in a while, maybe.'
'Save mine.'
'What goes?'

'I heard you leveled with the customers, Marlowe.'

'That's why I stay poor.'

'I still got two friends. You make it three and you'll be out of the red. You got five grand coming if you pry me loose.'

'From what?'

'You're talkative as hell this morning. Don't you pipe who I am?'

'Nope.'

'Never been east, huh?'

'Sure—but I wasn't in your set.'

'What set would that be?'

I was getting tired of it. 'Stop being so damn cagey or pick up your grand and be missing.'

'I'm Ikky Rossen. I'll be missing but good unless you can figure something out. Guess.'

'I've already guessed. You tell me and tell me quick. I don't have all day to watch you feeding me with an eye-dropper.'

'I ran out on the Outfit. The high boys don't go for that. To them it means you got info you figure you can peddle, or you got independent ideas, or you lost your moxie. Me, I lost my moxie. I had it up to here.' He touched his Adam's apple with the forefinger of a stretched hand. 'I done bad things. I scared and hurt guys. I never killed nobody. That's nothing to the Outfit. I'm out of line. So they pick up the pencil and they draw a line. I got the word. The operators are on the way. I made a bad mistake. I tried to hole up in Vegas. I figured they'd never expect me to lie up in their own joint. They outfigured me. What I did's been done before, but I didn't know it. When I took the plane to LA there must have been somebody on it. They know where I live.'

'Move.'

'No good now. I'm covered.'

I knew he was right.

'Why haven't they taken care of you already?'

'They don't do it that way. Always specialists. Don't you know how it works?'

'More or less. A guy with a nice hardware store in Buffalo. A guy with a small dairy in KC. Always a good front. They report back to New York or somewhere. When they mount the plane west or wherever they're going, they have guns in their briefcases. They're quiet and well dressed and they don't sit together. They could be a couple of lawyers or income-tax sharpies—anything at all that's well mannered and inconspicuous. All sorts of people carry briefcases. Including women.'

'Correct as hell. And when they land they'll be steered to me, but not from the airfield. They got ways. If I go to the cops, somebody will know about me. They could have a couple Mafia boys right on the city council for all I know. The cops will give me twenty-four hours to leave town. No use. Mexico? Worse than here. Canada? Better but still no good. Connections there too.'

'Australia?'

'Can't get a passport. I been here twenty-five years—illegal. They can't deport me unless they can prove a crime on me. The Outfit would see they didn't. Suppose I got tossed into the freezer. I'm out on a writ in twenty-four hours. And my nice friends got a car waiting to take me home—only not home.'

I had my pipe lit and going well. I frowned down at the one-grand note. I could use it very nicely. My checking account could kiss the sidewalk without stooping.

'Let's stop horsing,' I said. 'Suppose—just suppose—I could figure an out for you. What's your next move?'

'I know a place—if I could get there without bein' tailed. I'd leave my car here and take a rent car. I'd turn it in just short of the county line and buy a secondhand job. Halfway to where I'm going I trade it on a new last-year's model, a leftover—this is just the right time of year. Good discount, new models out soon. Not to save money—less show off. Where I'd go is a good-sized place but still pretty clean.'

'Uh-huh,' I said. 'Wichita, last I heard. But it might have changed.'

He scowled at me. 'Get smart, Marlowe, but not too damn smart.'

'I'll get as smart as I want to. Don't try to make rules for me. If I take this on, there aren't any rules. I take it for this grand and the rest if I bring it off. Don't cross me. I might leak information. If I get knocked off, put just one red rose on my grave. I don't like cut flowers. I like to see them growing. But I could take one because you're such a sweet character. When's the plane in?'

'Sometime today. It's nine hours from New York. Probably come in around five-thirty p.m.'

'Might come by San Diego and switch or by San Francisco and switch. A lot of planes from both places. I need a helper.'

'Damn you, Marlowe—'

'Hold it. I know a girl. Daughter of a chief of police who got broken for honesty. She wouldn't leak under torture.'

'You got no right to risk her,' Ikky said angrily.

I was so astonished my jaw hung halfway to my waist. I closed it slowly and swallowed.

'Good God, the man's got a heart.'

'Women ain't built for the rough stuff,' he said grudgingly.

I picked up the thousand-dollar note and snapped it. 'Sorry. No receipt,' I said. 'I can't have my name in your pocket. And there won't be any rough stuff if I'm lucky. They'd have me outclassed. There's only one way to work it. Now give me your address and all the dope you can think of—names, descriptions of any operators you have ever seen in the flesh.'

He did. He was a pretty good observer. Trouble was, the Outfit would know what he had seen. The operators would be strangers to him.

He got up silently and put his hand out. I had to shake it, but what he had said about women made it easier. His hand was moist. Mine would have been in his spot. He nodded and went out silently.

It was a quiet street in Bay City, if there are any quiet streets in this beatnik generation when you can't get through a meal without some male or female stomach-singer belching out a kind of love that is as old-fashioned as a bustle or some Hammond organ jazzing it up in the customer's soup.

The little one-story house was as neat as a fresh pinafore. The front lawn was cut lovingly and very green. The smooth composition driveway was free of grease spots from standing cars, and the hedge that bordered it looked as though the barber came every day.

The white door had a knocker with a tiger's head, a go-to-hell window, and a dingus that let someone inside talk to someone outside without even opening the little window.

I'd have given a mortgage on my left leg to live in a house like that. I didn't think I ever would.

The bell chimed inside and after a while she opened the door in a pale-blue sports shirt and white shorts that were short enough to be friendly. She had gray-blue eyes, dark red hair, and fine bones in her face. There was usually a trace of bitterness in the gray-blue eyes. She couldn't forget that her father's life had been destroyed by the crooked power of a gambling-ship mobster, that her mother had died too.

She was able to suppress the bitterness when she wrote nonsense about young love for the shiny magazines, but this wasn't her life. She didn't really have a life. She had an existence without much pain and enough money to make it safe. But in a tight spot she was as cool and resourceful as a good cop. Her name was Anne Riordan.

She stood to one side and I passed her pretty close. But I have rules too. She shut the door and parked herself on a sofa and went through the cigarette routine, and here was one doll who had the strength to light her own cigarette.

I stood looking around. There were a few changes, not many.

'I need your help,' I said.

'The only time I ever see you.'

'I've got a client who is an ex-hood, used to be a troubleshooter for the Outfit, the Syndicate, the big mob, or whatever name you want to use for it. You know damn well it exists and is as rich as Midas. You can't beat it because not enough people want to, especially the million-a-year lawyers who work for it.'

'My God, are you running for office somewhere? I never heard you sound so pure.'

She moved her legs around, not provocatively—she wasn't the type—but it made it difficult for me to think straight just the same.

'Stop moving your legs around,' I said. 'Or put a pair of slacks on.'

'Damn you, Marlowe. Can't you think of anything else?'

'I'll try. I like to think that I know at least one pretty and charming female who doesn't have round heels.' I swallowed and went on. 'The man's name is Ikky Rossen. He's not beautiful and he's not anything that I like—except one thing. He got mad when I said I needed a girl helper. He said women were not made for the rough stuff. That's why I took the job. To a real mobster, a woman means no more than a sack of flour. They use women in the usual way, but if it's advisable to get rid of them they do it without a second thought.'

'So far you've told me a whole lot of nothing. Perhaps you need a cup of coffee or a drink.'

'You're sweet but I don't in the morning—except sometimes, and this isn't one of them. Coffee later. Ikky has been penciled.'

'Now what's that?'

'You have a list. You draw a line through a name with a pencil. The guy is as good as dead. The Outfit has reasons. They don't do it just for kicks anymore. They don't get any kick. It's just bookkeeping to them.'

'What on earth can I do? I might even have said, what can *you* do?'

'I can try. What you can do is help me spot their plane and see where they go—the operators assigned to the job.'

'Yes, but how can you do anything?'

'I said I could try. If they took a night plane they are already here. If they took a morning plane they can't be here before five or so. Plenty of time to get set. You know what they look like?'

'Oh, sure. I meet killers every day. I have them in for whiskey sours and caviar on hot toast.' She grinned. While she was grinning I took four long steps across the tan-figured rug and lifted her and put a kiss on her mouth. She didn't fight me but she didn't go all trembly either. I went back and sat down.

'They'll look like anybody who's in a quiet well-run business or profession. They'll have quiet clothes and they'll be polite—when they want to be. They'll have briefcases with guns in them that have changed hands so often they can't possibly be traced. When and if they do the job, they'll drop the guns. They'll probably use revolvers, but they could use automatics. They won't use silencers because silencers can jam a gun and the weight makes it hard to shoot accurately. They won't sit together on the plane, but once off of it they may pretend to know each other and simply not have noticed during the flight. They may shake hands with appropriate smiles and walk away and get in the same taxi. I think they'll go in the same taxi. I think they'll go to a hotel first. But very soon they will move into something from which they can watch Ikky's movements and get used to his schedule. They won't be in any hurry unless Ikky makes a move. That would tip them off that Ikky has been tipped off. He has a couple of friends left—he says.'

'Will they shoot him from this room or apartment across the street—assuming there is one?'

'No. They'll shoot him from three feet away. They'll walk up behind and say "Hello, Ikky". He'll either freeze or turn. They'll fill him with lead, drop the guns, and hop into the car they have waiting. Then they'll follow the crash car off the scene.'

'Who'll drive the crash car?'

'Some well-fixed and blameless citizen who hasn't been rapped. He'll drive his own car. He'll clear the way, even if he has to accidentally on purpose crash somebody, even a police car. He'll be so damn sorry he'll cry all the way down his monogrammed shirt. And the killers will be long gone.'

'Good heavens,' Anne said. 'How can you stand your life? If you do bring it off, they'll send operators after you.'

'I don't think so. They don't kill a legit. The blame will go to the operators. Remember, these top mobsters are businessmen. They want lots and lots of money. They only get really tough when they figure they have to get rid of somebody, and they don't crave that. There's always a chance of a slipup. Not much of a chance. No gang killing has ever been solved here or anywhere else except two or three times. The top mobster is awful big and awful tough. When he gets too big, too tough—pencil.'

She shuddered a little. 'I think I need a drink myself.'

I grinned at her. 'You're right in the atmosphere, darling. I'll weaken.'

She brought a couple of Scotch highballs. When we were drinking them I said, 'If you spot them or think you spot them, follow to where they go—if you can do it safely. Not otherwise. If it's a hotel—and ten to one it will be—check in and keep calling me until you get me.'

She knew my office number and I was still on Yucca Avenue. She knew that too.

'You're the damnedest guy,' she said. 'Women do anything you want them to. How come I'm still a virgin at twenty-eight?'

'We need a few like you. Why don't you get married?'

'To what? Some cynical chaser who has nothing left? I don't know any really nice men—except you. I'm no pushover for white teeth and a gaudy smile.'

I went over and pulled her to her feet. I kissed her long and hard. 'I'm honest,' I almost whispered. 'That's something. But I'm too shop-soiled for a girl like you. I've thought of you, I've wanted you, but that sweet clear look in your eyes tells me to lay off.'

'Take me,' she said softly. 'I have dreams too.'

'I couldn't. I've had too many women to deserve one like you. We have to save a man's life. I'm going.'

She stood up and watched me leave with a grave face.

The women you get and the women you don't get—they live in different worlds. I don't sneer at either world. I live in both myself.

At Los Angeles International Airport you can't get close to the planes unless you're leaving on one. You see them land, if you happen to be in the right place, but you have to wait at a barrier to get a look at the passengers. The airport buildings don't make it any easier. They are strung out from here to breakfast time, and you can get calluses walking from TWA to American.

I copied an arrival schedule off the boards and prowled around like a dog that has forgotten where he put his bone. Planes came in, planes took off, porters carried luggage, passengers sweated and scurried, children whined, the loudspeaker overrode all the other noises.

I passed Anne a number of times. She took no notice of me.

At 5:45 they must have come. Anne disappeared. I gave it half an hour, just in case she had some other reason for fading. No. She was gone for good. I went out to my car and drove some long crowded miles to Hollywood and my office. I had a drink and sat. At 6:45 the phone rang.

'I think so,' she said. 'Beverly-Western Hotel. Room 410. I couldn't get any names. You know the clerks don't leave registration cards lying around these days. I didn't like to ask any questions. But I rode up in the elevator with them and spotted their room. I walked right on past them when the bellman put a key in their door, and went down to the mezzanine and then downstairs with a bunch of women from the tea room. I didn't bother to take a room.'

'What were they like?'

'They came up the ramp together but I didn't hear them speak. Both had briefcases, both wore quiet suits, nothing flashy. White shirts, starched, one blue tie, one black striped with gray. Black shoes.

A couple of businessmen from the East Coast. They could be publishers, lawyers, doctors, account executives—no, cut the last; they weren't gaudy enough. You wouldn't look at them twice.'

'Faces?'

'Both medium-brown hair, one a bit darker than the other. Smooth faces, rather expressionless. One had gray eyes, the one with the lighter hair had blue eyes. Their eyes were interesting. Very quick to move, very observant, watching everything near them. That might have been wrong. They should have been a bit preoccupied with what they came out for or interested in California. They seemed more occupied with faces. It's a good thing I spotted them and not you. You don't look like a cop, but you don't look like a man who is not a cop. You have marks on you.'

'Phooey. I'm a damn good-looking heart wrecker.'

'Their features were strictly assembly line. Each picked up a flight suitcase. One suitcase was gray with two red and white stripes up and down, about six or seven inches from the ends, the other a blue and white tartan. I didn't know there was such a tartan.'

'There is, but I forget the name of it.'

'I thought you knew everything.'

'Just almost everything. Run along home now.'

'Do I get a dinner and maybe a kiss?'

'Later, and if you're not careful you'll get more than you want.'

'You'll take over and follow them?'

'If they're the right men, they'll follow me. I already took an apartment across the street from Ikky—that block on Poynter with six lowlife apartment houses on the block. I'll bet the incidence of chippies is very high.'

'It's high everywhere these days.'

'So long, Anne. See you.'

'When you need help.'

She hung up. I hung up. She puzzles me. Too wise to be so nice. I guess all nice women are wise too.

I called Ikky. He was out. I had a drink from the office bottle, smoked for half an hour, and called again. This time I got him.

I told him the score up to then, and said I hoped Anne had picked the right men. I told him about the apartment I had taken.

'Do I get expenses?' I asked.

'Five grand ought to cover the lot.'

'If I earn it and get it. I heard you had a quarter of a million,' I said at a wild venture.

'Could be, pal, but how do I get at it? The high boys know where it is. It'll have to cool a long time.'

I said that was all right. I had cooled a long time myself. Of course, I didn't expect to get the other four thousand, even if I brought the job off. Men like Ikky Rossen would steal their mother's gold teeth. There seemed to be a little gold in him somewhere—but little was the operative word.

I spent the next half hour trying to think of a plan. I couldn't think of one that looked promising. It was almost eight o'clock and I needed food. I didn't think the boys would move that night. Next morning they would drive past Ikky's place and scout the neighborhood.

I was ready to leave the office when the buzzer sounded from the door of my waiting room. I opened the communicating door. A small tight-looking man was standing in the middle of the floor rocking on his heels with his hands behind his back. He smiled at me, but he wasn't good at it. He walked toward me.

'You Philip Marlowe?'

'Who else? What can I do for you?'

He was close now. He brought his right hand around fast with a gun in it. He stuck the gun in my stomach.

'You can lay off Ikky Rossen,' he said in a voice that matched his face, 'or you can get your belly full of lead.'

He was an amateur. If he had stayed four feet away, he might have had something. I reached up and took the cigarette out of my mouth and held it carelessly.

'What makes you think I know any Ikky Rossen?'

He laughed and pushed his gun into my stomach.

'Wouldn't you like to know!' The cheap sneer, and empty triumph of that feeling of power when you hold a fat gun in a small hand.

'It would be fair to tell me.'

As his mouth opened for another crack, I dropped the cigarette and swept a hand. I can be fast when I have to. There are boys that are faster, but they don't stick guns in your stomach.

I got my thumb behind the trigger and my hand over his. I kneed him in the groin. He bent over with a whimper. I twisted his arm to the right and I had his gun. I hooked a heel behind his heel and he was on the floor.

He lay there blinking with surprise and pain, his knees drawn up against his stomach. He rolled from side to side groaning. I reached down and grabbed his left hand and yanked him to his feet. I had six inches and forty pounds on him. They ought to have sent a bigger, better-trained messenger.

'Let's go into my thinking parlor,' I said. 'We could have a chat and you could have a drink to pick you up. Next time don't get near enough to a prospect for him to get your gun hand. I'll just see if you have any more iron on you.'

He hadn't. I pushed him through the door and into a chair. His breath wasn't quite so rasping. He grabbed out a handkerchief and mopped at his face.

'Next time,' he said between his teeth. 'Next time.'

'Don't be an optimist. You don't look the part.'

I poured him a drink of Scotch in a paper cup, set it down in front of him. I broke his .38 and dumped the cartridges into the desk drawer. I clicked the chamber back and laid the gun down.

'You can have it when you leave—if you leave.'

'That's a dirty way to fight,' he said, still gasping.

'Sure. Shooting a man is so much cleaner. Now, how did you get here?'

'Nuts.'

'Don't be a fool. I have friends. Not many, but some. I can get you for armed assault, and you know what would happen then. You'd be out on a writ or on bail and that's the last anyone would hear of you. The biggies don't go for failures. Now who sent you and how did you know where to come?'

'Ikky was covered,' he said sullenly. 'He's dumb. I trailed him here without no trouble at all. Why would he go see a private eye? People want to know.'

'More.'

'Go to hell.'

'Come to think of it, I don't have to get you for armed assault. I can smash it out of you right here and now.'

I got up from the chair and he put out a flat hand.

'If I get knocked about, a couple of real tough monkeys will drop around. If I don't report back, same thing. You ain't holding no real high cards. They just look high,' he said.

'You haven't anything to tell. If this Ikky came to see me, you don't know why, nor whether I took him on. If he's a mobster, he's not my type of client.'

'He come to get you to try and save his hide.'

'Who from?'

'That'd be talking.'

'Go right ahead. Your mouth seems to work fine. And tell the boys any time I front for a hood, that will be the day.'

You have to lie a little once in a while in my business. I was lying a little. 'What's Ikky done to get himself disliked? Or would that be talking?'

'You think you're a lot of man,' he sneered, rubbing the place where I had kneed him. 'In my league you wouldn't make pinch runner.'

I laughed in his face. Then I grabbed his right wrist and twisted it behind his back. He began to squawk. I reached into his breast pocket with my left hand and hauled out a wallet. I let him go. He reached for his gun on the desk and I bisected his upper arm with a hard cut. He fell into the customer's chair and grunted.

'You can have your gun,' I told him. 'When I give it to you. Now be good or I'll have to bounce you just to amuse myself.'

In the wallet I found a driver's license made out to Charles Hickon. It did me no good at all. Punks of his type always have slangy aliases. They probably called him Tiny, or Slim, or Marbles, or even just 'you'. I tossed the wallet back to him. It fell to the floor. He couldn't even catch it.

'Hell,' I said, 'there must be an economy campaign on, if they send you to do more than pick up cigarette butts.'

'Nuts.'

'All right, mug. Beat it back to the laundry. Here's your gun.'

He took it, made a business of shoving it into his waistband, stood up, gave me as dirty a look as he had in stock, and strolled to the door, nonchalant as a hustler with a new mink stole.

He turned at the door and gave me the beady eye. 'Stay clean, tin-horn. Tin bends easy.'

With this blinding piece of repartee he opened the door and drifted out.

After a little while I locked my other door, cut the buzzer, made the office dark, and left. I saw no one who looked like a lifetaker. I drove to my house, packed a suitcase, drove to a service station where they were almost fond of me, stored my car, and picked up a rental Chevrolet.

I drove this to Poynter Street, dumped my suitcase in the sleazy apartment I had rented early in the afternoon, and went to dinner at Victor's. It was nine o'clock, too late to drive to Bay City and take Anne to dinner.

I ordered a double Gibson with fresh limes and drank it, and I was as hungry as a schoolboy.

On the way back to Poynter Street I did a good deal of weaving in and out and circling blocks and stopping, with a gun on the seat beside me. As far as I could tell, no one was trying to tail me.

I stopped on Sunset at a service station and made two calls from the box. I caught Bernie Ohls just as he was leaving to go home.

'This is Marlowe, Bernie. We haven't had a fight in years. I'm getting lonely.'

'Well, get married. I'm chief investigator for the sheriff's office now. I rank acting captain until I pass the exam. I don't hardly speak to private eyes.'

'Speak to this one. I need help. I'm on a ticklish job where I could get killed.'

'And you expect me to interfere with the course of nature?'

'Come off it, Bernie. I haven't been a bad guy. I'm trying to save an ex-mobster from a couple of executioners.'

'The more they mow each other down, the better I like it.'

'Yeah. If I call you, come running or send a couple of good boys. You'll have time to teach them.'

We exchanged a couple of mild insults and hung up. I dialed Ikky Rossen's number. His rather unpleasant voice said, 'Okay, talk.'

'Marlowe. Be ready to move out about midnight. We've spotted your boyfriends and they are holed up at the Beverly-Western. They won't move to your street tonight. Remember, they don't know you've been tipped.'

'Sounds chancy.'

'Good God, it wasn't meant to be a Sunday school picnic. You've been careless, Ikky. You were followed to my office. That cuts the time we have.'

He was silent for a moment. I heard him breathing. 'Who by?' he asked.

'Some little tweezer who stuck a gun in my belly and gave me the trouble of taking it away from him. I can only figure they sent a punk on the theory they don't want me to know too much, in case I don't know it already.'

'You're in for trouble, friend.'

'When not? I'll come over to your place about midnight. Be ready. Where's your car?'

'Out front.'

'Get it on a side street and make a business of locking it up. Where's the back door of your flop?'

'In back. Where would it be? On the alley.'

'Leave your suitcase there. We walk out together and go to your car. We drive by the alley and pick up the suitcase or cases.'

'Suppose some guy steals them?'

'Yeah. Suppose you get dead. Which do you like better?'

'Okay,' he grunted. 'I'm waiting. But we're taking big chances.'

'So do race drivers. Does that stop them? There's no way to get out but fast. Douse your lights about ten and rumple the bed well. It would be good if you could leave some baggage behind. Wouldn't look so planned.'

He grunted okay and I hung up. The telephone box was well lighted outside. They usually are in service stations. I took a good long gander around while I pawed over the collection of giveaway maps inside the station. I saw nothing to worry me. I took a map of San Diego just for the hell of it and got into my rented car.

On Poynter I parked around the corner and went up to my second-floor sleazy apartment and sat in the dark watching from my window.

I saw nothing to worry about. A couple of medium-class chippies came out of Ikky's apartment house and were picked up in a late-model car. A man about Ikky's height and build went into the apartment house. Various other people came and went. The street was fairly quiet. Since they put in the Hollywood Freeway nobody much uses the off-the-boulevard streets unless they live in the neighborhood.

It was a nice fall night—or as nice as they get in Los Angeles' climate—clearish but not even crisp. I don't know what's happened to the weather in our overcrowded city, but it's not the weather I knew when I came to it.

It seemed like a long time to midnight. I couldn't spot anybody watching anything, and no couple of quiet-suited men paged any of the six apartment houses available. I was pretty sure they'd try mine first when they came, but I wasn't sure if Anne had picked the right men, or if the tweezer's message back to his bosses had done me any good or otherwise.

In spite of the hundred ways Anne could be wrong, I had a hunch she was right. The killers had no reason to be cagey if they didn't know Ikky had been warned. No reason but one. He had come to my office and been tailed there. But the Outfit, with all its arrogance of power, might laugh at the idea he had been tipped off or come to me for help. I was so small they would hardly be able to see me.

At midnight I left the apartment, walked two blocks watching for a tail, crossed the street, and went into Ikky's drive. There was no locked door, and no elevator. I climbed steps to the third floor and looked for his apartment. I knocked lightly. He opened the door with a gun in his hand. He probably looked scared.

There were two suitcases by the door and another against the far wall. I went over and lifted it. It was heavy enough. I opened it—it was unlocked.

'You don't have to worry,' he said. 'It's got everything a guy could need for three–four nights, and nothing except some clothes that I couldn't glom off in any ready-to-wear place.'

I picked up one of the other suitcases. 'Let's stash this by the back door.'

'We can leave by the alley too.'

'We leave by the front door. Just in case we're covered—though I don't think so—we're just two guys going out together. Just one thing. Keep both hands in your coat pockets and the gun in your right. If anybody calls out your name behind you, turn fast and shoot. Nobody but a lifetaker will do it. I'll do the same.'

'I'm scared,' he said in his rusty voice.

'Me too, if it helps any. But we have to do it. If you're braced, they'll have guns in their hands. Don't bother asking them questions. They wouldn't answer in words. If it's just my small friend, we'll cool him and dump him inside the door. Got it?'

He nodded, licking his lips. We carried the suitcases down and put them outside the back door. I looked along the alley. Nobody, and only a short distance to the side street. We went back in and along the hall to the front. We walked out on Poynter Street with all the casualness of a wife buying her husband a birthday tie.

Nobody made a move. The street was empty.

We walked around the corner to Ikky's rented car. He unlocked it. I went back with him for the suitcases. Not a stir. We put the suitcases in the car and started up and drove to the next street.

A traffic light not working, a boulevard stop or two, the entrance to the freeway. There was plenty of traffic on it even at midnight. California is loaded with people going places and making speed to get there. If you don't drive eighty miles an hour, everybody passes you. If you do, you have to watch the rearview mirror for highway patrol cars. It's the rat race of rat races.

Ikky did a quiet seventy. We reached the junction to Route 66 and he took it. So far nothing. I stayed with him to Pomona.

'This is far enough for me,' I said. 'I'll grab a bus back if there is one, or park myself in a motel. Drive to a service station and we'll ask for the bus stop. It should be close to the freeway.'

He did that and stopped midway on a block. He reached for his pocketbook and held out four thousand-dollar bills.

'I don't really feel I've earned all that. It was too easy.'

He laughed with a kind of wry amusement on his pudgy face. 'Don't be a sap. I have it made. You didn't know what you was walking into. What's more, your troubles are just beginning. The Outfit has eyes and ears everywhere. Perhaps I'm safe if I'm damn careful.

Perhaps I ain't as safe as I think I am. Either way, you did what I asked. Take the dough. I got plenty.'

I took it and put it away. He drove to an all-night service station and we were told where to find the bus stop. 'There's a cross-country Greyhound at two twenty-five a.m.,' the attendant said, looking at a schedule. 'They'll take you, if they got room.'

Ikky drove to the bus stop. We shook hands and he went gunning down the road toward the freeway. I looked at my watch and found a liquor store still open and bought a pint of Scotch. Then I found a bar and ordered a double with water.

My troubles were just beginning, Ikky had said. He was so right.

I got off at the Hollywood bus station, grabbed a taxi, and drove to my office. I asked the driver to wait a few moments. At that time of night he was glad to. The night man let me into the building.

'You work late, Mr Marlowe. But you always did, didn't you?'

'It's that sort of business,' I said. 'Thanks, Jimmy.'

Up in my office I pawed the floor for mail and found nothing but a longish narrowish box, Special Delivery, with a Glendale postmark.

It contained nothing at all but a freshly sharpened pencil—the mobster's mark of death.

I didn't take it too hard. When they mean it, they don't send it to you. I took it as a sharp warning to lay off. There might be a beating arranged. From their point of view, that would be good discipline. 'When we pencil a guy, any guy that tries to help him is in for smashing.' That could be the message.

I thought of going to my house on Yucca Avenue. Too lonely. I thought of going to Anne's place in Bay City. Worse. If they got wise to her, real hoods would think nothing of beating her up too.

It was the Poynter Street flop for me—easily the safest place now. I went down to the waiting taxi and had him drive me to within three blocks of the so-called apartment house. I went upstairs, undressed, and slept raw. Nothing bothered me but a broken spring—that bothered my back.

I lay until 3:30 pondering the situation with my massive brain. I went to sleep with a gun under the pillow, which is a bad place to keep a gun when you have one pillow as thick and soft as a typewriter pad.

It bothered me, so I transferred it to my right hand. Practice had taught me to keep it there even in sleep.

I woke up with the sun shining. I felt like a piece of spoiled meat. I struggled into the bathroom and doused myself with cold water and wiped off with a towel you couldn't have seen if you held it sideways. This was a really gorgeous apartment. All it needed was a set of Chippendale furniture to be graduated into the slum class.

There was nothing to eat and if I went out, Miss-Nothing Marlowe might miss something. I had a pint of whiskey. I looked at it and smelled it, but I couldn't take it for breakfast on an empty stomach, even if I could reach my stomach, which was floating around near the ceiling.

I looked into the closets in case a previous tenant might have left a crust of bread in a hasty departure. Nope. I wouldn't have liked it any-how, not even with whiskey on it. So I sat at the window. An hour of that and I was ready to bite a piece off a bellhop's arm.

I dressed and went around the corner to the rented car and drove to an eatery. The waitress was sore too. She swept a cloth over the counter in front of me and let me have the last customer's crumbs in my lap.

'Look, sweetness,' I said, 'don't be so generous. Save the crumbs for a rainy day. All I want is two eggs three minutes—no more—a slice of your famous concrete toast, a tall glass of tomato juice and a dash of Lea and Perrins, a big happy smile, and don't give anybody else any coffee. I might need it all.'

'I got a cold,' she said. 'Don't push me around. I might crack you one on the kisser.'

'Let's be pals. I had a rough night too.'

She gave me a half smile and went through the swing door sideways. It showed more of her curves, which were ample, even excessive. But I got the eggs the way I liked them. The toast had been painted with melted butter past its bloom.

'No Lea and Perrins,' she said, putting down the tomato juice. 'How about a little Tabasco? We're fresh out of arsenic too.'

I used two drops of Tabasco, swallowed the eggs, drank two cups of coffee, and was about to leave the toast for a tip, but I went soft and left a quarter instead. That really brightened her. It was a joint where you left a dime or nothing. Mostly nothing.

Back on Poynter Street nothing had changed. I got to my window again and sat. At about 8:30 the man I had seen go into the apartment house across the way—the one about the same height and build as Ikky—came out with a small briefcase and turned east. Two men got out of a dark-blue sedan. They were of the same height and very quietly dressed and had soft hats pulled low over their foreheads. Each jerked out a revolver.

'Hey, Ikky!' one of them called out.

The man turned. 'So long, Ikky,' the other man said.

Gunfire racketed between the houses. The man crumpled and lay motionless. The two men rushed for their car and were off, going west. Halfway down the block I saw a limousine pull out and start ahead of them.

In no time at all they were completely gone.

It was a nice swift clean job. The only thing wrong with it was that they hadn't given it enough time for preparation.

They had shot the wrong man.

I got out of there fast, almost as fast as the two killers. There was a smallish crowd grouped around the dead man. I didn't have to look at him to know he was dead—the boys were pros. Where he lay on the sidewalk on the other side of the street I couldn't see him—people were in the way. But I knew just how he would look and I already heard sirens in the distance. It could have been just the routine shrieking from Sunset, but it wasn't. So somebody had telephoned. It was too early for the cops to be going to lunch.

I strolled around the corner with my suitcase and jammed into the rented car and beat it away from there. The neighborhood was not my piece of shortcake any more. I could imagine the questions.

'Just what took you over there, Marlowe? You got a flop of your own, ain't you?'

'I was hired by an ex-mobster in trouble with the Outfit. They'd sent killers after him!'

'Don't tell us he was trying to go straight.'

'I don't know. But I liked his money.'

'Didn't do much to earn it, did you?'

'I got him away last night. I don't know where he is now, and I don't want to know.'

'You got him away?'

'That's what I said.'

'Yeah—only he's in the morgue with multiple bullet wounds. Try something better. Or somebody's in the morgue.'

And on and on. Policeman's dialogue. It comes out of an old shoebox. What they say doesn't mean anything, what they ask doesn't mean anything. They just keep boring in until you are so exhausted you slip on some detail. Then they smile happily and rub their hands, and say, 'Kind of careless there, weren't you? Let's start all over again.'

The less I had of that, the better. I parked in my usual parking slot and went up to the office. It was full of nothing but stale air. Every time I went into the dump I felt more and more tired. Why the hell hadn't I got myself a government job ten years ago? Make it fifteen years. I had brains enough to get a mail-order law degree. The country's full of lawyers who couldn't write a complaint without the book.

So I sat in my office chair and disadmired myself. After a while I remembered the pencil. I made certain arrangements with a .45 gun, more gun than I ever carry—too much weight. I dialed the sheriff's office and asked for Bernie Ohls. I got him. His voice was sour.

'Marlowe. I'm in trouble—real trouble,' I said.

'Why tell me?' he growled. 'You must be used to it by now.'

'This kind of trouble you don't get used to. I'd like to come over and tell you.'

'You in the same office?'

'The same.'

'Have to go over that way. I'll drop in.'

He hung up. I opened two windows. The gentle breeze wafted a smell of coffee and stale fat to me from Joe's Eats next door. I hated it, I hated myself, I hated everything.

Ohls didn't bother with my elegant waiting room. He rapped on my own door and I let him in. He scowled his way to the customer's chair.

'Okay. Give.'

'Ever hear of a character named Ikky Rossen?'

'Why would I? Record?'

'An ex-mobster who got disliked by the mob. They put a pencil through his name and sent the usual two tough boys on a plane. He got tipped and hired me to help him get away.'

'Nice clean work.'

'Cut it out, Bernie.' I lit a cigarette and blew smoke in his face. In retaliation he began to chew a cigarette. He never lit one, but he certainly mangled them.

'Look,' I went on. 'Suppose the man wants to go straight and suppose he doesn't. He's entitled to his life as long as he hasn't killed anyone. He told me he hadn't.'

'And you believed the hood, huh? When do you start teaching Sunday school?'

'I neither believed him nor disbelieved him. I took him on. There was no reason not to. A girl I know and I watched the planes yesterday. She spotted the boys and tailed them to a hotel. She was sure of what they were. They looked it right down to their black shoes. This girl—'

'Would she have a name?'

'Only for you.'

'I'll buy, if she hasn't cracked any laws.'

'Her name is Anne Riordan. She lives in Bay City. Her father was once chief of police there. And don't say that makes him a crook, because he wasn't.'

'Uh-huh. Let's have the rest. Make a little time too.'

'I took an apartment opposite Ikky. The killers were still at the hotel. At midnight I got Ikky out and drove with him as far as Pomona. He went on in his rented car and I came back by Greyhound. I moved into the apartment on Poynter Street, right across from his dump.'

'Why—if he was already gone?'

I opened the middle desk drawer and took out the nice sharp pencil. I wrote my name on a piece of paper and ran the pencil through it.

'Because someone sent me this. I didn't think they'd kill me, but I thought they planned to give me enough of a beating to warn me off any more pranks.'

'They knew you were in on it?'

'Ikky was tailed here by a little squirt who later came around and stuck a gun in my stomach. I knocked him around a bit, but I had to let him go. I thought Poynter Street was safer after that. I live lonely.'

'I get around,' Bernie Ohls said. 'I hear reports. So they gunned the wrong guy.'

'Same height, same build, same general appearance. I saw them gun him. I couldn't tell if it was the two guys from the Beverly-Western. I'd never seen them. It was just two guys in dark suits with hats pulled down. They jumped into a blue Pontiac sedan, about two years old, and lammed off, with a big Caddy running crash for them.'

Bernie stood up and stared at me for a long moment. 'I don't think they'll bother with you now,' he said. 'They've hit the wrong guy. The mob will be very quiet for a while. You know something? This town is getting to be almost as lousy as New York, Brooklyn, and Chicago. We could end up real corrupt.'

'We've made a hell of a good start.'

'You haven't told me anything that makes me take action, Phil. I'll talk to the city homicide boys. I don't guess you're in any trouble. But you saw the shooting. They'll want that.'

'I couldn't identify anybody, Bernie. I didn't know the man who was shot. How did *you* know it was the wrong man?'

'You told me, stupid.'

'I thought perhaps the city boys had a make on him.'

'They wouldn't tell me, if they had. Besides, they ain't hardly had time to go out for breakfast. He's just a stiff in the morgue to them until the ID comes up with something. But they'll want to talk to you, Phil. They just love their tape recorders.'

He went out and the door whooshed shut behind him. I sat there wondering if I had been a dope to talk to him. Or to take on Ikky's troubles. Five thousand green men said no. But they can be wrong too.

Somebody banged on my door. It was a uniform holding a telegram. I receipted for it and tore it loose.

It said: ON MY WAY TO FLAGSTAFF, MIRADOR MOTOR COURT. THINK I'VE BEEN SPOTTED. COME FAST.

I tore the wire into small pieces and burned them in my big ashtray.

I called Anne Riordan.

'Funny thing happened,' I told her, and told her about the funny thing.

'I don't like the pencil,' she said. 'And I don't like the wrong man being killed—probably some poor bookkeeper in a cheap business or he wouldn't be living in that neighborhood. You should never have touched it, Phil.'

'Ikky had a life. Where he's going he might make himself decent. He can change his name. He must be loaded or he wouldn't have paid me so much.'

'I said I didn't like the pencil. You'd better come down here for a while. You can have your mail readdressed—if you get any mail. You don't have to work right away anyhow. And LA is oozing with private eyes.'

'You don't get the point. I'm not through with the job. The city dicks have to know where I am, and if they do, all the crime reporters will know too. The cops might even decide to make me a suspect. Nobody who saw the shooting is going to put out a description that means anything. The American people know better than to be witnesses to gang killings.'

'All right, but my offer stands.'

The buzzer sounded in the outside room. I told Anne I had to hang up. I opened the communicating door and a well-dressed—I might say elegantly dressed—middle-aged man stood six feet inside the outer door. He had a pleasantly dishonest smile on his face. He wore a white Stetson and one of those narrow ties that go through an ornamental buckle. His cream-colored flannel suit was beautifully tailored.

He lit a cigarette with a gold lighter and looked at me over the first puff of smoke.

'Mr Philip Marlowe?'

I nodded.

'I'm Foster Grimes from Las Vegas. I run the Rancho Esperanza on South Fifth. I hear you got a little involved with a man named Ikky Rossen.'

'Won't you come in?'

He strolled past me into my office. His appearance told me

nothing—a prosperous man who liked or felt it good business to look a bit western. You see them by the dozen in the Palm Springs winter season. His accent told me he was an easterner, but not New England. New York or Baltimore, likely. Long Island, the Berkshires—no, too far from the city.

I showed him the customer's chair with a flick of the wrist and sat down in my antique swivelsqueaker. I waited.

'Where is Ikky now, if you know?'

'I don't know, Mr Grimes.'

'How come you messed with him?'

'Money.'

'A damned good reason,' he smiled. 'How far did it go?'

'I helped him leave town. I'm telling you this, although I don't know who the hell you are, because I've already told an old friend-enemy of mine, a top man in the sheriff's office.'

'What's a friend-enemy?'

'Lawmen don't go around kissing me, but I've known him for years, and we are as much friends as a private star can be with a lawman.'

'I told you who I was. We have a unique setup in Vegas. We own the place except for one lousy newspaper editor who keeps climbing our backs and the backs of our friends. We let him live because letting him live makes us look better than knocking him off. Killings are not good business any more.'

'Like Ikky Rossen.'

'That's not a killing. It's an execution. Ikky got out of line.'

'So your gun boys had to rub the wrong guy. They could have hung around a little to make sure.'

'They would have, if you'd kept your nose where it belonged. They hurried. We don't appreciate that. We want cool efficiency.'

'Who's this great big fat "we" you keep talking about?'

'Don't go juvenile on me, Marlowe.'

'Okay. Let's say I know.'

'Here's what we want.' He reached into his pocket and drew out a loose bill. He put it on the desk on his side. 'Find Ikky and tell him to get back in line and everything is okay. With an innocent by-stander gunned, we don't want any trouble or any extra publicity.

It's that simple. You get this now,' he nodded at the bill. It was a grand. Probably the smallest bill they had. 'And another when you find Ikky and give him the message. If he holds out—curtains.'

'Suppose I say take your grand and blow your nose with it?'

'That would be unwise.' He flipped out a Colt Woodsman with a short silencer on it. A Colt Woodsman will take one without jamming. He was fast too, fast and smooth. The genial expression on his face didn't change.

'I never left Vegas,' he said calmly. 'I can prove it. You're dead in your office chair and nobody knows anything. Just another private eye that tried the wrong pitch. Put your hands on the desk and think a little. Incidentally, I'm a crack shot even with this damned silencer.'

I flipped the nicely sharpened pencil across to him. He grabbed for it after a swift change of the gun to his left hand—very swift. He held the pencil up so that he could look at it without taking his eyes off me.

I said, 'It came to me by Special Delivery mail. No message, no return address. Just the pencil. Think I've never heard about the pencil, Mr Grimes?'

He frowned and tossed the pencil down. Before he could shift his long lithe gun back to his right hand I dropped mine under the desk and grabbed the butt of the .45 and put my finger hard on the trigger.

'Look under the desk, Mr Grimes. You'll see a .45 in an opened holster. It's fixed there and it's pointing at your belly. Even if you could shoot me through the heart, the .45 would still go off from a convulsive movement of my hand. And your belly would be hanging by a shred and you would be knocked out of that chair. A .45 slug can throw you back six feet. Even the movies learned that at last.'

'Looks like a Mexican standoff,' he said quietly. He holstered his gun. He grinned. 'Nice work, Marlowe. We could use a man like you. I suggest that you find Ikky and don't be a drip. He'll listen to reason. He doesn't really want to be on the run for the rest of his life.'

'Tell me something, Mr Grimes. Why pick on me? Apart from Ikky, what did I ever do to make you dislike me?'

Not moving, he thought a moment, or pretended to. 'The Larsen case. You helped send one of our boys to the gas chamber. That we don't forget. We had you in mind as a fall guy for Ikky. You'll always be a fall guy, unless you play it our way. Something will hit you when you least expect it.'

'A man in my business is always a fall guy, Mr Grimes. Pick up your grand and drift out quietly. I might decide to do it your way, but I have to think about it. As for the Larsen case, the cops did all the work. I just happened to know where he was. I don't guess you miss him terribly.'

'We don't like interference.' He stood up. He put the grand note casually back in his pocket. While he was doing it I let go of the .45 and jerked out my Smith and Wesson five-inch .38.

He looked at it contemptuously. 'I'll be in Vegas, Marlowe—in fact, I never left Vegas. You can catch me at the Esperanza. No, we don't give a damn about Larsen personally. Just another gun handler. They come in gross lots. We *do* give a damn that some punk private eye fingered him.'

He nodded and went out by my office door.

I did some pondering. I knew Ikky wouldn't go back to the Outfit. He wouldn't trust them enough even if he got the chance. But there was another reason now. I called Anne Riordan again.

'I'm going to look for Ikky. I have to. If I don't call you in three days, get hold of Bernie Ohls. I'm going to Flagstaff, Arizona. Ikky says he will be there.'

'You're a fool,' she wailed. 'It's some sort of trap.'

'A Mr Grimes of Vegas visited me with a silenced gun. I beat him to the punch, but I won't always be that lucky. If I find Ikky and report to Grimes, the mob will let me alone.'

'You'd condemn a man to death?' Her voice was sharp and incredulous.

'No. He won't be there when I report. He'll have to hop a plane to Montreal, buy forged papers, and plane to Europe. He may be fairly safe there. But the Outfit has long arms and Ikky won't have a dull life staying alive. He hasn't any choice. For him it's either hide or get the pencil.'

'So clever of you, darling. What about your own pencil?'

'If they meant it, they wouldn't have sent it. Just a bit of scare technique.'

'And you don't scare, you wonderful handsome brute.'

'I scare. But it doesn't paralyze me. So long. Don't take any lovers until I get back.'

'Damn you, Marlowe!'

She hung up on me. I hung up on myself.

Saying the wrong thing is one of my specialties.

I beat it out of town before the homicide boys could hear about me. It would take them quite a while to get a lead. And Bernie Ohls wouldn't give a city dick a used paper bag. The sheriff's men and the city police cooperate about as much as two tomcats on a fence.

I made Phoenix by evening and parked myself in a motor court on the outskirts. Phoenix was damned hot. The motor court had a dining room, so I had dinner. I collected some quarters and dimes from the cashier and shut myself in a phone booth and started to call the Mirador in Flagstaff.

How silly could I get? Ikky might be registered under any name from Cohen to Cordileone, from Watson to Woichehovski. I called anyway and got nothing but as much of a smile as you can get on the phone.

So I asked for a room the following night. Not a chance unless someone checked out, but they would put me down for a cancellation or something. Flagstaff is too near the Grand Canyon. Ikky must have arranged in advance. That was something to ponder too.

I bought a paperback and read it. I set my alarm watch for 6:30. The paperback scared me so badly that I put two guns under my pillow. It was about a guy who bucked the hoodlum boss of Milwaukee and got beaten up every fifteen minutes. I figured that his head and face would be nothing but a piece of bone with a strip of skin hanging from it. But in the next chapter he was as gay as a meadowlark.

Then I asked myself why I was reading this drivel when I could have been memorizing *The Brothers Karamazov*. Not knowing any good answers, I turned the light out and went to sleep.

At 6:30 I shaved, showered, had breakfast, and took off for Flagstaff. I got there by lunchtime, and there was Ikky in the restaurant eating mountain trout. I sat down across from him. He looked surprised to see me.

I ordered mountain trout and ate it from the outside in, which is the proper way. Boning spoils it a little.

'What gives?' he asked me with his mouth full. A delicate eater.

'You read the papers?'

'Just the sports section.'

'Let's go to your room and talk about it.'

We paid for our lunches and went along to a nice double. The motor courts are getting so good that they make a lot of hotels look cheap. We sat down and lit cigarettes.

'The two hoods got up too early and went over to Poynter Street. They parked outside your apartment house. They hadn't been briefed carefully enough. They shot a guy who looked a little like you.'

'That's a hot one,' he grinned. 'But the cops will find out, and the Outfit will find out. So the tag for me stays on.'

'You must think I'm dumb,' I said. 'I am.'

'I thought you did a first-class job, Marlowe. What's dumb about that?'

'What job did I do?'

'You got me out of there pretty slick.'

'Anything about it you couldn't have done yourself?'

'With luck—no. But it's nice to have a helper.'

'You mean sucker.'

His face tightened. And his rusty voice growled. 'I don't catch. And give me back some of that five grand, will you? I'm shorter than I thought.'

'I'll give it back to you when you find a hummingbird in a salt shaker.'

'Don't be like that.' He almost sighed, and flicked a gun into his hand. I didn't have to flick. I was holding one in my side pocket.

'I oughtn't to have boobed off,' I said. 'Put the heater away. It doesn't pay any more than a Vegas slot machine.'

'Wrong. Them machines pay the jackpot every so often. Other-wise—no customers.'

'Every so seldom, you mean. Listen, and listen good.'

He grinned. His dentist was tired waiting for him.

'The setup intrigued me,' I went on, debonair as Philo Vance in an S. S. Van Dine story and a lot brighter in the head. 'First off, could it be done? Second, if it could be done, where would I be? But gradually I saw the little touches that flawed the picture. Why would you come to me at all? The Outfit isn't naive. Why would they send a little punk like this Charles Hickon or whatever name he uses on Thursdays? Why would an old hand like you let anybody trail you to a dangerous connection?'

'You slay me, Marlowe. You're so bright I could find you in the dark. You're so dumb you couldn't see a red, white, and blue giraffe. I bet you were back there in your unbrain emporium playing with that five grand like a cat with a bag of catnip. I bet you were kissing the notes.'

'Not after you handled them. Then why the pencil that was sent to me? Big dangerous threat. It reinforced the rest. But like I told your choirboy from Vegas, they don't send them when they mean them. By the way, he had a gun too. A Woodsman .22 with a silencer. I had to make him put it away. He was nice about that. He started waving grands at me to find out where you were and tell him. A well-dressed, nice-looking front man for a pack of dirty rats. The Woman's Christian Temperance Association and some bootlicking politicians gave them the money to be big, and they learned how to use it and make it grow. Now they're pretty well unstoppable. But they're still a pack of dirty rats. And they're always where they can't make a mistake. That's inhuman. Any man has a right to a few mistakes. Not the rats. They have to be perfect all the time. Or else they get stuck with *you*.'

'I don't know what the hell you're talking about. I just know it's too long.'

'Well, allow me to put it in English. Some poor jerk from the East Side gets involved with the lower echelons of a mob. You know what an echelon is, Ikky?'

'I been in the Army,' he sneered.

'He grows up in the mob, but he's not all rotten. He's not rotten enough. So he tries to break loose. He comes out here and gets himself a cheap job of some sort and changes his name or names and lives quietly in a cheap apartment house. But the mob by now has agents in many places. Somebody spots him and recognizes him. It might be a pusher, a front man for a bookie joint, a night girl. So the mob, or call them the Outfit, say through their cigar smoke: "Ikky can't do this to us. It's a small operation because he's small. But it annoys us. Bad for discipline. Call a couple of boys and have them pencil him." But what boys do they call? A couple they're tired of. Been around too long. Might make a mistake or get chilly toes. Perhaps they like killing. That's bad too. That makes for recklessness. The best boys are the ones that don't care either way. So although they don't know it, the boys they call are on their way out. But it would be kind of cute to frame a guy they already don't like, for fingering a hood named Larsen. One of these puny little jokes the Outfit takes big. "Look, guys, we even got time to play footsie with a private eye." So they send a ringer.'

'The Torrence brothers ain't ringers. They're real hard boys. They proved it—even if they did make a mistake.'

'Mistake nothing. They got Ikky Rossen. You're just a singing commercial in this deal. And as of now you're under arrest for murder. You're worse off than that. The Outfit will habeas corpus you out of the clink and blow you down. You've served your purpose and you failed to finger me into a patsy.'

His finger tightened on the trigger. I shot the gun out of his hand. The gun in my coat pocket was small, but at that distance accurate. And it was one of my days to be accurate.

He made a faint moaning sound and sucked at his hand. I went over and kicked him hard in the chest. Being nice to killers is not part of my repertoire. He went over backward and stumbled four or five steps. I picked up his gun and held it on him while I tapped all the places—not just pockets or holsters—where a man could stash a second gun. He was clean—that way anyhow.

'What are you trying to do to me?' he whined. 'I paid you. You're clear. I paid you damn well.'

'We both have problems there. Your's is to stay alive.' I took a pair of cuffs out of my pocket and wrestled his hands behind him and snapped them on. His hand was bleeding. I tied his show handkerchief around it and then went to the telephone and called the police.

I had to stick around for a few days, but I didn't mind that as long as I could have trout caught eight or nine thousand feet up. I called Anne and Bernie Ohls. I called my answering service. The Arizona DA was a young keen-eyed man and the chief of police was one of the biggest men I ever saw.

I got back to LA in time and took Anne to Romanoff's for dinner and champagne.

'What I can't see,' she said over a third glass of bubbly, 'is why they dragged you into it, why they set up the fake Ikky Rossen. Why didn't they just let the two lifetakers do their job?'

'I couldn't really say. Unless the big boys feel so safe they're developing a sense of humor. And unless this Larsen guy who went to the gas chamber was bigger than he seemed to be. Only three or four important mobsters have made the electric chair or the rope or the gas chamber. None that I know of in the life-imprisonment states like Michigan. If Larsen was bigger than anyone thought, they might have had my name on a waiting list.'

'But why wait?' she asked me. 'They'd go after you quickly.'

'They can afford to wait. Who's going to bother them? Except when they make a mistake.'

'Income tax rap?'

'Yeah, like Capone. Capone may have had several hundred men killed, and killed a few of them himself, personally. But it took the Internal Revenue boys to get him. But the Outfit won't make that mistake often.'

'What I like about you, apart from your enormous personal charm, is that when you don't know an answer you make one up.'

'The money worries me,' I said. 'Five grand of their dirty money. What do I do with it?'

'Don't be a jerk all your life. You earned the money and you risked your life for it. You can buy Series E Bonds—they'll make the money clean. And to me that would be part of the joke.'

'*You* tell *me* one good sound reason why they pulled the switch.'

'You have more of a reputation than you realize. And suppose it was the false Ikky who pulled the switch? He sounds like one of these over-clever types that can't do anything simple.'

'The Outfit will get him for making his own plans—if you're right.'

'If the DA doesn't. And I couldn't care less about what happens to him. More champagne, please.'

They extradited 'Ikky' and he broke under pressure and named the two gunmen—after I had already named them, the Torrence brothers. But nobody could find them. They never went home. And you

The Pencil

can't prove conspiracy on one man. The law couldn't even get him for accessory after the fact. They couldn't prove he knew the real Ikky had been gunned.

They could have got him for some trifle, but they had a better idea. They left him to his friends. They just turned him loose.

Where is he now? My hunch says nowhere.

Anne Riordan was glad it was all over and I was safe. Safe—that isn't a word you use in my trade.

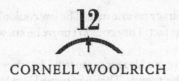

12

CORNELL WOOLRICH

One Drop of Blood

I. THE CRIME—AND THE EVENTS LEADING UP TO IT

He didn't premeditate it, and yet, he told himself afterward, it all turned out better than if he had. Much better. He might have done all the wrong things, he told himself. Picked the wrong place, the wrong time, the wrong weapon. Too much careful planning ahead might have made him nervous, as it had many another. In the effort to remember *not* to forget something, he might have forgotten *something else*. How often that had happened!

This way, there was nothing to forget—because there had been nothing to remember in the first place. He just walked through the whole thing 'cold', for the first time, without having had any rehearsal. And everything just seemed to fall into place—the right place, by itself. These hair-split timetables are very hard to stick to. Impromptu, the way he did it, the time element doesn't become important. You can't trip over a loose thirty seconds and fall flat on your face when there aren't a loose thirty seconds to trip over.

The situation itself was old and trite. One of the oldest, one of the tritest. Not to him, of course, and not to her—it never is to those involved. It's always new, first-time new.

To begin with, he was single, and had no troubles whatsoever to deal with. He had a car, he had a job, he had health, and he had good looks. But mainly, he had freedom. If he came home at ten o'clock or if he came at two, if he had one drink or if he had a few, there was no one but himself to keep score.

He was the personification of the male spirit, that restless roving spirit that can only get into trouble because it didn't have any trouble to start with, that had no other way to go but—from lack of trouble into a mess of trouble.

And so we find him one star-spiked May evening, in a $95 suit, with $75 in his wallet, with a new convertible waiting outside to take him in any direction he wanted to go, and with a girl named Corinne in his arms—a very pretty Corinne too, dexterously dancing and spinning around together, breaking apart, coming together again, and above all (a favorite step of theirs) making an overhead loop of their two hands so that she could walk through it, turn, then go back through it again. All in excellent time and in excellent rhythm to the tune of *The Night They Invented Champagne*, played by an excellent band.

Beautiful to watch, but what a fatal dance that was, because—it was their first together. They should have turned and fled from each other in opposite directions.

Instead they went out to the car. She patted it admiringly as he beamed, proudly possessive as only a young male car-owner can be. Then they drove to where she lived, sat a while and watched the stars, and kissed and kissed, and watched the stars . . . and that was it.

Another night, another dance, same car, same stars, same kisses—or same lips, anyway. She got out to go in. He got out to keep her from going in. Then they both got in the car again and went to a motel . . . And that was it again.

After some time had gone by she asked him about marriage. But she didn't get much of an answer. He liked it the way it was. She hadn't asked him soon enough, or in the right order of things. So, afraid that she would lose him altogether, and preferring to have him this way rather than no way at all, she didn't ask him again.

It was a peaceful, comfortable existence. It was definitely not sordid—she was not a sordid girl. She was no different, in effect, from any other girl on her street who had stepped out and married. Only she had stepped out and not married. He was the first man she had ever loved, and it stopped there. The only thing was, she had left freedom of action, freedom of choice, entirely in his hands—which was a tactical error of the worst sort in the never-ending war between the sexes. She was a very poor soldier, for a woman. They were not actually living together. They were keeping company, one might say, on a permanent basis.

At any rate, one night when he called to take her out, she complained of not feeling well. In fact, it was easy to see she wasn't shamming, and noticing that she was alternately shivering and burning up he sent for a doctor and remained there while the doctor examined her. (She spoke of him as her fiancé whenever it became necessary in front of a third person.) It was nothing serious—merely an attack of the flu, but she had to go to bed.

He would not—to give him some credit—have walked out on her then and there; but she was feeling so miserable that for her part she wished he would leave her alone. So, noticing this, he kissed her—a mere peck—and left.

His original intention—at least, from the door to the car—was to go to his own apartment and make the best of an unexpected solitary evening. But the stars were at their dirty work again, and his wrist watch didn't help either (9:48); he was 28 and *didn't* have the flu, so—

Her name was Allie.

And she wasn't going to be like Corinne—he found that out right from the start. She could enjoy the stars, sure, and she could kiss, sure, but she'd take up both those occupations on his time, as his officially credited fiancée or his lawfully wedded wife—not on her own time, as a free-lance, if you get the distinction.

And her sense of timing was much better, too. He came out three or four kisses short the first meeting. So he wanted to see her again, to try to make up the shortage. But she always knew just when to stop. He was still a couple short the second meeting, so that made him want to see her a third time. By then he was so hopelessly in hock to her that his only chance of clearing up the debt was to marry her, and try to work it out on a lifetime payment plan.

She was a five-star general in the battle of the sexes. And it must have been inborn, because she'd never heard a shot fired until she met him.

At first he managed to sandwich the two of them in together. He saw Allie a couple of nights in the week, saw Corinne a couple of others. In fact, he would have liked to continue his three-way-stretch arrangement indefinitely; the difficulty, however, lay not with them but with himself. Soon more and more nights with Corinne reminded him of the night she'd had the flu: the stars above and the wrist watch were there, but not Corinne's stars any more and not Corinne's time. A waste of Allie's time, instead.

Finally there were no more nights with Corinne—just one last station-break and the program went off the air.

'You've lost interest in me. I'm not blind. I've noticed it for some time now.'

'That's the chance you have to take,' he told her, 'when you're in love.'

'But why did it happen to you?' she wanted to know, 'and not to me? Shouldn't we both come out even?'

'You don't come out even in love,' he told her. 'Someone always has to come out behind.' And then he added, 'I'll call you up some night.' Which is the way some men say goodbye to a woman.

She'll find somebody else, he thought; she was easy for me, she'll be easy for the next one. And he shrugged her off.

But there are three things in this world you can't shrug off: death, taxes—and a girl who loves you.

Now they were in the homestretch, Allie and he. Now when they looped their hands above their heads on the dance floor, her engagement diamond blazed toward the lights, proclaiming, 'This is mine. Hands off.' Not to jewel thieves, but to stealers of men.

Now all the tribal customs were brought to bear—everything the world insists shall surround the lawful mating of a man and a woman. The meetings with the relatives from far-off places; the luncheons, dinners, parties, showers; the choosing of a trousseau; the finding of their first home; even the purchase of the furniture that was to go into it.

Now the date was set, the license applied for, the church reserved, the flowers and the caterers and the champagne arranged for. Now even the blood tests were taken, and they were both declared pure. All that remained was the marrying and the honeymoon.

Now the boys got together and gave him his bachelor party, his last night to howl. And the howls were something to hear. Three separate times around town they were arrested *en masse*, and twice the arresting officers not only released them but even accompanied them for a short part of the way, and the third time wished them well and urged them only to 'keep it down, boys'. Then finally the last two survivors, the diehards whose pledge had been to see him safely home, had him at his door, and after much fumbling with keys, and draping of arms across shoulders, and swaying and tottering, they thrust him inside, closed the door, and left him.

And suddenly he was sober, stone-cold, ice-cold sober, and the whole party had been a waste of liquor—at least, for him.

Corinne was sitting there. Waiting for him.

'You took so long to get back,' she complained mildly. 'I knew you still lived here, but I thought you'd never get back.'

'Had a little party,' he said. He was starkly sober, but his tongue hadn't yet quite caught up with the rest of him. A warning bell started ringing: I wonder if she knows, I wonder if she knows.

'I'm not criticizing,' she went on. 'You're free to go out with your pals—free every night in the week. It's only natural, so what's the harm?'

The warning bell stopped suddenly. There was silence. She doesn't know, he told himself, *and she's not going to know from me.*

Business of fooling around with a cigarette, so he'd use up time and wouldn't have to say too much to her. Maybe she'd go away.

'I know it's late,' she said.

He looked at the wrist watch that had played such a double-crossing part in their little story. Meaning, it is late.

She doesn't want to start over again, does she? For Pete's sake, not that! Love is a one-way street.

'Aren't you working?' he asked. 'Don't you have to get up early in the morning?'

'I haven't been working since last week,' she said. Then, understandingly, 'You're tired; I know.'

'Aren't you?'

'Yes, but I do have to talk to you about something. I've got to. It's very important.'

Now he knew, more or less. There were only two things a girl could possibly want from a man, in all the world, in all this life: love or money. And since love was out, that left only money. Another thing told him: she was much too tractable, noticeably taking pains not to antagonize or ruffle him in any way.

'Won't it keep till tomorrow?' he said by way of acquiescence. 'I'm beat. Completely beat. I'll come over to see you tomorrow.'

'But will you?' she asked, frowning, but still with that air of not wanting to push him, not wanting to crowd him.

'Aw, for the love of Mike, Cor,' he said impatiently, 'when did you ever know me to break my word to you?'

It was true. He never had—not in the little things.

She had to accept that—it was the best she could get.

'I've moved since the last time I saw you,' she said, and gave him the new address.

'All right, I'll be there, Allie,' he promised. He was almost nudging the door inch by inch right in her face, anxious to get rid of her.

For a moment he lost an inch or two. 'Allie?' she said. 'Who's Allie?'

'That's Al,' he said quickly. 'Fellow I go around with—with him tonight. I'm so used to saying his name every five minutes or so.'

He finally got the door shut and went 'Whew!'—from the shoelaces up. Money, he said, that's all it is—she wants money. That hint about not working. All right, I'll give her some. Wind the thing up that way. She was entitled to something after all, he supposed.

He took five hundred out of his savings account the next day, during his lunch-hour. The nick it made wasn't too bad. There was still plenty to cover the honeymoon expenses and the first few months of married life. And he was making a good salary.

Then right in front of the bank, coming out, he met Dunc, Allie's brother. Dunc glanced up at the bank facade, then at him, and said, 'Look, if you could use a little extra—I know how it is at a time like this, I went through the mill myself three years ago.'

Bing! another two hundred and fifty from Dunc, smack in his palm. His face didn't even change color. After all, they were both going to be in the same family, weren't they?

First, he thought, I'll put two fifty of my own back. Then he thought, why be a rat—let her have it all, it's only money. So she was coming out pretty good for a last year's leftover crush; she had no kick coming. She'll fall all over my neck, he thought complacently. But no fooling around tonight; I'm going to unwind her arms and give them back to her.

The bungalow was 'way out at the end of nowhere—dim in the growing darkness. Even the road in front of it wasn't paved yet, just surfaced with some kind of black stuff. But there were going to be other bungalows—he could just make out the skeleton frames of some of them already starting up in a straight line past hers, getting thinner as they went along, until there were only foundations, then just a bulldozer.

She had it fixed up real pretty, the way women like to do, even women with broken hearts. Chintz curtains fluttering out the windows, like vermilion lips coaxing to be kissed.

She didn't even give him a chance to get onto the porch and ring the bell. She was waiting there for him. She had on a little apron to match the curtains. Last year's love, playing house all by herself.

'I wasn't sure you were really coming.'

He raised his brows. 'Did I ever break my word to you?'

'No,' she said. 'Not your word. Only—'

She had cocktails frosting in a shaker.

'You used to like martinis best,' she said.

'I don't like martinis any more,' he said, and let that sink in.

She traced a finger on the frosting of the shaker and made a little track, shiny as a mirror. 'I've got to talk to you.'

'We don't have to,' he said. 'This talks better than anything. This talks best.' He'd taken the money out and laid it down.

'What's that for?' she said, her face suddenly white with shock and insult and hurt.

'Well, if you don't know why, don't ask me.'

She sat in a chair for a few moments getting over it—or, it would be more correct to say, getting familiar with it. She had a slow temper. Until this moment, as a matter of fact, he hadn't known she had any temper at all.

Then she got up, and her face was unlike any face he'd ever seen her wear before. She flung the words point-blank at him.

'You don't have to do *this* to me! You don't have to do *this*!'

'Then what else is there?' In all honesty he couldn't understand her outrage. He'd lost her train of thought, and the situation was becoming an irritant.

'What *else* is there? You have to stand by me, that's what else there is! I can't go it alone!'

Now his voice went up, almost into a wail of incomprehension. 'Stand by you! What does that mean?'

She took her open hand and slammed it down on the table, so hard that the ice in the shaker went *tlink!* 'I'm going to have your baby, that's what that means!'

The shock was dizzying. He had to reach out and hold on to something for a moment.

'How do I—?'

'There never was another man in my life, that's how you know.' And he did know.

'All right,' he said.

'All right what?'

'I'll take care of everything. Hospital and—'

Now finally she screamed piercingly at him in her passion and torment, and she wasn't the kind to scream. 'Hospital? I don't want a hospital, I want a husband!'

The second shock, on top of the first, completely unbalanced him. The rest was just physical reflex, not mental reaction at all.

She said only one thing more in her life. In her entire life.

'You're going to marry me, do you understand? You're going to *marry* me!'

The object was suddenly in his hand, as though it had jumped into his hand of its own accord. He hadn't seen it before, hadn't even known it was in the room.

She died at almost the very first blow. But he kept striking on and on and on, to the point of frenzy, to the point of mania, to the point of sheer hallucination. And then she was gone, and it was over. And the thing that a hundred other men, a thousand other men, had done, and that he'd thought he'd never do—now he'd done it too. And the thing he'd read about a hundred times, a thousand times, now he wasn't reading about it, he was living it. And he liked it much better the other way.

He looked at the object he was still holding, and he realized he actually didn't know what it was even now. What could have been more unpremeditated than that? Some sort of long curving blade, razor-keen. Then at last he identified it—more by hearsay than by actual recognition. A Samurai sword, souvenir of the long-ago war with Japan. He remembered now she had once mentioned she had a brother who had served in the Pacific theater—only to come back and

217

die in a car crash not long after. Many men had brought these back with them at the time.

He let go, and it dropped with a muffled thud.

After a while he located the bracket she had driven into the wall. It must have been hanging up there. When he went over to it he found, on the floor underneath, the severed cord it had hung by and the empty scabbard. His subconscious mind must have recognized it for a weapon, for he had no recollection whatever of snatching it down, and yet he must have, in the blinding red explosion that had burst in his brain and ended in murder.

In the beginning he was very mechanical, as the glaze of shock that coated him all over slowly thawed and loosened. He tipped the cocktail shaker into one of the two glasses and drank. He even ate one of the two olives she'd had ready at the bottoms of the two glasses. Not calloused. His instinct told him he needed it, if he wanted to try to live. And he wanted to try to live very badly. Even more so now that he'd looked at death this close with his own eyes. Then he poured a second one, but let it stand. Then he emptied what remained in the shaker down the sink.

It seemed hopeless. There seemed no place to begin. The room was daubed with her, as though a house painter had taken a bucket of her blood, dipped his paint brush in it, then splashed it this way and that way and every which way all over the walls. He was splattered himself, but fortunately he was wearing a dark suit and it didn't show up much; and that part of the job could wait until later.

The first thing to do was to get her out of here. All the little hers . . . He went to her closet and found a number of opaque plastic garment bags—even more than he needed, in fact . . . and finally he zippered them up securely and let them lean there a moment.

Then he went out to his car, opened the trunk compartment, and made room. He went around to the front seat, got the evening newspaper that he remembered having left there, and papered the entire trunk with it, to prevent any errant stains or smears. It was so incredibly unpeopled out here that he didn't even have to be furtive about it. Just an occasional precautionary look around him.

Then he went in again, brought out the garment bags, put them in the trunk, and locked it. He stepped back into the bungalow to put out the lights, took her key with him so he'd be able to get back in again, got in his car, and drove off.

And as far as that part went, that was all. There was nothing more to it.

He drove steadily for some hours. And strangely enough, at a rather slow pace, almost a desultory glide. He could do that because, again strangely enough, he felt no panic whatever. Even his fear was not acute or urgent. It would be untrue to say that he felt no fear at all; but it was distant and objective, rather than imminent and personal—more on the level of ordinary prudence and caution. And this must have been because it had all come up so suddenly, and blown over so suddenly, that his nerves hadn't had time to be subjected to a long, fraying strain. They were the nerves of an almost normal person, not of a man who had just taken another person's life.

He even stopped once, left the car, and bought a fresh pack of cigarettes at a place he saw was still open. He even stayed there for a few moments, parked in front of it, smoking, then finally slithered on again.

At last his driving stopped being directionless, took on purpose, as he finally made up his mind about a destination. There was very little noticeable change in it, and he still didn't hurry. He simply made fewer haphazard turns and roundabouts, and perhaps stepped it up another five miles per hour.

Even with a target, he still continued driving for several more hours. The metropolitan section was now left far behind. On the final lap he was purring steadily along a road that paralleled a railroad right-of-way. An occasional pair of lights would blink past him going the other way. There was nothing for anyone else to see or recall—just a relaxed silhouette behind the wheel, with a red coal near its lips, and tooling by. Although a good, wide road, it was not a main artery of traffic.

More than half the night had now gone by, but he still drove on. This had to be done, and when a thing has to be done, it should be done right, no matter how much time it takes.

At last, as he neared the outskirts of a large-sized town, the railroad tracks broadened into numerous sidings, and these blossomed finally into strings of stagnant freight cars of assorted lengths, some only two or three coupled together, others almost endless chains.

He came to a halt finally by the side of the road, took out a flashlight, and left the car. He disappeared into one of the dark lanes between the freight cars, an occasional soft crunch of gravel the only indication of his movements. He was gone for some time, taking his time in this as in everything else. Almost like a shopper shopping for something that exactly suits him, and refusing to be satisfied with anything else.

When he came back to his car there was very little more to it. He went out to the middle of the road, stood there first looking up one way, then down the other. When he was sure there were no lights approaching even in the remotest distance, he stepped over to his car, moving deftly and quickly but still by no means frightenedly, opened the trunk, and took out the garment bags. He propped them for a moment against the car while he took the precaution of closing the trunk, so that it might not attract attention in case anyone should drive by while he was gone.

Then, half supporting and half trailing the garment bags, he disappeared into the lane of his choice between the parallels of freight cars—the one that led to the freight car he had found with its door left unfastened. There was the sound of the slide grating open, then in a few moments the sound of it grating closed again. And that was all.

When he came back to the car he was alone, unburdened.

The drive back was as uneventful as the drive out. If he had been of a cynical nature, he might have been tempted to ask: What's there to a murder? What's there to worry about?

In due course he came back to the point where the route that led out to her bungalow diverged from the route that would eventually bring him to his own apartment. He didn't even hesitate. He took the road home. He was taking a gamble of a sort, and yet it wasn't as great a gamble as it appeared; he felt now that the longer odds were in his favor, and besides, there was nothing more he could do in her bungalow at this time. She had told him she had stopped working. There was a good chance no one would go there to seek her out during the course of the next day or two. And if someone should, there was an even better chance they would not force entry into the bungalow.

So he decided to go home, leave the bloodstained room the way it was for the time being, and not return until after he'd had a chance to make the necessary preparations for cleaning it up.

He set his alarm for nine, and slept the three hours remaining until then. Which is three hours more sleep than the average murderer can usually get on the first night following his crime.

When he awoke it was Saturday morning, and without even breakfasting he went to a paint store completely across town from where he lived and explained to the clerk that his so-and-so of a landlord wouldn't paint for him; so he was going to do the job himself and be damned to him.

The man in the paint store was sympathetic. 'What color you want?' he asked.

'What color would you advise?'

'What color is it now?'

He picked it out with positive accuracy on a color chart the man showed him.

'Well, your best bet to cover that would be either a medium green or a medium brown,' the clerk said. 'Otherwise the color on now is going to show through and you'd have to give it two coats.'

He thought of the color of dried blood and promptly selected the brown—a sort of light cinnamon with a reddish overtone. Then he bought a like shade of glossy paint for the woodwork, a ladder, and the requisite brushes and mixing fluids. Then he went to a clothing store—not a haberdashery but the sort of outlet that sells work clothes—and purchased a pair of overalls, and added a pair of gauntlets so that he wouldn't get any paint under his fingernails. Such a thing could be the devil to pay.

Then he went back to where he'd killed her.

It was only just past mid-morning when he got there. This time he drove off the unpaved roadway, detoured around to the back of the bungalow, and parked directly behind it in such a way that the house itself hid his car.

There was really no need for this precaution. Being Saturday, the neighborhood was empty—no workmen, no residents; but he felt better taking every possible safeguard, even against an unlikely prowler.

Then on foot he circled around to the front and examined the porch before unloading anything from his car. It was just as he had left it. There was every evidence that his gamble had paid off, that no one had come near the bungalow since it had happened. From a remark she had dropped at his place when they were setting up what had turned out to be the murder appointment, he knew she had no telephone. She was on the waiting list but they hadn't got to her yet. From their old days together he remembered she had never been much of a newspaper reader, so it was extremely improbable she would have regular delivery service, especially in this deserted section. As for milk, there were no signs of that either; she must have brought home a carton from the grocery store whenever she needed it. Finally, the mail slot opened directly into the house itself, so there was no way of telling from the outside whether the mail had been picked up by its recipient or not.

There wasn't a single thing that wasn't in his favor. He almost marveled at it himself.

He gave another precautionary look around, then opened up the front door with her key, and went in.

For a moment—and for the first time—his heart almost failed him. It looked even worse than he'd remembered from the night before. Maybe he'd been too taken up with removing her to give it due notice. There was only one wall that was completely sterile. Two more were in bad-to-middling shape. But the fourth was practically marbleized, it had such veins and skeins twining all over it. It resembled nothing so much as a great upright slab of white-and-brown marble.

He could see what had caused the marbleized effect. It wasn't that the blood had spurted of its own accord: it was the strokes of the Samurai sword that had splashed it like that—all over everything.

It was too big a job; he felt he could never swing it.

And then he reminded himself: you got rid of her body, didn't you? If you did that, you can do this too.

He then did another of those incongruous things that he kept doing all the way through. He picked up the shaker from the night before, got out the gin and the vermouth, and made himself two more martinis. He left out the olives though.

Feeling more confident now, he changed to his work clothes. He even took off his shoes and remained in his socks. Paint spots on shoes could be just as hard to remove and just as incriminating as paint underneath fingernails.

When he began the new paint job he realized that he didn't have to be too finicky about it—they couldn't arrest you just because your painting wasn't up to major league standards. The daubing went as fast as a speed-cop's motorcycle on the way with a ticket. Almost before he knew it, he had all four sides done, including the one that hadn't needed it. This latter he threw in by way of artistic flourish. The room would have looked queer with three walls one color and the fourth another.

The ladder folded, the buckets out of the way, the overalls and gauntlets stripped off, he stood in the center of the room and took a comprehensive look at his handiwork—and drew a deep sigh. Not only of relief, but somewhat of cocksure pride.

It might not have been the best paint job that had ever been done, but it guaranteed one thing: the walls were bloodless; the damning stains were completely covered up.

The furniture, of course, was going to be a different matter. Fortunately, it wasn't outsized, the room itself being fairly small. He rolled up the rug and stood it in a corner, just inside the front door.

This part of the program, he knew, would be less arduous than the walls, but it was also going to be a good deal more risky. It necessitated arson.

He slipped out and made a tour of inspection of the skeleton bungalows that sprouted past hers, giving the interior of each one a quick glance.

The first three were too close to hers for his purpose—the inference might be a little too easy to draw. The one at the opposite end was nothing but a gouged-out foundation and poured concrete. The next-to-the-last already had its two-by-fours up, but no flooring or roofing. The next one in had enough wooden construction—plus a lot of shavings—to be ideal: it was like starting a fire in an empty lathe-basket.

Three trips were necessary. He carried the rolled rug, the removable cushions from settee and chair, a small end-table, a parchment lampshade, and whatever else had been stained beyond hope of cover-up, to the unfinished bungalow. He didn't forget to include the suit he had worn the night before. He made a pyre of these, topped it off with the paint-impregnated overalls, gauntlets, and brushes, and poured on the highly-inflammable residue from the paint cans.

Then he drained gas from his car, using a receptacle he'd brought from the bungalow, leaving just enough in the tank to get him home, and liberally doused it not only on the mount itself but on the wood around it.

He turned his car around, facing in the direction he was to go, killed the engine, and sat waiting, looking all around him. Finally he started the engine again, very softly, like a newborn kitten purring, picked up a furled newspaper, took a lighter out of his pocket, clicked it twice to make sure it was in working order, got out of the car, leaving the door open in readiness, and went inside the unfinished house.

He came out again at a run—this was the first time since he'd killed her that he moved fast—jumped in the car and started off with a surge. He only closed the door after he was careening along, foot tight to the floor. This part of the operation, if no other, was split-second schedule, and not a stray moment could be spared.

For as long as the place remained in sight behind him he could see no sign of flickering flame, of incipient fire. After that—who was around to care?

He got out in front of his own door, locked the car, tossed his keys jauntily up into the air and caught them deftly in the same hand.

Upstairs, he sprawled out in a chair, legs wide apart, and let out a great sigh of completion, of finality.

'Now let them say I've killed her.' Then, sensibly, he amended it to: 'Now let them *prove* I killed her.'

II. THE DETECTION—AND HOW THEY PROVED IT

They did neither the one nor the other. They started very circumspectly, very offhandedly, in a very minor key—as those things often happen.

A ring at the doorbell.

Two men were standing there.

'Are you—?'

'Yes, I'm—'

'Like to ask you a few questions. Mind if we come in?'

'Come in if you want. I have no objections. Why should I?'

'Do you know a Corinne Matthews?'

'I did at one time.'

'When was the last time you saw her?'

'What is this—June, isn't it? Either late February or early March. I'm not sure which.'

'Not since then?'

'You asked me a minute ago and I told you. If I'd seen her since then, I'd say so.'

'Not since then. That's your statement?'

'My statement, right.'

'Any objection to coming downtown with us? We'd like to question you in further detail.'

'You're the police. When you ask people to come downtown with you, they come downtown with you. No objection.'

They came back again that evening. He went down again the next day. Then back again, down again. Then—

Down again for good.

Held on suspicion of murder.

A back room. Many different rooms, but a back room in particular.

'I suppose now you're going to beat the hell out of me.'

'No, we're not going to beat the hell out of you—never do. Besides, we're too sure of you; we don't want anything to backfire. Juries are funny sometimes. No, we're going to treat you with kid gloves. In fact, you're even going to wear kid shorts when you squat down in the old Easy Chair.'

'Is that what I'm going to do,' he asked wryly, 'for something I didn't do?'

'Save it,' he was advised. 'Save it for when you need it, and you're going to need it plenty.'

All through the long weary day identification followed identification.

'Is this the man who bought a pack of cigarettes from you, and handed you in payment a dollar bill with the print of a bloody thumb on one side and the print of a bloody forefinger on the other?'

'That's him. I thought it was an advertising gag at first, the prints were both so clear. Like for one of them horror movies, where they stencil bloody footprints on the sidewalk in front of the theater, to pull the customers inside. I couldn't help looking at him while he was pocketing his change. I didn't call him on it because I could tell the bill wasn't queer, and he acted so natural, so nonchalant. I even saw him sitting out there smoking for a while afterwards. Yes sir, that's him all right!'

'I don't deny it.'

'Is this the man who bought a can of Number Two russet-brown paint from you? *And* gloss. *And* brushes. *And* a folding stepladder.'

'That's him.'

'I don't deny it.'

'Is this the man who bought a pair of overalls from you? And a pair of work gloves?'

'That's him.'

'I don't deny it.'

Room cleared of identifying witnesses.

'Then you took the materials you've just confessed you bought and went to work on the living room at One Eighty-two.'

'That I don't admit.'

'You deny you repainted that room? Why, it's the identical shade and grade of paint you bought from this paint store!'

'I didn't say I denied it. What I said was, I don't admit it.'

'What does that mean?'

'Prove I painted there. Prove I didn't paint somewhere else.'

They knew they couldn't. So did he.

'Show us where you painted somewhere else, then.'

'No, sir. No, *sir*. That's up to you, not up to me. I didn't say I painted somewhere else. I didn't say I didn't pour it down a sewer. I didn't say I didn't give it away as a present to a friend of mine. I didn't say I didn't leave it standing around some place for a minute and someone stole it from me.'

The two detectives turned their backs on him for a minute. One smote himself on the top of the head and murmured to his companion, 'Oh, this man! He's got a pretzel for a tongue.'

The plastic garment bags and their hideous contents were finally located. Perhaps all the way across the country in some siding or railroad yard in Duluth or Kansas City or Abilene. They didn't tell him that outright, in so many words, or exactly where, but he could sense it by the subtle turn their questioning took.

They had their *corpus delicti* now, but they still couldn't pin it on him. What was holding them up, what was blocking them, he realized with grim satisfaction, was that they couldn't unearth a single witness who could place him at or near the freight yard he'd driven to that night—or at any other freight yard anywhere else on any other night. The car itself, after exhaustive tests and examinations, must have turned out pasteurizedly pure, antibiotically bloodless. He'd seen to that. And the garment bags had been her own to begin with.

There was nothing to trace him by.

Even the Samurai sword—which he had had the audacity to send right along with her, encased in a pair of her nylon stockings—was worthless to them. It had belonged to her, and even if it hadn't, there was no way of checking on such a thing—as there would have been in the case of a firearm. Being a war souvenir, it was nonregisterable.

Finally, there was the total lack of an alibi. Instead of counting against him it seemed to have intensified the deadlock. From the very beginning he had offered none, laid claim to none, therefore gave them none to break down. He'd simply said he'd gone home and stayed there, and admitted from the start he couldn't prove it. But then they couldn't prove he'd been out to the bungalow either. Result: each canceled the other out. Stand-off. Stalemate.

As if to show that they had reached a point of desperation they finally had recourse, during several of the periods of interrogation, to stronger measures. Not violence: no blows were struck, nothing was done that might leave a mark on him afterward. Nor were any threats or promises made. It was a sort of tacit coercion, one might say. He understood it, they understood it, he understood they did, and they understood he did.

Unsuspectingly he accepted some punishingly salty food they sent out for and gave to him. Pickled or smoked herring. But not water.

A fire was made in the boiler room and the radiator in one of the basement detention rooms was turned on full blast, even though it was an oppressively hot turn-of-spring-into-summer day. Still no water.

As though this weren't enough, an electric heater was plugged into an outlet and aimed at his straight-backed chair. He was seated in it and compelled to keep two or three heavy blankets bundled around him. In no time the floor around his feet had darkened with the slow seep of his perspiration. But still no water.

Then a tantalizingly frosted glass pitcher, brimming with crystal-clear water and studded with alluring ice cubes, was brought in and set down on a table just within arm's reach.

But each time he reached for it he was asked a question. And while waiting for the answer, the nearest detective would, absently, draw the pitcher away—just beyond his reach—as if not being aware of what he was doing, the way a man doodles with a pencil or fiddles with a paperweight while talking to someone. When he asked openly for a drink he was told (for the record): 'Help yourself. It's right there in front of you. That's what it's here for.' They were very meticulous about it. Nothing could be proved afterward.

He didn't get a drink of water. But they didn't get the answers they wanted either. Another stalemate.

They rang in a couple of ingenious variations after that, once with cigarettes, another time by a refusal of the comfort facilities of the building. With even less result, since neither impulse was as strong as thirst.

'All we need is one drop of blood,' the detective kept warning him. 'One drop of blood.'

'You won't get it out of me.'

'We have identified the remains, to show there *was* a crime—somewhere. We've found traces of blood on articles handled by you—like the dollar bill you gave the storekeeper—to show, presumably, that you were involved in some crime—somewhere. We've placed *you* in the vicinity of the bungalow: metal bits from the overalls and remains of the paint cans and brush handles in the ashes of the fire. Now all we've got to do is place the crime *itself* there. And that will close the circuit.

'One drop of blood will do it. One single drop of blood.'

'It seems a shame that such a modest requirement can't be met,' was his ironic comment.

And then suddenly, when least expected, he was released.

Whether there was some legal technicality involved and they were afraid of losing him altogether in the long run if they charged him too quickly; whether it was just a temporary expedient so that they could watch him all the closer—anyway, release.

One of the detectives came in, stood looking at him.

'Good morning,' he said finally to the detective, sardonically, to break the optical deadlock.

'I suppose you'd like to get out of here.'

'There are places I've liked better.'

The detective jerked his head. 'You can go. That's all for now. Sign a receipt and the property clerk will return your valuables.'

He didn't stir. 'Not if there are any strings attached to it.'

'What do you want, an apology or something?'

'No, I just want to know where I stand. Am I in or am I out—or what.'

'You were never actually under arrest, so what're you beefing about?'

'Well, if I wasn't, there sure has been something hampering my freedom. Maybe my shoelaces were tied together.'

'Just hold yourself available in case you're needed. Don't leave town.'

He finally walked out behind the detective, throwing an empty cigarette pack on the floor. 'Was any of this in the newspapers?'

'I don't keep a scrapbook. I wouldn't know,' said the detective.

He picked one up, and it was, had been, and was going to be.

The first thing he did was to phone Allie. She wouldn't come to the phone—or they wouldn't let her. She was ill in bed, they said. That much he didn't disbelieve, or wonder at. There was also a coldness, an iciness: he'd hurt these people badly.

He hung up. He tried again later. And then again. And still again. He wouldn't give up. His whole happiness was at stake now.

Finally he went back to his own apartment. There was nothing left for him to do. It was already well after midnight by this time. The phone was ringing as he keyed the door open. It sounded as if it had been ringing for some time and was about to die out. He grabbed at it.

'Darling,' Allie said in a pathetically weak voice, 'I'm calling you from the phone next to my bed. They don't know I'm doing it, or they—'

'You don't believe what you've been reading about me?'

'Not if you tell me not to.'

'It was just a routine questioning. I used to know the girl a long time ago, and they grabbed at every straw that came their way.'

'We'll have to change everything—go off quietly by ourselves. But I don't care.'

'I've got to see you. Shall I come up there?'

'No,' she said tearfully. 'Not yet. You'd better wait a while first. Give them a little more time.'

'But then how am I going to—?'

'I'll dress and come out and meet you somewhere.'

'Can you make it?'

'I'm getting better every minute. Just hearing your voice, hearing you say that it was not true—that's better than all their tranquilizers.'

"There's a quiet little cocktail lounge called "For Lovers Only". Not noisy, not jammed. The end booth.'

Her voice was getting stronger. 'We were there once, remember?'

'Wear the same dress you did that night.'

It was on all over again. 'Hurry, I'm waiting for your hello-kiss.'

He pulled his shirt off so exuberantly that he split the sleeve halfway down. He didn't care. He shook the shave-cream bomb until it nearly exploded in his hand. He went back to the phone and called a florist.

'I want an orchid sent somewhere—end booth—she'll be wearing pale yellow. I didn't ask you that, but what does come after the fifteen-dollar one? Then make it two fifteen-dollar ones. And on the card you just say this—"From a fellow to his girl." '

And because he was young and in love—completely, sincerely in love, even though he'd killed someone who had once loved him the same way—he started, in his high spirits, in his release from long-sustained tension, to do a mimic Indian war-dance, prancing around the room, now reared up high, now bent down low, drumming his hand against his mouth. 'O-wah-o-wah!'

I beat it! he told himself, I've got it made. Just take it easy from here in, just talk with a small mouth—and I'm the one in a thousand who beat it!

Then someone knocked quietly on his door.

Less than an hour after going to bed, one of the detectives stirred and finally sat up again.

His wife heard him groping for his shoes to put them back on. 'What's the matter?' she asked sleepily. 'You want a drink of water?'

'No,' he said. 'I want a drop of blood.'

'If you couldn't find a drop of blood in the daytime how are you going to find it at night?'

He didn't answer; he just went ahead pulling his pants on.

'Oh, God,' the poor woman moaned, 'why did I ever marry a detective?'

'Oh, God,' he groaned back from the direction of the door, 'what makes you think you have?'

'O-wah-o-wah!'

Someone knocked quietly on his door.

He went over to it, and it was one of them again.

He looked at the intruder ruefully—confidently but ruefully. 'What, again?' he sighed.

'This time it's for real.'

'What was it all the other times, a rehearsal without costumes?'

'Hard to convince, aren't you? All right, I'll make it official,' the detective said obligingly, 'You're under arrest for the murder of Corinne Matthews. Anything-you-say-may-be-held-against-you-kindly-come-with-me.'

'You did that like a professional,' he smirked, still confident.

The detective had brought a car with him. They got in it.

'This is going to blow right up in your face. You know that, don't you? I'll sue for false arrest—I'll sue the city for a million.'

'All right, I'll show you.'

They drove to the bungalow that had been Corinne Matthews', and parked. They got out and went in together. They had to go through the doorway on the bias. The detective had him on handcuffs now—he wasn't taking any chances.

The detective left it dark. He took out his flashlight and made a big dazzling cartwheel of light by holding it nozzle-close against one section of the wall.

'Take a good look,' he said.

'Why don't you put the lights on?'

'Take a good look this way first.'

Just a newly painted, spotless wall, and at one side the light switch, tripped to OFF.

'Now look at it this way.'

He killed the flashlight, snapped up the wall switch, and the room lit up. Still just a newly painted, spotless wall, and at one side the light switch, reversed now to ON.

And on it a small blob of blood.

'That's what I needed. And look, that's what I got.'

The accused sat down, the accuser at the other end of the hand-cuffs, standing, his arm at elbow height.

'How can a guy win?' the murderer whispered.

'You killed her at night, when the lights were on, when the switch was up like this, showing ON. You came back and painted in the day-light hours, when the lights were not on, when the switch was down, showing OFF. We cased this room a hundred times, for a hundred hours—*but always in the daytime too*, when the lights were not on, when the switch was down, showing OFF. And on the part of the switch *that never showed in the daytime*, the part marked ON, the way it is now, there was one drop of blood that we never found—until tonight.'

The murderer was quiet for a minute, then he said the final words—no good to hold them back any more. 'Sure,' he said, 'it was like that. That's what it was like.'

His head went over, and a great huff of hot breath came surging out of him, rippling down his necktie, like the vital force, the will to resist, emptying itself.

The end of another story.

The end of another life.

NOTES

1

'Thou Art the Man' by Edgar Allan Poe (1809–49). First published in *Godey's Lady's Book* (Nov. 1844). Born in Boston and educated at private schools, Poe was dismissed from both the University of Virginia and West Point. He published his first poems in 1827 and his short stories began to appear in 1833. The first of his three pioneering detective stories about C. Auguste Dupin, 'The Murders in the Rue Morgue', was published by *Graham's Magazine* in 1841, a publication which he later edited. In ill health and suffering from a nervous breakdown, he died in Baltimore at the age of 40.

2

'The Stolen Rubens' by Jacques Futrelle (1875–1912). First published in 1907 by Associated Sunday Magazine, Inc. Born in Georgia, Futrelle moved north and became a staff member of the *Boston American*. The first of his Thinking Machine tales, 'The Problem of Cell 13', appeared serially as a contest story in the paper in 1905 and soon became one of the most popular of American detective stories. He followed it with a variety of other fiction, including nearly fifty more stories about the Thinking Machine. Futrelle and his wife were aboard the maiden voyage of the *Titanic* in 1912. She survived but he perished with the ship.

3

'The Second Bullet' by Anna Katharine Green (1846–1935). First published in *The Golden Slipper and Other Problems for Violet Strange* (1915). A native of Brooklyn who lived much of her life in Buffalo, New York, Anna Katharine Green was the first important woman mystery writer in America. Her book *The Leavenworth Case* (1878) was the first best-selling mystery novel and launched a lengthy and productive career during which she produced thirty-three novels and six collections of short stories. Born during Poe's lifetime, she lived well into mystery's Golden Age, publishing her final novel three years after the début of Agatha Christie.

4

'The Age of Miracles' by Melville Davisson Post (1869–1930). First published in the *Pictorial Review* (Feb. 1916). Born in West Virginia, Post practised criminal and corporate law for eleven years, drawing upon his knowledge for *The Strange Schemes of Randolph Mason* (1896) and its sequels about an unscrupulous lawyer. These were followed by his twenty-two tales about Uncle Abner, a deeply religious man who solves crimes in rural Virginia shortly before the Civil War. One of the great American contributions to the detective story, the stories were collected in *Uncle Abner, Master of Mysteries* (1918) and *The Complete Uncle Abner* (1977).

5

'The Shadow' by T(homas) S(igismund) Stribling (1881–1965). First published in 1934 by *Red Book Magazine*. A native of Tennessee, Stribling had various careers as an editor, teacher, and lawyer before publishing his first book in 1917. His fourteen novels were all mainstream work, often set in the backcountry of Tennessee and Alabama. *The Store* (1932) was the most highly regarded, bringing him the Pulitzer Prize for Fiction. His only mysteries, the Henry Poggioli stories, are found in the classic *Clues of the Caribbees* (1929) and *Best Dr. Poggioli Detective Stories* (1975), though some from the 1930s remain uncollected.

6

'The Episode of the Nail and the Requiem' by C(harles) Daly King (1895–1963). First published in *The Curious Mr. Tarrant* (1935). Born in New York City and an honors graduate from Yale University, King published three books on psychology before turning to mystery writing in the 1930s. He produced six novels, notably *Obelists Fly High* (1935), and a collection of Trevis Tarrant short stories. All were published first in England, and the Tarrant stories had to wait forty-two years for an American edition. He all but abandoned detective fiction after 1940, returning to his studies at Yale.

7

'His Heart Could Break' by Craig Rice (Georgiana Ann Randolph, 1908–57). First published in *Ellery Queen's Mystery Magazine* (Mar. 1943). A Chicago native who became, briefly, the best-known of America's women mystery writers, Craig Rice published her first novel *8 Faces at 3* in 1939 and followed it with twenty more novels and three screenplays during the 1940s alone, including ghost-written mysteries for Gypsy Rose Lee and George Sanders. She seems to have used a ghost writer during the final years of her life. *Trial by Fury* (1941) is usually considered the best of her books.

8

'The House in Goblin Wood' by Carter Dickson (John Dickson Carr, 1906–77). First published in *Ellery Queen's Mystery Magazine* (Nov. 1947). Born in Pennsylvania, John Dickson Carr married an Englishwoman early in his career and lived in England from 1932 to 1948, returning for a time in the mid-1950s. In addition to some seventy novels and fifty short stories he wrote nearly one hundred radio plays for the BBC and CBS. A master of the locked room, exemplified by

Notes

The Three Coffins (1935, British title *The Hollow Man*), his books also included numerous historical mysteries and a biography of Sir Arthur Conan Doyle.

9

'The Dauphin's Doll' by Ellery Queen (Frederic Dannay, 1905–82, and Manfred B. Lee, 1905–71). First published in *Ellery Queen's Mystery Magazine* (Dec. 1948). Cousins Dannay and Lee, both born in Brooklyn, won a contest with their first novel, *The Roman Hat Mystery* (1929). They published thirty-seven novels and eight short-story collections over the next forty-two years, most about super-sleuth Ellery Queen. They also founded *Ellery Queen's Mystery Magazine*, which Dannay edited until his death. Their most notable novels were *Calamity Town* (1942) and *Cat of Many Tails* (1949).

10

'The Splinter' by Mary Roberts Rinehart (1876–1958). First published in *Ellery Queen's Mystery Magazine* (Sept. 1955). Born in Pittsburgh, Rinehart published her first novel *The Circular Staircase* in 1908 and was a popular mystery writer for the next half-century, drawing upon her early nurse's training for the character of Nurse Hilda Adams in some books. Usually considered a woman's writer and known for inventing the 'Had I But Known' device in her books, she was still an important contributor to the romantic mystery. True to the old cliché, in one of her twenty mystery novels the butler did it.

11

'The Pencil' by Raymond Chandler (1888–1959). First published in the (London) *Daily Mail* (6 Apr. 1959). A Chicago native, Chandler was educated in England and became a naturalized British subject, reverting to his American citizenship late in life. Holding a variety of jobs, he did not become a full-time writer until 1933 when he began selling stories to *Black Mask* magazine. His first two novels, *The Big Sleep* (1939) and *Farewell, My Lovely* (1940), established him as a major American mystery writer. Chandler followed them with five other novels, notably *The Long Goodbye* (1953).

12

'One Drop of Blood' by Cornell Woolrich (George Hopley-Woolrich, 1903–68). First published in *Ellery Queen's Mystery Magazine* (Apr. 1962). Born in New York City, Woolrich achieved fame with his six 'black' novels beginning with *The Bride Wore Black* (1940). He also wrote as 'William Irish', producing the notable novel *Phantom Lady* (1942). His life, lived mainly in hotel rooms, was as dark and lonely as his fiction, but his influence on crime writing and films cannot be overstated. Hitchcock's classic film *Rear Window* was one of many based on a Woolrich story.

ACKNOWLEDGEMENTS

Raymond Chandler, *The Pencil*, first published in the *Daily Mail* (London) (6 Apr. 1959), © Philip Marlowe B.V. courtesy of Ed Victor Ltd. Literary Agency, London.

Carter Dickson, *The House in Goblin Wood*, first published in *Ellery Queen's Mystery Magazine* (Nov. 1947). Reprinted by permission of Harold Ober Associates Incorporated. Copyright © 1947 by John Dickson Carr. Copyright renewed 1975 by John Dickson Carr.

Ellery Queen, *The Dauphin's Doll*, first published in *Ellery Queen's Mystery Magazine* (Dec. 1948). Copyright © 1948 by Mercury House Publications and reprinted by permission of the author's estate and its agents, Scott Meredith Literary Agency, L.P., 845 Third Avenue, New York, NY 10022.

Craig Rice, *His Heart Could Break*, first published in *Ellery Queen's Mystery Magazine* (Mar. 1943). Copyright © 1943 by Mercury House Publications and reprinted by permission of the author's estate and its agents, Scott Meredith Literary Agency, L.P., 845 Third Avenue, New York, NY 10022.

Mary Roberts Rinehart, *The Splinter*, first published in *Ellery Queen's Mystery Magazine* (Sept. 1955). Copyright © 1955 Henry Holt & Co., New York, and reprinted by permission of the artist's estate.

Cornell Woolrich, *One Drop of Blood*, first published in *Ellery Queen's Mystery Magazine* (Apr. 1962). Copyright © 1962 by Mercury House Publications and reprinted by permission of the author's estate and its agents, Scott Meredith Literary Agency, L.P., 845 Third Avenue, New York, NY 10022.

OXFORD

MORE OXFORD PAPERBACKS

This book is just one of nearly 1000 Oxford Paperbacks currently in print. If you would like details of other Oxford Paperbacks, including titles in the World's Classics, Oxford Reference, Oxford Books, OPUS, Past Masters, Oxford Authors, and Oxford Shakespeare series, please write to:

UK and Europe: Oxford Paperbacks Publicity Manager, Arts and Reference Publicity Department, Oxford University Press, Walton Street, Oxford OX2 6DP.

Customers in UK and Europe will find Oxford Paperbacks available in all good bookshops. But in case of difficulty please send orders to the Cash-with-Order Department, Oxford University Press Distribution Services, Saxon Way West, Corby, Northants NN18 9ES. Tel: 01536 741519; Fax: 01536 746337. Please send a cheque for the total cost of the books, plus £1.75 postage and packing for orders under £20; £2.75 for orders over £20. Customers outside the UK should add 10% of the cost of the books for postage and packing.

USA: Oxford Paperbacks Marketing Manager, Oxford University Press, Inc., 200 Madison Avenue, New York, N.Y. 10016.

Canada: Trade Department, Oxford University Press, 70 Wynford Drive, Don Mills, Ontario M3C 1J9.

Australia: Trade Marketing Manager, Oxford University Press, G.P.O. Box 2784Y, Melbourne 3001, Victoria.

South Africa: Oxford University Press, P.O. Box 1141, Cape Town 8000.

OXFORD BOOKS

THE OXFORD BOOK OF ENGLISH GHOST STORIES

Chosen by Michael Cox and R. A. Gilbert

This anthology includes some of the best and most frightening ghost stories ever written, including M. R. James's 'Oh Whistle, and I'll Come to You, My Lad', 'The Monkey's Paw' by W. W. Jacobs, and H. G. Wells's 'The Red Room'. The important contribution of women writers to the genre is represented by stories such as Amelia Edwards's 'The Phantom Coach', Edith Wharton's 'Mr Jones', and Elizabeth Bowen's 'Hand in Glove'.

As the editors stress in their informative introduction, a good ghost story, though it may raise many profound questions about life and death, entertains as much as it unsettles us, and the best writers are careful to satisfy what Virginia Woolf called 'the strange human craving for the pleasure of feeling afraid'. This anthology, the first to present the full range of classic English ghost fiction, similarly combines a serious literary purpose with the plain intention of arousing pleasing fear at the doings of the dead.

'an excellent cross-section of familiar and unfamiliar stories and guaranteed to delight' *New Statesman*

ILLUSTRATED HISTORIES IN
OXFORD PAPERBACKS

THE OXFORD ILLUSTRATED HISTORY
OF ENGLISH LITERATURE

Edited by Pat Rogers

Britain possesses a literary heritage which is almost
unrivalled in the Western world. In this volume, the
richness, diversity, and continuity of that tradition
are explored by a group of Britain's foremost literary scholars.

Chapter by chapter the authors trace the history
of English literature, from its first stirrings in Anglo-
Saxon poetry to the present day. At its heart towers
the figure of Shakespeare, who is accorded a special
chapter to himself. Other major figures such as
Chaucer, Milton, Donne, Wordsworth, Dickens,
Eliot, and Auden are treated in depth, and the story
is brought up to date with discussion of living
authors such as Seamus Heaney and Edward Bond.

'[a] lovely volume . . . put in your thumb and pull
out plums' Michael Foot

'scholarly and enthusiastic people have written inspiring essays that induce an eagerness in their readers to return to the writers they admire' *Economist*

Oxford ✿ Paperbacks

OXFORD

ON HORSEBACK THROUGH ASIA MINOR

Frederick Burnaby

With a new introduction by *Peter Hopkirk*

In the savage winter of 1876, Captain Frederick Burnaby rode 1,000 miles eastwards from Constantinople to see for himself what the Russians were up to in this remote corner of the Great Game battlefield. With war between Turkey and Russia imminent, he wanted to discover, among other things, whether the Sultan's armies were capable of resisting a determined Tsarist thrust towards Constantinople.

Frederick Gustav Burnaby was no ordinary officer. For a start he was reputed to be the strongest man in the British Army. Nor was he all brawn, being fluent in seven languages and possessing a vigorous and colourful prose style—as readers of this Great Game classic will discover.

With his redoubtable manservant Radford, he spent five months riding across some of the cruellest winter landscape in the world before hastening home to write this best-seller.

Oxford ✿ Paperbacks

ON SECRET SERVICE EAST OF
CONSTANTINOPLE

THE PLOT TO BRING DOWN THE
BRITISH EMPIRE

Peter Hopkirk

Under the banner of a Holy War, masterminded in
Berlin and unleashed from Constantinople, the Ger-
mans and the Turks set out in 1914 to foment violent revolutionary uprisings against the British in
India and the Russians in Central Asia. It was a new
and more sinister version of the old Great Game,
with world domination as its ultimate aim.

Here, told in epic detail and for the first time, is the
true story of behind John Buchan's classic wartime
novel *Greenmantle*, recounted through the adventures and misadventures of the secret agents and
others who took part in it.

Pieced together from the secret intelligence reports
of the day and the long-forgotten memoirs of the
participants, Peter Hopkirk's latest narrative is an
enthralling sequel to his best-selling *The Great
Game*, and his three earlier works set in Central
Asia. It is a highly topical tale in view of recent
events in this volatile region where the Great Game
has never really ceased.

'an enthralling story'
Observer

'a story which no single book has told before'
Sunday Telegraph

Oxford ⚙ Paperbacks

OXFORD

SETTING THE EAST ABLAZE
ON SECRET SERVICE IN BOLSHEVIK ASIA

Peter Hopkirk

As the European revolution failed to materialize,
Lenin decreed, 'Let us turn our faces towards Asia.
The East will help us to conquer the West.'

Pieced together from secret reports and eye-witness
memoirs, this is the first book to tell the story of the
Bolshevik attempt to spread Marxism throughout
Asia and its frustration by British Indian intelligence
agents. An extraordinary story of the intrigue and
treachery of the Great Game, its key players include
Chinese warlords, Muslim visionaries, and a White
Russian baron who roasted his Communist captives
alive.

'a classic example of truth outpacing fiction'
Times Literary Supplement

'the stuff of a dozen adventure movies'
New York Times

OXFORD

TRESPASSERS ON THE ROOF OF
THE WORLD
THE RACE FOR LHASA

Peter Hopkirk

Hidden behind the Himalayas and ruled over by a God-king, Tibet has always cast a powerful spell over travellers from the West.

In this remarkable, and ultimately tragic narrative, Peter Hopkirk recounts the forcible opening up of this medieval land during the nineteenth and twentieth centuries,—of the extraordinary race between agents, soldiers, missionaries, mountaineers, explorers, and mystics from nine different countries to reach Lhasa, Tibet's sacred capital. His story with its remarkable cast, concludes with the ultimate act of trespass—the Chinese invasion of 1950.

'as vivid and gripping as a John Buchan novel'
Evening Standard

'a rich harvest of harrowing adventures which Hopkirk recounts in fascinating detail'
Daily Telegraph

OXFORD

FOREIGN DEVILS ON THE SILK ROAD
THE SEARCH FOR THE LOST TREASURES OF CENTRAL ASIA

Peter Hopkirk

The Silk Road was the great trans-Asian highway linking Imperial Rome with distant China. Along it travelled precious cargoes of silk, gold, ivory, plants and animals, art and knowledge. A thousand years after it fell into disuse, a Swede, Sven Hedin, stumbled onto one of its lost towns and began a race to plunder the art treasures buried beneath the desert sands. Defying local legends of vengeful demons, archaeologists carried off vast quantities of wall-paintings, sculptures, silks, and manuscripts.

In examining this contentious chapter in China's history, Peter Hopkirk recalls the intrepid men who, at great personal risk, led these daring raids.

'a book which, once opened, is difficult to put down'
Daily Telegraph

'highly readable'
Times Literary Supplement

'opens a window onto a fascinating world'
Financial Times

OXFORD

THE GREAT GAME
ON SECRET SERVICE IN HIGH ASIA
Peter Hopkirk

For nearly a century the two most powerful nations on earth—Victorian Britain and Tsarist Russia—fought a secret war in the lonely passes and deserts of Central Asia. Those engaged in this shadowy struggle called it the 'Great Game', a phrase immortalized in Kipling's *Kim*.

When play first began the two rival empires lay nearly 2,000 miles apart. By the end, some Russian outposts were within 20 miles of India.

This book tells the story of the Great Game through the exploits of the young officers, both British and Russian, who risked their lives playing it. Disguised as holy men or native horse-traders, they mapped secret passes, gathered intelligence, and sought the allegiance of powerful khans. Some never returned.

'A terrific collection of yarns; an invaluable work of imperial history.'
Observer

'brilliant'
Daily Telegraph

'highly entertaining'
Independent on Sunday

BUDDHISM

Damien Keown

'Karma can be either good or bad. Buddhists speak of good karma as "merit", and much effort is expended in acquiring it. Some picture it as a kind of spiritual capital—like money in a bank account—whereby credit is built up as the deposit on a heavenly rebirth.'

This Very Short Introduction introduces the reader both to the teachings of the Buddha and to the integration of Buddhism into daily life. What are the distinctive features of Buddhism? Who was the Buddha, and what are his teachings? How has Buddhist thought developed over the centuries, and how can contemporary dilemmas be faced from a Buddhist perspective?

'Damien Keown's book is a readable and wonderfully lucid introduction to one of mankind's most beautiful, profound, and compelling systems of wisdom. The rise of the East makes understanding and learning from Buddhism, a living doctrine, more urgent than ever before. Keown's impressive powers of explanation help us to come to terms with a vital contemporary reality.'
Bryan Appleyard

ARCHAEOLOGY

Paul Bahn

'Archaeology starts, really, at the point when the first recognizable 'artefacts' appear—on current evidence, that was in East Africa about 2.5 million years ago—and stretches right up to the present day. What you threw in the garbage yesterday, no matter how useless, disgusting, or potentially embarrassing, has now become part of the recent archaeological record.'

This Very Short Introduction reflects the enduring popularity of archaeology—a subject which appeals as a pastime, career, and academic discipline, encompasses the whole globe, and surveys 2.5 million years. From deserts to jungles, from deep caves to mountain-tops, from pebble tools to satellite photographs, from excavation to abstract theory, archaeology interacts with nearly every other discipline in its attempts to reconstruct the past.

'very lively indeed and remarkably perceptive . . . a quite brilliant and level-headed look at the curious world of archaeology'
Professor Barry Cunliffe,
University of Oxford

A Very Short Introduction

CLASSICS

Mary Beard and John Henderson

This *Very Short Introduction* to Classics links a haunting temple on a lonely mountainside to the glory of ancient Greece and the grandeur of Rome, and to Classics within modern culture—from Jefferson and Byron to Asterix and Ben-Hur.

'This little book should be in the hands of every student, and every tourist to the lands of the ancient world . . . a splendid piece of work'
Peter Wiseman
Author of *Talking to Virgil*

'an eminently readable and useful guide to many of the modern debates enlivening the field . . . the most up-to-date and accessible introduction available'
Edith Hall
Author of *Inventing the Barbarian*

'lively and up-to-date . . . it shows classics as a living enterprise, not a warehouse of relics'
New Statesman and Society

'nobody could fail to be informed and entertained—the accent of the book is provocative and stimulating'
Times Literary Supplement